VICIOUS REBEL

82ND STREET VANDALS

HEATHER LONG

Copyright © 2021 by Heather Long

Photographer: Eric McKinney

Cover: Crimson Phoenix Creations

Editing: Leavens Editing

Proofreading: Bookish Dreams

All rights reserved.

No part of this book may be reproduced in any form or by any electronic or mechanical means, including information storage and retrieval systems, without written permission from the author, except for the use of brief quotations in a book review.

*This one is totally for my #girlgang.
You rock in so many ways.*

SERIES SO FAR

Savage Vandal
Vicious Rebel

FOREWORD

Dear Reader,

Thank you for picking up *Vicious Rebel*. If you haven't read *Savage Vandal*, please stop and go grab that book first. This is a continuation of that story. When I first conceived of Emersyn and the Vandals, I knew it was going to be something special. As cheesy as that sounds, some stories click like magic in your brain. Even when you know they are going to push you, make you sad, and uncomfortable, you simply cannot wait to immerse yourself in their world.

There are some really dark and twisted places that *Vicious Rebel* goes. Please understand that some of the material may make you uncomfortable and it's supposed to, because it's part of their story. There are situations that some may find triggering regarding sexual assault and violence.

When we started off this journey together in *Savage Vandal*, I promised you a wild ride. Make sure your seat belts are tightened, this is definitely one of the turbulent parts.

And now, as always, the housekeeping notes:

For those of you who have never read a reverse harem before, first let me thank you for picking this up and giving it

FOREWORD

a shot. Second, a reverse harem means the heroine will not make a choice in this book or any other between the guys in her life. It may take her a while to reach that conclusion, but it's the journey that drives it. There are many ways to frame this kind of relationship, currently reverse harem fits it very well.

Also, this is the second book in a series. While there may be no specific happy endings at the end of each of these books, there will be one to the whole series, that I promise you. Some of these books will have cliffhangers, largely due to the size of the story, but the happy ending has to be earned as part of the journey.

Thank you again for reading Emersyn's story and I truly hope you enjoy it!

xoxo

Heather

THE VANDALS

82nd Street Boys
　Jasper "Hawk" Horan
　Kellan "Kestrel" Traschel
　Rome "Hummingbird" Cleary
　Vaughn "Falcon" Westbrook
　Liam "Mockingbird" O'Connell
　Freddie "Unknown" Dunlap

Unknown
　Raptor

Not a Vandal
　Mickey "Doc" James
　Emersyn "Dove, Sparrow, Starling, Swan, Little Bit, Boo-boo" Sharpe

CHAPTER 1

EMERSYN

Nightmares came to life with the press of a hand over my mouth and nose. The scents of something like turpentine, oil, and soap threatened to suffocate me. The band of arms were so tight, I almost forgot how to breathe. Fear coiled around, its venom a paralytic in my system as I was all but rushed into a shadowy spot between two buildings. Off the street. Away from people. In the darkness… No. As the sunshine slipped from view and the shadows crowded in to blind me, I fought.

Wildly maybe.

But I fought.

I wasn't going to let *him* take me.

No.

I hadn't come this far…

I bit down into the meaty part of the hand over my mouth and kicked my feet back at the person holding me. I missed with the first swing, but the second slammed into a knee.

"Fuck." The heated curse exploded against my ear. "Goddammit, princess."

Princess...

Bile burned in my throat, and I fought to get my teeth into his hand again. I didn't want any part of him touching me, much less his flesh. The moment I found purchase, I gritted down and he yanked his hand away. Cold air slapped my face, and I curled my hands up to dig my nails into his forearm. I didn't remember him being this strong, but I didn't care.

"Fuck me. Stop, princess."

I slammed my head back into his face, and spots flickered in front of my eyes. There were windows above us. And I thought I could see flour dust rising somewhere. Maybe a bakery. The trash in the alley smelled too. All of it raced at me, like sensory overload. The arms crushing me released abruptly.

The pounding of feet against concrete, even as I stumbled forward, had me twisting. My assailant turned away to look back the way we'd come, and a blur of motion caught him right in the chest and threw him to the ground.

Like a reel played in slow motion, the pair of men grappled as they rolled, and then as suddenly as the fight started, it ended with one man pinning the other with his legs while he held his arm in a lock. That man—Doc—stared up at me. "You okay, Little Bit?"

Fear ballooned in my gut, and I blew out a ragged breath before my gaze fell to the blond in the brutal hold.

It wasn't my uncle.

It was Liam.

Relief swam through me, and I staggered away, barely catching myself on the side of a dumpster before what little food I'd eaten that day came up. The sour taste burned my throat, and my eyes sparked tears. I couldn't suck in a breath for the retching hurling out of me.

The shakes hit next and I didn't have time for this, but it was like every part of the panic unfurled in my system and left me a trembling, sniveling mess.

"Easy, Little Bit." The warmth of Doc's voice penetrated the shell around me a moment before a heavy hand settled on my back. "Easy, I've got you."

"What the fuck, Doc?" Liam demanded. Their conversation came from a million miles away. "You tried to break my goddamn arm."

"Why the hell were you dragging her off the street?" The growl in Doc's words reverberated over me, but I couldn't make myself focus on it, not when I was trying to remember how to breathe.

My uncle's face flooded my mind's eye, and I squeezed my eyes shut to try and blot out the image. Music. Dance. The Vandals.

Anything but my uncle.

"'Cause she took off on Rome's watch. You think Jasper's gonna get over that shit? No. So I came to see what the fuck she was doing, and don't think I didn't see her hook up with you."

"You didn't see shit," Doc snarled back, and I closed my eyes as the heaving finally eased and wiped at my mouth with the back of my hand. But before I could even connect, Doc pressed a napkin into my hand as he helped me ease upright. I stared at him, then over at Liam, then back again. "You with us, Little Bit?"

"What the fuck is wrong with the little hellspawn?"

Hellspawn.

I laughed.

It wasn't a very friendly sound. If anything, it sounded a

lot like crying.

"Ignore the prick, Emersyn." Doc touched my cheek lightly. "How fucking hard did you grip her?"

"She was fighting," Liam said with a scowl and crossed his arms. "Why don't you ask if she's had her shots since she bit me."

I cut a look over at him. "You followed me." The words sounded so normal, and yet everything inside me still shook. "Why?"

"Why?" he parroted, cocking his head to the side and staring at me before glancing over his shoulder back at the street. "How about we get the hell back to the clubhouse with her before the guys realize she left?" That wasn't directed at me.

"She wanted out," Doc said, curling his arm around me. I shouldn't lean into him. In fact, the best thing to do was walk out of this alley and keep walking.

"I don't care." The disdain in Liam's voice made me frown. "Jasper will put another hole in Rome if he thinks he let her go."

"He can't do anything about her escaping," Doc said patiently, like it was the most rational thing in the world. "The obligation of the prisoner is to escape."

"Let me repeat," Liam said, arms falling to his side as he took a step toward us. A shadow of a bruise formed on his cheek, and there were scrapes on his neck, plus more bruises on his knuckles. "I. Don't. Care. They want her there, Rome was left to look after her, she's going back… She already got him stabbed once. I'm not letting it happen a second time."

"Wait." Finding my voice shouldn't be this hard. I pushed away from Doc and forced myself to stand on my own two feet. The problem was, I wanted to curl up against him and hide there. Doc *felt* safe. Safety was always a lie. "What do you mean I got him stabbed?"

The attack.

The three guys who came at us when we'd been at the park. Correction, the three guys had come at *me*. I'd trusted Rome had my back and he had.

I took a step toward Liam. The dismissive coolness in his eyes cut at me. "He was hurt."

"Yes, princ—"

I didn't even realize I'd moved until my fist cracked against the side of his nose. The faintest sound of crunching bone made me wince. So did the spray of blood.

"You cunt," he snapped as he put a hand up to his face. Lucky for me, he didn't hit back, but Doc was already hauling me backward and putting himself between us.

"Watch your mouth," Doc chastised him.

"I don't care if he calls me cunt," I said. "I told you, don't call me princess. You do it again, and it'll be your balls I smash."

I was no princess. The word even tasted filthy in my mouth.

"Noted, Hellspawn." He spit out blood, then touched his nose carefully before glaring at me. "Hellspawn fits better anyway."

I'd take it.

Doc glanced at me again. "Look, let's get you out of here and back to the hotel."

"No," I said and shook my head. "Not the hotel." Not after seeing him there. I should have known he'd make it there. As long as I'd been with the company, I'd had some safety. Even enduring Eric, I could survive that. But the company had moved on and now he was looking for me.

They'd haul me home.

Probably commit me.

Worse, they'd lock me up in that mausoleum and he'd come to check on me daily.

No.

The bile burned the back of my throat again, and I choked back the urge to vomit. Somehow, I went from standing to sitting in that nasty alley, the cold air perfumed with bits of trash and exhaust while Doc massaged the back of my neck as I tucked my head down between my knees.

"She's crazy," Liam murmured.

"She's traumatized, you overbearing little shit. Stop freaking out about your brother for thirty seconds and look at this girl. She hasn't done a damn thing to any of you, and yet you're treating her like she's a damn possession." The ferociousness in Doc's voice had me lifting my head again.

He'd gone toe-to-toe with Jasper and hadn't flinched when Jasper pulled a gun on him. Right now, he glared at Liam like he was ready to tackle him too. It took me a moment to register that a trickle of blood escaped the corner of his mouth.

"You're hurt."

Liam rolled his eyes and threw his hands up as he half stomped away, and I reached up to try and dab the blood on Doc's face.

"I'm fine, Little Bit. Trust me, a cut like that isn't going to hurt me." He stood and pulled me up to my feet with him. "Can you focus on me a second?"

I stared into his eyes, and a part of me wanted to cry. When I'd kissed him in the truck, there'd been some real regret in me. I hadn't wanted to say goodbye, and at the same time, I hadn't wanted to leave him without some acknowledgement that he'd come through for me.

"You're in shock." He said it almost too softly. "What happened to you?"

"Nothing," I said slowly. "I just—" I had no idea what to do.

"You won't go to the hotel?" It was a question.

I shook my head.

"I'm guessing you don't want to go with Liam." It wasn't a question. Rome's twin glared at me, but it wasn't hate in his eyes.

Worry.

He was worried about his brother.

"I—I don't know," I said slowly. "I need to think."

That wasn't really an answer. But I needed to go somewhere. Right? I'd just managed to escape. I couldn't go back.

I rubbed a hand over my face and winced. My mouth hurt. So did my head. My nails had bits of blood under them. "Will Jasper really hurt Rome?"

"Fuck, I don't know," Liam said, shocking me. There was a puffiness to his nose, and blood still decorated his face as he drew closer to us. "If he could pin it on me and shoot me, he'd probably leave Rome alone. But they're turning the city upside down looking for fucking Freddie, and all he wanted was for Rome to make sure you were safe."

Freddie.

My heart clenched.

"They haven't found him yet?"

Liam stared at me, eyebrows up. "I have no clue. I've been following you for the last couple of hours. Then your boyfriend."

"Shut the fuck up," Doc ground out. "Don't even joke about that."

"Hey, Doc, just calling it like I see it. I saw her kissing you before she got out of the truck, and you sure pulled up conveniently when she was out there walking."

"Wait," I said, waving aside the posturing bullshit. "You followed me? I didn't see you."

"You weren't supposed to." Liam smirked.

"I walked for a long time and you just let me go?" Suspicion curved through me. That sounded remarkably convenient. "I thought you were worried about your brother."

"Yeah," Doc murmured. "If you were that interested in protecting Rome, why let her get that far at all?"

"I just wanted to see where you were going," Liam said.

"And?" Because there was more to this.

He leaned over and spat blood onto the pavement. "And I debated just letting you go. Fine? Is that what you want to hear, Pr—Hellspawn?"

The fact he edited himself went a long way for me. "Why did you change your mind?"

"Fuck if I know." Liam glared at me, then at Doc. "You know what? This shit is not worth it. My nose fucking hurts —nice hit, by the way." He said that to me as almost an aside. "You ever want to work on that southpaw, you let me know. You take her back, and I'm getting out of here. This side of town gives me hives."

"Hey, Mockingbird," Doc said before Liam even made it halfway down the alley. "You're trying too hard."

The other man flipped him off, and then he was gone.

Leaving me alone with Doc.

"Where do you want to go, Emersyn?" I should have expected the question. I had expected the question. The problem was I didn't have any kind of answer.

Not anymore.

"I don't have anywhere to go," I admitted after a long time. There was one person I could call. Maybe. Well, no maybe. But I still wasn't sure I should involve her.

Doc sighed and tilted his head back to stare at the sky.

"I'm sorry," I told him. "You don't have to worry about me. I'll figure this out." Bit by bit, the trembling abated, and I stopped chasing my own mental tail. I needed a plan. Understanding the need for one was the first step.

Making one would be the second step.

I went to touch his arm, then curled my fingers against my palm. Doc had done more than enough. Now he'd even gotten into another fight for me. "Thanks, Mickey."

He let me get three steps away before he said, "Where are you going, Little Bit?"

"You don't have to worry," I said over my shoulder. "I'll figure it out."

His sigh followed me another three steps. On the fourth one, he was quiet. By the fifth one, I was sure he'd let me go. Yet, it didn't surprise me to find him standing next to me when I reached the next street.

When he held out his hand to me, I stared at it for a long moment. Taking it meant going back. At least with Doc. Taking it meant trusting him.

Taking it meant taking a risk.

"It's cold out here, Little Bit," he said. "Let's at least get something warmer in you again, and we'll take some time for you to make your decision."

"Jasper won't like it."

"I don't care." His words practically echoed Liam's, and a small smile escaped me. "Let me help you."

"You already have."

"Fine," he said with an impatient sigh. "Let me help you *more*."

I blew out a breath. "I have nothing to pay you back with right now..." And honestly, I had no idea what I was getting him into if he was in the middle of all of this. He wasn't a Vandal, right?

"Tell you what, you let me worry about me while I worry about you. Then you can focus on what you want to do next, but in the meanwhile, I got your back."

Sometimes, you have to fall before you fly...

And every flight required a leap of faith.

When he held out his hand this time, I took it.

CHAPTER 2

EMERSYN

Doc led me to his truck and tucked me inside, snapping the belt into place before he closed the passenger door and circled the truck to get back behind the wheel. The cold barely touched me anymore. Not saying a word, he started the engine, and then we were back on the road. He'd parked a block away from the hotel.

Traffic seemed heavier leaving than when we'd driven in. Course, it was later in the morning. Rush hour, maybe? It occurred to me I didn't even know what day of the week it was. I'd lost all track of time and reason. I could still feel the weight of Vaughn's hands and the heat of his kisses. I was in the passenger seat of a truck not only heading away from my own escape, but also back toward the people who kidnapped me.

Irony could go fuck itself.

I flicked a look at the side mirror and caught sight of a motorcycle behind us. Liam? I only paid attention because it was a stunning shade of blue. Pretty. Then I looked forward again. Doc left me to my thoughts. He'd taken us through another drive-thru for coffee, huge cups for each of us. I warmed my icy hands on the cup as he pressed it into them. The heat of his hands on mine lingered as he closed my fingers around the beverage.

For a split second, I glanced up to find him watching me. I licked my lips and glanced down and away. Doc saw way too much. "I suppose I should ask where we're going." It wasn't really a question, it was just me giving voice to some words. I still couldn't believe how close I'd come to walking right into my uncle.

"I'm taking you to the clinic," Doc said. "Let you have some time to figure out what you want to do."

His clinic. "Oh fuck, I've kept you from your work."

"Stop," he ordered in a soft voice before his hand settled on my knee. There was nothing suggestive about the contact. If anything, it was a source of deep comfort. His hand rested there, offering strength not demanding anything. "You haven't done anything to me. You haven't done anything to anyone. I told you I would help you, and I meant it. You got out of there on your own, but Liam's not wrong—they are going to start looking for you the moment they figure out you're gone."

My stomach bottomed out.

"The clinic might be one of the places they look, but we have some time and my place isn't far. I'd offer the apartment, but I'm doing immunizations this afternoon and I want to be there before the line starts. I can get you inside without too many eyes on you. I also want you somewhere you can feel comfortable, that isn't another cell." Maybe he didn't want to leave me alone at his place in case I disappeared?

The flutters in my belly gained some altitude. I slanted a

look at him and sighed. "Thank you. I really don't want to get in the way of your work." At least this way, I'd find out the name of his clinic and stuff. "Are you the only one who works there?"

"Most days," Doc said easily, driving one-handed and keeping his eyes focused on the traffic. "Two days a week, I have a nurse volunteer come in so I can see female patients without them being uncomfortable. If I have one that really needs an exam, I ask them to bring a family member or girlfriend…"

I frowned and took a sip of the coffee. "Why?" The moment the question passed my lips, I shook my head. "That was stupid. You need someone there to not only make them feel comfortable but also so no one can accuse you of being inappropriate. I forget that not everyone is used to having their body on constant display."

"Everyone should feel comfortable with their physician," Doc informed me, and he gave me a measured look when we stopped at a traffic light. "And your body should only ever be on display if you choose to do that."

Avoiding that knowing gaze, I glanced at the side mirror. The blue bike was visible a few cars back.

"Liam's still following us," Doc said. "Which means he'll know you're going to be at the clinic."

I sighed. I tried to work up the energy to care… "Will Jasper really hurt Rome?"

"I can't say for sure," Doc answered with a sigh of his own. "Hawk's a pain in the ass, but he means well."

Surprise flickered through me, and this time, I half twisted to look at Doc. He flexed his fingers on my knee and chuckled in this deep baritone that I swear went straight to my cunt. His kindness alone made him appealing. The way he spoke to me and helped me, even more, the way he treated me were all alluring, but that chuckle?

It was sexy as fuck, and I sucked in a deeper breath of air, all of it filled with the scent of coffee and something far more male.

Really not the time to be thinking with my pussy.

Just, not the time.

"Seriously," Doc continued, as if my reaction had been to his earlier statement and not to him. Probably a good thing. "He's a good kid. Just…life hasn't always been kind to them, and the boys look after each other."

"He put a gun to your chin," I reminded him. "Just because you were helping me bathe."

"No, he put a gun to my chin because he found me with you naked and vulnerable in the bathtub."

"But…" What the hell was with Jasper and that? I barely knew him. I mean, what I did know was hot and oddly attractive, despite his kidnapping and surly tendencies. The man had them build me a freaking studio. He'd been kinder to me in ways even the people who were supposed to love me never had been. At the same time, he was frustratingly mute on a lot of topics.

And he refused to let me go.

"Little Bit, you were in a vulnerable spot. And you were hardly in a position to fend me off if I got handsy."

I rolled my eyes. "You're not the type, but people like Jasper are why you have to have someone with you when you examine a woman." All right, that made sense. "But he doesn't understand."

"He doesn't have to understand," Doc said with another light squeeze to my knee before releasing it. "He wants to keep you safe. They have given their word to protect you, and they take that seriously."

"And that's the part I really don't get." It sounded like everything I could have ever wanted. "I've never met them before and they…" I trailed off, the accusation of kidnapping dying on my tongue. I'd brought it up before, but I was free now and I didn't want Doc reporting this.

Of course, he hadn't reported it.

"Are you a Vandal?" The question came out abruptly as Doc maneuvered across a few lanes of traffic to exit the highway.

"No," he answered without elaboration. "And I can't tell you why they made the oath, but I can tell you that they meant every word. It's why they took your partner."

I grimaced.

Eric.

"He was only someone I performed with," I corrected. Was he still in that cell being tortured? A wash of heat went through me at the idea of him suffering. For all the weeks I had been there, apparently so had he, and from the state I'd found him in, they'd been generous with their abuse.

"But he hurt you." It wasn't a question.

I could shrug it off, but I didn't. "Yes."

Doc nodded. "He won't. Ever again."

No complaints here. Maybe I should feel some sense of guilt or remorse. No matter how terrible a human being he had been, he was still a human being.

I searched for a scrap of pity.

Nope, fresh out of fucks to give where he was concerned. "Good."

Another of those sexy chuckles fell from Doc's lips as he turned. The farther we drove, the sadder the town looked. A little more rundown. A little more worn. The buildings were older. The paint chipped. It wasn't dirty though. The streets were thick with people. Vendors. Kids were heading to school, based on their backpacks. Stores were opening.

They had a neighborhood grocer. The man was wheeling out crates of fruits and veggies to put in a stand just outside the front door. On another corner, there was a huddle of business suits—not expensive or smart, but definitely cleaned and pressed—waiting for a bus that rumbled up as we were passing.

Even though the blue bike remained in the side mirror, I focused on the people filing onto the bus. Some had earbuds in, listening to music or maybe podcasts. Others chattered. Still more just wore a resting bitch face as they climbed aboard. The light changed, and Doc pulled away, the bus vanishing behind me.

The streets were numbered in this part of town. At least all the cross streets we passed. Some of the buildings began to look a little more disreputable. The level of disrepair grew, and while there were shops, they grew fewer and farther in between.

At the next light, a mural on the wall of one of the buildings blew me away. It was a stunning painting of kids playing on a playground. It was a colorful scene with the children kicking a ball around, while another kid swung on a swing and still another jumped on the back of one. All told, there were five boys playing ball, but there were others in the background. One stood on the far side of a fence, like he couldn't get into where the others were.

Doc pulled away before I could make out more details. We turned at the next cross street, and there was another mural. I gaped at it, and Doc slowed the truck. It was a series of dancers. They were adorable, little girls in pink tutus going through their routines. It threw me back to when dance had been fun. There was a girl in the background dancing away from the others.

That could have been me. Lots of times it *was* me.

I laughed.

"Rome did these," I said as Doc put his foot down on the accelerator.

"He's very talented," Doc explained unnecessarily. "No

VICIOUS REBEL

one ever knows what he's going to create. He's done a few around town. Usually on the worst buildings or…"

"Falling apart playgrounds."

"Abandoned ones, yeah. There's not enough money for all the things here, but he tries to make them a little prettier. When he disappears for a few days, you can usually expect something beautiful to show up."

Now, I kind of wanted to go hunting them. "Do you know where they all are?"

"Some of them," Doc said with a glance at me, and then we circled a building and pulled into a pothole pitted parking lot in the back. We were the only vehicle. It wasn't hard to believe this was the clinic, it fit right into the aesthetic of this area of town. Dilapidated, unkempt, but even if it was *poor*, it was lived in.

The Vandals lived here. When they'd taken me to Doc's for the test, it hadn't been that long of a drive from the warehouse. I wasn't sure which way it was, but I could guess. The air was chilly as I opened the passenger door, but Doc circled the vehicle before I could slip out and then he was there offering me a hand.

His truck was parked in a shaded area, but the lot itself had a lot of rough gravel and it was definitely uneven. When I wrote his clinic a check, I was going to make sure he got this repaved. Maybe I could even fix up Rome's park.

Would he still paint if it was fixed?

I'd have to ask.

No sooner did I take Doc's hand than the blue bike rumbled to the opening of the lot. With his helmet on, Liam's face was obscured. Doc followed my gaze, but he wore an unreadable expression. Was Liam planning on dragging me back, or was he just making sure Doc took me to the clinic so he could report to Jasper later?

Instead of following us though, he nodded and then

rumbled away on the bike. I let out a long breath, and Doc glanced down at me. "I told you, you're safe."

"What about Freddie?" I asked as I let him guide me inside. He had to unlock three deadbolts to get the door open. It sounded heavy when he pulled it open.

"The guys are already looking for him." Doc didn't sound too concerned. "Knowing Freddie? He probably found a hookup and went home with a new pussy."

Doc grimaced.

"Sorry…"

"It's fine," I said, waving off his apology. "Contrary to what the guys think, I'm not going to fall apart at the mention of a pussy, or a dick for that matter." Doc had tattoos all down half his body to cover his scars. Did they go all the way down his leg? Did he pierce his dick too? Curiosity roused in me like a sleepy cat.

He chuckled, locking up before he led the way up a grayish white hallway. The antiseptic smell promised that despite the hints of peeling tile and cracked paint in the corners, the clinic was clean.

We passed open doors that revealed a couple of exam rooms. A third one revealed an office. The desk was neat, save for a stack of files on the corner and what looked like bobbleheads lined along the front of it, not that I got a lot of time to look. Doc guided me to a set of stairs and up.

There was a sitting room of sorts up here, or more like a living room. There were a couple of arcade games, bean bags, books, and a big television with a couple of video game consoles. The room seemed to take up the length and breadth of the clinic below, and there was a divided off area with a little kitchenette.

That was where Doc headed. He filled the coffeemaker with water and started a fresh pot. "You can make yourself comfortable here. There's a little bathroom around the corner. It's Monday, so the teens that use this won't be here until after school. If you haven't made a choice by then, I can run you back to my place or you can settle in my office. That won't have the entertainment that this has."

I set my coffee cup down on a table and glanced around. Arms folded, I turned in a little circle. Posters decorated most of the walls, but there was another mural. This one was all video game characters battling across different platforms.

More of Rome's work?

Was there anything he couldn't do?

The bean bags were a mishmash of darker primary colors. The carpet was the same. One could almost imagine if it were brighter colors, this wouldn't look out of place in a kindergarten class, but it didn't feel like a little kid's place. It felt…lived in, open, and welcoming. The posters ranged from music to movies, some of them were older. There was even a…

"That's a poster of me." I stared at the one in the corner.

Doc glanced up from the kitchen at my whispered words, and the shock on his face wasn't imagined. The poster was from one of my first shows. I wasn't even prominent in it, but I was there. I was the kid in the circle dangling from the ceiling.

I'd been eight.

It was my first tour.

"That's you?" Doc asked as he joined me, his voice rough. "Which one?"

When I pointed to me in the circle, he blew out a ragged breath. When he glanced at me, he looked like he'd seen a ghost.

"Mickey?"

"It's okay," he said, but he didn't sound like he had earlier. Gone was the cool assurance, and in its place was a guarded fear. Maybe not fear, but definitely disturbance. "It really is okay, Little Bit. I should have put it together. And I was at that show." He said, indicating the poster. "Everything in here is something one of us has been to."

He'd been at that show?

I barely even remembered where we'd been performing, but it hadn't been here. "Oh."

A faint smile creased his lips. "Don't worry about it, just take it easy. Watch some television and think about what you want to do. There's not a phone up here, but there's a hardline in my office. I can send someone to grab a new cell phone for you, if you'd rather…" He shot a look at his watch and rubbed my arm gently before he headed for the stairs. "I gotta get this place open, you'll be fine here."

Not waiting for my response, he vanished down the stairs. I stared after him for a moment, then glanced back at the poster.

He'd been *at* the show. That had been ten years earlier.

I was more confused than ever. I dropped into one of the bean bags and ran my hands over my face.

And I still had no idea what the hell to do or who to call. Lainey's face danced across my mind's eye, and I grimaced. I wanted to talk to her *so* bad. At the same time, my uncle might have figured out about her. What if he was watching her? What if he went after her?

Right now, my best bet was the people I'd escaped.

How fucked up was that?

CHAPTER 3

JASPER

No one had seen Freddie. Not since we left him to look after Emersyn. No one could even tell us when he left. Not Emersyn, not the rats. I could go ask her, but Kellan and Vaughn both vouched for her not knowing anything else. Cagey bastards were hiding something. I'd deal with that and them later. After we figured out where the fuck Freddie went. The last thing we needed was someone missing while the 19 Diamonds were nursing their wounds.

A pair of rats met me at the corner of Pike and 60th. If we kept heading south, we'd be in 19 Diamonds territory. "What did you find?"

JD shook his head. "I checked his usual dealers, Hawk. None of them have sold to 'im. They swore they wouldn't either. Not after the beatdown you and Kestrel delivered last time." He checked his phone. "We've covered most of our territory. I don't think he'd try to buy here. They all know better."

They knew better. They sold here under our protection. The two dealers who wouldn't play ball and continued to sell to Freddie didn't sell anything anymore to anyone. As it was, we monitored closely who was selling and who was buying. The rules hadn't changed, nor had the penalty for breaking them.

"Get Shaun and Ripper," I said before heading toward my car. The old muscle car looked like a beaten-up piece of shit. But I didn't care about looking cool. All I cared about was that it was solid steel. Nothing on this car would buckle unless something considerably larger hit it.

I'd long-since scratched the racing itch and left that for Raptor and Kestrel. Fuck... Just the thought of Raptor made my jaw clench. It wasn't time.

I fired off a text to Vaughn and Kellan to see if they'd found anything, while I debated my next move. The 19 Diamonds would not be welcoming if they caught us in their territory. Not that I needed anyone to invite me in.

But was I really looking to pick a fight?

The simple *Nothing* they sent in response didn't bode well.

Engine started, I stared out the front window as JD slid into the seat next to me.

"Shaun and Ripper are on the way. They worked their way all the way up to 115th. They didn't find him either. Checked at Ms. Thompkins too."

"He doesn't go there alone anymore," I mused aloud, but I got why they checked. I'd said no stone unturned. And the rats were out kicking a lot of stones over. Freddie had burned his bridges with Ronnie. Veronica Thompkins could lay a beatdown on a grown man without breaking a sweat, and Freddie could irritate a saint. She didn't put up with him, and he didn't tempt fate.

We'd been looking for hours. It was already midafternoon, and we were no closer to tracking him down than we'd been when we set out. I rubbed my phone against my lower lip.

The one thing about JD I liked was the rat knew how to keep his mouth shut. Most of the time. If he could learn to keep his zipper up, he might make it past his year. He wouldn't. Almost none of them would. The year was grueling for a reason.

Fuck it. If Freddie was there, I was going to get him. I could kick his ass later, but he had to be alive for me to do that.

"Tell Ripper and Shaun we're heading toward The Smokestack."

"That's—" JD shut up when I glanced at him and just sent a text.

I called Kellan. He wouldn't like it. He never did.

"Yeah?" he answered.

"Smokestack. Fifteen minutes. Don't be late."

"Fuck me," Kellan groaned. "You really do want to start a war."

"If Freddie went to score, he wouldn't do it here. He's nowhere else he should be. That means he's probably in their territory, and they were already pissed."

"And whose fucking fault is that?" The complaint rolled right off me. It didn't matter how irritated he was, he'd be where he needed to be.

"Call in more rats, we may need the distraction."

We could do more, just the three of us, than most of the rats.

"Liam's at the clubhouse," Kellan suggested.

"I don't care." He shouldn't be there either, but the guy kept showing up for Rome. Short of kicking Rome, which I would never fucking do, I had to deal with it. It meant Liam would keep showing up until we put a bullet in him or someone else did. Since we wouldn't do that to Rome, we were stuck with him.

Didn't mean I planned on sharing shit with him.

"I meant to tell him so he can watch Rome's back. If we're all heading into 19 Diamonds…"

Emersyn was at the clubhouse with Rome. He needed to be there while still nursing that stab wound, whether he took it seriously or not.

Fuck.

"I'll take care of it."

I texted Rome to check in and got a middle finger in response.

That was about par for the course.

Asshole.

So I sent Liam a text. *Watch for 19D. Heading South.*

There was no response from Liam. Not even an acknowledgement.

But the fucker read the text.

He'd watch Rome's back. Rome would watch Emersyn's. I pulled off a block away from the Smokestack. The old bar sat squarely in Old Town. Dingy, shitty piece of real estate, and the bar offered all manner of sins. It was great on those nights when we were just looking for a fight. But it wouldn't be *open* for another couple of hours.

During the day, it belonged to the 19D only.

It was also a good place to score some E if you were looking for it, along with eight-balls and other drugs. They were a lot looser on what they distributed. They also took a bigger slice of the pie and didn't give as much of a damn about who they hurt. The only rules they bothered to enforce were the ones we made them enforce.

JD was out of the car without saying a word, and I flipped open the glove box and pulled out a set of brass knuckles. Some jobs called for a knife. Some for the gun.

This one?

This required a few broken jaws.

And that was if Freddie wasn't there.

The 19D needed to be reminded of their place. They shouldn't have shown up at ours in the first place. I circled the car and opened the trunk for my bat. Better to be prepared.

Kellan and Vaughn pulled up behind me with three more cars slotting in neatly behind them. They met me on the sidewalk, and the rats arrayed around us. Nine of them, three of us.

Twelve was not a big number.

Ten was fewer.

But two had to stay with the cars.

Without a word, because the boys and I didn't need that, we divvied up the rats' assignments. While there might be tension and secrets inhabiting the ever widening gulf between us, we still moved together.

"Do we even know if Freddie's here?" was Kellan's only question. Like me, he wore a jacket to cover the gun he kept tucked at the small of his back and the second weapon in the shoulder holster.

The clouds that threatened earlier had blown back in, and lightning flashed in the distance. "Unless he's shacked up with some new pussy, he's here, or worse, he's in Royals' territory looking to score."

"Maybe stop cutting him off closer to home," Vaughn suggested in a dry drawl that I didn't even acknowledge. None of us wanted Freddie flushing his life down the toilet, and if he had even an ounce of restraint, I might not be such a hard-ass.

But he'd OD'd the last time, and if Doc hadn't still been at the clinic when we rolled in with him, we might have been burying him instead of listening to him cuss us out for the next week when we detoxed him.

It had sucked.

For all of us.

"We go in, we round up who's there, kick out the pussy and the civilians, and then get some answers."

I didn't hurt pussy.

Period.

None of us did. We all had our weird little hang-ups about it.

Correction, I did and Vaughn did. Kellan held no such illusions. He just shook his head. "I'll question them."

Fine by me.

Course, he had a way of looking at them, and they either pissed their pants or threw their panties at him. It could be downright entertaining when I could afford to be amused by it. Right now, the only things I wanted were to find Freddie, make sure he was fine, then get back to Emersyn. I'd damn well kissed her the night before, then shit went down, and I hadn't fucking seen her since.

That rasped over every nerve like rough sandpaper. As much as I hated doing it, I boxed up my thoughts of her and secured them in the back of my mind. Fucking Freddie had better be okay, or I'd kill him and everyone else involved.

The rats followed us, fanning out. One by one, they peeled off, including one heading up to a roof to give us eyes on high. Our route back to the cars would be protected, and we'd have warning if they'd been compromised. No one left unattended wheels when strolling into someone else's territory.

Define irony.

I'd cut the finger off the 19 Diamond who walked into my territory looking for his men. Now, here we were, in search of one of our own. Now ask me if I gave a fuck about irony?

By the time we reached the red curtained doors to the

club, there were four rats still with us. More than enough to get the job done.

I rolled my head from side to side, cracking the vertebrae, then nodded to Vaughn. He took doors first. Not that he was bulletproof or anything, but he was just that fucking fast. The speed at which he took doors and the guards on them was equivalent to a freight train. The crunch of fist on bone and the hollow explosions of harsh releases of breath were my cue to follow. I caught the guy swinging for Vaughn's back with my bat. The crunch of bone in his arm sent him staggering.

It was also the moment that literally cracked the silence of our assault. Kellan hit the stairs with two of the four rats right behind him. The room was thick with a haze of smoke. The room reeked of dope, and it left our targets in a literal lazy state of response.

More than a few were too out of it to even notice we'd invaded or respond until we were literally on top of them. The girls noticed though. I'd give them that. One girl pulled off a cock she'd been riding and hopped from one foot to the other as she jerked down her skirt.

I pointed to the other side of the room with the bat, and she went. Fifteen minutes after storming inside, we had fourteen males present—all 19 Ds—and eight women. Two were club bitches, from the looks of them, the rest were just whores hanging out for a good time.

Trusting Kellan to deal with them, I studied those present. Meeks wasn't here, nor was his second, a weaselly little fuck named Twister. Middle management made for a good second in some groups. Twister might be a useless, skinny shit in a fight, but the man could spin shit into dough and they made a pretty penny off him.

Vaughn stood like my silent shadow as I swept my gaze over the men in front of me. Some of them were too stoned to take this seriously. Hell, we were all gonna be a little high before we walked out of here. The bar wasn't called The Smokestack for nothing.

I rested the bat against my shoulders, hooking my hands over the ends as much to keep them away from the guns and the knives as to give myself time to choose carefully.

Honestly, I knew maybe two of the faces. Three if I counted the bartender, but he was old-school Braxton Harbor and while he was a 19D, it was more because they owned The Smokestack than anything else and it offered him a form of protection. I dismissed him immediately. He knew everything and would share exactly nothing.

That was how he kept his cushy position.

Fuck it.

"I'm only asking this once," I began, keeping my voice at a civil tone and perfectly pleasant.

I was aware of the conversation going on to my left, where Kellan was interrogating the ladies. The fact that no fewer than three had sighed and tittered with laughter said he'd worked his magic, so I shoved them out of my mind. He'd pull me into the conversation if he got anything useful from them.

"I'm looking for Freddie Dunlap." I didn't miss the recognition flickering in some eyes but not in others. One pair of unfocused eyes took on a sharper look. I'd keep track of those. The guy would need to be slightly less stoned to motivate. "Be straight with me, and we'll leave you intact. Play games, you'll lose."

I nodded to the first guy on the left, his bald, tatted head shining under the muddy red lights. That was the other part of this bar's weird aesthetic. It had high backed booths, lots of dope to smoke and vape, and red lights to give the illusion you'd descended into Hell.

Unfortunately for them, Hell didn't scare us.

"Have you seen him?"

"Like I'm telling you shit," the man spat out, finding his balls or his voice for the first time since we'd stormed the club. Okay.

I did warn them.

A split second before I took a step toward him, I spotted the axe affixed to the wall behind him. It seemed decorative, only the way the edge gleamed, it really wasn't. Sidestepping them, I passed the bat over to JD, and he accepted it without question before I gripped the axe and pulled it down.

Well, would you look at that? It had balance to it, a good, solid feel in my hand, and fit my grip like it had been made for me.

I tested the edge with a thumb and then sucked the blood that welled up from the cut. Sharp enough.

Time to make a point.

I returned to the first guy to offer a challenge to my question. "I'll do you a favor," I told him as kindly as I could muster. "I'll let you choose. Righty or lefty?"

"What?" The man stared at me like I'd sprouted a second fucking head. To my left, Kellan had gone dead silent, and his attention was now on me.

Everyone's was.

Good.

I liked having to demonstrate lessons only once.

"Are you a righty or a lefty?" I eyed the man in question. He had about three seconds to give me an answer, because while I might be kind enough to give him a choice, I wasn't going to be waiting around on it all day.

"Right-handed," the guy said slowly, almost warily, like it had sunk in.

"Hold out your left," I told him. "And thank me."

He didn't move a muscle. "What the fuck for?"

I smiled. "Because I'm giving you the opportunity to only

lose a hand. You make me come for it, and it might be the whole arm."

He didn't believe me.

It was almost more fun when they didn't. At first.

Unfortunately, I wasn't in the mood to play. I wanted Freddie's whereabouts and straight answers to my questions.

"Vaughn."

Seizing the guy by the back of his neck, Vaughn slammed him forward and not so gently bounced his head off the table before slamming his left arm down. Bracing him with a knee to his back, he eyed me, and I read the facts on his face. He was about to get covered in blood. No two ways about it.

"You should thank my brother too." I closed the gap. "After you apologize for inconveniencing him."

"Fuck you," the man spat, even as blood trickled down his forehead.

I had intended to send one of the rats for ice. Well, if he couldn't be bothered to be polite, I couldn't be bothered to help him preserve his chances.

With one direct swing, I slammed the axe down through his wrist. The edge went clean through flesh, the muscle, the tendon, and the bone to bite into the table beneath. Blood splattered, and one of the guys promptly threw up.

Weak fucker.

The mouthy one didn't have much to say beyond screaming.

Without a word, Vaughn just wrapped a towel around the end of the guy's wrist to staunch the bleeding. Not that it would give him long.

"Who wants to go next?" I smiled, already picking my target in the wild-eyed stoner whose pupils had begun to shrink as reality sank in. "Freddie Dunlap. Have you seen him?"

CHAPTER 4

KELLAN

A fucking axe. Jasper had picked a fucking axe off the wall. Thankfully, he hadn't spotted the katana hanging there as well. I'd grab it on our way out, though I was pretty sure walking an axe out of here wasn't just something that could be overlooked. The cops weren't stupid or all on the take. A lot of them knew we kept our streets relatively clean and they cut us some slack.

Bloody axes and full-on swords weren't going to win us friends or influence people, no matter how effective Jasper found it for his questioning. The second guy he pointed to dropped into a dead faint after pissing himself. I swallowed a sigh, studying the women lined up against the stairs.

They didn't know much, but I wouldn't say they knew nothing. Darla, the bleach bottled blonde tipped girl with the black hair was a 19D. Last I checked, she belonged to a couple of the guys. Not that I cared beyond she'd have a better idea of what was what. Conversations would happen around her.

I gave her points for not flinching at the severing of the guy's hand, and I was also rather grateful when he passed out from the pain. At least he wasn't screaming anymore. The harsh scent of urine punched through the heavier smoke of the room. The sickly scent would cling to my nostrils for days to come, and I already wanted to wash my clothes.

Fuck, I hated the stench here.

Darla shifted her stance and cut her gaze to me when she thought I wasn't looking. Hesitation marked her expression, and she sucked on her lower lip for a moment before shifting her gaze back to the guys. Vaughn hauled another one forward. We couldn't really maim our way through the 19 Diamonds, no matter how much damage Jasper had on display.

Freddie hadn't vanished like this in a while. I'd checked with the cops and the hospitals. He hadn't been pinched and he hadn't OD'd. I'd seen the way he looked at Emersyn. Something kept him from coming back, and it wasn't Vaughn.

A flash of rumpled, defiant Emersyn in the middle of Vaughn's bed flashed through my eyes. Fuck me sideways. That was going to go so goddamn wrong. What the fuck had Vaughn been thinking?

You know exactly what he was thinking, the pernicious little voice in the back of my head taunted. *He wanted her, she needed something, and he gave it to her.*

The first time she'd turned that want on me, I'd damn near caved. But we weren't good for her, and now...

Now was not the time to think about this. Jasper had no clue, and it was safer for everyone if it stayed that way. I didn't think he'd go after Vaughn. Not for more than a fist fight, and Vaughn could more than hold his own. But we so didn't need that shit.

Darla shifted again when Jasper demanded, "Freddie Dunlap. Where is he?"

This time, when her gaze flicked to me, I pinned her with a look and she gulped.

"Where is he?" I kept the question soft. The girls were dead silent like they didn't want the crazed guy with the axe noticing them. Not that I could blame them.

"I'm—" Darla began, then grimaced. She cut a glance back to the drama unfolding behind me. I kept my gaze on her.

The swing of the axe would come any moment, if she wanted to save the guy's hand, she better speak up now.

"He showed up looking to score with one of the girls from Mama's." The statement was only a fragment of the story. Freddie wouldn't wander into 19D territory on a whim. Not even for pussy.

"And?"

"Look, if I tell you—" A sharp scream punctuated the air behind me, and she blanched beneath the red lights. Those hard eyes cut to mine, and her jaw tightened. If anything, she looked like she was going to be sick.

"He's next door at Bernie's," the girl next to Darla said and then winced when Darla slapped her. I caught Darla's wrist when she would have swung her hand again. Tears filled her cold eyes, but I ignored Darla and focused on the brunette who'd spilled the beans.

"How do you know?"

"Because I got him here from Mama's," she admitted and offered up her own life. No wonder she'd been dead silent and pale since we arrived. "There was a reward if you found a Vandal alone and let them know."

Let them know. The 19Ds.

"How long?" If it happened in the last twenty-four, it was

Meeks. If not, then it was old shit rearing its head, and the Bay Ridge Royals sticking their fingers into everything was more than enough to destabilize the peace here.

The last thing any of us needed was a gang war, but between Jasper severing body parts and Meeks pushing an agenda, we were well on our way.

Another reason to get Emersyn the fuck out of here.

Darla tried to jerk herself free, but I shackled her wrist without a look. When she would have swung her free hand, I twisted the arm up behind her back and pushed her face first against the wall. I didn't slam her or do any other damage. If she kept struggling, she'd keep inflicting pain on herself.

"Just a couple of days. Some of the 19Ds were supposed to leave you a present, and then they didn't come back…"

The fuckers at the playground.

"Freddie's next door at Bernie's. Upstairs, backroom overlooking the alley. He was pretty high when they dragged him out of here for singing."

Only fucking Freddie would get bagged by a rival gang and then piss them off by being too cheerful about it.

"Hawk," I said over my shoulder. "Got a location."

"I've got it here, go," Vaughn said without Jasper responding verbally. I jerked my head toward the girl, and she hurried away from the wall and toward the doors. Darla hissed as I let her go.

JD moved to cover her while I headed for the doors with Jasper.

"I'm Candy," the girl told us.

"I don't care," Jasper informed her as he pushed the door open to the street. Thank fuck he left the axe behind. Candy winced, but I put a hand at the small of her back to keep her moving.

For her sake, Freddie better be in one piece. Bernie's shop next door to The Smokestack was one of those international bodegas where they sold a little bit of everything. I'd been in here once, and a five-foot-eight paunchy guy with a receding hairline ran the place, unironically named Bernie.

I welcomed the first wash of fresh air I sucked into my lungs. It might also have smelled of exhaust fumes, but I didn't give a damn. Even the competing scents of roasting peppers and spicy meat were a welcome reprieve from the more cloying nature of the scents inside of the club.

Bernie eyed us as we came inside. He was behind the register, stacks of cigarettes behind him. "I don't want any trouble."

"Keys." I ordered as I flipped the lock on the inner door and the sign to the *closed* side. There was a rat outside watching the front, but better to avoid surprises. "Keep your hands where I can see them."

The man passed over a set of keys and then raised his hands. "Like I said, no trouble."

Right.

I tossed the keys to Jasper, who caught them one-handed. He weaved through the store toward the back stairs, and the clunk of his boots hitting the steps as he went up them echoed through the shop. Somewhere, coffee hissed into a pot, the scent of it edging into the others and reminding me it'd been hours since we took a break, much less got food or coffee.

I'd kill for a cup right now.

Above our heads, the clunk of boots continued as I kept an eye on Candy and Bernie. She had her arms folded over her chest like that would keep her safe, and she looked anywhere but at me.

A double thump echoed.

Relief flickered through me. At my exhale, Candy cut me a glance. "Am I free to go?"

I didn't answer her while I tracked the movement from

above. Jasper didn't waste any time bringing Freddie down, and goddammit, he was more than fucked. His gaze was all over the place. His hair was stringy with sweat and his grin loopy.

"Kestrel," he greeted me as he staggered, despite Jasper mostly carrying him. Lurching forward, he tried to hug me, and I grimaced at the state of him. "It's been a hot minute, where you been?"

I flicked a look to the thunderous fury on Jasper's face and pulled out my phone. One text went out to Vaughn and the rats with us. Our cars would be on the way, and we'd leave them to clean up their own mess.

Freddie staggered against me and then focused on Candy. "Oh, I remember you."

She looked nervous. Freddie kept patting my chest, and I was used to dealing with doped out Freddie so I ignored it.

"She's the chick who offered me a blowjob and an eight-ball."

Great.

"She didn't give me either." He rolled his head to look at me. "That's pretty shitty, you know?"

Copper tinged some of the stress sweat rolling off of him.

"Yeah, Freddie, but you gotta just stop sticking your dick in everything, man. Particularly pussy that just wants to sell you out."

"Ah, they were fucking hysterical. Thought they'd get me high and I'd spill, so I started with kindergarten." His laughter cut through the silence, and Jasper just looked more pissed.

"Who?" He fired that one word like a bullet.

"I don't think I should tell you," Freddie said. "You're not being very nice to me."

"We'll deal with it later," I said more to Jasper than to

Freddie. We wouldn't get much out of him while he was this fucked up.

"Oh shit," Freddie said abruptly. "I'm starving." He tried to pull away from me to head over to the counter, and I dragged him back.

"Later," I told him.

We didn't need him puking in the car.

Jasper grabbed a carton of cigarettes and dropped three crumpled twenties on the counter. Then he eyed Candy. "Disappear."

My phone chirped, and I hauled Freddie toward the door. The lock turned, and I didn't have to glance back to know Candy had already taken off running for the backroom and out of the store.

Bernie stayed right where he was, his expression stone but his hands where I could see them.

"Put him in my car," Jasper ordered as the five vehicles pulled up smoothly.

Fine by me. I all but shoved Freddie into the backseat of Jasper's car. He didn't wait for me or the rats before he replaced the rat driving his car and peeled out with a screech of tires. Hopefully, the ride back to the clubhouse chilled him out some.

"Should we clean up?" JD asked, and I shook my head.

"That's their problem. Get out of here and scatter. Keep an ear to the ground."

Unsurprisingly, Vaughn was the last out of The Smokestack, and he exited shirtless, carrying a bag over one shoulder. Most of the blood had been cleaned off, but he would still need a shower when we got back. I popped the trunk as I slid into the driver's seat, and he set the bag inside it.

The weight as it landed in the trunk told me it likely had more than the axe in there.

Even before Vaughn fully closed the door, I pulled out,

and the rats streamed away behind us. Two of them followed me to the next corner, then turned away. In the distance, the hollow scream of a siren followed by a powerful bleating of a horn suggested paramedics had been dispatched.

"We're going to catch hell for that," Vaughn said.

I shrugged a shoulder. "They should have answered the question."

"He's out of control," Vaughn commented quietly.

"No," I said, disagreeing. "If he were out of control, it would have been a full-on bloodbath."

"He cut the asshole's hand off."

Yeah. Not much I could say to that.

"What's next? He really starts dismembering people?"

I chuckled. "We dismembered a guy yesterday." Or had he already forgotten?

"Fuck me," Vaughn muttered as he ran a hand over his face.

"No thanks. Pretty sure you already dipped where you weren't supposed to."

"Don't be a jealous prick." He rolled his head from side to side. "You wouldn't have sent her away either."

Bullshit. I had turned her down. The light in her eyes when she'd flirted with me had vanished when she realized I was one of the people who'd taken her. The tough shell she wore couldn't fully disguise the hurt, and I'd been a dick enough to lean into that. Her getting attached was a bad idea.

Her fucking Vaughn was a worse one.

"You want her, man," Vaughn said quietly, and I scowled as I adjusted my grip on the wheel. The urge to punch him thrummed through me, and I stuffed it down with every other impulse I'd curbed since we'd found out she was coming to town with her show.

"Wanting and having are two different things," I

reminded him. "She's not ours, Vaughn. This world isn't for her…"

"This world is a fuck load safer for her than the other one." Those words rocked me, and I frowned. "Don't play like you don't know that. Asshole partner abusing her. Management riding her and letting the pain go on because it made them money. Then someone fucked with those silks *after* I did my check, because I know they were damn secure."

I believed him on the last. None of us would mess around where her safety was concerned.

"And you said someone went for her in the parking garage at the hotel."

"That could have been a drunk driver." It was weak. Neither of us believed it.

"That family of hers leaves her out on the road months at a time. She was miserable, the pain in her performances? The rawness of it? You don't make that shit up, and she isn't that good of an actress."

On that, he was wrong—she was probably better than any of them realized. She hid those injuries from me in the first few days like they were nothing. Even her body lied when she wanted it to. The sheer amount of control she had over it… No kid should have to control themselves that much.

I'd taken the long way back to the clubhouse. We didn't have a tail, but that didn't really matter. It wasn't like the 19Ds wouldn't know who hit them and where to hit back. We'd have to be vigilant over the next few days.

Rome and Freddie both needed to stick close to home. Neither were good at it. They moved to their own beats. Fuck. Emersyn was still there.

Maybe this would be the impetus for Jasper letting her get back to some semblance of a real life. Or something.

I knew the answer to that without even bringing it up.

It wasn't until we turned toward the clubhouse itself that Vaughn asked, "Are you going to tell him?"

"Fuck no," I rumbled and let out a humorless laugh. "He's already in a dickish mood. Just don't fuck her again."

"No."

I cut a look at him. "Vaughn…"

"You heard me, I said no. If she wants me, I'm not turning her down." Instead of combative, it sounded like a promise. "She deserves good things."

"And you think that's us?" I couldn't help but scoff.

"I think we're a hell of a lot better than what she had. At least we give a damn if she's hurt and there are no new bruises on her. She can take a deep breath, and she can move… Goddamn, can she move."

My dick twitched at the last. Particularly with the emphasis he put on move. Not a good plan. Just, none of this was a good plan. Sooner or later, Raptor would find out. Or worse, Jasper would find out about Vaughn and then Raptor would.

We didn't need this grief in our life, especially if we had a turf war in the offing. Neither of us said a word as the double wide doors rolled back and I pulled into the clubhouse. Rats kept watch, and the doors closed behind us.

A familiar dark blue bike sat parked off to the side. Liam was still here. At least he'd had Rome's back. Vaughn headed inside with the bag, and I followed him. Freddie's singing carried as we entered, and the door behind me made a thud as I closed it. I was so not in the mood for Freddie's shit, but the soft sound of Emersyn's laughter was like a balm to my soul.

"Careful, Dove," Vaughn said ahead of me, and it took me a couple of steps to close the gap and see what he meant. Freddie was hunched over a bucket and seated on the sofa next to her. The sound of Freddie's retching wasn't much better than his singing, but instead of being turned off by it, Emersyn kept rubbing his back.

Something inside of me unclenched at her swift glance from Vaughn to me, then back again. The curve of her lips, the gleam in her eyes... Fuck me, I'd missed her today.

Nothing good was going to come from this.

Freddie threw up again, and I stripped off my jacket.

Nothing good.

CHAPTER 5

EMERSYN

It was early evening when Jasper rolled in with a staggering Freddie in tow. The smell of cloves, smoky fruits, and bitter chocolate clung to the air, underscored by the tobacco as Jasper exhaled a stream of smoke. Freddie had all but collapsed next to me on the sofa, puncturing the tension in the showdown between Liam and Doc. Rome and I hadn't said a word to each other, but he'd taken one look at me and then just nodded.

Maybe I was reading too much into it, but it felt like forgiveness, so I'd go with it. Thankfully, he didn't hesitate to bring a bucket over to where Freddie had begun to heave. I'd really rather he didn't throw up on me.

"How bad?" Doc asked, switching gears from the combative pose he'd adopted when Liam challenged our arrival. Oddly, Liam hadn't challenged *me*, just Doc. If anything, Liam had taken my return even better than Rome.

"Hey, Doc," Freddie managed before another gag took

him. I concentrated only on breathing through my mouth and not just because of the smell of the vomit, but the sour odor of sweat combined with the acridness of the urine weren't doing him any favors. My stomach twisted at the next choking cough that came from Freddie before he threw up again.

"Come on, Little Bit," Doc said, moving to tug me up from the seat so he could take my place. "How much did you do?"

Jasper caught my arm and tugged me a little farther away. Freddie seemed to fight to track where I was going, but his eyes were dancing all over the place and his skin was shiny. When Freddie finished retching, Jasper grasped the bucket and carried it out. My stomach lurched, but this wasn't the worst I'd seen.

I caught Rome staring at me, and then I glanced back at Freddie. He was a mess.

"I have Narcan," Doc said. "But I don't want to use it without knowing what you did." His focus remained on Freddie.

"Went to get food," Freddie said, the fun in his voice plummeting toward misery. "Sorry, Boo-Boo, got a little turned around. But we didn't have shit in the kitchen, and I can't cook anyway."

"It's fine," I said, folding my arms. "Though I hope you weren't picking up the drugs for me."

"Nah," Freddie said with a crooked grin that was all bad boy sass, like he'd been caught doing something he shouldn't have. "Unless you wanted some. 'Cause I know some places to score."

"No, she doesn't want you to score," Jasper snarled as he clapped Freddie in the back of the head and slammed the bucket down next to him on the floor. "Tell Doc what the fuck you took, then what the hell they gave you before we got there."

"You know, Hawk, you're an asshole." Freddie glanced up at him, not even an ounce of remorse in his expression. "We all know you got a crush on Boo-Boo, so be nice to her, 'cause she's pretty and she's nice. She smells good too."

I cut my gaze away and caught Liam rolling his eyes, and I swore for just a moment, the corners of his lips twitched. A hand danced against my back, and I glanced over my shoulder to find Rome holding a hand out to me.

Jasper glared down at glassy-eyed Freddie, and for once, Doc wore a similar expression. Compassion infused that anger, since they needed more information if they wanted to help him.

Taking Rome's hand, I let him pull me toward the kitchen. Doc and I had only gotten back minutes ahead of Jasper. We'd barely even made it inside before he'd arrived, dragging Freddie with him.

"Get him ice," Rome suggested. "The crushed will help."

That was a good idea, especially since he was sweaty. I opened the freezer and stared at the nearly empty appliance. There was an entire bag of crushed ice already there, in addition to the cubes in the ice maker. He turned the sink on while I filled an oversized tumbler with the ice.

When I turned around, he had a pair of washcloths soaked and squeezed out in his hands. Without a word, he passed them to me.

"Rome—" I started, but he pressed his fingers to my lips. Cool and still damp from the sink, they sent a chill through me. The calmness in his eyes washed over me, and he just gave me the barest shake of his head. I frowned until his gaze flicked past me.

Liam stood in the doorway, staring at both of us. To be honest, my hand still hurt from where I'd punched him. Not that it appeared I'd done any damage. His faint smirk and shake of his head seemed more aimed at his brother than me.

In fact, they were both just staring at each other, and yeah, that was my clue to get out of the way.

The last place I needed to be was trapped between them. If they told Jasper I was gone, then they told him. I'd deal with that fallout.

Freddie was sitting alone and miserable, while Doc and Jasper were locked in a hushed if intense conversation. Pale and wan, Freddie's sad condition tugged at my heart as I perched on the sofa next to him. With care, I traded him the bucket for the ice chips.

"Oh, Boo-Boo," he said with a rough groan. "You're a goddess."

"Uh huh." I nudged his chin to face away from me so I could wipe his brow and then his cheeks. "Don't breathe on me. You reek."

He grimaced. "I'm a mess."

"Apparently," I said, agreeing with him. At least he'd gotten most of the vomit into the bucket and not on his clothes. "Did you have to dumpster dive while you were at it?"

He let out a weak chuckle before he tucked his head against my shoulder. Ice dribbled from the corner of his mouth toward the round neck of my leotard. I hadn't really changed since I'd put on the dance clothes and used them to disguise my intentions earlier.

Despite my earlier success, I was right back here and no closer to answers than I'd been when I left. Except that it was my choice to be here now.

"I wanted to get you food, then I thought, you know, a little bit wouldn't hurt."

"They always say the first taste is free," I told him, carefully wiping around his face and then looking at his hands. "Suck on the ice. That will help with the dry throat."

He let out an indelicate belch, and thankfully, I hadn't

tried to do more than breathe through my mouth yet. "I know better," he mumbled, and if he weren't talking into my shoulder, I probably wouldn't have heard it. "Hawk's gonna kick my ass. Supposed to stay clean. Then I go wandering after pussy into 19D, know better than that, but she was at Mama's and I figured I could get you ribs."

The groan he let out was such a pained sound, and it jerked both Doc and Jasper's attention toward us. Slate-gray eyes locked on mine. The last time I'd seen Jasper, he'd kissed me. My lips tingled at the memory. Then he'd snarled and stormed out.

With a sigh, I dragged my gaze away from him back toward Freddie. He really did smell like a distillery rolled around in a trash can outside a fast-food strip joint.

I could use a shower already, so I kept that complaint to myself. "It's fine," I told him.

"But I never got you food. I was supposed to get you food and keep you safe while they dealt with the 19Ds, and instead, I wander off and leave you alone in…" He didn't really finish the thought as another bout of retching took him, and I angled his head over the bucket.

He wasn't the first person's head I had to keep up while they puked their guts out. The door slammed, the only precursor to Vaughn and Kestrel returning.

I swore my whole body shivered when I locked eyes with Vaughn. He was shirtless, which left all that gorgeous, colorful skin on display. His tattoos rippled and flexed as he moved, and it took monumental effort to push my gaze back up to his. Particularly now that I knew what those muscles felt like under my hands, my thighs, my ass…

"I hate my life," Freddie moaned, and I rubbed his back. The last thing he needed was platitudes and laughing at him probably wasn't fair, but he was kind of cute, even if he was a mess.

"It could be so much worse," I promised him, and he answered with another violent hurl.

"Careful, Dove," Vaughn cautioned me, and I tightened my thighs and tried to suppress my smile. Two words. Two words in that beautiful voice, and liquid heat pooled in my belly. Didn't matter that Liam surveyed all of us like he was a cop in an interrogation or Rome leaned against the wall like he was the only thing keeping it up. It didn't matter that Freddie emptied his stomach or that Jasper studied us both like he wanted to find an answer.

To be honest, the look on Jasper's face was probably the kindest I'd seen on him around Doc since I'd arrived. As for Doc, I'd avoided his troubled eyes as much as possible. While I didn't care if Jasper and the rest figured out I'd gotten away, I didn't want Jasper targeting his ire at Doc.

That thought sobered my lust right up.

Still, I tried not to smile as I glanced at Kestrel. My heart fisted as he let out a breath, and just like earlier with Jasper, Kestrel trapped me in his gaze. There was so much going on behind his eyes, but I didn't speak whatever language it was in. As hungry as I was to know more, it wasn't a good idea.

Though to be honest, I wasn't sure what was a good idea and what wasn't.

Not anymore.

"I want to die," Freddie moaned, and Doc let out an aggrieved sigh, then almost as one, he and Jasper stalked over to where I was sheltering him. The looks on their faces worried me.

"He's coming down," I told them. "And sobering up. It's a miserable place to be."

"We know, Little Bit," Doc assured me. "Don't worry. We're not going to hurt him."

"Of course we're not going to hurt him." Jasper snarled the words out like they were stuck between his teeth and he needed to bite them off. With a harsh exhale, he shook his head, then ran a hand over his face. "I'm tired. He's tired. It's been a long day and night. Let us take him, clean him up, and Doc can put him on IV fluids. I don't suppose you can stick around and keep an eye on him?"

The actual niceness in Jasper's tone caught me flatfooted. And I wasn't alone. Kestrel's brows raised, but Vaughn looked more amused than surprised. He rubbed his thumb against his lower lip, and it took effort to not track the motion.

"Well, after that sweet talk, how can I resist?" Doc said almost lightly and shot me a grin. I couldn't help it—a smile escaped with another laugh hot on its heels. This was probably one of the most bizarre situations I'd ever been in.

One of… No, the most bizarre. Period.

I licked my lips and shifted so that Jasper could haul Freddie up. Doc rescued the bucket and handed it off to Liam, who just took it and carried it into the kitchen. The dynamics present were as foreign to me as the thoughts Kestrel kept hidden away or the mumbled ravings that Freddie spilled.

"You know, I told them about the playground and the sandbox," he was saying to Jasper, patting his chest as Jasper all but carried him. The size differential between them seemed even more exaggerated. "They just don't get why tag was important, or why I was always safe when you were it because you always got the others first… Wait!"

Jasper slowed.

"Someone feed Boo-Boo," Freddie ordered, trying to swing around to look at me. "I put her in Vaughn's room so she could watch TV—Oh, hey, Boo-Boo! You're not supposed to be down here, Jasper said keep you out of the way so you were safe."

The lines of Jasper's back had gone stiff as a board. "Leave it, Freddie. C'mon."

"Fuck, I screwed up again, Hawk. Didn't I? I didn't get pinched. I promise. I wouldn't even have followed that pussy, except she said they had better ribs at the pig and poke place down in the Bowery. Besides, the prettiest pussy is right here, so I don't need to follow pussy."

"Freddie," Jasper growled. "Shut up. It's fine. Let's get you upstairs…"

I didn't get the rest of it, but Freddie hadn't shut up as Jasper hauled him out. Doc let out a sigh. "Someone grab my med kit and bag from the truck?"

Kestrel held out his hand for the keys that Doc tossed, then he nodded to me before he headed up the stairs. Kestrel spun on one heel and stalked back out. Then it was me, Vaughn, Rome, and Liam.

"Come on, Dove," Vaughn said, holding out a hand. "Let's get you cleaned up, then we'll get food."

"I'll get food," Rome said, and I looked over at him. He'd said so little. "What do you want?"

His gaze was on me, not them.

"I'll get it," Liam cut in. "And she can eat whatever the hell we get her."

Rome flipped him off but didn't look away from me. "You want ribs?"

"Is it safe to go out?" It was the only question that came to mind. Because even as I wiped my damp hands against my leggings, Liam's earlier words and Freddie's ramblings collided. There was blood on Vaughn too. He'd narrowed the distance to where I sat, and I had little choice but to take his hand.

Not that I minded. The warmth of his skin sliding over mine sent another shudder through my system. Today had been…a lot. On so many levels.

"It'll be fine. I'm fast," Rome told me. "What do you want, Starling?"

Liam rolled his eyes. But I hadn't missed the way his mouth tightened or the fact he flexed his fists. More, the temperature in the room shifted as Vaughn tucked me behind him and Rome put himself between us and Liam.

"Is there a place that does grilled cheese and fries?" Honestly, it sounded like the best thing ever. Way too many carbs, but I didn't care.

Liam and Rome glanced at each other.

"There's a diner on 86th and Grand," Vaughn said. "It's safe."

"What about everyone else?" Okay, I should have just let it go and not pushed, but I wasn't the only one here. The corners of Rome's mouth curved, and he gave me a shrug.

"Don't worry, Hellspawn. They're not so fucking delicate in their choices."

Rome thumped his brother, and Liam, the ass, laughed.

"We'll get pizza," was all Rome said, and then he shoved at his brother and it was just me and Vaughn.

With my hand in his, Vaughn led the way upstairs, and I shouldn't have been surprised that he took me straight to his room or that I followed him inside without an argument. Three steps in, and then Vaughn invaded my space. One finger under my chin, he tilted my head back, then his mouth was on mine.

I forgot how to breathe or object or the dozen other thoughts that had tangled in my head not thirty seconds earlier. Despite smelling like he'd been in a dessert flavored smoke factory with hints of copper sticking to him, Vaughn tasted like heat, sin, and escape.

Falling wasn't hard when he was lifting me up before I could even land.

CHAPTER 6

EMERSYN

Words formed, burst, then tried to reform as Vaughn stroked them right out of my mouth. A thousand things I could say, and none of them made it past the gatekeeper of his lips. Sliding my hands into his hair, I fisted the softness of it as he continued to hold my mouth captive.

Thick, powerful fingers dug into my ass as he lifted me. Drunk on the taste of him, I groaned as he began to move. The rasp of his denim against my leggings reminded me of how thin they were, and I swore I soaked right through them.

Three steps, and we were in the bathroom. I barely recognized myself in the mirror as he cut on the lights and shoved the door closed without letting go of me once. I'd worked with plenty of dancers not even half that coordinated.

The press of his mouth to my chin then down my throat let me suck in a ragged breath. His skin was so damn hot under my fingers. The raw demand to lose myself in him communicated beautifully. I wanted out of my clothes so I could writhe against him. Somewhere along the way, I'd hooked my thighs to his hips, and he maneuvered us in the bathroom, turning on the water, all the while still kissing me and massaging my ass. We never lost contact as I rolled my hips to grind against the very present erection.

I forced my eyes open, determined to see and savor him rather than just drown in sensation. The colorful pattern of art on his skin rippled as he moved, and I dug my fingers into the bunched muscle of his shoulder and…

"Vaughn," I groaned, then jerked away from his lips as I ran my fingers over his shoulder.

"Hmm, Dove?"

"You're bleeding."

He stilled for a moment, then twisted, still holding me as steam began to billow from the shower. The red speckles on his back couldn't be anything else. If I hadn't been so intent on consuming him, I'd probably have noticed the coppery odor. There were streaks on his back, almost like it had…

I wiggled, more to get down than to turn either of us on, even if the thickness of his erection reminded me of just how good he'd felt moving inside of me. Reminded me of the sexy piercing gliding against my inner walls and lighting me up.

But he was bleeding.

And Freddie had been a mess…

"The 19Ds. Freddie said something about them." I wasn't even sure what a 19D was other than a poorly numbered bralette of some kind.

"Dove." Vaughn's low growl caught me off guard, even as he set me on my feet. He slid a hand up to my chin, capturing it and effectively fixing my gaze on him. "They're no one who will be allowed near you. The ones who hurt Freddie have been dealt with. He's safe. So are you."

"I'm not worried about me." I frowned at him. "My problems are..." I ground my teeth together, but instead of pushing me, Vaughn focused those dangerous for my good sense topaz eyes on me. Their influence demanded I listen and beckoned me to choose. "My problems aren't whatever the 19D are. They're different."

I leaned back against the wall, exhausted all of a sudden, as if that confession pulled it out of me. All afternoon while I'd sat upstairs in Doc's clinic and even after he'd moved me down to his office, I hadn't been able to sort an easy solution to my problem.

There'd never been one.

"I want to tell you," I admitted. "Even if you're not asking. Maybe because you aren't asking. But I don't know how much I want to confide in you is because I like riding your dick and how much of it is because I want to trust you."

The corners of his mouth dipped a fraction, and I swore his gaze grew heavier where it rested on me. The breath backed up in my lungs. I hadn't lied about wanting to confess. Maybe telling someone would help. Or maybe it was another fool's errand. Every other time...

This wasn't other times. I'd never had another time like this. Kidnappers that I returned to of my own volition, even after I'd escaped. Doc had stared at me for a long moment when I asked him to bring me back. His silence had gone on so long, I'd finally said we could call Liam if that would be easier for him.

Then, as now, I hadn't wanted to confront the questions in his eyes, even if I'd wanted to explain myself, and I wasn't sure I had the words. Vaughn... Everything about him beckoned to me, and maybe I just needed to get laid but that wasn't fair to either of us.

Fuck me.

Why did life have to be so goddamn complicated?

"You like my dick," Vaughn said finally, the darkness in his gaze retreating for a twinkle. Relief sagged through me and I almost hated myself for it, but he was letting me off the hook.

"I do," I told him, and then I dropped down to my knees as I tugged his zipper down and then helped him peel out of the denim. He paused me only long enough to toe off his shoes, blood spattered across them as well. I glanced up to find Vaughn watching me.

I could ask.

But he'd said the blood wasn't his.

He could ask me.

But I'd said I wasn't sure I was ready to tell.

We let each other off the hook. Not letting go of his gaze, I leaned forward to nuzzle a kiss to his navel. I could study the tattoo there. Hell, I could study any of the tattoos decorating his beautiful body. But I'd rather taste him.

The heat of his skin scorched my fingertips as I shoved the pants down. The shower kept running, and we were probably using up all the hot water. I didn't think Vaughn cared.

I didn't.

His cock bumped against his stomach as I freed it, red and thick just like I remembered it. The piercing fascinated me, I wasn't going to lie. I half forgot to finish yanking his jeans down as I wrapped a hand around his engorged length and stroked up the satiny skin, even as I teased one of the silvery knobs with my tongue.

Eyelids half lowered, Vaughn stared down at me and rubbed a thumb against his lower lip as I explored the piercing with my tongue. Everything outside of the room faded away as I opened my mouth and slowly swallowed against the tip. His jaw clenched, but he didn't thrust forward. In fact, the muscles along his chest and arms rippled as though he held himself back.

Sucking against the tip, I rolled my tongue over the saltiness of the pre-cum already beading along his slit. I hadn't really gotten to play with his dick as much as I might have wanted. With every stroke, I took him deeper into my mouth.

Slow, even strokes pushed him against my throat, and I could get him only so far before I had to swallow around the gag. Each time I pulled him out, I nibbled and sucked on the piercings before rolling my tongue over the head. His dick grew hotter in my palms, and his eyes were so laser focused on me, I swore my cunt tingled for the moment he took off the leash.

All at once, I wanted to push him. I wanted to see how far I could go before he would demand more. I alternated between thrusting him deep and swallowing around him and double fisting his cock so I could stroke it away from my lips.

Each time I pushed him, he held himself in check. He let me play. This sexy beast of a man seemed intent on letting me do whatever the fuck I wanted. Then he growled, "Dove."

Everything in me clenched.

Yes. Please.

I pulled off his cock and licked my lips. "Yes, Vaughn?"

"Get naked, or I'm going to rip those pants open so I can fuck you with them on."

He did not have to tell me twice. My soaked panties had long since disintegrated, and I didn't take my gaze off him as I stripped down and dropped the clothes where they landed.

It wasn't until I'd stripped that everything about him seemed to arrest. Nipples peaked and aching while I rubbed my thighs together, as if that would alleviate the need to feel his cock pounding into me again, I almost held my breath waiting for him to move.

"What happened to fucking me?" I demanded. He traced fingers around my upper arm and then across my breast bone with such utter gentleness, it almost brought me to tears.

"You're hurt."

Two words, and it almost sucked all the oxygen out of the room. I glanced down at the faint shadows of bruises smudging my skin. I'd barely even noticed them.

"I'm not."

The hand he'd been so gently tracing over me with locked around my throat in a grip that was both kind and demanding. How the fuck he did that, I had no idea. With his thumb, he tilted my head back as he stared at me.

"Don't ask me," I begged him, and his eyes narrowed.

"Dove…"

"It doesn't hurt, and I bruise easily. The only thing I want to feel right now is you. So please don't ask me."

I didn't want to lie to him. The bruises went across my upper arms too, probably from where Liam had picked me up. Lifting my left hand, Vaughn stared down at the knuckles. The bruises there were a lot more noticeable, but he only turned my hand over to look at the palms.

I'd banged them up during my escape.

"I need you to trust me, Dove," he admitted. The roughness of his palm as he cupped my cheek was a stark contrast to the gentleness of his actions. "But you're trusting me with your body—that's a start."

Then his mouth was on mine, thank fuck, and he slid his arm around me.

"Up." I felt more than heard the command as he sucked against my tongue. Or maybe I imagined it. But I pushed up as he lifted, and between us, I lined him up and then sank down on him.

The fullness of him pushing into me was intense. Even as

wet as my cunt was, I groaned, and his answering moan sounded nearly as tortured. The water was still somewhat hot as he pushed us underneath it, and then I was against the shower wall as he set a punishing pace.

Every brush of his piercing against my inner walls sent them spasming, and I fought to match him, but each time I thought I had it, he would shift and slow down or speed up. I dragged my nails across his scalp and let my body go loose. Even my nipples rubbing against his chest ached for more contact.

Vaughn grunted, and then the bite of his teeth dragged on my lower lip. "Look at me, Dove," he ordered, and I forced my eyes open again. "See me." Thrust. "Feel me." Thrust. "Take me."

The trembling began in my toes and shivered its way up my legs until my thighs were quaking. Every time he pushed into me deep, he ground against my clit, and it just added to the spasms. Heat uncoiled and flashed through me, and I kept my eyes open and on his as I splintered.

His grin turned fierce, triumphant as he pushed me through that orgasm. A scream tore from my throat at every hot pulse of his piercings hitting that spot inside me.

"Trust me," he demanded as I shook and quaked around him. The clamping down of my cunt didn't slow him. If anything, it spurred him on, and then I swore I came again. Everything went liquid, my muscles, my thoughts, and my fears.

The hot water sluiced it away, and I strained up to meet his kiss, answering the only way I could right now. I answered him with *me*. Vaughn came with a shout, the heat of his release rushing out to fill me, and I clung to him as he pumped his hips once, twice more before burying his face against my throat.

"Trust me, Dove," he whispered in a rough voice as we

panted. "I won't disappoint you. I promise."

The words ate at me, even after he eased out of my cunt and helped me wash his hair. They nibbled around my consciousness as I soaped up his back and then ran my hands over the tight muscles of his ass. They sank into my bones as he massaged my breasts and then he followed me as we rinsed off and left the shower behind for towels.

Vaughn yanked the door open to his bedroom after he hung his towel up. "I'll get you something of mine to wear," he offered, but he didn't move from the doorway. Everything about him went rock hard still.

"I already know she's in there. Neither of you are very discreet." Kestrel's voice crackled, cold and hot at the same time. "Or quiet."

"What do you want?" Vaughn didn't respond to his comments. Instead, he just strolled out into the room nude and went over to the closet. Taking a page from his book, I leaned against the doorframe. My damp hair clung to my shoulders, but I still had the towel wrapped around my torso.

Kestrel cut a look at me rather than answering Vaughn, and I raised my brows. The coolness in his blue-green eyes kept his secrets hidden. "Have you really thought this through, Sparrow?"

"Leave her alone," Vaughn ordered. "And don't be a dick to her." He had dragged on sweatpants in the closet, hiding that magnificent ass and gorgeous cock. At least his chest was still on display.

"I'm not being a dick," Kestrel retorted. "Interesting that was the first place you went."

They glared at each other. Tension spiked, and the air seemed to get even colder. I swore it looked like Kestrel wanted to take a swing at Vaughn, and from the way Vaughn opened and closed his fists, he'd welcome it.

I cleared my throat. Both gazes swung toward me

abruptly, and they landed with force that had me shivering. Vaughn swore and yanked a drawer open. He crossed to me without a word and pulled a shirt over my head. It was soft and huge, and it smelled just like him.

My nipples beaded at the thought, even as I let the towel fall away. The only thing between me and their eyes was this red cotton.

"That's a good color on you," Vaughn commented, brushing his knuckles along my jaw.

"Goddammit, Falcon," Kestrel swore abruptly as he stood. "Jasper is *here*. As soon as he's done with Freddie, where do you think the first place he's going to go is?"

They both glanced at me again, and Vaughn's jaw tightened. My stomach bottomed out. Had I lost an ally that fast? Not that we'd put a label on the sex. It had been great, but it didn't have to mean anything. I folded my arms and waited.

"You know what, I don't care," Vaughn said with a slice of his hand through the air. "Dove wants to stay here, she can stay here. She wants to go to her room, she can go there. We brought her here to keep her safe, not to keep her prisoner."

My heart buoyed.

Kestrel raked a hand over his face.

"Jasper doesn't own her, and he isn't the only one with a right to care about her." As much as I loved Vaughn's words, I really needed them to remember something.

"I'm still here, and it would be great if you remembered that and stopped talking about me in the third person."

Pinning me with a look, Kestrel sighed. The defeat in his eyes hurt me. I couldn't even explain why, but I just wanted to chase it away. Something.

"Sparrow, I know you don't have a reason to trust me and I burned that bridge with you, but I need you to listen to me because if you don't, dumbass over here is gonna get himself killed."

"No, I'm not," Vaughn assured me.

"Yes," Kestrel said, ignoring him. "He is. Jasper…"

Their phones both beeped, and Kestrel glanced at his as Vaughn walked back into the bathroom.

"Fuck," Kestrel swore. "The twins are back with food, and they would like us to let you out of whatever cupboard we're hiding you in."

"And Jasper will be down in a minute," Vaughn finished for him.

The question was, did I go and pretend this didn't happen and cover with Jasper? Or did I maintain the fact that Jasper didn't own me and push it?

Neither man said anything. They were both waiting.

I could feel it.

Pivoting, I returned to the bathroom and scooped up my clothes. Regardless of my audience, I pulled the leggings back on. Kestrel's eyes narrowed at me, but he didn't comment.

"I'm not making any promises," I told them. "But I don't want to cause any problems, either."

"Trust me, Dove," Vaughn murmured as he pressed a kiss right behind my ear. "You are not the problem." He shifted around me to go and get a clean shirt, and I locked gazes with Kestrel again. He only mouthed the words 'thank you.'

I nodded.

He was right—we had burned some bridges when I found out who he was. But maybe we could build some new ones. Folding my arms, I waited until they were both ready to go. Kestrel checked the hallway before I left Vaughn's room.

I needed to understand these guys, how they worked and where their friendships were in relation to each other. Not everyone who came and went here was close. Some were definitely closer than others—like Freddie and Jasper, which seemed like a weird combination. Other relationships were more strained—like Jasper and everyone else.

Or Liam.

I needed to know where I stood. And who I could trust.

Because I was here.

As much as I might not want to admit it…I needed their help.

CHAPTER 7

EMERSYN

If I thought going down for food that night would solve anything, I was wrong. Not only did Jasper not make an appearance for food, Doc only dropped in for a couple of minutes to grab some before he carried it upstairs.

He and Jasper remained shut away with Freddie. Vaughn got a phone call and then left with Liam burning out behind him, and then it was just me, Kestrel, and Rome. My grilled cheese and fries were amazing, but not enough of a conversation starter.

I half expected Rome to ask questions, but he didn't. All he said was, "Going out."

"Watch your back," Kestrel told him as he stood.

"Should you be going out alone?" I had no idea what was going on, but it seemed a fair question to ask.

Rome only glanced at me, his faint smile almost but not quite a smirk. Clearly, he was thinking if I went out by myself why shouldn't he? But he still didn't say anything as he tugged my hair gently on his way past.

Then it was me and Kestrel.

Alone.

I cleaned up my trash and then glanced around the kitchen for something to do, but there really wasn't anything.

"C'mon, Sparrow," Kestrel said, handing me a beer. "Let's go watch some TV until you're up for sleeping."

Despite how long I tried to wait, Vaughn didn't come back and neither did Rome. By the third beer, my yawns were cracking my jaw, and I had a feeling that was Kestrel's intention.

He walked me up, told me goodnight, and then left me in my room, alone. The next three days were like nothing had ever happened with Jasper, Vaughn, or Doc for that matter.

First, I didn't see any of them, and I was too worried about Freddie to get butthurt over it. Okay, correction, I was too worried to get upset over the absolute lack of Jasper and Doc, but that didn't explain Vaughn *unless* he was taking a shift looking after him. Detoxing was a bitch.

I'd offer to help, but I didn't know where he was.

And I'd tried a couple of the doors, they were either locked or the rooms were empty. Not exactly encouraging participation. Weird thing was that no one watched me as closely. Or at least they didn't seem to be.

Kestrel was there in the mornings, since he woke me up each day and made breakfast. I tried to help one day, but he just kept waving me at the table with the cracked seal around the edges and the splits in the chairs. Rome breezed in, smelling of sunshine, cold air, and paint, then he was gone again.

Something Doc had said to me kept circling around and around in the back of my mind. *When he disappears for a few days, you can usually expect something beautiful to show up.* No

Rome meant no Liam. When Kestrel left, I either watched television or I went to the studio.

Most days, I went into the studio. I was still trying to figure out what to say. I'd work out how to approach the topic with Vaughn, but the end of the day would come and go without any sign of him. On the fourth day, I ignored the breakfast Kestrel had fixed, poured my coffee, and walked the hell out of their clubhouse.

I'd found a pack of Jasper's cigarettes tucked into the corner of the sofa and the lighter had been under it. I might have cleaned up one afternoon after I'd torn the place apart in frustration.

They even had a vacuum tucked away in a cubby. The rat who'd found me throwing everything in the living room had stared at me with a dirty smirk and vicious eyes. I'd dealt with grubby little sycophants like him all my life. When I stared at him with no expression, his smirk fell away and he finally stammered an 'excuse me' before he ducked out.

It was the first time I'd seen any of the rats come inside since I'd been back, and I hadn't been hiding in my room. Admittedly, I spent hours in the studio, and one night, I'd snuck out of my room and down to Vaughn's, but his door had been locked and he didn't come when I knocked.

I needed Freddie to show me how to pick locks. That would be a useful skill. Which brought me full circle to heading outside. I was in dance capris, one of Vaughn's shirts that I'd kept over a dance leotard, heavy socks to shield my feet, and a pair of running shoes I'd found in my stuff.

"Sparrow," Kestrel called, but I kept moving.

The door banged as I strode out of it. There were guys out in the warehouse. More rats probably. Why did they call them *rats*? Couldn't they come up with a more attractive name?

They're a street gang, what do you expect? I ignored the little voice in my head as I made for the exit Rome and I had used that lead to the quiet little alley. An alarm shrilled when I hit the crash bar and opened the door. It cut off before I'd even taken three steps.

The cold air was downright bitter, and frost nipped at my nose as I lifted a cigarette to my lips and lit it. Fuck, it was cold out here. Colder than the day I'd left. There was even a hint of frost on the alleyway, or maybe it was just icy here.

Behind me, the door cracked open as a breeze stirred a lone paper flyer loose from behind a trash can and sent it sliding down the alley in the direction of the street. The cigarette smoke burned my throat and helped settle my quaking hands.

Well, the illusion of it anyway.

I had jitters worse than Freddie had when he'd been throwing up his lungs.

A heavy jacket dropped on my shoulders, and I didn't look back. Kestrel wore the heavier leather jacket the last couple of days when he left. I guess that should have been my first clue about how cold it was out here.

"If you wanted to come outside..." He didn't finish the sentence.

I picked an imaginary loose hair from my lower lip before sucking in a deep breath of the smoke. On the exhale, I aimed it upward. "Thank you for not insulting me with some bullshit platitude about just asking you."

"Well," he said slowly, circling around me to lean against the wall. In his hand was a cup of coffee, and the steam curled up from it.

It reminded me of my own, and I swallowed a mouthful, actually enjoying the way it burned down my throat before hitting my stomach. It wasn't so hot that it scalded but definitely hot enough to chase away the chill.

Across from me, Kestrel watched me with those enigmatic eyes housing all their secrets. "We both know that if you wanted to leave, you could have. You've had plenty of time over the last few days."

I froze. Someone had told him? Did it matter who? The idea of Rome or Doc telling on me kind of hurt a little. And Liam? I didn't know what to do with that. Then again, it didn't really matter, did it? He knew. "Then why chase me out here?"

"Because it's fucking freezing," Kestrel answered easily. "And you don't have any money or car keys. I'm also pretty sure you don't know how to drive."

I glared at him. "I took driver's ed."

"But did you pass it?" He raised his eyebrows as he lifted the cup of coffee for a sip.

What a dick.

Still, his eyes almost seemed to gleam with some suppressed mischief.

"Wouldn't you like to know?" I muttered, then took another deep draw on the cigarette. It wasn't doing shit for my mood, but it helped to get out here.

"I would. Especially if I plan on getting you a car to drive."

The cigarette fell from my fingers. He stepped forward and on it while I stared at him.

"I didn't..." I'd rather masturbate with sand paper than admit that. Grimacing, I stared down at my coffee cup. "I didn't fail it, but I couldn't get enough practice hours in before I had to leave for the next show."

"How many hours did you practice?"

I got another cigarette out, and he crossed over to light it for me. "Thank you."

"See, that wasn't so hard, Sparrow. We used to do this every day."

I glared at him, but honestly, my heart just wasn't in it. After days of being relatively ignored, it was nice to just talk to him. "What's with all the bird names?"

"You answer my question, and I'll think about answering yours."

"How the hell is that fair? I already answered one."

"We weren't negotiating then." The fucker grinned at me. When I didn't respond, he tilted his head, and I swore everything in me clenched. "C'mon, Sparrow. Play with me."

"You think you're charming."

"I know I am," he admitted without an ounce of shame or bravado. "That's not why I want you to play."

I turned to look down the alley and took another long drink of the coffee. "Fifty-five or fifty-six. Something like that." Honestly, I was pulling that number out of my butt. I couldn't remember what the form said.

"But you finished the class?"

"Yes, I finished the class, and why are you asking me two questions?"

"Why are you answering it?"

I scowled, and his smile grew a little wider.

"Birds fly free. They choose where they land."

That was…elegant and beautiful. "Except if someone clips their wings."

"That's why we don't let anyone clip us, and we'll tear free the jesses anyone tries to put on the others." The quiet certainty offered a far more provocative threat.

I licked my lips. "Like Freddie?"

One nod. "And you."

That took us too close to a vulnerable and sensitive place. I frowned and glanced at the cigarette again. "Freddie doesn't have a bird name."

"Ask him when he's feeling better."

"What if I want to ask you?"

"Just because you ask doesn't mean I'll tell you." The dare in his eyes said the rest—we could keep playing the question game, or I could let it go.

"Fine," I exhaled. "I'll ask him later."

A car horn honked in the distance. Trucks rumbled by. Somewhere, I swore there was a louder, lower pitched horn. It reminded me of those at train crossings, but I didn't remember seeing any of those.

"You want to go to work with me today, Sparrow?"

"Where's work?" I glanced at him.

"Not here," he offered, and when I narrowed my eyes, he flashed another smile. "I work at a shop down the road. It's not that far, but far enough that you'll be out. Probably not the most comfortable." The last was said with a hint of a shrug.

"Do you think Freddie will be out today?"

"No, Sparrow. They took him to Doc's clinic so Doc could let him sleep off the worst of it. It's not easy to get everything out of his system without the tremors and delirium setting in, and if we keep him out, then at least we can get his system clean before he starts trying to wander off and score again. At least when he's sober, there's a chance he makes better choices."

"That's why I haven't seen Jasper or Vaughn?"

He nodded. "They're taking turns sitting with him. Vaughn's got work too. You missing them?"

I'd finished my second cigarette, and it had definitely done what the first hadn't—it had eased my agitation. "It would be weird if I was."

"It would be weirder if you weren't." He shrugged.

"How did you know?" I met his stare.

"Know what?"

"That I left."

The corners of his mouth tipped, and he dropped his chin. "I didn't, for sure, until just now."

Fuck.

Goddammit.

Before I could spin away though, he caught my arm and dragged me back to him. To be fair, it wasn't like he was gripping me that tight. I could yank away. Leaning into my space, he studied me.

"Sparrow, you relaxed. Before, you were jumpy as fuck around all of us. Even Vaughn."

"I didn't feel very jumpy when I fucked him."

"Good, if you were, I'd have to beat the shit out of him." The simplicity of the statement lent a lot more weight than all the yelling in the world. "And I make it a point of noticing things, particularly since you've been hellbent on escape since you got here, and you've been left alone for days and didn't try to leave."

My heart sank. It was one thing to admit it to myself, but another to admit it to them.

"I'm not mad," he said quietly, and that last bit pulled my attention upward. "We want you to feel safe here. Even if you don't belong here."

Why did those last few words hurt?

"I thought you brought me here to protect me."

"We did." He stroked the inside of my arm with his thumb. The quiet tone kept me riveted because I didn't want to miss a single word. "Doesn't mean this place is good for you, or that we are."

I frowned.

"But you're here, Sparrow, and nothing is going to happen to you here."

I licked my lips. "The threat…it's gone, right?" Was I testing him?

Maybe.

"Your former dance partner is gone," he admitted. "He won't lay a finger on you again."

"Then—" His cool eyed frown silenced my next question

"That wasn't the only threat. Someone cut your silks the night of the performance."

Surprise flickered through me. Oh. Shit. I'd almost forgotten that.

"And someone, it may be nothing, but someone tried to run you down in the parking lot."

"You said it was a drunk driver." Yes, that was an accusation.

"I didn't want you afraid."

The laughter escaping me might have bordered a little on the hysterical.

Okay, so it crossed the border into a lot hysterical.

"So you bring me here?"

"That was Jasper's idea," Kestrel admitted, drawing me right up next to him so he could tuck an arm around me. The warmth had me leaning into his side, even if I shouldn't. "And as much as I hate to admit it, I think he was right."

"Can I ask why?"

"You can."

I snorted. "Will you answer me?"

"Not yet, Sparrow." He brushed a strand of my hair back away from my face.

"Why not?"

"You still don't trust us yet."

I frowned.

"But you're closer." He turned us both toward the door to go back inside. Probably a good plan since the coffee was gone.

"How do you know?"

He kept one hand at my back as he reached for the door to open it. "You came back."

I paused to study him, the noise inside not really registering or the fact that we had an audience now.

"And you're still here," he finished. "It's as good a place to start as any."

CHAPTER 8

VAUGHN

"Grabbing food," Doc said as he leaned in the door. "You two should shower and get some sleep. I think we're past the worst."

Jasper glanced up from where he'd set up vigil near the head of the bed. "You go." The roughness of a three-day growth covered his cheeks, his usually neat beard having grown. "I don't want to leave him alone."

"He's going to sleep," Doc offered. "He'll be al—"

"I said I wasn't leaving him alone, Doc. Let it go." The curt tone rolled right off Doc, and I pushed up from the broken chair I'd been sitting in until my ass had gone numb. I needed a shower. Hell, I needed food, a shower, and about ten hours of horizontal time asleep with my girl.

The dare in her dark eyes seemed an ever-present phantom in my mind. My own personal ghost. Not that I didn't have many. Still, she was the best of all of them, and I'd barely gotten any time with her.

Fuck, she probably thought I'd hit it and quit it by now. She'd need an apology. And a gift.

Probably some groveling.

I had zero fucks in that department. I'd make it up to her on my knees and with my face buried in her cunt until she came so hard and so often, she blacked out.

That would be a good start.

Doc retreated into the hallway as I stepped out. The clinic had been the best location. Doc could monitor him, keep him sedated while we flushed his system, and since we didn't really know what the hell he'd taken this time, we needed the help.

Especially when he flipped out and tried to have a seizure back at the clubhouse. I was here to spell Jasper out, even if he refused to leave the room and hadn't slept in more than thirty-minute bursts in that chair. The clinic was closed currently, and it was nearly sundown. Doc wasn't usually open on the weekends unless he was doing a vaccination clinic.

"You should get him to take some time for real sleep."

At Doc's advice, I glanced over my shoulder. "Give it a rest. You know he's not going to. Freddie falls off the wagon, and Jasper takes it as a personal failure. It's one thing when he gets pinched by the cops and tossed in jail for a few days. This…"

I shook my head. It wasn't just the drugs. It was the fact he had some cracked ribs and a concussion. There were signs that they'd burned his feet. None of us discussed the torture, we'd just catalogued it.

The 19Ds were going to be in a world of bloody and brutal hurt as soon as Freddie came through this. It wasn't a matter of if, but when. At the moment, we were all better off with Jasper preoccupied with Freddie. Might give Kellan and me time for damage control.

"You guys left a bloody mess down at the Smokestacks," Doc said as he followed me up the stairs. The community center upstairs was a great option for local kids to come and hang out after school. A safe place out of the weather and away from the dealers.

Doc's was a haven.

No one disturbed it. Not even us.

Especially not us.

I stripped off my shirt, ignoring the fact that Doc still followed me.

"Doc, you know better than to ask questions." What he didn't know, he couldn't testify to. In the bathroom, I yanked the knob to turn on the water before I scrubbed a hand over my face. I could use a shave, but I'd save that for back at the clubhouse. "If you plan on hanging out, want to grab me some clean clothes out of our bags?"

The look he shot me was less than friendly, but I ignored it. He had a right to his opinions. He went out of his way for us a lot and took a lot of shit for it. Still, I was too fucking tired to play this game right now. The door closed behind him, and I ducked under the water.

This wouldn't be anywhere near as pleasant as my last shower, so I made quick work of cleaning up and was already toweling off by the time Doc came back. I'd throw the clothes I'd stripped out of into the washer before I went back to kick Jasper out.

"I'm going for food," Doc said, repeating his earlier sentiment from where he stood in the middle of the common room, staring at the posters on the wall. There were a lot of them. Movies. Musicals. Even a symphony. Two for ballets.

People would freak if they knew they all had a personal meaning to us.

"So you said," I told him, but instead of heading back

downstairs to find the washer, I waited Doc out. "But you're still here."

Silence greeted my statement.

A full minute passed before he finally said, "Why did you guys take Emersyn?"

Surprise snapped through me. First and foremost, we hadn't told Doc anything about this. It wasn't *our* secret to tell. Nor would we. I'd carry it to my grave.

"It doesn't matter." The lie flowed off my tongue easily. "Don't ask questions, Doc. You know better."

"I do," he said, then cut a look at me. "What I don't know I can't reveal. This time, however, I helped put that girl back together and I've left her in your care."

Something about the way he said that last sentence tickled the back of my mind.

"I know the hell she went through, maybe better than any of you," Doc continued. "But she's not one of you. So why did you take her? And how long are you planning on keeping her?"

The hell she wasn't. The idea of letting her go flushed anger through me. I'd already told him to not ask questions, so I walked away.

I walked away before I punched him. The idea of her leaving pissed me off.

It pissed me off way more than it should.

Doc didn't let it go though, he followed me all the way down the stairs and to the mechanical room where the washer and dryer were stacked. I threw my vomit stained clothes inside.

The weight of his stare bored into me. When I was done starting the washer, Doc blocked my exit from the room.

"You don't want to do this, Doc," I informed him. Personally, I liked him. He was a solid guy. But if he kept this up, I would push back.

"Answer my question," Doc ordered. "You owe me that much. Particularly where *she* is concerned."

"Why the fuck do you care so much?" Jasper demanded in a harsh tone, and Doc half twisted away from me to face the hall. Probably better than letting Jasper be at his back in this mood. "You're a doctor. You helped us put her back together. Your interest in her ended there. So did your need to know."

"You don't get to decide that," Doc stated in a colder voice than I'd ever heard out of him before. "None of you do. I grant you a lot of latitude. I do that as a favor." Every word held an element of warning and threat. Over Doc's shoulder, I couldn't miss Jasper's eyes narrowing or the way his expression turned foreboding.

"She's not yours, Doc." The words were like an incendiary device.

"She's not a possession," Doc countered. "She's not your bitch to mark and keep."

The earlier anger billowed into a detonation of fury. She didn't belong to either of them. *But* she had shared herself with me.

"What did you call her?" Jasper had a gun in his hand, and Doc stood between me and him. Three things happened that I could not explain. Jasper's bloodshot eyes were a little wild. The gun he pulled out never actually made it up to be aimed at Doc. In fact, Jasper barely made it to Doc before Doc had disarmed him and wrenched an arm behind Jasper as he slammed Jasper against the wall.

I took two steps forward, but Doc pointed the gun at me and I stopped. I'd take the hit if I had to, but Jasper's face was a rictus of pure rage. Doc hadn't done anything but defend himself, and fine…fair.

Withdrawing a step, Doc released Jasper, then gave him a shove into the room with me.

"Now," Doc said in that same cool voice he'd used earlier.

I'd seen him stop wholesale slaughter using that tone. He'd backed down more than one would-be gangster with an axe to grind or some meth head flying on a bad dose. "Let's get a few things straight. I help the Vandals because you kids need it. I look after your injuries. I patch you up. I clean up Freddie when he falls off the wagon."

Jasper exhaled and started forward a step, but I gripped his shoulder. He shot me a dirty look but stopped. Doc wasn't pointing the gun anymore. Better to keep it that way. "Just listen," I advised. We could still take him if we had to, but I really didn't want it to come to that.

"I'm not one of your rats to push around, and you're going to learn you catch a lot more flies with honey than vinegar," Doc continued.

"I'd catch plenty with your bloated corpse too," Jasper countered. "Your point?"

"Explain why Emersyn is here. I checked. Raptor's in the hole. There's no way he knows."

Oh.

Shit.

Jasper gave a little jerk. I glanced at him. Raptor was in the hole? What the hell happened to land him in solitary?

"She doesn't belong here. The injuries I got, you brought her in pretty damn beat up. But that problem has been dealt with." It wasn't a question, and neither of us confirmed or denied it.

However, *that* particular problem was in so many different pieces and scattered for fish bait. He wouldn't be appearing again.

Ever.

"But she's *healthy* now, and in one piece. So why are you keeping her? You damn well know Raptor will tear your head off your shoulders when he finds out, if he doesn't already know."

Fuck. I hadn't considered that. If he did know, it may be why he'd ended up in solitary. At the same time... "She needs us," I answered before Jasper could, and he shot me a look. I ignored him. Unlike him, I had been paying attention to her. I'd tasted her pleasure and her pain.

Worse, I'd felt the fear she ruthlessly tried to bury and the flinches that told me so much worse had happened to her.

"She needs to be with us where she is safe and she can heal the wounds we can't see."

That earned me a measured look from Doc and a deeper frown from Jasper. "What do you know?"

"Enough," I said with a shrug. "You weren't the only one backstage and watching her before shit went sideways with the dick. More, I've seen how she is now. How she watches and gauges our actions and reactions before she does things, like she isn't positive we won't react negatively. And more... she's still here."

That got Jasper's attention more effectively than slapping him. "You think it means something she hasn't tried to escape again?"

I shrugged. "Of course it means something. What exactly? I have no idea. But I agree with you that she needs to stay with us." I ignored the surprise in his expression. "Try getting to know her, Hawk, and stop snarling at her. You might find out more. When she trusts us enough to tell us where the other threats are..."

"We'll eliminate them."

"Agreed." Doc's singular nod and the hard emphasis he put on both syllables confirmed we were in lockstep on that issue.

I didn't think Doc could shock me more than he had when he disarmed Jasper.

I was wrong.

He stripped down the gun, unloading it and removing the

clip before he handed it back to Jasper. "The next time you pull that on me, you better shoot me, because I'm done with the attitude."

"What do you mean by agreed?" Jasper took the gun back slowly and didn't seem in a rush to put it together.

"Exactly what I said. Now go shower and change, you reek. Vaughn, keep an eye on Freddie or get some shut eye. I'm going for food. When Freddie's well enough to go back, I'm going to pick up Emersyn to spend some time here…"

"What?"

"Excuse me?" Jasper's words crashed into mine.

"You heard me," Doc said, leveling us both. "When Raptor asks, he's damn well going to know she had *all* of our protection, that includes mine. But you go ahead and fight me on this. I dare you."

With that, he turned and stalked away from us. It wasn't until the door closed at the end of the hall that Jasper turned to look at me. "What the hell was that?"

"I think Doc's smitten with Dove." And that might be putting it mildly.

Instead of saying anything, he slammed his fist into the door then left the room, and his feet hit the stairs with noisy thumps. I exhaled and rubbed my face before I went looking for my phone. I didn't have it in these pants, it was still in the room where we'd been looking after Freddie.

Dove didn't have a phone, though. That was something we needed to change. She wasn't a prisoner, and being able to reach out to her would be nice. Nicer, would be her reaching out to us.

Freddie was still out and snoring. He looked way too damn young at the moment, even with the dark shadows under his eyes. It was too close to how he'd looked…

Yeah, I shoved that thought out of my mind and dropped into a chair with my phone and sent a message off to Kestrel.

He didn't answer, but then he was probably at the shop. If it was loud there, he wouldn't hear his phone. I let Rome know Freddie seemed to have turned the corner.

Rome: *Good.*

One word, but better than nothing. Still...

Me: *How is Dove?*

The response was slow coming.

Rome: *Beautiful.*

I chuckled. Well, she was that. Exhaustion wore at me, but I fought it off until a freshly showered and wearing clean clothes Jasper returned to the room. He had pillows and a sleeping bag with him. Rather than find a room, he just set up on the hard tile floor.

We'd certainly slept on worse.

"I don't want to start anything," Jasper said slowly. "But you need to know something."

I waited.

"I'm not letting her go." He glanced at me, and I raised my brows. "To you. To Doc. To anyone. I've never wanted anyone the way I want her."

"And if she doesn't want you?" I kept the challenge out of my voice because now wasn't the time.

"She does," he said slowly, but in a tone that held a hell of a lot more confidence in himself than I had. "I kissed her. She kissed me back."

Fuck.

"You're my brother..." he began, but I shook my head.

"I'm not backing off," I informed him. "You aren't the only one who cares and has cared for a long time." She was in my blood and already embedded deeper in my skin than any ink I used. "If I were a wagering man, I'd say Doc isn't going to retreat either."

Because in all the years since he came back and Raptor

got sent up, Doc hadn't once challenged Jasper the way he had today.

"If we're calling dibs on Boo-Boo," Freddie mumbled in a raw voice, "count me in."

It wasn't a joke and it shouldn't be funny, but I wasn't the only one who looked at Freddie with real relief, and Jasper actually laughed.

"It's about time you woke your ass up," Jasper said, and Freddie groaned.

"I'm a burrito, Hawk. I'm going to lay like broccoli. My head is splitting."

"Yeah," Jasper answered him. "Go back to sleep. We'll be here when you wake up."

A yawn stretched his jaw, and then Freddie made a face. "I smell like ass."

"Yes," I told him. "You do."

Jasper snorted. "He's smelled worse."

"Yeah," I agreed. "But we all smelled like a dumpster then."

"It wasn't a dumpster," Freddie groaned.

"No, it was a compost heap," Jasper teased, and something in me relaxed a fraction. Being on the edge constantly had begun to take its toll on Jasper, and it had been a long time since this guy had come out to play. "You wanted to help out at the community garden 'cause you figured we'd score food."

"Yeah," Freddie said, his eyes half closed but his grin widening. "It worked."

"And you smelled like shit," I pointed out. Literal shit. They were using compost and manure, and we had to shovel it.

Worst. Job. Ever.

Freddie groaned as he laughed. "But I keep thinking about those tomatoes. So juicy…"

Yeah. The food had been good, even if it had made him sick because we gorged on too much of it.

His laughter faded away, and his breathing evened. But he really had turned the corner, and when I glanced over, Jasper had his chin tucked into his chest and his arms folded while he stretched his legs out. The light snores punctuated Freddie's deeper breaths.

Rubbing the back of my neck, I stretched out in the chair to wait for Doc. The sooner we got Freddie better, the sooner I got to see Dove again. On my phone, I opened up the web page that led to her videos. I'd watched all her dances and silk performances a hundred times.

Still, I watched them again, and I searched for...something. Something to tell me what secrets she still housed. Secrets that once we exposed, we could deal with and keep her safe.

Because no matter what anyone said, I would make sure she was all right first and foremost.

Even if it meant letting her go.

CHAPTER 9

EMERSYN

It was the second morning in a row that Kestrel took me with him to the auto body shop where he worked. I almost hated to admit how excited I was to roll over when he knocked on the door to my room.

"Breakfast downstairs in fifteen, Sparrow. We can grab some fancy coffee for you on the way to the shop."

No argument from me. I dressed warmer than I had the day before, though. I didn't have any heavy sweatshirts of my own that weren't half cut up for dancing. When I mentioned that, Kestrel walked into his closet and came out with a heavy black and gray pullover cable knit sweater.

He eyed me a beat, then my feet. "You have heavier shoes?"

I glanced down at the running shoes I had on over double socks. The yoga pants weren't that warm either.

"Not really, what's wrong with these?"

"They won't protect your toes if something heavy falls on

them. You need steel-toed boots for the shop."

"That's what you said yesterday, and I basically stayed in the office." Where they made the awful coffee and it smelled like week-old gym socks. The peeling linoleum and desk that only stayed even because there was a half-torn and mutilated paperback propping up one broken foot weren't so bad in the face of the others.

The corners of his mouth twitched. "Here." He tugged the sweater over my head. The act was so like Vaughn, I rolled my eyes and laughed. The action pulled some tendrils from my braid, but this wasn't a performance and I didn't need to be perfect.

In fact, a little messy seemed to fit right in. Something Kestrel pointed out when I'd come all the way back with grease on my nose from where he'd tapped it and I hadn't seen it until I was getting ready for bed.

The night before had also been some of the best sleep I'd had in weeks. I needed to up my workouts. I hadn't danced the day before, but I would today. I would also work on stretching out at the shop so I could walk right into the studio when I got back.

"You didn't want to stay in the office," Kestrel reminded me as I tucked my arm into the sleeves and he smoothed the sweater over my hips. It dwarfed me like it was a sweater dress, and if I had the right boots, it would look pretty snazzy with the yoga pants.

Not that I was going for fashion. Kestrel hooked one of the loose tendrils around his finger, and the barest pull kept me in place as he studied me.

He was waiting for a response to his earlier comment, and I rolled my eyes. "It smells in the office."

A soft huff of laughter teased my cheek before he pressed a kiss to it and then let me go. Surprise rippled through me, but he was already moving, and he gave my ass a playful tap.

"Move it, Sparrow, we need to feed that growling stomach of yours since there's no reason to starve yourself."

I barely covered the thrill that went through me at the action. This Kestrel was so different from the other one. I hurried after him and tempted fate since it might piss him off. "What changed?"

"Hmm?" He slowed his longer strides until I was keeping pace with him easily. The warm scent combination of his soap and something with more leathery undertones filled my nostrils, and I took a deep breath.

"You were all cool stares and 'grr.'" For lack of a better example, I hooked my fingers like they were claws and bared my teeth at him.

Kestrel eyed me for a beat, then deadpanned, "I was a T-Rex?"

"That's not a T-rex," I retorted.

"That's definitely a T-rex," he confirmed with a wink before leading the way down the stairs. Most so-called gentlemen would let a lady go first. But Kestrel always went ahead of me, and he always descended at my pace as though wanting to be in range. I had zero doubt that if I missed a step, he'd catch me.

That sent a balloon of warmth to fill me. It was ridiculous, and I should put a pin in it right now and pop it, but…

"Never mind," I muttered, and Kestrel turned as he passed the last step and caught me with his hands on my hips and lifted me up and then down.

"Don't be like that Sparrow, I'll try not to growl. Besides, T-Rex can't reach much with their hands, and I promise you, mine can reach everywhere they need." Then he gave me a very deliberate wink as the hands in question rested on my hips for a few seconds longer than necessary. And all too soon, he let me go before he walked away and left me to stare after him.

Heat swept through me, igniting brain cells along the way. Kestrel was flirting with me.

I hadn't imagined that.

A throat clearing behind me sent my pulse rabbiting, and I glanced back to find Rome studying me from above on the steps. Questions lingered in his eyes, and he tilted his head. With a flick of a look past me, he lifted his chin and then waited.

"We're going to have breakfast before I go to the shop with Kestrel," I explained. "Want to join us?"

He snorted, but it lacked any real derision. With deliberate slowness, he descended the steps until he stood next to me and I had to tilt my head up. It was the first time I'd really been alone with Rome since he took me out painting.

Since…

"Can I ask you a question?"

Eyebrows quirked, he waited.

I licked my lips. "Liam told me I got you stabbed."

The eyebrows descended, and his eyes narrowed.

"Are you all right?"

"You didn't get me stabbed," he said rather than answer the question. "Liam was being a jerk. Ignore him. I do."

"Sparrow, get that ass in here if you want to eat." The lure of coffee scenting the air accompanied Kestrel's call. Despite the statement about *if*, I rather suspected we wouldn't leave until I'd eaten something.

He'd done the same thing the day before when lunchtime rolled around. I hadn't been all that keen on the greasy diner we'd gone to, but I'd finally chosen something on the menu after some prodding. I made a face, and Rome curled his fingers and held out his hand.

"You can go with me," Rome offered. "If Kestrel is bothering you."

"Hey," Kestrel called, and I half jumped as if I'd been caught, guilty of something. "I'm not bothering her."

"No?" Rome asked him. "Move *that* ass?"

The question was almost innocent. And I said almost, because something flickered in Rome's expression that had been present the night on the playground.

"Don't be a jackass," Kestrel drawled. "She has a nice ass, and I was teasing her. We're becoming friends."

That announcement surprised me, and I wasn't alone. Rome took a step forward as though to put himself between me and Kestrel. I stopped him with a hand to his arm. "He wasn't being a jackass," I informed Kestrel. "I was asking him about something Liam said and your yelling kind of interrupted that."

"What the hell is Liam doing talking to you?" The silky smooth question held not one whit of anger, but that made it a little more terrifying. Rome sighed.

"Liam doesn't want her around me."

Wait.

I twisted to face him and gripped his forearm when he didn't pull away. "He said that?"

Rome gave a little shrug, then seemed to smile almost sheepishly. "Ignore Liam. I do."

"Yeah," Kestrel said. "Ignore him. Now, Sparrow, let's eat." He caught my free hand in his, the warmth of his fingers slotted between mine. Outside of when he'd had to help me while I recovered and the one time he tackled me in the garage on the way to the theater, Kestrel didn't touch me.

Something electric slammed through me. Like the connection jolted from a supercharge, lighting me up from where Kestrel held my hand to where my hand rested on Rome's forearm. Before Kestrel could take a step though, Rome twisted his arm under my grip and grasped my forearm as well.

"If she doesn't want to go with you," Rome stated coolly, "she doesn't have to. You had her yesterday. Let her come play with me today."

"We already have plans today," Kestrel said smoothly. "Come to the shop with us. You can work on the back wall. We finally finished patching it, so it's free for you to paint."

Then I could have company and divide my time between the shop and the back. I glanced at Rome, mentally crossing my fingers he'd agree. I loved watching him paint. After meeting my look, Rome glanced past me to Kestrel.

"You took her yesterday." He slid his hand down my forearm until our fingers tangled together.

"And I'm taking her today. Sparrow and I have plans. You can come or you can stay," Kestrel told him, and I raised my eyebrows.

"What if she doesn't *want* to go with you?"

"What if we don't talk about me like I'm not here." I squeezed their hands, both of them, and then pulled away. Only neither let me go, and I rebounded right back to where I'd been standing—firmly between them.

"It's fine," Kestrel soothed, but the corners of his mouth kept twitching upward. "Rome's just fucking with us. He wants to go, but he doesn't want to want to go, and it's better if we make it hard for him so he has to agree. That way when Liam bitches about it, Rome can just flip him off because it's not like he makes it easy for anyone."

The assessment spilled out of him so easily, I had to wonder how many times he had actually said it. Or at least thought it.

Rome lifted his free hand and very slowly raised his middle finger at Kestrel.

"See?" Kestrel said, and I laughed. It was ridiculous and kind of adorable. And oh so human.

"Food," I announced. "Then come with us?" I offered the invitation to Rome again. "Please?"

His eyes locked on mine, and he gave the barest of nods. "If you want. Will you dance later?"

The question surprised me, but they both started walking and pulling me along with them to the kitchen. I managed to free myself and pounced on the coffee already sitting on the table waiting for me. Kestrel diverted over to the side and started putting cream cheese on a bagel.

My stomach was quite enthusiastic about that idea. Rome gave my gurgling tummy an amused look, and I ignored him as I took a long swallow of the coffee. We'd lingered in the hallway so long, it wasn't hot anymore, but it was still more than warm enough for me to just drink.

It wasn't until Kestrel slid the bagel in front of me and said, "Not to push, but we're running a little tight on time if you want your coffee."

"We don't have to," I offered. "I mean, the coffee at the shop is terrible, but you have the soda machine."

"We'll make time," he insisted. "Eat your bagel. Not much else in here. We need to send the rats shopping."

There was that name again. "I don't know that I'd trust a rat with my food."

Rome chuckled, but he never stopped staring at me, and then it hit me—I hadn't answered his question yet. "I was going to use the studio tonight when we got back. I didn't have time yesterday and I was tired after all day in the shop. It's a lot more work than I expected it to be."

That earned Kestrel's frown. "What is?"

"Doing *nothing*." I lifted my shoulders in a half shrug before I took a bite of the still warm bagel and closed my eyes as the cream cheese half melted in my mouth. A little moan escaped me. This was way better than I'd imagined and I was starving.

They were both eyeing me as I polished off the bagel and the coffee. Rome had a bagel in front of him, and he slid it over to me.

"Aren't you hungry?"

Kestrel was busily eating his own bagel, with peanut butter on it that actually looked interesting, but I preferred the cream cheese.

"Eat."

"Thank you." I grinned and didn't waste any time devouring it. As much as I probably shouldn't have, I was starving. Rome shifted his weight, and I caught the smug look he sent at Kestrel. The vague movement in the corner of my eye was Kestrel flipping him off.

I had to suppress another laugh because I didn't know where playful Kestrel had been hiding, but I hoped he never left.

Rome agreed to come with us, and we had to wait for him to go grab his gear. Kestrel walked me out to the car in the main warehouse, holding my hand again, which was only a little weird.

There were rats working out there. Some on cars, some moving boxes. I had no idea what was in the boxes. I mean, their whole place was in a warehouse. Did they steal stuff? Process it?

I mean, they could be drug dealers for all I knew. That was a humbling thought. Freddie had been stoned and drunk the other night. The hurt in his eyes had been clear for everyone to read. It made me ache to think about it.

The Vandals were a gang. It was easier to forget when it was just me and Kestrel or me and Vaughn. Honestly, with all of them, except maybe Liam and Jasper.

Liam was an enigma, and Jasper?

The fact he'd kissed me in the studio before storming out and disappearing for a few days? It seemed to be a habit these guys were forming. Kiss Doc, he disappears. Kiss Jasper, he disappears. Have sex with Vaughn, he takes off.

Okay, admittedly, we'd had really great sex and he was helping with Freddie. At least, that was what Kestrel said.

"Hey," Kestrel murmured, pulling me back to the present, and I stared at him blankly. "JD is going to the store to shop, is there anything you need?"

The other man fixed more of a dead-eyed stare on my face. It felt kind of slimy. I folded my arms, because at least Kestrel's oversized sweater gave me a kind of armor. It shielded me from the other man's eyes.

"No," I answered because it didn't matter if I did want something. I didn't want *that* man getting anything for me.

"You sure, princess? They're buying."

I hadn't even seen Rome arrive, but the words had barely left JD's mouth before Rome punched him so hard, the crack of bone echoed through the garage. All activity within the warehouse ceased.

I flinched back, and Kestrel whirled on him. "What the fuck, Rome?"

"Don't call her princess," Rome ordered the man now groaning on the ground and clutching at his face. Blood spurted from his nose and soaked his shirt. Glaring around the huge room, Rome pinned every single person in place.

"Do you understand?"

One by one, mutters of assent rippled across the whole warehouse.

"Make sure everyone understands," Rome continued, then glanced at me. Fire seemed to blaze in those eyes, and my pussy clenched, even as heat rushed through me. He'd done that for me. Because I hated that name.

Couldn't stand it.

'Thank you,' I mouthed, and he gave me a single nod.

Kestrel stared down at JD, then at Rome and finally at me.

"Let's go, kids, before we end up having to take one of these assholes to the hospital." But he didn't follow us to his car immediately, instead, he helped JD up and said something to him. The other man nodded, and I kept my eye on them as I climbed into the backseat, despite Rome's protests. He finally settled in the passenger seat while we both waited for Kestrel.

After Kestrel turned his back and started toward us, JD glared in our direction and then at Kestrel. The thrums of desire gave way to trepidation.

"Don't worry, Starling," Rome whispered. "We've got this."

And I wanted to believe him, but that man looked pissed, largely because Rome had just punched him because of me.

Hooking his arm behind the seat, Rome held out his hand to me. I clasped it, and he squeezed my fingers.

"Don't worry," he repeated. "Think about what you want painted on the shop."

"What I want painted?"

"Yes, tell me what would make you happy, and I'll paint it."

Kestrel slid into the driver's seat at that sentence and he snorted, half laughing and half glaring. "You're a real dick."

I couldn't see his face, but I damn well knew Rome smiled because it was audible in his next words. "Bigger than you."

It was the strangest retort, and at the same time, hilarious. When I laughed, Kestrel nodded and started the engine. I forgot about JD and the warehouse and the rats. I still hadn't figured out how to tell them—any of them—what I needed to, and yet here they were, going out of their way to make me safe.

More, to make me *feel* safe.

And they were doing it.

For real.

CHAPTER 10

ROME

My neck tingled with the awareness of her presence in the backseat. She'd taken the spot directly behind mine and put her seatbelt on. While I approved of the safety, I'd rather she were able to lean up between the seats where I could see her more easily.

As it was, I kept my gaze fixed on the side mirror for the glimpses of her it revealed. On the way to the coffee shop, Kestrel took the longer way around. For someone in a hurry, he didn't take the easiest or fastest routes. I flexed my left hand. The punch had left my knuckles aching.

I didn't like JD. I didn't like the way he looked at Starling. I really didn't like it when he talked to her. Then he called her the one word she'd been adamant she didn't want applied to her. If I had to break every one of the rats' faces, they would get the message.

Despite the traffic pattern, Kestrel navigated to the wrong lane, and I finally understood what he planned. I sighed, and he shot me a grin. I didn't even bother to raise my hand when I flipped him off. Somehow, he'd figured out where I'd been working.

Curling my fingers into my palm again, I cracked my knuckles. I'd finished late the night before. They didn't want me out working on my own while the 19Ds were being problematic. Liam had crawled up my ass the last few days. Where I went, he appeared. I'd already gone through my stuff to make sure he hadn't placed a tracker on me. Might seem like a stretch, but they made cheap tracking devices these days, and you could get them at most electronics stores.

I wouldn't put it past my brother. He worried too much.

The soft inhale of breath from behind me made all the hairs on my body stand up. Kestrel must have heard it too, because he slowed enough that someone behind us blasted their horn and then flipped us off as they jerked around us in traffic.

It had taken me a few days to finish the whole side of the old goods warehouse that once served as an exchange hub between the incoming freight trains and the port. The stockyards were right next door, though neither was used anymore. The city had been threatening to knock them down for years, but they still stood.

The warehouse had been one of our favorite hangouts when we were younger. We'd learned a lot inside those old brick walls. Maybe my latest piece would help inspire change in this part of the neighborhood. I stared at my work. It wasn't my best. I'd changed my mind a third of the way through and started over.

Still, traffic all along the road had begun to slow. I glanced at the side mirror, hoping to see her reaction. The little inhale was one thing, but I wanted to know what she thought of the dancer I'd put up along the east-facing side of the building.

"Nice, man," Kestrel murmured, and I nodded. My brothers always appreciated the work, even if none of them really cared about the art itself. I had a feeling he cared more about this one. Kind of like I did.

It was Starling up there. Well, the silhouette of her. I knew every single line of her body, from the dip of her waist and the faint flare out from her hips, to her thighs where taut muscle demonstrated her strength.

She had a near perfect figure. Curves softened her muscular frame. The symmetry of her facial features beckoned to the artist in me, but so did the rest of her. When she danced, she was everything. Everything good about the world could be isolated down to the movement of her body as she conveyed a wealth of emotion and stories.

That was why I had to change the painting. It was her up there. I knew every line of it, but I kept her in shadow. The first bits had been her eyes. Those indelible dark pools that reminded me of mysterious woods and aged whiskey all in the same breath.

Not that I'd seen much in the way of forests outside of books and television. Within those eyes, I'd seen so much torture, pain, and loss. Putting it on the side of a building seemed like an invasion, and I'd no more put her on display than I'd let that fuck JD call her princess.

Instead, I'd redone it, detailing the lines of her body in motion as she danced in the silks. I'd let my mind fill in the blanks for her musculature. Smooth, clear lines as she hung suspended in the air. A fragment of the beauty she could convey there for everyone to see.

"Rome...it's beautiful."

They weren't just words coming from her. The breathiness punctuating every syllable coupled with how her voice hushed and her whole body leaned forward held me riveted. The glassiness in her eyes sent a spike of terror through me, but the shimmer of tears didn't fall as she blinked them away.

"This is where you've been the last few days?"

The question held some element of reproach maybe. I wasn't always good at the cues, but I could swear I heard something akin to scolding in the way she asked that question. That she'd even noticed I wasn't around was something.

"Yes." The need to paint it had been burning inside of me, and as soon as I'd been able to slip away, I had. This was hell and gone from 19D territory. Not that I cared if they came after me. I could hold my own.

Then her fingers brushed my shoulder, and I made myself sit still. I didn't normally care for people touching me, but we'd already moved past the warehouse and the painting was gone. She dug her fingers into my shirt, and then it hit me. She was squeezing my shoulder.

"Thank you," she whispered in a lower voice, and I locked eyes with her in that side mirror. The moment I looked at her, the corners of her mouth lifted and the darkness in her eyes retreated. The darkness there didn't frighten me either. I'd take it on if she needed me to.

With care, I covered her fingers with my own, and her smile grew. Was she happier about the painting or that she'd seen what I'd been doing?

"I'll take you the next time," I promised her.

"You're going with her now," Kestrel said in a kind of low growl that he usually reserved for Jasper, and I grinned. Pissing Kellan off was almost as fun as ticking off Liam.

It was also a lot harder.

One point for me.

"I meant on a day for just her and me. Right now, we're going with you."

"I know what you meant." Oh, someone didn't want me hanging out with Starling. I tilted my head to look at him.

She hadn't pulled her hand away, and when I slid a finger beneath hers, she hooked her fingers with mine. It couldn't be comfortable for her, but she was still leaning forward, stretching the seatbelt.

Someone was unhappy with it. "Don't be a dick," I reminded him. "Your name isn't Jasper."

Kellan side-eyed me right up until Starling burst into laughter. The sound washed through the vehicle, warming it more than the sunshine or the heaters could.

I grinned. It had been my words that made her smile and laugh like that. She squeezed my fingers and pulled her hand away. I missed the contact, but I was also glad for the fact I'd made her happy.

"Asshole," Kellan muttered under his breath, and I chuckled at the look he shot me. A snort echoed from the backseat, and Kellan glanced over his shoulder. "Keep it up, Sparrow. I'll make you help change out spark plugs today and do oil changes."

"Who says I can't do those things?" The dare in her voice had me shaking my head.

"I guess we're going to find out."

It was my turn to frown a little. If she was helping Kellan in the garage, she wouldn't be out back with me painting. Probably his intent.

Yes. We were going to see about that.

~

"KEL," I SAID AS I WALKED INTO THE GARAGE. HE'D HAD HER attention for the last hour as he taught her how to pull spark plugs from the ugly old Ford in the bay.

"She's almost done," he assured me, but he didn't move from where he was half wrapped around her and guiding her hand to the different parts. They'd changed the oil, and her laughter as she'd drained the oil pan had been refreshing. Working on cars was not exciting or fun, but she seemed to be enjoying herself right down to the "smelly" overalls—her words when Kellan had insisted she pull them on.

The only other mechanic working today was Old George, and he was half deaf in both ears and preferred to just do his work and ignore us. That he'd found a smile for Starling said a lot more about her than she realized. She made things better.

"No," I said shaking my head and leaning against the slender section of wall between the open bay doors. The position was on purpose, because we had company across the street, and I didn't want them being able to track what I said or didn't say.

I used my phone to send him a text, and when his phone chirped, he leaned back from Starling and wiped his hands on an old towel to clean off the grease before he pulled his phone out of his pocket.

Me: *Two men. Gray LeSabre across the street. Been there for an hour.*

Rolling his head from side to side, Kellan's expression never changed as he read the message. Despite the lack of any noticeable shifts, the air around him charged as he raked a hand through his hair and then shoved the phone back into his pocket.

Starling held up the spark plugs with a satisfied smirk. "You owe me twenty bucks," she informed Kellan, and I swore my eyebrows shot up. Kellan bet her money she couldn't do something?

"Well, so I do," Kellan said with a nod. "Good job. Tell you what, how about I pay you later before we grab dinner?"

"I find those terms acceptable." There was a smudge of grease on her cheek, but her face was flushed from the exertion, despite the damp chill in the air. The interior of the garage was always cold in the winter. Didn't ever seem to bother Kellan, but I preferred to sit around waiting where it was warmer. "So, what's next?"

"What's next is you go into the office and maybe make us a pot of coffee?"

The look on her face said she had zero interest in doing that. "The coffeemaker in there is disgusting."

I kept an eye on the Buick via the mirror in the corner of the garage that let Kellan see behind him when he was in there working. Our two watchers were still parked there, one of them was out of the car and standing near the corner of the chicken place smoking a cigarette. The other had his phone to his ear.

Maybe I was being paranoid.

Or maybe they were cops and the garage—and by default, Kellan—was under observation.

I got cop vibes off them, or least some kind of investigator. I'd avoided too many of them back when we first started cutting out of the group home. We couldn't afford anyone knowing where we were going.

"There's cleaner in the little kitchen in the back of the office." The suggestion from Kellan earned him so much stink eye, I almost laughed. I'd thought her arrogant and spoiled when I first met her, but she was none of those things.

I also had no idea if she even knew *how* to clean out a coffee pot, but it wasn't important. I'd run down the street after we dealt with these guys and buy a whole new coffeemaker if necessary. I'd get her coffee too.

Hands on her hips, she glanced over at me, and I offered a small smile. Looking at Kestrel, she said, "Fine, but I'm going to help Rome after. He's been waiting."

I had been, but more, I'd been waiting because I wanted to spend the time with her, and if I went back there without her, I'd lose track of everything. I didn't want to miss the time.

"Yeah yeah, you've done a lot up here, Sparrow." He tugged her ponytail gently. "Bring me a fresh cup when it's ready?"

She rolled her eyes like it was such an imposition, but it was hard to miss the quick flash of a smile on her lips. Being included was important to her. I filed that away. I didn't care when they included me or not. I could go days without seeing my brothers. They knew how to reach me if they wanted something.

"Rome," she said, focusing on me. "Do you want coffee?"

"Please." Not really, but she wanted to be included. I could do that. "If you have enough."

"Cream and sugar?"

"Whatever he has." I could pretty much drink it in any format. "Surprise me."

Kellan only snorted a little, but she nodded and then plucked the rag from his hands to wipe her own as she headed into the office. It was warmer in there, but better, it was out of sight. Tucked into the back of the garage, it wasn't designed for customers so much as for Kellan and the other mechanics to do the paperwork they never wanted to do. The little kitchen behind it had an ancient fridge and a microwave along with the coffeemaker.

As soon as the door closed behind her, Kellan moved to the supply cabinet as though looking for spark plugs.

"How do you want to play this?" he asked without turning around.

I glanced at the mirror. One guy was still in the driver's seat, but the guy who'd been smoking…was gone.

Frowning, I pushed off the wall and walked out of the bay as though I just wanted to stretch. Traffic hummed past. There were customers coming and going around the chicken place despite the early hour. I studied the street, then glanced back toward Kellan.

"We're missing one."

He pulled out a wrench and then his wallet. "Stay here," he told me and then strode out of the garage and waited for a car to pass before he jogged across the street. The guy in the Buick started the engine, even as Kellan approached. He looked for all the world like he was heading for the chicken place too.

A split second before Kellan got to the passenger door, the car jerked away from the curb and burned rubber getting away. The scream of tires on pavement irritated me.

We stood there, both of us, staring after the car, and then I glanced at Kellan again.

Maybe I had overreacted.

Or maybe the other guy took a walk when Starling vanished from our sight in the garage. I was already running for the office before the first crash echoed out.

CHAPTER 11

EMERSYN

Make coffee. Despite the face I made at the request, a little bit of pride sparked in my gut. I'd pulled the spark plugs myself. Granted, Kestrel had to help me adjust my grip twice and my fingers were a mess. Not that my manicure hadn't been shot for months, but I'd broken a nail when we'd changed the oil.

Honestly, I needed to keep them clipped anyway, and I'd been getting lazy about that. It was a good reminder. The office was tucked in the back of the garage, and it was warm in there, warmer than outside anyway. It also smelled way worse than the garage itself.

At least out there, fresh air came in with the exhaust from passing cars and helped to dispel the competing scents of motor oil, transmission fluid, and whatever that gunk was Kestrel had to scrape off to open the box thingy with the spark plugs.

Cars kind of stunk. Sweat. Dirt. Oil. Grit. But it was also

kind of fun, and Kestrel had been super patient about showing me how to do things, even when I had no idea what I was doing.

"No bad habits to unlearn," he'd told me with a grin. Maybe I'd been really hard on him in the beginning. Then again, the sting of his betrayal had also eased. I'd expected a lot from a guy I'd only known a handful of days.

I'd known him a lot longer now. The door to the kitchen was a swinging door, so I backed through it 'cause I had grease on my hands. Though to be honest, there were little bits of grease here and there, plus smudgy fingerprints. Old George, the guy who worked with Kestrel, and Kestrel both had these stained cloths in their back pockets. I'd wrinkled my nose at them the day before, but I got it now.

The kitchen was kind of disgusting, but nowhere near as bad as the bathroom. Thankfully, I had strong thighs and calves, so my ass never touched that seat, and I could hold it for a long time if I had to.

Kestrel had actually looked a bit embarrassed the day before when I walked out of there. Honestly, there wasn't enough soap on the planet. Speaking of soap, I searched the kitchen and eyed the old cake bar on the sink side with distrust.

Not happening.

With my foot, I opened the cabinet below.

Jackpot.

Dish soap.

It was half stuck to the bottom of the cabinet, and I refused to wonder why. With my elbow, I turned the water on, and it screeched as it hurtled through the pipes to spurt out of the nozzle before it began running in a stream. It was ice cold, but I wanted my hands clean more than I cared about warm water.

I'd just gotten a handful of soap when a door at the back

of the kitchen swung open. Oh shit, I hadn't even realized it was there. The guy stepping inside wasn't anyone I'd been introduced to. Maybe he was another mechanic? Or the owner? I gave him a quick smile as I soaped up my hands.

"Good morning," I said, greeting him, and then focused on washing my fingers. There was oil darkening the corners of each nail. Hopefully, that came out easily. I might need a brush or something.

The guy at the door had stopped there for a beat, like his eyes needed to adjust. I supposed it was a little brighter outdoors than in. At least his entrance had shoved some cold air through the kitchen, and it helped dispel the sour odor of whatever died in here…

I shot the guy another glance when he didn't move. There was letting your eyes adjust, and then there was rude.

A shiver that had nothing to do with the cold—either the temperature of the room or the water—raced up my spine. He stared at me. My shoulders stiffened, and I raised my chin. Shutting off the water, I shook the droplets from my hands.

There was no hand towel easily visible, but the overalls Kestrel had tucked me into were not only oversized and rolled up several times, but mostly clean. So I wiped my hands on the top.

The man took a single step forward, his eyes narrowed. The scent of cigarettes wafted off him, made sharper and more pungent by the chill he'd carried. Worse was the sour odor of sweat under it all.

There was a grease stain on his shirt, and despite the fact he wore a button-down with a jacket, he had no tie and the collar was undone. Rumpled, like he'd slept in the suit.

His hair was too long. His belly too wide. His shoes too cheap. And when he opened his mouth, his teeth were just a little too stained. Everything about his clothes said cheap, business attire. Everything else said he played dress-up and was intensely uncomfortable.

Except his eyes.

They were bloodshot, narrow, and mean-looking above the flushed jowls and unshaven cheeks. If the smell wafting off of him wasn't so distasteful, the unkempt nature of his appearance would have glared warning signs at me.

Call me a snob, but I'd had my share of bad encounters.

This guy was trouble in great, drenched in garbage neon letters. With all the noise out in the bays, I wasn't sure the guys would hear me if I started yelling. The newcomer took another step in my direction, and not once had he looked away from me.

Since I was wearing the mechanics overalls and I was basically a shapeless blob, it wasn't my attractive appearance that appealed to him.

"Take a picture, it lasts longer." The cool words leapt off my tongue as I glared at the guy. Sweat gathered at the base of my spine, and the earlier shiver turned into razor blades of ice.

"Emersyn Sharpe."

After weeks with the Vandals, the very last thing I wanted was to be recognized. Even when I'd wanted to escape them, this guy would not have been my eighteenth, much less my first, choice.

The door to the office was behind me and even then, I had to get through another door to get back to the garage. There was the door behind him that I hadn't even noticed with its crash bar to get out. I guessed it should have been locked?

Stinky clapped a hand onto my arm, and I reached for the coffee pot at the same time. It was one of those old-school coffee pots you always saw in diners, with the heavy balloon bottom and the narrow black mouth and a heavy handle made out of the same black plastic. It was stained, like one too many pots of coffee had been brewed in it.

The coffee the day before had been sludge. I wouldn't be surprised if it had stained my insides. But the pot was heavy, and there was already coffee in it. It was also still hot, and the sludge was definitely sludge.

I locked my fingers around it, even as Stinky hauled me toward his pot belly.

No.

Thank.

You.

I swung the pot, and it crashed against the side of his head, spraying us both with burnt coffee and chunks of glass. Fortunately, it missed my face, though pain sliced at my arm.

Stinky let out a roar, and though his hand on my arm loosened, he hadn't by any means let me go. He struck out blindly and I ducked the first swing, but he yanked me toward him and then nailed me with the back of his hand.

Pain bloomed against my face as I banged into the counter.

It was still a win though, since he let me go. He roared as he charged at me, and I had two choices—fight him or get away.

Yeah, fight wasn't really an option. The guy was twice my size.

I hopped up onto the counter and then, holding on, I slammed both of my feet into his chest. Between his rush forward and my momentum, I managed to absorb some of the shock of his charge, even as I drove my feet into his gut.

The chest might have been better, but I was aiming for his diaphragm under the layers of flab. His air whooshed out of him with a wheeze, and I rolled sideways, trusting my own balance and ignoring the glass I hit on the counter to get away from him. I was on the other side of him and closer to the door to the outside.

Not ideal, but better than nothing.

I bolted for it.

He got a hand around my ponytail. Pain lit up my scalp as he hauled me backwards. I swore some strands tore loose, and then all of a sudden, his grip on me was gone and I stumbled forward, barely catching myself on my hands before I fell on my face.

A gurgle of sound filled the narrow kitchen galley, and I twisted, hands braced against the floor, ready to snap my foot out and kick again. This time, I'd go for his groin. Should have done that in the first—

Something warm splattered against my cheek. The guy's face had already been bloodied and burned from me hitting him with the coffee pot, but it was Rome who had him down on the ground.

Silent.

Vicious.

Delivering a brutal beating as he rained punches down on the guy's head and face. Something crunched, the bone making a sickening kind of wet noise, and the guy just…stopped.

Everything stopped.

Even Rome paused with one hand on the guy's throat, the other raised in the air. Blood spattered the cabinets, his shirt, his fists, and the floor. It puddled out where it trickled between the splashes of burnt coffee and broken glass.

Blazing, fury filled eyes locked on mine. I swore they burned where they stroked over me, and without a doubt, Rome's gaze seemed to blast through the layers of clothing as though he could see right down to my marrow.

"How much of that blood is yours?"

The question floated in the air so softly, I wasn't sure I'd actually heard him right.

"None. I think." To be honest, nothing hurt.

The door behind me jerked open, and Rome glided, fucking glided, to his feet like a dancer, picked me up, and put me behind him as he faced the door. The flawless execution stole my breath. I'd known he fought like a fallen angel that night at the playground, but I hadn't truly seen him move.

Not like this.

The line of muscle blocking my view relaxed a fraction, and I leaned around him to find Kestrel standing there.

Then the door behind us, the one into the office, slammed open, and I jerked around and backed right into Rome, who had his arms around me. He tucked me between him and Kestrel as another familiar blond head appeared.

"Fuck." Liam's voice crashed through the room, and the world slowed. Kestrel's hands settled on my shoulders, and he turned me to him. Like Rome before him, he looked me over.

"You bleeding anywhere, Sparrow?"

"I don't think so." It took me far longer to get the words out. "I broke the coffee pot on his face. Some of the glass might have gotten me. The coffee was still hot."

"He's dead." Liam's voice pulled me around, and I stared at where he was kneeling, careful of the blood, and had two fingers to the neck of Stinky with a ruined face.

Because his face was ruined.

It was so much meat.

My stomach revolted, but before I could even process that, a finger tugged my attention back to Kestrel.

"Eyes on me, Sparrow." The soothing, soft tone seemed perfect for the silence bearing down on all of us. "Clean that up." The last he said over my shoulder, then his gaze was on me. "Sparrow, I need you out of this." Kestrel didn't wait for me to respond, just started undoing the overalls.

"I'll grab a tarp," Liam said.

"Clean up," Kestrel repeated, but he was tugging the overalls down my arms and then pulling them free down my legs and encouraging me to step out. "Come on, Sparrow. I need to make sure there's no blood on you."

The water turned on in the sink. Kestrel tossed my overalls at the body. Rome stripped out of his shirt, and it landed on the body too. There was blood all over his arms and his chest where it had soaked through the fabric.

The tattoos looked like they wept tears of blood. I started to glance down at Stinky again, but Kestrel was in front of me and guiding me over to Rome. "Clean her up while I help Liam." But he didn't just move away, he waited until Rome glanced at him then me then back with a nod before leaving us.

Rome didn't seem to have the same objections to the soap I'd had, and he lathered it up his arms and then over his face and his chest. The blood washed away, turning the water pink for several long moments before it rinsed clear. He reached above, pulling open a cabinet. He set a roll of paper towels down on the counter.

Kestrel and Liam were both back, Kestrel with a mop and broom, Liam with a heavy piece of tarp. Then Rome had my hands in his, and he began to wash them with the same efficiency he'd done himself, only his hands were warm on mine. He washed away the blood and the chill, cleaning around my nail beds and then under them.

He even got the grease I hadn't been able to get earlier. The towels were dampened, and he washed my face. I closed my eyes at the gentle touch, not wanting to think how red the water had turned when he'd rinsed my hands.

Not the first time I'd gotten blood on my hands.

"The sweater needs to go, Starling," Rome told me in an almost regretful voice, and it was the only warning he gave me before he lifted it up and over, leaving me in the thin T-shirt beneath. He tossed the sweater toward his brother, who already had the body completely rolled up in the tarp.

The glass and the coffee on the floor were gone. The blood vanished under Kestrel's mop. The strong scent of peroxide filled the air. I'd have expected bleach, but I didn't get a chance to ask as Rome cupped my chin in his gentle hand.

He tilted my head one way and then the next. A moment later, Liam joined him, twin mirrors of concern as they studied me. I'd never felt so stripped before.

"There," Liam said. "Side of her neck. Something nicked her. But it's not deep."

Rome ran his fingers over my scalp, and tingles raced through me at the contact. It was gentle as hell and had my toes curling in my shoes.

"Liam," Kestrel said from behind me, and at least that took one blazing gaze off of me.

"Does it hurt anywhere else?" Rome asked me in a soft voice as Liam moved away. I shook my head. "Did he touch you anywhere else?"

I glanced down at my arm. There were three red marks, livid against my flesh where his fingers had bitten through the overalls and the sweater. But it didn't really hurt.

Gliding his fingers over the spots, Rome frowned.

"It's fine," I told him. "The coffee hurt more than he did."

"The bruise on your cheek says he hit you."

I'd forgotten that, in the panic and rush. "He might have. I was getting away."

"You were."

"I didn't know him."

"Me neither," Rome agreed. "But I got a picture on my phone. We'll find out."

"I mean, I didn't know him, but he knew who I was."

The words halted all the activity in the kitchen, and the three men exchanged a look, one I didn't need a dictionary to translate.

They were surprised.

They were also *pissed*.

"Rome," Liam all but growled as he tossed something. His twin caught the set of keys. "My bike's out back with my jacket and an extra helmet. Grab something for yourself and get Hellspawn out of here. I'll find you later."

Wait…

But no one gave me any options, because Kestrel nodded. "He had a friend. We're going to need to find him."

Whatever else he said to Liam after that I missed because Rome had threaded our fingers together and led me back out into the garage. The cold air hit me in a rush, and without the sweater or the overalls, my nipples went on point and so did all the hair on my body.

After he snagged some heavy black coat off a hook, Rome led me right out another door I hadn't seen in the far back of one of the bays. It went into a utility area and then out into the violently bright light of day. After the muddy light inside, it made my eyes water.

I was still shivering, so I didn't complain when he draped me in a heavy jacket that threatened to swallow me whole. He zipped it up, and then he put a helmet on my head.

"I've never ridden a motorcycle," I confessed.

The blue bike was the same one Liam had used to follow Doc and me when I got away.

"Just hold onto me," Rome said as he straddled the bike. "Put your feet here and here, wrap your arms around me, and hold on. I won't let anything happen to you."

He didn't have a helmet. The giant one he'd put on me smelled like Liam—mint and cloves. I straddled the bike behind him, threaded my arms around him, and leaned into his back.

As soon as I was secure, he walked the bike back, and it rumbled to life, vibrating beneath us like a growling tiger.

"Hold on, Starling," Rome called back to me, and then we were racing forward. He didn't even slow before he turned out into traffic, weaved through the intersection, and whipped away.

Somewhere back there, I'd left my frantically beating heart as the bike continued to accelerate.

Then we were flying.

FIRST IMPRESSIONS

EMERSYN

"Emersyn!" The snap of Marta's demand cut through my focus like a heated blade. I swore the woman did it on purpose. I had not mastered the latest series of movements for the *"Pride of Giselle"* that I was supposed to perform on opening night.

Dimitri Vankovich was one of the best choreographers in the country. The show was lucky to have him. I was a most fortunate girl to get to earn his tutelage. But he was also an asshole who changed his mind repeatedly, and every day, there'd been a new segment of the routine. He'd either removed something or added it.

I wouldn't fail.

"Yes, Marta?" I faced the company manager and my chaperone, who spent more time scolding me than she did managing anyone else, as she stomped toward me. A man followed in her wake, his stroll far easier than hers. If anything, he looked amused.

I couldn't stand the woman. But no one asked me about

whether I wanted her to be my chaperone. My fourteenth birthday, she had allowed the company to give me a cupcake with no frosting on it and to sing me happy birthday.

I wasn't actually allowed to eat it, because she thought my weight was already too much. I'd lost ten pounds since then.

"Your new partner has arrived."

My new what?

"Emersyn Sharpe, this is Eric Arlington." The blond giant behind her offered me a smile as he moved toward the stage I'd been working on. My practice room was too small for the leaps, and we were going to be adding silks to the choreography as soon as the techs got them added out here.

Dimitri had been apoplectic they weren't already available.

With ease, Eric hoisted himself on stage and held out his right hand to me as he approached. "It's a pleasure to meet you. You're a gifted dancer."

I raised a brow and then clasped his hand. He squeezed mine, and his smile deepened. He was tall. My head didn't quite reach his shoulders. His hands swallowed mine. I somehow didn't think lifts were going to be a problem.

"You should get changed, Eric," Marta said in that waspish tone of hers. "Then return here. Emersyn can run you through the program so far. He will be dancing *Giselle* with you. Dimitri will adjust the choreography later today."

"Sounds good," Eric said, giving her a salute, then winking at me when his back was to her. It would be nice to have an ally here. He held my hand a moment longer, then released it before he strolled toward offstage to where the dressing rooms were.

"Don't get any ideas," Marta scolded, reminding me that she was still present. "He's a grown man and you are still a little girl. If you are dancing together, I will be here for every moment."

I flashed her a smile I didn't feel. The polite smiles with the hint of manufactured warmth were something I'd mastered a long time ago. "The only thing I care about is if he can do the moves."

"Uh-huh."

Not that Marta would understand. She was trying to protect a purity and a chasteness that had died a violent death years earlier. As it was, I turned away and took my mark. Then, with only the music in my head, I began the routine from the top.

CHAPTER 12

EMERSYN

The thrill of riding the bike couldn't compete with the icy wind biting at me as we tore through the city. Rome rode the bike like it was an extension of himself, gliding smoothly around corners, weaving in and out of traffic. I hoped he knew where he was going, because I'd lost track somewhere along the way.

I didn't think I could find my way back if I tried. Holding Rome though, I trusted my understanding of muscle movement and shifted my weight when he shifted his. When his body flowed right, I leaned into it with him, and then left or center again.

If he danced, I would love to see it. There was a fluid elegance to how he handled the bike. The last place I expected to go was into a gated, underground garage in a really nice part of town.

The stores lining the sidewalks here were designer. More than one were the types that my mother shopped in. Everything about the area declared its affluent separation from where we'd been. Once below, he cruised deeper. The lack of wind helped, but my arms were so numb, even with the jacket, and I'd long since lost feeling in my toes.

After Rome parked, he rubbed my hands, which I'd tucked up under his jacket against his abs in an effort to keep them warm. They ached like hell to unlink from each other, and I hopped a little as I swung off the bike. Rome caught my arm when I stumbled. Oh, wow. I was cold.

He unbuckled the helmet and tugged it off my head. After he secured it on the bike, he pulled my hands into his. I was pretty sure his were just as cold. Neither of us had gloves on, but he kept rubbing them as he headed for the elevator.

"Where are we?" My jaw quivered, and my teeth began to chatter. Rome hit the button to summon the elevator, then typed in five numbers without making any effort to hide them. When he pressed the last one, the doors opened with a ding.

Warm air washed out to greet us, and I didn't hesitate to step into the vestibule with him. Once inside, he chose an upper floor and then kept rubbing my hands with his. Cold could burn if you got too cold. Thankfully, the helmet had protected my face and Rome had protected my chest, or my nipples and my nose would be ready to break off.

The elevator let us out on the twelfth floor. Rome guided me out and down the hall. From what I could tell, there were only three or four doors on this floor. So only three or four apartments?

The thick, plush carpet muffled our steps, and it was as expensive as the fancy marble tile inside the elevator. We were a *long* way from the clubhouse. The art on the wall was gallery purchased. At least two of them were Crowls.

At the end of the hall, Rome unlocked the door marked with only a two. He had a key card in his wallet. The electronic locks let go, and I stared a beat before he swung the door inward and ushered me inside.

If the elevator and hallway were quiet elegance, the interior of this apartment was an exercise in pure restraint. It was done in a series of grays and metallic tones to add some warmth without sheen. Lights came on at the flick of a switch. Two lamps, one at each end of the sofa, warmed the room with low-wattage light.

After the brightness outside, it seemed almost too dark. The walls were gunmetal gray. But there were paintings on each wall, each one done in vibrant colors and abstracts that made the whole wall seem like it had been designed to feature that single painting.

A gym was set up in one corner near floor to ceiling windows. A faux fireplace came to life in the center of the room. The electric fire offering a multitude of colors. Another spark of personality for what should be an almost institutional room.

Everything had a place, and everything was in it. I couldn't imagine anything further from Rome. He was more controlled chaos, and this was precise, orderly lines where nothing should be left out of place. I didn't even want to mess up the sofas or the chairs by disturbing their lines.

As he made his way through the room, Rome hit various buttons—one turned on another set of lights, one in the galley kitchen with the black marble floors and another that illuminated the workout equipment in the corner. A treadmill, weight bench, and what looked like a rowing machine waited for their next occupant. The vertical blinds along the windows retracted until the natural light from outside filtered through what had to be double-paned and treated glass.

The light couldn't blaze through, so it wouldn't fade the carpet, but if it was like the stuff on...well, like the stuff I'd seen before, it would also prevent others from seeing inside at night, even when the lights were on.

"Tea or coffee?" Rome asked abruptly, and I twisted to find him standing in the kitchen doorway. He eyed me for a moment. "Take off the coat and the shoes. Go take a shower. I'll find you clean and warmer clothes, then put those through the washer and dryer."

He didn't wait for my response before he disappeared into the kitchen. I wanted to argue, but I was freezing and needed a minute.

Maybe I needed more than a minute.

"Okay."

There was only one hallway, so I followed it down to find two rooms. They were both bedrooms, so I just eeny meeny miny moe'd the choice and finally took the door on the left. Like the living room, it had a wall of windows looking out over the city.

The bed in the center was huge, and there was more abstract art over the bed itself. Then a pair of framed photos on the bedside table. I resisted the urge to snoop, but I did take off the motorcycle jacket and set it down on the foot of the bed.

It was the single messiest thing in the room. The covers had been tossed back like whoever slept there just rolled out of bed and left. The bathroom door was ajar, and I flipped on the light switch.

It was as clean and modern as the rest of the apartment. Dark walls, dark tile, and bright lights gave it the atmosphere of a cave but a warm one, like a kind of sanctuary, and the counter was clean and neat.

After swinging the water on inside the oversized glass shower stall, I stripped out of the clothes I had on. There was some blood on my leg, and I froze at the sight of it. I didn't think I'd gotten blood on my pants. I picked up my shoes and inspected them carefully. Nothing jumped out, but there was another spot on my socks.

A shudder of revulsion went through me, and I hurriedly pulled off the rest before rushing under the hot water. I didn't even care if it scalded my too cold skin, I just closed my eyes and braced my hands on the wall as the water poured over me.

The pressure was amazing. The heat began to seep into my bones, and the spill of water hid the tears escaping from the corners of my eyes as the shakes took me.

We'd killed someone.

Again.

I counted myself in on the action because I'd been in the middle of that fight when Rome came in. The man had been there for *me*. If not for me, then Rome wouldn't have had to kill him.

The violent trembling worked its way up and down my body. Eventually, even when the cold was gone and the shaking subsided, I lifted my head and glanced around for the shampoo.

The first dollop to hit my hand smelled of cloves, mint, and something distinctly male.

This was Liam's place.

A weird little laugh eddied through me as I began to work the shampoo into my hair. Liam lived large compared to the other Vandals. But they didn't always seem to treat him like he was one. Not that I wanted to pretend I understood any of it.

In no time, I'd washed and conditioned my hair. I didn't know why he had conditioner, but I didn't intend to ask. Maybe he entertained overnight guests and he was a fucking gentleman. Or maybe I was just a snob, but most of the guys on tour used the combo bottles. What did I know?

Just because he'd been a dick to me didn't mean he was a

dick all the time. And he was related to Rome, so there had to be something nice about him.

There was a stack of thick fluffy towels waiting for me and clean clothes on the vanity. I hadn't even heard Rome come in. I dried off and mostly toweled my hair until it wasn't soaking. Finger combing would have to do.

The clothes turned out to be an oversized, much faded T-shirt and an old pair of sweatpants. They had a tie I could pull tight to cinch them to my waist. There were no panties, and that was fine. I really didn't want to borrow some other woman's panties anyway. The shirt was a pale, pale gray, and there was no mistaking my nipples beneath the fabric, but whatever.

The door opened to the bedroom, and the air was cooler, less humid than in the bathroom, but the scent of Liam's shampoo followed me as I padded back out to the living room. Rome stood by the windows and turned at my arrival. His hair was damp and slick, his face freshly shaven.

Like me, he'd changed into clean clothes, though his fit him far better than mind did me. "I made hot cocoa," he told me, "if you're still cold, and there's food. It's not much. Mostly microwave meals."

"I could eat."

His eyes lit at my response.

"Thank you for the towels and the clothes. I feel much better." Not a lie. I did.

"It wasn't your fault," Rome told me as he led the way to the kitchen. If I wanted to know what he was talking about, I'd have to follow, or I could look out the windows at the view. The ocean was visible in the distance. Kind of gray and stormy-looking with the leaden clouds above it, but also stretching out to the horizon.

I bet it was really pretty when the sun shone.

The sound of a milk steamer in the kitchen pulled me

around, and I tracked after him. There was a huge, fancy cappuccino maker set up on the counter. I tried not to gape, but the coffeemaker at…I hesitated to say home, but where the Vandals lived, had to be thirty years old, and I swore the one at the garage was older still.

Not that it had a carafe anymore, but I shook that off. Not what I wanted to focus on.

It took no time before Rome filled the mugs with frothy milk and stirred the chocolate up. My stomach growled at the rich scent now filling the air, and Rome flashed me a real smile.

"What do you mean it's not my fault?"

"The guy at the garage," he said as he added a dollop of whip cream to the cup before holding it out to me. "He shouldn't have been there. He was trying to hurt you."

"He was trying to take me," I admitted. "He knew who I was. I guess…maybe he recognized me."

Rome nodded once. "He had a partner. Don't worry, Liam and Kellan already scooped him up."

I shook my head slowly and stared down at the hot cocoa. The first sip coated my lip in whip cream, but the hot chocolate itself was divine. It warmed me all the way to my toes. "I should feel bad about that," I half mumbled.

"Why?"

Nothing disingenuous lived in the question. "They tried to hurt you. To take you. They don't deserve your compassion, Starling."

"It's not compassion," I argued, though without a lot of heat to it. I took another sip as I tried to cobble my thoughts together. When I raised my head, I met Rome's curious gaze head-on. "There's a reward for finding me. I saw it on the news. They probably just thought they were rescuing me for an easy fee. Or maybe they didn't care if they were rescuing me and just wanted to kidnap me for their gain."

I gave a little shrug.

"I don't know that it's a crime that deserves death."

"We don't know what they would have done or why they chose to act as they did. They could have called your location in if they just wanted a reward."

Pure fear jolted through my system at the suggestion, and if Rome hadn't closed his hands over mine on the mug, I'd have dropped it. My heart thundered, slamming against my ribs like it wanted to escape. Oh fuck. What if they called him? What if he knew I'd been seen at the mechanic's shop? I didn't have to go back, but it could lead them to Kellan and maybe to Rome. What if they took pictures?

"Starling," Rome said, and apparently, he'd been repeating it for a while. He pulled the mug from my fingers and then wrapped his arms around me in a tight hug. Eyes closed, I tucked my face against his shirt and just held on. "Starling, you're safe."

"You don't know that," I finally managed to squeeze out. "What if they called them? What if they know where I am?"

"Then we'll deal with it," Rome said, his hand flat against my back before he began to rub in slow circles. "No one will hurt you. We won't let them."

But it could bring a world of hurt down on them. They didn't know. They couldn't. His arms flexed as they tightened, squeezing me hard, and I craved it, pushing against his chest like I could hide away in there.

I was not a coward. I hated that even the thought of going *home* reduced me to some quivering mess.

"Starling, I promise. We won't let anyone hurt you. Not even us."

I let out a little laugh. They hadn't hurt me. Yes, they'd kidnapped me, and I'd been hurt when I got there, but that was because Eric hurt me. Vaughn and Kellan had stood up for me. So had Jasper.

They had taken care of me, even when I didn't know who they were. I still had no idea *why* they'd taken me or why they were working so hard to make me comfortable, but I had been safe with them.

All the threats I'd faced had come from outside the Vandals, and they'd been there to protect me.

"You've had to kill for me twice now," I whispered.

"I'd kill a hundred men if you needed it," Rome said as if it were the simplest thing in the world. "The only thing that matters to me is your happiness and your safety."

I believed him. As scary as that declaration was, I believed him and I appreciated it. When I pulled back a little, he loosened his grip and tilted his head down to study me as I gazed up at him.

"I know I was all about escape…"

"That's over now," Rome murmured. "You went. You came back. Nothing more has to be discussed."

I didn't deserve him.

A smile tugged at the corners of my mouth. "Just like that?"

"Just like that." He nodded. "We have three things in life. The people we choose. The work we do. The life we make. You're one of my people. I will always choose you."

My heart squeezed. "You don't know me."

"I know you enough. I know you here." He slid his hand over my heart, then raised it to cup my face. "And in here. You don't see the world like I do. That's okay. But I see you."

Apprehension shivered through me.

"I've always seen you. I thought you were in a good place. But your eyes…" He stroked my cheek. "They've grown sadder and sadder, Starling. It's like all the darkness that haunts you gathers there, but that darkness doesn't frighten me."

I swallowed.

"Your world was supposed to keep you safe."

A laugh slipped out. It was more of a scoffing sound, but he gave me a slow nod.

"Exactly. Your world wasn't protecting you. So now we will. I will. You will always be safe with me." The warmth of his fingers traced up my cheek and then over my brow before he retreated to my jaw line and finally to my lips. My breath caught at the gentleness there. "My world isn't kind."

"No," I agreed. "It's not. And I don't want you to get hurt."

Then another smile turned up the corners of his mouth. "I'm okay. I've fought the darkness before."

My gaze dipped to his mouth, then back up again as he continued to cradle my face against his palm.

"Will you trust me to look after you?" Rome asked. "Trust me even if you aren't ready to trust all of us?"

I already did trust him. I wasn't even sure when that happened. Licking my lips once, I nodded, but I didn't get the words out that followed before Rome kissed me. With his hands cradling my face to hold me still, Rome took possession of my mouth as though kissing me was where he belonged.

His lips were so damn soft and warm where they moved against mine. I opened to the silky thread of his tongue seeking entrance, and the first stroke brought me up on my tiptoes. Heat bloomed and electricity sizzled as he delved his tongue hungrily against mine. All I could taste was chocolate, sweetness, and Rome.

Digging my fingers into his shoulders, I tried to get higher, and he dropped his hands down to my hips and lifted me in one smooth motion, not once letting go of my mouth. He deposited me on the counter and pulled back briefly, his eyes hooded and his gaze heated as he swept it over me.

I spread my legs, and he stepped forward into the cradle of them. I didn't know which of us reached for the other first, but I craved the touch of his lips like I craved air. My nipples strained against the T-shirt as I rubbed against him and sucked on his tongue.

He threaded a hand into my damp hair, tilting my head this way and that as though desperate to deepen the kiss.

"I can still make you food," Rome offered in between kisses, and I laughed a little. It was insane and sweet and perfectly him.

"I'm not hungry yet," I promised him. Then he was kissing me again, and I stopped worrying about anything beyond where we were. Right here, this moment. It was the purity of chaos.

Just like him.

BROTHER MINE

ROME

"Let's go boys," the woman said with a snap of her fingers. I kept thinking of her as the woman. Mostly because she didn't call us by our names. So I didn't want to use hers.

"We're not dogs," Liam grumbled as he climbed out of the backseat first, then I clambered after him. Everywhere we went and everything she said, the woman snapped her fingers. Follow her. *Snap snap.* Eat your food. *Snap snap.* Hurry up. *Snap. Snap.*

We'd parked on the street in front of a low-slung brown house. It was just that—brown. Brown brick. Brown roof. Brown dirt. Brown porch. Brown door.

There was even a brown bike lying in the dirt of the chain link yard.

"Boys," the woman said, snapping her fingers, and Liam nudged me. He had his backpack on, but I just held mine to my chest. The house we'd stayed at the night before had lots of kids in it, and one of them had tried to take my backpack.

Liam's knuckles were still scraped and red from where

he'd hit the other kid. His right ear was redder where the woman had grabbed him and yanked him off the other boy. When she was scolding him, I stomped that boy's hand. His screams got Liam out of trouble, and the woman looked right past me as everyone rushed to help.

They always looked past me. I didn't care. I wouldn't smile for them. I didn't laugh. I didn't want to talk to them. I talked to Liam.

That was enough.

But my teddy was inside the bag, and I didn't want to lose it. Everything I owned was in my bag, including two coloring books and some broken crayons. Liam stuffed my clothes into his to make room.

Where he went, I went. So, what did it matter?

"Boys," the woman said with another snap of her fingers as she climbed the porch. She was already knocking on the door, or she would have seen Liam stick his middle finger and his tongue out at her.

"I hate that bitch," Liam muttered, and I elbowed him. I agreed, but if he said it too loud, she'd go after his ears again.

He shoulder checked me back and then flashed me a smile. I wanted to smile for him. I really did. But it was hard. Never seemed to bother Liam much though. The door to the house was open, and another lady stood there, her flushed face and harried expression giving way to a real smile.

"Well, I expected you an hour ago," she scolded. At Liam's snicker, I glanced up. The new lady glared at the woman with disapproval. "These boys look half starved...and twins. Goodness. You look exactly alike."

"This is—"

But the lady stopped the woman before she could finish her statement or the snap of her fingers. "No, no. I read their profiles. Let me guess." She studied us. The wisps of her hair pulling free from the bun made a kind of crinkly reddish-brown halo around her face. The light shining in the window behind her added to the effect.

It was kind of cool.

"You're Liam," she said after a beat, nodding to my brother, and then she focused her gaze on me as she lowered herself to a crouch. Liam had already begun to drift in front of me. I didn't like the attention. "And you're Rome."

"He is," Liam volunteered for me. "And we're both starving."

"I knew it." She sounded downright cheerful about that. "Well come on in, both of you. I saved you both bacon and there's pancakes. I'll have to reheat them real quick."

All at once, my stomach growled as Liam darted forward. He had a hand on my arm, holding onto me long enough to make sure I followed him inside before he let me go.

The women talked behind us, but Liam cut right across the cluttered room that had toys everywhere. The television was on, blaring away, and a baby stood at the edge of a pen staring at the cartoons with a bottle in his mouth. He barely noticed us.

It was so much louder in here. Brighter too.

Shouts beyond the window climbed in volume as a backdoor slammed open and three boys rolled in, yelling and wrestling with each other.

They stopped dead when they saw Liam and me. I hugged my backpack tighter, and Liam cut off their view of me.

"Boys," the nice lady from the door called as the door clicked closed. "Our new arrivals are here. Do not start anything."

"We won't," the first boy said, his dark eyes intense. "Just came to get a drink."

"Well outside, I'll bring juice out in a minute. Let's let Liam and Rome settle in before they deal with you scamps."

All three boys laughed at the description and let her

hustle them outside. Liam looked over his shoulder at me, and I gave a little shrug.

That went way better than I'd thought. Then she was calling us to the table. We had to wash our hands in the kitchen, and Liam held my backpack while I did mine. Then we had piles of food in front of us, and I had no idea what to eat first.

The baby in the living room let out a laugh, and I looked over in time to see the toddler climb right out of the pen. The woman laughed as she scooped the baby up.

Weird.

"I like her," I told Liam in a little voice. He snorted and stuffed another piece of bacon in his mouth, but he didn't disagree with me.

CHAPTER 13

JASPER

"So I'm all clear, Doc?" Freddie asked for the fifteenth time in the last twenty minutes. Despite the fact he was clean and hadn't had a drop of alcohol or a touch of drugs in almost a week, the jitters weren't something he could hide. I leaned against the wall behind the clinic and just took a long drag on the cigarette.

Vaughn rolled his eyes, then his neck. The fucker had been in a sour mood for the last two days, but he'd stuck around, even when the last place he'd wanted to be was here. The fact Kellan kept us *updated* on Emersyn helped.

She's fine.

Sleeping.

Busy.

The responses had grown shorter, terser, and far less illuminating until he'd just stopped answering altogether. When I'd asked Doc to message him, Kestrel hadn't even answered his question. Clearly, he knew where we were, and the asshole kept sending me to voicemail.

I scratched at my beard as Freddie paced around in another circle. I wasn't the only one watching him. Doc had only removed his IVs an hour earlier, and he'd finally kept down solid food without puking up his guts. All good signs, but he needed to stay clean, and every damn time he fell off the wagon, it seemed to get a little harder.

Fuck my life.

We'd figure it out.

As much as I felt like hell, Doc and Vaughn both looked it. None of us had really slept for longer than a couple of hours here or there. Freddie groaned and turned to face Doc.

"C'mon, Doc, cut me loose. I need to find some pussy and some food and some company that isn't your three ugly mugs and maybe not in that order. In fact, I could find food with the prettiest pussy I've seen, and that would be a hell of a lot better than this."

I lowered my hand from where I'd been pinching the bridge of my nose in time to catch Vaughn smacking Freddie right upside the head.

"Holy fuck, ow, man," Freddie grumbled, then shot us a sheepish grin. "I'm just playing. You know I'll treat Boo-Boo right."

"Freddie, I love you like a brother, but I will break both of your kneecaps and make sure you have to have your jaw wired shut if you don't dial down the discussion about her perfect pussy." While I hadn't stared at it like some kind of creeper, I had no doubt about its beauty. Not when she was so fucking perfect.

Hot.

Tempestuous.

Wild like a controlled fire.

"Someone's got blue balls," Freddie said without an ounce

of remorse. "You should be more laid back like our buddy Vaughn here. I know he got some pussy recently. It always gives him that kind of growl to his glow."

"He needs rehab," Doc cut in before either Vaughn or I could respond. "Serious rehab this time, Freddie. You can't keep doing this crap to you or to anyone else."

"Look, Doc, I know I slipped…"

"Save it," Doc said with a wave of his hand. "You're good at telling everyone sorry, and I think you even mean it. But you have a problem and you have the tools to at least even out your life. This time, you came out of it with a concussion and some cracked ribs. You're lucky they didn't amputate a body part, considering Jasper's recent actions."

I scoffed, but Doc wasn't wrong. The sun had come out earlier in the day, but it had vanished behind another wall of clouds. Winter in the Harbor meant stormy skies and cold wind and oftentimes more rain than any of us ever needed. "Is he good to go or not, Doc? I'll keep someone on him for the next few days."

While I didn't want to agree with him, Doc wasn't wrong —Freddie needed handling. We'd taken all the time at the clinic we could, but I couldn't run the Vandals from here, and so far, Kestrel hadn't brought Emersyn around.

Then again, she didn't need to deal with Freddie high or detoxing, no matter how kind she'd been to him that first night. The compassion and kindness she'd shown him were rare in our world. A flash of the haughtiness in her eyes from the first night we'd met flashed through my mind.

It would be easy to dismiss her as a stuck-up princess, but she was nothing like that at all. Fuck, I'd missed her the last few days. Having her so close at the clubhouse all the while keeping my distance had been a kind of hellish salvation. She was *there*. Safe. No one could *touch* her there.

The bruises on her body healed. The shadows beneath

her eyes faded. The hollowness of her body filled in. What seemed at times the near translucence of her grew more solid and stable. The steady burn of her resentment had also eased.

Killing Eric had helped.

Giving her the studio helped more.

The taste of her lingered on my lips, even as I took a last drag on the cigarette. Even the long days and nights since hadn't chased that memory away. First, I'd had to deal with the 19 Diamonds, then Freddie's disappearance, and finally, his detox.

All I wanted to do was go back to that fucking kiss and pin her back to that wall where we could take our time. I wanted to find all the different ways she liked being kissed, and I wanted to feel the drag of her fingers against my skin.

Dragging my mind back to the present with a vicious grip, I glared at Freddie. I didn't need to be sporting a semi of any kind around any of these assholes. "We'll talk about rehab," I said, breaking through Freddie's tirade before he could get wound up.

He shot me a wounded look as he raked a hand through his hair and shoved the locks away from his face. He could use a damn haircut while he was at it, but one battle a time.

Pinning Freddie in place, I raised my eyebrows. "We will talk about rehab. There are places we can send you." Before he could object, I continued, "I get it. The last thing you want to do is be sent away. Not particularly a fan of the idea, but this shit has to stop, Freddie. There's only so many holes we can drag you out of. This time…this time cut it awfully close. If they hadn't been so intent on making you suffer, they could have slit your throat before we even knew you were gone."

The rebellion in Freddie's expression fled. The words

gutted him. Or maybe it was my tone. At the moment, I didn't care what worked, only that it worked.

"And you can't be with Emersyn like this."

It was a last-minute call, but it hit him like a slap in the face.

"She deserves better," I reminded him. "You can fight this. We'll have your back. But you gotta do the work, man."

"Jasper's right," Vaughn offered up, and Freddie twisted to look at him and then Doc.

"Don't look at me," Doc told him. "I'm on Jasper's side in this. Little Bit doesn't need to hurt because you want to drown your pain."

Well, I wouldn't have put it like that.

"She cares about you, Freddie, hell if I know why, but she does. And seeing you like you were that night hurt her."

I frowned. She'd been taking care of him, rubbing his back and soothing him. What the fuck had I missed?

More to the point, what had Doc seen?

"I'll do better," Freddie said slowly. "Just…don't kick me out. You guys are my family. I don't have anything outside of you guys. I don't…I don't want to go away." He swallowed hard and grimaced as he tried to take a deep breath. Cracked ribs were a bitch, and he'd be hurting for a while. "If I do the work, maybe I can do one of those outpatient places?"

The last thing I wanted to do was cut him off. We never left family behind. "Maybe," was all I said though. "And we have to see the work, Freddie. We can't be watching you twenty-four-seven."

"I can hang out with Boo-Boo when you guys are…"

"No," Vaughn said before I could. "You're not putting this on her. She already felt bad that you fucking disappeared when you were supposed to be looking after her."

Shoulders hunching, Freddie sighed. "I fucked up."

"Yeah," I told him. "You did. Worse, you fucked our trust.

You're not out, Freddie, but you're not all the way in anymore, either."

His eyes rounded, and even Vaughn looked startled.

"Get your shit and let's get out of here. We've taken up enough of Doc's space and his time."

"C'mon," Vaughn said, clasping a hand on Freddie's shoulder and guiding him back inside all the while shooting me a side eye. Yeah yeah, I got it. We didn't abandon anyone, and what I'd just said probably sounded an awful lot like I was considering it.

I wasn't.

I'd no sooner leave Freddie behind than I'd willingly cut off my own hand. But maybe it was time Freddie knew that even my patience had limits.

"I'll come by daily," Doc offered. "Do piss tests for a while. That will encourage him to stay clean."

"And if you get to see Emersyn, all the better, right?" I should have just kept my mouth shut, but Doc's interest in her was just…

"Exactly," Doc said with an easy smile. "Get used to it, Jasper. I'm not going anywhere."

"Fuck you, Doc."

"You're not my type, and you should have told me who she was when you brought her here in the first place."

"You didn't *need* to know." I dropped the last bit of the cigarette and crushed it with my boot before glaring at him. "You're not one of us. You made that clear. Remember?"

"This is not a Vandals thing."

"The hell it isn't," I countered. "You tell yourself whatever stories you want, but you enlisted, you went away. You went to school. Made yourself a whole other life. Then you come back here to grace us with your presence after a near decade long absence?"

Uh-huh. He could fuck right off.

"It wasn't like that," Doc began, and I cut a hand through the air.

"It was *exactly* like that. You know it. I know it. Raptor knows it. You tell yourself whatever story helps you sleep at night." Then, because we had enough battles, I blew out a breath. "You want to see Emersyn, fine. You can see her as long as she wants to see you, but only at the clubhouse. You're not taking her anywhere."

Not without one of us, and I had zero intention of letting him make any moves on her. Fuck, he was old enough to be her father.

Doc just gave me a look and said nothing. He could hide so much behind those granite eyes of his and that expressionless face. The door opened, and Freddie led Vaughn out. Vaughn tossed me one of the duffels and then lifted his chin toward his car. "Am I taking Freddie?"

"I got him."

"Thanks, Doc," Freddie said, shaking Doc's hand. "I'll clean my act up. You'll see."

"I'll be by tomorrow," Doc told him before he walked away.

I waited until he had the door open to say, "Hey, Doc…"

The other man glanced back at me, and I nodded to him.

"Thank you. We owe you one."

And I paid my debts.

"No," Doc said. "You don't. Friends never owe friends debts."

Then he disappeared inside the building, and I scowled. We were not friends. I'd pay back the damn favor. In the car, Freddie leaned back with an exhausted sigh. All his earlier energy seemed to have evaporated, and he looked pale.

"You good?"

"Just hungry," Freddie admitted. "I know maybe I should stay here…"

"But you don't want to." I got that.

"No. There's no stuff at the clubhouse. I mean, there's weed, but…"

Weed wasn't the problem. "Lay off it anyway, okay?"

"I will."

I blew out a breath. "How about I swing by and get us some tacos?"

Freddie's whole expression lit up. "Oh, man…now you're talking my language."

Chuckling, I shook my head. Some things never changed. Freddie was always hungry.

"Jas?"

"Hmm?"

"Thanks for coming to get me."

"Shut up, punk," I murmured and then ruffled his hair. He groaned at the action, then laughed.

It didn't take long to buy enough tacos, burritos, and chalupas to feed a damn army, though I would have to hit the books at some point this week and check our accounts. I didn't usually let them go this long.

There was a lot of activity at the clubhouse. Rats were loading a truck, so we must have had a shipment come in. As I pulled in, Kestrel met us with Liam of all fucking people. What the hell was he doing here?

Goddammit. The guy just kept showing back up.

"Problems?" Freddie asked, and I shrugged.

"Who the hell knows. Take the food inside and settle in."

Freddie hesitated, scanning the warehouse. I'd already done the same. She wasn't out here. As soon as I was out of the car, Kestrel headed for me. Vaughn pulled in right behind me, and it looked like he'd hit a store too.

I paused at the sight of the flowers and quirked a brow. He just met my gaze with a stare. For Emersyn.

Goddammit, everyone wanted a piece of her.

Sucking in a breath, I focused on Kestrel. "What's going on?"

"We have a problem," he began, and that was never good. All business, Kestrel detailed what happened at the auto shop, from the attack on Emersyn to the fact he and Liam had to track down the second guy.

That guy was currently in the fridge awaiting interrogation. The guy who went after Emersyn was dead.

"They're PIs, as far as I can tell," Kestrel continued as the anger began to pound away in my blood. "Looking for her. I don't know if it's for her family or what, but…"

He hesitated, and I raised my eyebrows. "Don't get shy on me now, asshole. You took her the fuck out of here where she's *safe* and exposed her. So let's finish it. But what?"

His jaw set and Kestrel glared at me, but the flex of his jaw said a lot more for his current mood. He was pissed, but not because I was questioning him or challenging what the hell he'd been thinking. That was definitely a conversation we were going to be having.

"But there's a reward that's been placed for any and all information leading to her successful recovery, and Liam told me there's a bounty out on her now."

What the fuck? I swung my head to look at him. "Since when?"

"Since five days ago."

Since the day we'd gotten Freddie back. I ran a hand over my face.

"Jasper?" Freddie asked. "Is this because of me?"

"No," I told him. Kestrel echoed it, but Vaughn frowned.

"Where is Dove now?"

"About that…"

I closed my eyes and counted slowly, fisting my temper in both hands, before I opened them and raised my brows at Kestrel. "Yes, Kellan," I said slowly, even as Vaughn loomed at my shoulder. Apparently, he was on my side in this argument. "Where is Emersyn?"

"She and Rome took off on my bike," Liam answered. "I told him to get her out of there. We didn't know how many might be around, and I stuck around to deal with the mess. He probably took her to my place."

Yeah. I was done.

"Get in the fucking car," I told him as I pivoted to go to the car. "Freddie, inside, eat, shower, sleep. Don't touch the liquor and don't touch the weed. Kestrel, try to keep an eye on him and do a better job than you did with Emersyn."

I didn't wait for a single response as I slid into the driver's seat. Liam apparently took that particular command well. He folded into the seat next to me, and I was already accelerating as I hit the controller for the door. It was late in the day, the sun had already gone down, and traffic was thick as assholes working their banker's hours went home to their suburban houses after they stopped off to bang their mistresses or fucked a hooker in an alleyway.

Story of my fucking life.

"Jas…"

"Don't." I shook my head. "Don't Jas me."

Liam sighed and tilted his head back. "Fine, Hawk. She's safe at my place. I'm not connected with you guys as much, and it's in Royals' territory…"

I cut him a look as I took the next turn and headed for the loop to head to the far side of the city. "Not really selling this to me."

"She's with Rome."

There it was. The one person we both trusted. The only link we had left. I still didn't know why Rome had chosen to stay with us when Liam left, or why Liam had left him with us and didn't take him. I sure as shit wasn't gonna kick Rome out the door, but at the same time…

"Rome isn't going to let anything happen to her."

I pulled out a cigarette and got it lit before I cracked the window. "Why the hell do you keep coming around? If you want to be here, be here. You don't. So stay with your new friends." Bitterness swelled in me. I still had no idea why he'd decided to ditch us five minutes after Raptor ended up in jail. He hadn't even waited for them to move him upstate before he walked away.

"Does it matter?" He sounded tired. As tired as I was. The last three years had been…

"Yes, it matters. You left your brother—"

"I never left my brother," he cut in. "Don't start with that shit. I'll *always* have his back. I could have yours too if you'd stop being such a fucking dick about everything. I'll have hers too. *That* was why I was there today, by the way, and you're fucking welcome, since you and Vaughn were locked away with Freddie the desperate."

"Leave him alone."

"You coddle him," Liam snapped. "He's never going to stand on his own feet because he doesn't *have* to. He knows no matter how far he falls, you'll go and get him."

"That's what family does. You used to know that."

I blew out a stream of smoke.

"Sometimes you have to fall," Liam muttered. "You want an omelet, that means you break some eggs."

"When I want your opinion, I'll be sure to draw a dick on my face ahead of time, 'cause that's how smashed I'd have to be."

He ignored me after that, and I was fine with it. He wasn't wrong about Freddie, but I had no idea what the hell else to do. If we sent him away to one of those lock-in rehabs, I didn't know if he'd survive. Freddie needed us, and isolation freaked him out. He acted like everything was a party, but his triggers... Fuck, I wasn't sure even I knew where they all were.

Liam snorted when I pulled up to his building. Yeah, I knew where the fancy fucker lived. He gave me the code to get us in and then directed me where to park. The bike was sitting there. That was a good sign.

The ride up in the elevator was silent. I ignored all the cushy signs and the security cameras. The place gave me hives. At the door to his place, he took the lead. The interior was dark, save for the fireplace flickering colorfully and the exterior lights visible through the windows.

It was the light of the hall slanting into the room that revealed Rome wrapped completely around Emersyn on the sofa. She was tucked up to his chest, her eyes closed and her body utterly relaxed. There was a shadow of a bruise on her cheek, but otherwise, she was perfect.

"Lucky bastard," Liam muttered. Fuck it. I needed an outlet. I punched the asshole.

BLACK AND GRAY

JASPER

"Jasper." Ms. Stephanie pulled over one of the chairs in the classroom and took a seat on it. Everyone else was outside playing. I'd had to stay inside for recess. "We talked about this."

I nodded, not looking up from where I colored on the page. I was using the black and the gray crayons. I'd taken every single one of them. That was what had started the problems. But until Ms. Stephanie came in, I hadn't been willing to take them out from where I'd hidden them.

Ms. Stephanie never took away from me what I'd rightfully collected. At her little sigh, I stole a peek at her. She rubbed at the corner of her eyes. Ms. Stephanie was a pretty lady, with dark hair and eyes. She had a pretty smile. But she always seemed tired.

I was probably the reason she was tired.

Mommy said it was always my fault she couldn't sleep. Then Dad put her to sleep forever, and they put Dad in jail.

The crayon snapped in my fingers, and I glared at it. Then tossed it in the trash can in the corner. *Plink. Plink.* Both pieces landed.

I picked up a new black crayon and went to work on the outfits again. Stupid coloring assignment.

"Jasper," Ms. Stephanie said again. "Do you mind if I color with you?"

"Only if you use the black and gray." If she tried to put that green or blue on here, I'd... Well, I couldn't hit her like I had that other boy, but I'd tear up the page. That would be fair.

"Is that what prompted the fight?" She picked up the gray crayon and studied what I was doing before she began to shade in the cloud. That was perfect. It had been a dark and rainy day. The clouds had been getting grayer and grayer until they were almost black all day long.

"I guess." I shrugged.

"You guess, or you know?"

I stole another look at her and saw she wasn't focused on me but on the page. "I guess. I get into fights for lots of reasons. Most of the time, what the other kids say isn't why I did it."

She nodded, then traded her gray out for another black once all the clouds were done. I'd almost gotten all the people into black clothes, but one of the guys had an umbrella and she colored it black too. We sat like that for the next hour, coloring the page, adding touches of black and gray to the trees, until it was all done.

When we finished, she studied the picture with her chin propped in her hand. A knock on the door made me sigh, and I lined the crayons back up. Ms. Stephanie murmured, "We need to go now. The detectives have some questions."

"They always have questions."

"I know," she said softly, then hesitated, but when she ran

her hand over my hair, some of the tension leached out of me. "I know all this is hard, sweetheart. But they really do need your answers, then I'll take you for ice cream after. I have another boy I have to pick up today. Would you like to meet him?"

I eyed her. "Why?"

Instead of scolding me, she chuckled. "Because he's almost as suspicious as you are, and he's new to the system. I thought maybe you could give him some pointers."

Right.

I shrugged. "I don't care."

With care, she took the coloring page out of the book for me, and when she offered it to me, I shook my head. Nodding once, she slipped it into her bag.

"All right." When she stood and held out her hand, I didn't take it right away. I liked Ms. Stephanie, but that didn't mean I wanted to lean on her. The last six months had proved everyone was transient in my life. Everyone who mattered left.

I didn't want her to matter.

Then she wouldn't leave.

Or if she did, it wouldn't hurt.

No one stopped us leaving the school. No one questioned her or why she checked me out. In the car, she put me in the backseat and then tried to find out what my favorite music was, but I didn't care.

At the police station, I went into the room with the colorful walls and all the toys. The cops came in, and like Ms. Stephanie, they sat on the floor or on the little chairs like it made them one of us.

The questions started, all over again.

"When did your dad get home?"

"What did you and your mom do that day?"

"What did they fight about?"

"Did your dad ever hit you?"

"What about your mom?"

Every detail, and I answered the questions all the same. But I didn't look at them or Ms. Stephanie. I focused on the bird picture across the room. I wanted to be that bird. I wanted to fly away from here.

But I told them that Mommy took me to the zoo for my birthday. We'd looked at all the animals. She bought me popcorn. I got to feed the giraffes. She even let me go on the carousel. It had been a fun day. When Daddy got home, he'd been mad 'cause dinner wasn't ready. Mommy also forgot to pick up his beer.

The yelling started, and I got under the table like I always did. Mommy said if Daddy didn't see me when he was mad, he probably wouldn't hit me. But he kept hitting Mommy.

He hit her until she wasn't even crying anymore.

Then he dragged me out from under the table and made me go to bed. Mommy was on the floor for two days before the cops came.

Where did Daddy go after I went to bed?

I didn't know.

I didn't care.

Daddy broke Mommy.

Now I had to live somewhere else.

Finally, they let me leave.

"You did great, Jasper," Ms. Stephanie praised me as she guided me out. "I know you're tired of answering those questions. But it's important, and I'm so proud of you for being a strong little boy."

Except, I wasn't strong.

If I'd been strong, Mommy wouldn't be broken and I would have hit Daddy when he kept hitting her.

I didn't argue with Ms. Stephanie though. She meant well. She really did.

I'd forgotten all about the other boy until we made another stop. That was also when I realized I'd moved homes again. Did that mean I was moving schools? I'd stayed at three different group homes in the last few months. They moved me every few weeks.

At first, I'd thought it was an adventure. Now I knew better than to get attached.

To anything.

Or anyone.

"Jasper," Ms. Stephanie said as she led me into the yard where a dark-haired, dark-eyed boy watched us with all the suspicion I felt. "This is Milo. Milo, this is Jasper. He was the boy I told you about this morning."

I wasn't the only one to shoot her a sharp look. She'd told him about me.

"Why don't you two get to know each other while I take Jasper's things inside and talk to Ms. Joanie."

Neither of us said anything, and she left us alone to stare at each other. Milo squinted at me, then back at the house when a baby cried before he swung his gaze to look at me again.

"You want to play?"

"Not really," I told him. I wouldn't be here long. This kid would start something, we'd fight, and I'd end up somewhere else.

He shrugged. "Well, I'm gonna play over there." He pointed toward a row of toy cars and an old racing set. I'd had one like that. "It's better with two. But do what you want. Ms. Joanie will make us clean up before dinner."

Without another word, he walked away, and I sat down on the steps. I didn't play with him, and he didn't say anything else. Ms. Stephanie left with a wave and a kiss to the top of my head. Milo and I were out there all afternoon, not saying anything. But when the other kids got home, he did something weird.

He came to sit on the step next to me. Not saying a word, he just sat there, and so did I. None of the other kids bothered us.

CHAPTER 14

EMERSYN

The crash of a table and low-pitched snarls jerked me out of the most peaceful sleep I'd managed in a long time. My eyes snapped open as a pair of bodies fell next to the sofa. When I would have tried to roll out of the way, Rome's arms tightened around me, and we were suddenly over the back of the sofa and I was tucked behind him as the battle raged across the living room.

"What the hell?" All traces of sleepiness fled at the unrestrained violence. The pair on the floor staggered to their feet. Another pair of hits, flesh slamming into flesh followed by harsh breathing, ripped through the room. Rome made no move to intercede, and even though my heart slammed a mile a minute, I went for one of the lamps. There was a wall switch, and it turned up the lights in the room.

"Fuck." Jasper flinched as one of the brighter lights shown in his face. Liam's fist caught him next, and it was my turn to wince, 'cause the blow knocked Jasper back a couple of feet.

Not that it slowed him down, he just snarled and raced right at Liam, slamming his shoulder into Liam's midsection and driving him back toward the sofa Rome and I had been sleeping on.

Liam brought his fists together and drove them down at Jasper's back, landing a pair of blows before he crashed into the sofa, and then they were both knocking it over and landing on the far side.

Sidestepping the pair, Rome reached for me, and I gaped at him. A part of my brain was trying to process what the hell happened, and the rest of me couldn't believe he wasn't going to intercede.

Liam was a jerk, but he was his brother, right?

And Jasper?

I sighed. Jasper was Jasper.

The two were trading punches. Jasper took more than a couple in the gut, but then Liam swore as he narrowly missed Jasper's knee slamming into his crotch.

"This is ridiculous." I started forward, but Rome scooped me up by the waist and curled me to him as he walked us toward the kitchen.

"We can't let them just beat each other up."

"We can," he said, disagreeing with me, and then pressed a kiss to my nose. "It's good for them. Lets them get out all their feelings."

Once in the kitchen, he set me on the counter. It was the exact same position I'd been in earlier that evening. The night before? What day was it? But the same spot he'd kissed me for the first time. I wasn't the only one thinking about it, because his gaze dipped to my lips and his eyes warmed.

With his thumb, he traced my bottom lip. "Coffee? Or do you want to just go back to my room?"

My whole body clenched at the offer. We'd fallen asleep on

the sofa in between trading long, slow lazy kisses and little stories about things that didn't matter and were still safe to talk about. A crash from the other room burst the bubble around us, and I glanced toward the living room. Liam had Jasper pinned to the wall. But it didn't last long. Both of them were bleeding too.

"Are you sure we shouldn't stop this?" Another blow had me wincing.

"It's how they process their feelings," Rome told me, resting his forehead to the side of my head and bracing his hands on either side of me on the counter.

"With their fists?"

"It works for them." Rome shrugged. "I paint. You dance. We all have our process."

Flicking my gaze back to Rome, I sighed. "You know me almost too well."

"I've watched you for a long time."

I almost laughed. "'Cause that's not creepy at all." In so many ways, it wasn't funny, but Rome's sudden smile pulled my laughter free. There was just a hint of red to his cheeks too, and it was the sweetest thing.

"Are you two for fucking real right now?" The grunting, panting explosion of sound came from Jasper, and I pulled my gaze from Rome's rather reluctantly to find Liam and Jasper both leaning, bloody, shirts torn, faces puffy in a promise to bruise. Both were also glaring at me and Rome.

"Yes," Rome said. "We were sleeping, and no one invited you two."

"It's my fucking place," Liam snarled.

"And you brought my damn girl here," Jasper finished.

I blinked at Jasper's description, and I wasn't alone in that. Rome cut Jasper a look that held not one ounce of friendliness. "She's not a possession."

"You know what I meant," Jasper said with an aggrieved

sigh. "Get your things, I'm taking you back." The last was directed at me.

"What if I don't want to go?" Because while I had chosen to go back to the Vandals, most of them didn't know it. Jasper didn't seem the type to keep it to himself if he had heard. I was also sick and tired of being talked about in the third person and ordered around.

"Then you don't have to," Rome and Liam answered almost in perfect sync. It was eerie and sweet. Their voices were so alike, and yet the cadence and the emphasis were different. I didn't think I'd mistake one for the other. Not again.

Right now, with Liam's cut eyebrow and busted lip, it would be extremely difficult to mistake him for Rome. Twisting around in front of me, Rome folded his arms and leaned back against the counter with one of my knees pressing against him on either side.

"Oh, for fuck's sake," Jasper said, sounding all at once as tired as I felt and as weary as Liam appeared. But the tightness of Liam's stance and the way he shifted his weight said he was ready to tear back into Jasper, despite how bad they both looked. "I'm not the damn enemy. *This* is Bay Ridge Royals side of town." The last he delivered to Rome. "You might be safe, but does that safety extend to her?"

"It does." The answer from Liam sent a jolt through Rome that I felt more than saw, but it was Jasper I kept my attention on. The corners of his mouth turned down, his eyes narrowed, and for the briefest of seconds, I swore there'd been hurt present.

"Well, that's just fucking gravy," Jasper said, sneer firmly in place. "You still don't get to decide this. She's under *our* protection. That means she belongs in *Vandals* territory. *With* Vandals."

There was so much he was saying without words. It was

like every answer I needed vibrated silent and unspoken in between the syllables of that possessive and rather insulting description. The slate gray of his eyes held an icy kind of heat as his gaze collided with mine.

"It's time to go," he said, not releasing my gaze. "I can't protect you here."

"Maybe she doesn't need your protection," Liam snarked, and that pulled Jasper's attention away, freeing me to breathe. Even as the two men muttered at each other, I turned his request over in my head. Despite the growl in his voice and the expression he wore, Jasper had been asking.

Maybe that was *how* he asked.

Tilting my head back, I stared up at the ceiling. We'd come here because someone had come looking for me at the body shop. I swallowed, then said, "Maybe the Vandals would be safer if I wasn't there."

That shut Jasper and Liam up. Both bloodied men stared at me like I'd sprouted a second head. Rome turned his head to glance back at me.

I threw my hands up. At least Rome didn't look at me like I was an idiot. "There's a lot about me you don't know," I told them, aware that they each had pieces of the puzzle. "Or maybe you already know and I'm trying to protect you for nothing. But it's worth saying that Rome's already had to kill for me twice, and I don't know if the threat will be greater or worse. Especially after this last one."

Liam gave me a slow nod, and I could have sworn there was just the barest suggestion of approval in his eyes. But Jasper sliced a hand through the air. "If they come for you, then they're coming here to die." Well at least he wasn't splitting hairs on that. "I told you, we will keep you safe. Maybe I've…demanded that you let us protect you, but, Emersyn, Swan…you're *safe* with us. I *need* you to come back with me, now. We have Freddie home…"

I straightened and tapped Rome's shoulder, and he shifted so I could hop off the counter. "Freddie's all right?"

"He's doing well enough," Jasper answered. "Doc cleared him to leave the clinic, and he's got the drugs out of his system. But it always takes him time to adjust."

"I'm glad. I was worried about him." I frowned, then glanced at Rome. "I want to go see him."

"Then we go back." Rome nodded. "I'll get our clothes." He walked toward the doorway and both Jasper and Liam went stock-still and stared at him, then me.

"Your clothes?" Liam repeated, with the barest hint of a teasing smile.

"She had blood on hers, and we needed to shower. Don't be an ass." At the curt words, Liam raised his hands.

"I was just checking. Besides, she looks good in your stuff." Liam gave me a slow smile, one where the blood oozing from his split lip really killed any charm he might have possessed. Then again, the last time someone hit him that I knew of, it had been me socking him in the nose.

Rome shoved his brother with a less than friendly push, and Liam laughed as the two vanished around the corner, leaving me alone with Jasper.

Folding my arms, I studied him. "Do you want to clean those up?" I nodded to his bruises.

He shook his head. "I've had worse, and I needed that."

Surprise rippled through me.

"Did the guy at the shop do that to your cheek?"

I raised a hand to my face. I'd almost forgotten about the bruise, but the moment he mentioned it, the faint swelling over my cheekbone throbbed. "He caught me with a backhand, but I was getting away. Him yanking my hair hurt worse." I shrugged. "But Rome got him."

"Good." Jasper took a step forward, then raised his bruised hand. "May I?"

More curious than anything, I nodded. He brushed his fingers gently against my jaw, then tilted my head so he could study it. I swore his eyes chilled a little more.

"Any other injuries?"

"Not really. I mean, the counter hurt when I bounced against it. But I feel fine." I grinned at him. The redness on my arm had already begun to fade, and the little cut on my neck didn't bother me at all. "You don't need to make a list of injuries for this guy. He's already dead."

Jasper met my smile with a faint one of his own. "His partner isn't."

Oh.

My amusement faded.

"Liam and Kestrel caught him," Jasper murmured, still touching my chin. The lightness of his fingers made for a barely there sensation. It was kind of weird. We hadn't really seen each other, much less been alone, since the night he kissed me and walked out so pissed off.

Considering I'd just made out with Rome and I'd had sex with Vaughn, now might not be the time to address it. My romantic life had gotten far more complicated in a very short time span, considering the absolute dregs it had been before.

"What's a matter?" At the coaxing note, I almost wanted to tell him, but I just shook my head.

"I'm tired." Not a lie. "I was sleeping, you see, and these two jerks decided to wake us up by beating each other up."

"Fair," he said, that almost smile back as his hand fell away from my face. "Next time, we'll try to be quieter about it."

Next time.

"I have your things, Starling," Rome said. "Do you want to change into them or just wear that back? You can, if you want. I also brought you thicker socks and another jacket."

Liam had also returned, cleaned up and in fresh clothes. No shirt though. He wore just gray sweatpants as he brushed up against me to get past. There was no mistaking it was intentional, because Jasper glared at him and then caught my hand and tugged me away from him.

"I'm fine like this," I said, because I really didn't need Jasper starting another fight. Not when I already owed Liam for his silence. "You're coming with us?" The last I directed at Rome, and Jasper made a face.

Oh, did Jasper not want him coming?

"Of course," Jasper said, sliding me in front of him and giving me a little nudge toward Rome and the living room. "If he wants." The living room was in shambles.

"We can't leave it like this," I said abruptly and felt more than saw all three of them stare at me. "This is a wreck. And you guys broke that frame." It was one of the beautiful paintings from the wall. Sidestepping carefully to avoid the glass, I retrieved the painting.

"It's fine, Hellspawn," Liam drawled. "I'd rather you take the junkyard dog back to his pen. I can clean this up tomorrow." Rome took the frame from me and set it down. "Besides, you two had a long enough day as it is."

Not rising to the bait, Jasper nodded to Rome, who passed him a coat, and then Jasper held it up for me. That was it, the guys were just letting this go? They beat each other bloody, wreck the living room, and that was that?

I would never understand men.

Ever.

"Thank you for letting us use your bike," I told Liam. "And you have a very nice place."

"It's always open to you, Hellspawn. Just make sure you leave the junkyard dog at home."

Jasper glared over his shoulder at Liam but gave me a gentle push toward the door. Rome said nothing, but then, I guessed the twins didn't need to say much. Liam followed us to the door, and I caught him watching us as the elevator arrived.

He winked at me and then closed the door.

The return to the clubhouse, as they all called it, seemed to take forever as Jasper navigated his way through the quiet streets. Rome sat in the backseat. I'd offered to go back there, but both he and Jasper had pointed at the passenger seat.

Curls of fog hung in the air, and the traffic around the center of town dwindled as we made our way past affluent nightclubs and dancing spots. More than one looked to be busy with lines out front, but then we were in the business district and fewer people occupied the sidewalks.

The absolute silence was both a blessing and a curse, but I had no idea what to say to fill the emptiness. As it was, I was fighting off yawns by the time we pulled into the warehouse. My jaw cracked with the force of them. I barely even got my seatbelt undone before Vaughn had my door open, and he reached in to tug me out.

"Dove," he said with an almost relieved sigh. "You are a sight for sore eyes."

"Hey," I managed before he lifted me clean off the ground and kissed me. The warmth of him invaded every sense. The warehouse and the chill faded away, even as the hum of danger lurked there. I'd missed him, and there was relief tangling up in the knot of feelings these guys were dragging out of me. For a few brief seconds, I stopped worrying about anything and sank into the contact as my whole body went soft and slick. The ache Rome had sparked earlier roared back to life.

Then reality crashed in, as Jasper's voice cut through the haze. "What the fuck do you think you're doing?"

FIGHT OR FLIGHT

VAUGHN

The group home had a whole different set of rules from the fostering I had been doing. They kept trying to place me, and I kept getting sent back. It had all kind of rolled off me at this point. Most people thought I was a lot older than I was, 'cause I was big. Lots seemed to expect me to do or know more. Then they decided I was slow or stupid because I wasn't who they thought I was.

Most of the time, I let it roll off me. Other times, I got into fights. I wasn't looking for a fight, but I'd gotten pretty good at it. Better to not start anything. I'd promised Mom the last time I saw her to not start fights. Just finish them. I kept telling myself that. I already owed her one apology, but that kid deserved a pop in the mouth for calling her the B word.

Mom was not a bitch.

"Boys," Ms. Stephanie called as she opened the door to my 'new' room. It was a little crowded. There were three bunk beds in there, for six beds total. The other kids in the room paused mid laugh to swing their gazes to the door. It was early. Ms. Stephanie had let me have one last breakfast with Mom before she had to go. I didn't know how she'd arranged it, but I was grateful. "This is Vaughn Westbrook. He's new to Channing House, and he's going to be your bunkmate."

That earned me even more suspicious looks from two of them, while a third barely glanced at us before he went back to whatever he was drawing. A kid who looked just like him leaned against the table next to where he worked, and the last stood nearest the door, his dark eyes locked on mine thoughtfully.

"He's huge," the kid said without an ounce of aggression, sounding more puzzled than anything.

"Milo," Ms. Stephanie scolded. "Manners."

"Ma'am, he's bigger than we are. Shouldn't he be with the older boys?" At least he asked and didn't assume. That was something.

"I'm nine," I informed the other kid, and he blinked.

"Bullshit," one of the others said as he pushed his way forward to stand next to Milo.

"Jasper," Ms. Stephanie said with a sigh, and Jasper actually shot her a sheepish look.

"Sorry, Ms. Stephanie. I know. Manners. But I'm nine. How can he be nine too?"

I shrugged. "I'm just big. Still nine."

"I'm Milo," Milo introduced himself. "This is Jasper." He indicated the kid next to him that Ms. Stephanie already identified. "That's Kellan. The kid drawing, that's Rome and his brother, Liam."

Kellan gave me a little smile and a shrug. Liam eyed me, but then transferred his attention to Ms. Stephanie. Rome didn't even look up. That was cool.

"Thank you, Milo," Ms. Stephanie said with a warm smile before she glanced at me. "Vaughn's not entirely new to the

VICIOUS REBEL

system, but this is his first time in a group home long-term." She rested a hand on my arm. "I trust you will look after him for me?"

"Yes, ma'am," Milo agreed. Jasper's lip curled, but the moment Milo elbowed him, his expression smoothed. Jasper didn't want me here. That was fine. If he left me alone, I'd leave him alone.

"Which one of the beds is open?" Ms. Stephanie asked. I'd guess it was the only one not made, which was the bottom bunk closest to the door.

Milo scratched the back of his neck. "I'd say this one, but Jasper will probably want to be closest to the door, and Liam and Rome have the one by the window. So if Kellan doesn't mind bunking with Jasper here at the door, Vaughn can take the bottom bunk over here with me up top. Unless you need the top?" The last was a question, but to be honest, he looked skeptical.

"Bottom is fine." I didn't really care where I slept. Jasper didn't argue, but he did head over to the bunk and start ripping stuff off it. Milo shook his head.

"Don't mind him. He doesn't like change."

Ms. Stephanie looked at me again. "I'll be back to pick you up next Friday, if you want. I know it won't be enough, but I can take you to see her weekly."

Relief swarmed through me. I'd been afraid to ask. Mom had been straight with me that this last weekend might be our last time together. As much as I hated it, there wasn't much I could do about it.

"I would," I said. "If it's not any trouble."

"Of course it's not any trouble." Then she glanced back at the room. "Anything you boys need to tell me?"

"Nope."

"No, ma'am."

"All good."

"Nothing."

Milo said nothing, he just shook his head, and I didn't believe any of them. From the look on Ms. Stephanie's face, she didn't either, but she let it go. While she lingered a few more minutes and helped me make up my bed, she finally left with the promise to see me at the end of the week. Friday seemed a long way away.

The other guys weren't saying much, but they were watching me. Liam and Kellan more than Jasper, but I caught him staring when I wasn't looking up. Milo was sprawled on his bed in the bunk above mine, flipping through some magazine. After I stored away the few items I'd been able to pack, I dug a book out of my backpack and settled down to read.

"When Jenkins is here, don't push any rules. He's a pasty guy with a bald spot," Kellan said. "He's usually only here on Tuesdays and Thursdays. But if someone gets sick, he shows up on the weekends."

"Don't let him catch you alone either," Liam said. "Though I think you might scare him." He actually sounded gleeful about that.

"Don't risk it," Jasper said abruptly. "Even if you're huge. The guy's trash."

"He won't," Milo said from above. "We stick together in here."

And that seemed to decide that.

Except Jasper eyed me.

"What?" I asked, because the longer he stared, the harder it was to focus on my book.

"Why is Ms. Stephanie coming to get you on Friday?"

"Dude," Kellan said, sliding a piece of gum into his mouth. "None of your beeswax." But he still looked at me as if waiting for me to answer.

Liam had picked up a ball and was tossing it into the air

and catching it, and his brother was still busily scribbling away. The sounds of his pencil scratching and Liam's ball hitting were the only sounds in the room.

I shrugged. "My mom's in hospice. So Ms. Stephanie is taking me to see her."

"She's in the hospital?" Jasper asked, frowning. "So you're just staying here until she goes home?"

I looked down at my book. I promised Mom I wouldn't cry, and right now, my eyes burned. Better not to cry in front of these guys, anyway. "No. Hospice means she isn't going to go home again."

The room went silent.

Though no one asked, I continued, "She's got cancer. She's not getting better. And she's too sick to take care of me. So I'm here."

"Is she going to die?" Rome asked into the silence and Liam grunted as he bumped his brother, but I met the other boy's eyes and nodded.

"Yeah. They did everything they could. But as long as she's in hospice, Ms. Stephanie promised to take me to see her."

The room went quiet again.

"Do you like to draw?" Rome asked, and Liam frowned.

"Some," I said. I lifted my arm where I'd doodled all over it in pen. It looked like the inside of a robot arm. It was mostly hidden under my shirt, 'cause people seemed to not like it that I drew on myself so much.

"You can use my pencils and draw with me if you want."

Kellan swung his head to look at Rome and so did Jasper. Above me, Milo chuckled. "See? He's gonna fit right in."

CHAPTER 15

EMERSYN

The flush of heat spreading through my system collided with a chill rippling over my scalp and down my spine at the nascent threat in Jasper's tone. Vaughn lifted his head but he made no move to put me down, and I had one arm around his neck as I clung to him with a lot more need than even I'd realized I possessed.

"Kissing her hello," he said in that panty-melting voice that made me glad I didn't have any on. As it was, I wanted to lock my thighs against his hips, and I needed to control that very visceral, physical demand. "I've missed her the last few days." Then he focused those topaz-colored eyes on me. "I have missed you, Dove, and I got you a couple of surprises."

The driver's side door slammed.

"Hawk," Kestrel called. "Take a breath."

It hadn't even been an hour since Jasper and Liam had beaten the shit out of each other.

"Boo-Boo!" Freddie called. "Thank fuck. Good company

is here again. Put her down, Vaughn. I need my hug. Especially if we're dolling those out."

Vaughn hadn't stopped looking past my shoulder. The set of his muscles, the firmness of his jaw, and the way he stared promised he wasn't backing down. He might not be glaring, but he wasn't budging and his arms tightened around me.

I'd missed him too. But I didn't want there to be another fight. Not...

"Put her down." The snap of command in Jasper's voice ripped through me and pissed me off at the same time. Just when I thought I understood him, he'd act like he had the right to tell everyone what to do. Maybe he did with the Vandals. He seemed to call all the shots, but dammit...

"Leave." Rome's order carried through the warehouse, echoing across the walls. "Now."

He walked into my line of sight, but he wasn't staring at me or Vaughn. Instead, he looked out to the warehouse where the rats were working. A truck had been unloaded, and there were crates they were moving around. We had an audience. Including the guy he'd punched earlier in the day for calling me 'princess.'

That guy leaned to the side and spit. It was gross as hell, and I jerked my gaze away from it.

"You ice that cheek yet, Dove?" Vaughn asked. Either he didn't notice or he didn't care about our audience or Jasper's attitude. Not much seemed to get past any of them. Even as Rome stared, the others were grabbing jackets and putting down tools. They didn't even finish their tasks. They just left.

"C'mon, Hawk, lighten up. You know we're all crazy about Boo-Boo," Freddie said, but I swore I could *feel* Jasper looming up behind me. The hum of conversations from elsewhere faded as doors slammed.

Then it was us.

In the warehouse.

Without an audience.

I twisted a little in Vaughn's arms, and he loosened only enough to set me down. As though if I asked, then that was all he needed. But he kept an arm around me as I turned. A sigh escaped me as I spotted Freddie.

He definitely looked a hell of a lot better than he had before. Still, he was pale, and the lights in the warehouse didn't do him any favors. His longish hair was lanky and in need of a good brushing. The shadows beneath his eyes were still present but not quite as pronounced.

It hadn't even been a week, but I swore he'd lost weight.

"I'm good, Boo-Boo," Freddie assured me, offering me a cocky smile that neither reached his eyes nor quite pulled his lips as wide. It was more a facsimile than the real thing.

"Seriously, Jasper," Kestrel said, pulling my attention to the bruised and battered Jasper. "Not now. Let's just work this shit out without…"

"Without what? One of you deciding to snake her out from under me?" Jasper demanded. "Was that why you were running interference with her the last few days? Trying to slide in between my girl's legs before I got back? Or were you and Vaughn plotting something? It's bad enough I found Rome all wrapped around her like he was her personal comfort blanket at fucking Liam's place. Now you're gonna pull this shit?"

"I'm cutting you some slack because it's been a long fucking week of long fucking days in a long year." There was no mistaking the aggravation in Kestrel's tone, and I'd almost cheer him on, except I was back on the "my girl."

"Hey, Boo-Boo." Freddie edged toward me. His hand brushed mine as he added, "Why don't we go inside and let them work out their issues in private…"

"Don't fucking touch her, Freddie," Jasper snapped, and then before I could say a word, he glared past me *and*

Vaughn. "And don't you deny it. I see it in your eyes too—you all think you have some claim."

I tapped Vaughn's arm. "Let go, please," I said softly, and though he sighed, Vaughn released me. Jasper reached out with one hand and before he even touched me, Rome had him in an arm lock and Kestrel hit from the other side. Vaughn swept me backward and then surged forward. His bulk blocked my view.

One minute, it was fine, and the next, they were all in a fight. Even Vaughn was in there. The only one avoiding it besides me was Freddie. He grimaced as he glanced from the four of them to me.

"What the actual fuck?" Doc swore from somewhere to my right, and I found him staring at them a lot like we were. It was a fucking free for all.

I twisted, looking around, and when I spotted what I wanted, I headed for it, only to have Doc catch me gently. "Go inside, Little Bit…"

"Stop it," I told him. As much as it would be easy to just lean on him and let him solve things. I'd been leaning on all of them and that shit stopped right the fuck now. "I know what I'm doing."

Maybe for the first time since I got here, I knew what it was too. His gaze skated over my face, and his eyes narrowed. It was a bruise. I wouldn't break. I pulled free and hurried over to the hose. It was connected to a spigot, and I gripped it and yanked the dial to turn the water on. Fortunately, this hose also came with a sprayer.

Probably for washing all their fancy cars.

Freddie stared at me with wide eyes and Doc actually bit back a smile as I marched toward the pile of men—boys—steadily beating on each other. I aimed and then braced my feet as I squeezed the control.

Water shot out of it in a stream, and what water splashed me was icy cold.

The four of them froze, all of them jerking somewhat bruised and battered looks in my direction. Rome's knuckles were open and bleeding. The cut across Jasper's eye had gotten a lot worse. Even Kellan looked like he had gotten nailed in the face. Drenched, they finally yanked apart and scattered.

After turning off the water, I traced my gaze over them one at a time and then focused on Jasper. He looked worse than when he'd had his fight with Liam, and I didn't care what Rome said about how they processed their feelings. Rome actually gave me a small smile, and Vaughn raked a hand through his damp hair and slicked it back from his face.

"To be very clear, I may not have asked to be here in the beginning…" I started.

"Emersyn—" Jasper cut in, and I narrowed my eyes.

"Shut up, Jasper. I'm talking this time. Me. Not you. For once, all of you are going to listen."

He blinked, and Kestrel let out a slow whistle. Even Freddie raised his hands and backed up a step. At my frown, he said, "I know that look. Not arguing with it."

Whatever. I flicked a look back at the boys. Even Vaughn, who I'd been so damn happy to see, and Rome, who'd made me feel safe and warm after a bad day. Kestrel, who'd supported me getting out of here and doing other things, and finally, Jasper, who needed something from me badly and I wanted to figure out what it was and if I was even capable of it.

But not at this price.

"As I was saying," I continued when they'd held the line silently. "I may not have asked to come here in the beginning, but I stayed because it was my choice. One *I* made."

Rome, Kestrel, and Doc knew what I meant. If the others didn't, well, right now wasn't the time to educate them.

"But this..." I pointed to all of them. "This fighting? Over me? Like I'm some bone?" Liam's reference to a junkyard dog flitted across my mind, and I swatted it away. "I've been owned my whole life. For the first time..." Tears burned in my eyes and clogged my throat. "For the first time, I have a chance to be free and none of you are taking that from me." I locked eyes with Jasper. "None of you. I'll die before I go back in shackles or a cage."

He flinched.

Rome's expression darkened, and the others looked away, but Jasper... He held my eyes.

Dropping the hose, I backed off a step. "I won't." Not for anything or anyone.

With that, I turned around and headed for the door. Doc stared at me, a taut frown pulling at his brow. A thousand questions burned in his eyes, and I just shook my head a little. Please don't ask me.

He didn't.

He let me go as I stormed past him. It took everything I possessed to move at a purposeful walk and not to run. A part of me wanted to hit the door on the far side of the garage and race out of it and keep running. But that part just wanted to get away from the violence. From the fear. From the fact I wanted them, even if I didn't want them to chain me.

Would it be so bad? some dark little part of me whispered. *Just let them take care of everything. Kill your enemies. At least so far, them owning you seems like an upgrade.*

Except I didn't want to be owned.

By anyone.

I didn't slow down inside, heading straight for the steps and up them. The hallway seemed almost too stark, too institutional after Liam's apartment with its clean lines and dark walls. My feet slowed at Vaughn's room, but I refused to stop. I kept going, past Rome's. Then down to Kestrel's.

The door was unlocked, and I let myself in.

"Dove!"

Vaughn's voice followed me, but I ignored him as I pushed into the room they'd given me. I hadn't meant to admit so much. Those words had been stuck inside for so long, it actually tore something loose to say them aloud.

I shut the door and crossed over to the bed. It was all neatly made and cleaned up. The ragged old bear that had been sitting there the night I arrived was back in place against the pillows. I scooped him up and wrapped my arms around him as I fell onto the bed sideways and stared at the painting on the wall that looked like it had been framed.

The depth. The colors. The world it offered seemed so much brighter than...

The door behind me opened. I didn't even have to look to know it was Vaughn. Saying nothing, he closed the door once more. A soft sigh pulled out of him. The rustle of clothing followed, and the damp clothes hit the floor in the bathroom.

He cut off the lights, plunging the room into darkness, and then he eased onto the bed behind me.

"I'm sorry, Dove," he murmured in that soothing voice. That was it. The simple apology. "I'm going to wrap an arm around you, okay? If you want me to keep my hands to myself, I will."

He waited, and I sighed. Rolling onto my back, I reached out a hand to him, and he caught my fingers in the dark. His relief was palpable as he pulled me against him. His bare skin was still damp and very chilly from my dousing.

"Do you want to talk about it?"

It wasn't the first time he'd asked me. The other night, I'd come so close to confessing, and then it wouldn't come out.

"I don't know how," I admitted. It was easier in the dark. He couldn't see me. With a light thumb, he stroked my hand as he raised it to his lips. The press of a kiss to my palm had me shuddering. "I can't believe I said it down there."

"You needed us to hear you," he responded, as if it were the most natural thing in the world. "We clearly weren't listening."

It wasn't funny, and at the same time, the sheepish note much like Rome's earlier expression seemed so out of place on him that a huff of laughter escaped me. "No, you were all too busy peeing on my leg."

"Well..." The faint curl of disgust in that single syllable suggested Vaughn wasn't a fan of the description. "I wouldn't say peeing on your leg. But...I get your point. In my defense, I've missed you. I got you a couple of presents to say sorry for being gone for so long."

"You didn't have to do that." It was almost automatic, my upbringing kicking in. One should never act like a present was expected or needed.

"Maybe not," he agreed, stroking a hand down the side of my face and then over my hair. "But I wanted to do it. The flowers were pretty, something that smelled sweet, like you do, and colorful. And because I wanted you to smile."

I did. Even if I couldn't see them, I liked the picture he painted of them.

"And I got you a phone, so I could talk to you and message you if there's a next time that I'm gone. I won't have to rely on the guys to pass you messages or leave you in the dark because you wake up and I'm gone."

"A phone?" The second word actually caught in my throat, and I moved to tilt my face toward him as if I could see him in the dark. Not once in all the months I'd been here had they given me *my* phone back, much less a different one.

"It's not fancy, just a burner. But I put all our numbers in, not just mine." I could almost hear the smile. "Though, I freely admit, mine is first and I'm speed dial one."

Unlocking my fingers from the teddy, I reached up to caress his face. "Thank you."

The tension in his muscles seemed to let go as he pulled me to him. His lips found mine in the dark, and I almost let the tears out at the sweet sweep of his mouth opening to mine like he could devour all the pain. Then to my horror, one tear did slide down my cheek. It salted the kiss, but rather than pull away, Vaughn stroked the tear away with his thumb, then moved his kisses up to my nose then my forehead and down to my ear.

"It's all right, Dove," he whispered. "I promise you're safe here. You are safe with all of us." The declaration threatened to take me out at the knees almost as much, because I wanted to believe it as he was making it. The coolness of his flesh seemed to grow hotter as he traced kisses down my throat.

I ran my hands over his bare chest. And it wasn't long before I realized he'd stripped everything off. When he tugged at the shirt and pulled it up, I freed myself only long enough to yank it up and over my head. His hands spanned my ribs, then he pulled my nipple into his mouth and liquid heat spilled through me.

Between us, we got rid of the sweatpants and the socks. In between long, bruising kisses, he massaged my breasts, and I cupped his balls and then stroked a hand down the length of his cock. It burned against my palm, and I loved exploring the piercing at the tip.

When he thrust two blunt fingers inside of me, I groaned. All the thoughts pinging around inside of me quietened as he soothed and seduced my body. I ached for him.

At my tug, he moved to his back and lifted me up. We could have been fumbling in the dark, but he trusted me to guide him and his strength held me suspended as I straddled his hips. The tip of his dick was a torment and a pleasure as I ran him back and forth against my slickness.

"I need you, Dove," he whispered, and I shuddered at that confession.

It was braver than anything I'd ever been able to admit. "I think I need you too," I said slowly, not quite trusting myself to get the words out. Then I sank down on him, and the world narrowed to where his body thrust up into mine.

I might have been on top, but Vaughn controlled the pace, stretching me with his ever upward push into my body. The piercing struck sparks inside of me.

"Play with your nipples, Dove," Vaughn ordered, and I dragged my hands off his chest to my own as he lifted and pulled me back down to him. I clenched around him. "Pinch them like it's me," he whispered. "Roll them between your thumb and your forefinger. Stretch them, twist them. Do it until it hurts, and then feel me fucking into you."

I moved to obey him, and the soft cries I stifled in my throat grew louder.

"Let go, Dove," he commanded. "Give it to me. Give me your pleasure and your pain."

The downward slam had me seeing stars as I swore he was even deeper inside of me than before, and I cried out.

"Yes…" He sounded almost triumphant, and then he tumbled me onto my back and wrapped my legs around his waist. "Grip me tight, sweet Dove. Grip me tight and let me ride you now."

I swore those were the last words I heard him say as he began to power into me, and it took all the strength I had in my trembling limbs to hold onto him. Then his mouth captured mine and his fingers replaced mine on my nipples. I dug my nails into his back as his muscles bunched and flexed.

I came in a rush of wetness, the orgasm spiraling out of control, but he didn't let up, not once. The punishing pace drove me up the bed, and I fought to keep him between my thighs. Then one of my legs was over his shoulder as he pulled me upward, folding me near in half as his cock took me deeper still, stretching me right to the edge, and when I came this time, I sobbed and clung to him.

He orgasmed on a ragged cry, pounding into me until he filled me up, and then we were clinging to each other, trembling. Light teased at my eyelids, and I opened them to find a pair of frosty gray eyes boring into mine. Jasper stood illuminated in the doorway, his attention riveted on us. I opened my mouth, but he turned and left, pulling the door closed with a *thud* behind him.

Shit.

BROKEN SET

LIAM

The conversation in the other room carried through the door. Not the words, just the tones and the inflections. Ms. Stephanie wasn't happy. But she didn't seem to be having much effect on the couple inside. Every couple of weeks or so, the group home got visitors.

Couples. Lawyers. Occasionally other social workers. They came through and studied us like animals in the zoo. Milo said to just ignore them, let them come in, look around, and leave. Most of the time, I agreed with him.

Most of the time.

But I'd seen his face a few weeks earlier. It was the day three kids were adopted out at the same time. Adopted, not placed. Adopted meant they weren't supposed to come back. One of the kids…

The door opened, and Ms. Stephanie glanced out and then down at me. She gave me the most insincere smile I'd ever seen on her face. It faltered, the corners turning down before the smile could even reach her eyes. No, those only held an apology.

"Liam, come in, I want you to meet the O'Connells." She cleared her throat as I stood and moved aside so I could see the couple in her office. The man studied me for a moment as he stood, then he stepped forward and held out his hand like we'd actually been introduced.

"Hello, Liam," he said. "My name's Jonathon and this is my wife, Mary." Mary was a quiet thing, but there was an inescapable hope filling her eyes that made me shift in place. I studied his hand for a moment, then shook it slowly. I wasn't sure what was going on. Most of the time, I could figure it out.

Today? Not so much.

We weren't even at the group home. Ms. Stephanie had picked *me* up. Just me. Not Rome. That was strange enough. Now, the couple was looking at me like I was an answer to a question they hadn't actually asked me.

Ms. Stephanie stepped between us, breaking the uncomfortable eye contact, and I half followed her to the desk. But she didn't go behind it so much as lean against it. "Liam, have you seen Jonathon and Mary at the group home the last couple of weeks?"

"Sure," I answered. It was automatic. Lots of people came through. Milo was right about ignoring most of them. I got the routine—they looked, but they didn't want us, the older kids. The broken ones. We were the ones who were stuck in place. That was fine…

"We've been watching you," Mary said, moving to perch on the chair closest to me. Soft floral scents tickled my nose, and I resisted the urge to sneeze. She seemed like a really nice lady. "Oh, hell—Crap!" Redness bloomed in her cheeks, and she put a hand over her mouth like she was horrified.

Mr. O'Connell appeared to be struggling not to laugh. I

didn't fight it. That was funny. Adults acted like they didn't cuss all the time. Like it was some secret language we kids weren't supposed to even know yet. I hated to fucking break it to her. I pretty much knew every single word. Even cunt. Thank you, Jasper, for that one. He knew a lot of good ones.

Mary's face relaxed, though the pink in her cheeks was in high bloom. She really was a nice lady. The smile in her eyes was nice. "Sorry, I'm excited."

"It's okay," I said, automatic at this point. "I can cuss already, so it's not new to me."

It was her turn to laugh, and she shot a look up at her husband before she glanced back at me. "You are a charmer."

"Sure," I agreed with a nod. Not sure what I was being charming about, but why not. "See, Jonathon, I told you. He's got a wonderful sense of humor."

I shifted on my feet and rubbed the back of my neck. It gave me an excuse to look at Ms. Stephanie. She still seemed awfully unhappy. We'd done something like this a month earlier. Me and Rome both that time, though Rome had just stayed silent the whole time. He didn't like strangers. I covered easily enough.

"He does," her husband said, but he studied me with a wrinkled brow. "Tell me, Liam—It's all right if we call you Liam, yes?"

"That's my name." Liam Darragh Cleary. The one thing I owned that was mine. That and my brother. We were the matched set. Mary bit her lip at my response as though trying to hold back her smile, though she failed. I waited a couple of extra seconds before I tacked on a, "I mean, yes, sir."

Jonathon chuckled. "You've got spirit, young man. You really do." Then he moved closer to Mary's chair. "And we've got an offer for you. We're hoping you'll take us up on it."

"Okay." I stretched the word out. A string of unease

plucked in the back of my mind. The discordant chord had me backing up a single step. I wanted to be able to see Ms. Stephanie's face. Whatever their offer was, she didn't like it.

"It's not an offer so much as... We applied to adopt you," Mary said, and everything inside of me chilled.

"What?" I jerked my head to look at Ms. Stephanie. They'd been discussing my adoption, and she was against it.

Adopted.

The word floated around inside of me like dust in a sunbeam, aimless and uncertain.

"Why?" I couldn't hold back that syllable. I didn't know them. Why did they want us? "Are you telling me so I'll talk to Rome?"

A split second later, understanding hit me.

Mary glanced at her husband, even as she bit her lip, and his expression tensed briefly. But the unhappiness in Ms. Stephanie's eyes explained everything.

They didn't want Rome.

CHAPTER 16

LIAM

My face still ached a couple of days later. The bruises from Jasper's fists had bloomed on my side and around my jaw. Not the worst I'd ever had and certainly not anything that would slow me down. Rome had been circumspect when I checked in with him the next day.

Well, circumspect might be generous. All he'd said was *fine*. That word held so many meanings that he could have meant anything from the damn clubhouse was on fire to he had another fucking knife wound. No, the verbiage didn't tell me shit. The speed at which he'd answered did.

He'd ignored me for a solid hour. Then answered.

My other half was irritated with me. That was fine. He could be irked with me all he liked. It was still my fucking apartment, and if he'd brought Hellspawn here to get laid, all he had to do was send me a message, then I wouldn't have let anyone up here.

At the moment, I ran on the treadmill, watching the sun

rise in the distance. The speed amped up with every mile, so did the incline. I alternated my workouts between interval training and pure cardio. I needed endurance.

Period.

Music blasted through the apartment, the thrumming beat a good accompaniment to push me. My phone buzzed in the holder, and I spared it a look.

Ambrose.

He could fucking wait.

The Bay Ridge Royal lieutenant had been up my ass all week about next week's event. I had it handled, but he was a fucking micromanager. I'd like to micromanage his balls and knock them up into his throat. But that wouldn't be politic.

A fact that kept him from being gelded daily.

I focused my attention back out the window. No, I had other problems to work on today. One that I'd been turning over in my head for the last forty-eight hours. A problem spelled Hellspawn.

Rome's feelings on the diminutive subject were quite clear. Jasper would be a problem. If I had to clear that ground, I would. Kestrel's interest was crystal clear too. Her presence was creating all kinds of disruption. Worse, I was *here* and not where I could keep an eye on her.

She definitely required keeping an eye on.

I was no closer to a solution by the time I finished my run than I'd been when I started. By the time I had a protein shake in one hand and the news pulled up on my phone, the first inklings of a plan began to form.

The pair of bounty hunters—or should I say would-be-bounty-hunters?—who'd showed up at Kestrel's. That couldn't be a one off. So what had Little Miss Hellspawn done to earn that kind of attention? Curious, I scrolled through my schedule. I had a couple of meetings lined up. I had time after to hit the cop shop and put out some feelers.

After I pulled on my gun belt and secured the shoulder holster, I tugged a jacket over it. I didn't go unarmed to business meetings. Just not a good idea.

I sent a text back to Rome. Every day, rain or shine, no matter what the fuck was going on, I sent him a message. Sometimes he answered. Sometimes he ignored me.

Me: *Does she like roses?*

The answer came within seconds.

A middle finger emoji.

Love you too, bro.

Still chuckling, I pocketed the phone, snagged my jacket, and headed out. The day flew by. Rome hadn't said anything else, and the other Vandals remained dead ass silent. Then, I'd only actually heard from Kestrel once in the last year, and that was *after* Rome had been stabbed.

They better fucking call me if something happened to him. I was dead to them for the most part these days, and I could live with being a ghost. But Rome and I had been separated enough. The system couldn't keep us apart, and I wasn't about to let anyone else.

The first meeting of the day took an hour. The accountant was a short guy with glasses, male-pattern baldness, and balls big enough to take me on without flinching. Today, he was all about taxes, interest, and diversifying. I listened more than he probably thought.

I also read all of his reports. The man was honest. Direct. He was worth the twelve percent I paid him. Enough to keep his hand out of the till and not enough to matter to my bottom line.

Apparently, we'd made more money this month than expected. The windfall was nice. I could use that to invest. Still, by the time I parted ways with Curtis, I was already sick of numbers. I cut across town. My second meeting was in 19 Diamonds territory with Meeks. The man was an asshole, but if I wanted to get access to Juan Ricardo, I had to make nice with Meeks.

Wallace Meeks was a dick. He'd earned the name Deuce because he was basically a pile of shit, no matter *why* he thought he had the name. That he was an enforcer for the 19Ds rather than an actual shot caller didn't matter. If I wanted to get to Ricardo, I had to go through him.

I'd been negotiating deals for months between the Bay Ridge Royals and the 19 Diamonds. The rough peace between the two gangs worked more like a minefield of unstable personalities armed to the teeth.

Good times.

The bar they'd set the meetup for was called the Blue Diamond. Not very original. The titty bar opened right at lunchtime and actually offered a buffet of meat, potatoes, beer, and boobs. All the boobs. Even the waitresses were topless.

The girl who took me to my seat had a pair of double Ds with blackberry-colored nipples on tight display. She moved ahead of me, the thong barely covering her shaved snatch, and her ass had just a hint of jiggle as she moved. The thick, full pouty lips would look mighty fine wrapped around my cock while she looked up at me with those liquid brown eyes.

She was every inch my type, and my dick didn't remotely give a fuck.

Honestly, my dick probably had a point—business before distractions.

Even sweet, curved distractions that leaned over me as I took a seat and brushed one of those breasts right against my cheek. All I had to do was shift, and I could suck that nipple against my teeth. My dick didn't even twitch.

"What would you like?" An offer for anything I wanted seemed to populate her tone. Pretty sure if I invited her to get on her knees, she would be right there.

I pressed a light kiss to the curve of her breast and tucked a fifty into her thong. "Just bring me a beer, sweet cheeks, another smile, and we're good."

I could have let my hand linger. I could have traced a line along her thong. I mean, she positively dripped "fuck me" energy, but nope. My dick passed on that buffet offer. She gave me a saucy wink and a pouty smile before sauntering off. I'd arrived before Meeks, and I'd taken a table near the far side of the horseshoe-shaped main platform.

There were three other poles and stages in the room, but they were close to the door. In this situation, it was better to have my back against a wall. My bike jacket rested over the back of the chair, and I stretched my legs out like I had all the time in the world.

The music changed, and a new dancer strutted out on the stage to catch the pole and swing herself around. She was in all fringe and very little else. Pretty sure the thong she wore was more a suggestion than actual fabric. The muscles in those thighs flexed as she climbed the pole and then flipped herself around.

My beer arrived with another offer of company. Double Ds straddled my leg and did a slow roll of her hips. I let my gaze drift over her appreciatively. More because a man sitting in a titty bar ignoring the titty got noticed. I peeled another fifty off from the cash in my pocket and slid it down her chest until she thrust her hips upward, and I folded it right over the V covering her pussy.

"Thanks, babe," I murmured. "I'm good."

She dipped her gaze to my crotch and I could almost taste her disappointment. My dick, however, remained indifferent. Picky little fucker. I took a long pull from the cold bottle. An image of disheveled dark brown hair, warm, almost whiskey-colored eyes with sleep rumpled cheeks and a crease along her face from Rome's shirt flicked through my brain, and my dick stirred.

Yeah.

I slammed the door shut on that for now and focused on where I was and what I was doing. One full beer and two full sets of dancers later, Meeks strolled through the door of the club. The fucker was an hour late, and I was the schmuck sitting here waiting.

He grinned in my direction as he and his little cohort made their entrance. The man had at least a half-dozen low-level bully boys with him. And that was what they were—bullies. The 19 Diamonds had been an upstart gang that moved into Braxton Harbor a little under five years earlier, and they'd been making noise.

Three years ago, they'd started making moves.

Now they were out growing the little patch of territory they'd claimed and wanted to push into other areas. They wanted more than smuggled cigarettes and tax-free booze along with pimping out their whores and the sex clubs they'd been opening.

Sex clubs that were bad for business across the whole of the Harbor. Because they'd started offering any kink a person could afford, including—if the rumors were true—snuff. That was just bad for business. But people came and went. The missing in the Harbor were nothing new, nor were the drug addicts and the whores.

Meeks took his time crossing the bar. The swagger in his step didn't match the watchfulness in his eyes or the fact he still sported bandages on his hand. Reattachment surgery really had come a long way. The same girl who brought me my beer brought me a second and one for Meeks.

He took a handful of her ass and bit down on her neck. She arched her whole body like she enjoyed the attention. The fact there were teeth marks on her flesh and her gaze never shifted from mine didn't seem to matter to him. He slapped one of her breasts, then dragged her mouth to his for a brutal kiss.

Bored, I glanced at my watch more to let her get away from the groping than because I really had other places to be. Meeks chuckled, and he took her chin in his hand.

"Give us ten minutes, then get us a room. I want my cock in that mouth."

She dipped her eyes in acquiescence, but it didn't quite hide her shudder of revulsion. He didn't miss it either. He slapped her breast and then cupped her pussy.

"Do a good job, and I'll fuck you nice and hard here. Don't, and it's the ass. Got it?"

"You'll like what my mouth can do, baby," she promised him in a breathy voice, and I kicked out a chair, aiming it to hit him in the thigh right next to the obscene boner he sported.

Meeks grunted and glared at me.

"Pocket your dick and sit down, or fuck off. I've wasted enough time on your shit today." I met his stare, unimpressed. "Three…"

Amusingly enough, I didn't even have to hit two before he released her and waved her away before he sat. "Didn't take you for such a cockblocker, O'Connell."

"Don't recall giving a fuck one way or the other," I responded and ignored her look of gratitude as she hurried away. She probably shouldn't be so happy that I helped. This dickhead would probably take it out on her later. I couldn't afford to care.

Not right now.

He snorted a grunt of laughter like we were friends.

We were not.

His guys ranged out around the room, watching his back

and the door. The paranoia was strong with this one. In fact, it was worse than it had ever been in the past.

Jasper had that effect on people.

"Well, I'm here," Meeks said before he took a long drink of his beer. I didn't bother sipping mine. One was enough, and I was working. "What did you want?"

"Stop starting shit with the Vandals."

His bottle crashed to the tabletop. "Are you fucking with me right now, rich boy? You fucking cocksuckers deal in yachts and imported pussy. The Vandals are Harbor business and no concern of yours."

I ignored all of that. What the Bay Ridge Royals did was not his concern. Nor where their interests lay. "Did I stutter? Gang war is bad for business."

With a snort of derision, he flexed his hand around the bottle. The skull face tattoo he'd been adding to his scalp pulsed as though it was as pissed as he was. "What fucking business do you have with them? Is this about your retard brother?"

Ignoring the bait, I kept my expression bland. "You're replaceable, Deuce, don't forget that. Juan Ricardo needs this deal with us more than he needs you."

The sudden flare of his nostrils confirmed that opinion.

"If you like, I can just set up the call with him. I'm doing you a courtesy. Stay out of Vandals' business and stop picking fights with them."

"Or what?" Meeks demanded, seeming to find his balls, or maybe he lost what was left of his marbles. It was debatable.

"Well, we'll start with the three hundred percent tax that will be added to all your incoming shipments for the next three months."

He paled.

I glanced around the club. "And this bar."

"What about it?"

"I'll take it too." I hadn't intended to, but fuck him. "You and your boys will leave, or you'll pay the going rate plus three hundred percent."

"Are you out of your fucking mind?" It came out edged in fear.

"We can take more." For the most part, the Bay Ridge Royals used the Harbor as a launching point for businesses elsewhere. But they had a lot of resources—resources I had access to, and I was their fixer here. The 19 Diamonds needed fixing.

He slammed back the full beer, then set the bottle on the table. Raising a hand for the waitress, he snarled, "Fine. We'll leave them alone. We only have one small piece of business left."

"And what's that?"

"It's not your concern."

I chuckled softly, and he shot me a look. The whites of his eyes were very visible. "You want to try that answer again."

The waitress brought him another beer, and he reached out to grab her.

"Three hundred percent," I reminded him, and his hand froze just inches from her. "And if she says no, I'll cut your balls off if you keep reaching for her."

The waitress jerked her eyes to me, and Meeks closed his hand into a fist. Had to hurt from the way the blood drained from his knuckles and his jaw clicked as he ground his teeth together.

"Fuck off," he told the waitress and spun to face me fully. Well, well, it was about time the dick started paying attention.

I ignored her look of gratitude as she obeyed and kept my attention on Meeks.

"What's that last piece of business?"

He really didn't want to tell me, but he couldn't find a way around it. What he had to say, I really didn't like.

I'd deal with it.

After he was done and *after* he'd paid, Meeks and his people fucked off out of the bar. I leaned back in the seat and turned the idea around in my head. Bounties came in all shapes and sizes. The Bay Ridge Royals negotiated enough international product in flesh and drugs that we made it a point to know who carried and offered markers.

I informed the manager of the change in ownership and the new rules. I also sent over a handful of new security guards to deal with the place for now. The 19 Diamonds would hit back, or Meeks would. My waitress got a new best friend in the form of a guy to pick her up and drop her off, just in case Meeks got stupid.

Which he would.

'Cause he was a fucker.

Outside, I pulled on my jacket as I straddled my bike, then I made a call. The broker knew my number and answered on the first ring. "I thought we were up to date on our accounts." Wisely, he kept his tone even and civil.

"I need information."

His relieved exhale said more about the Royals' reach than it did me. I was fine with that. It was useful right now. "What can I do for you?"

"Word on the street is there's a bounty out on Emersyn Sharpe."

"There is," the broker confirmed. "Quarter of a million. It's gone up in the last week."

That was a lot of money. "Who's offering it?"

"You know that's not how this works."

"Sure, I do. I also know I have privileges others don't. I want to meet with the buyer."

Silence. "You have a lead?"

"You'll never hear it from me."

More silence.

"If this gets out…"

I snorted. Who the fuck was I going to tell? "Are we going to have a problem?"

He swore. I waited.

"I'll make the arrangements."

"Name."

Another pause.

"Bradley Sharpe."

I frowned. "Her father?"

"No," the broker answered. "Her uncle. And a word of advice—don't cross him."

Now I definitely wanted to meet him.

"Set it up."

Looked like I'd be seeing Hellspawn sooner rather than later.

SLOW DOWN AHEAD

KELLAN

The rain started early in the day. Mom and Nana argued for an hour over whether I should go to wait for the bus or one of them would drive me. Dad just let them argue while he drank his coffee and shot me a wink. I hid my own smile as I ate my toast.

I'd started first grade this year. I was more than old enough to take the bus. I'd argued with Mom all summer. She drove me every day for kindergarten, but I was a big boy. I wanted to ride with my friends. I didn't worry too much though. Mom had already said I could. Nana just wanted to fuss, or that's what Dad always said when Mom got upset with her.

"Don't worry, it's just Mom, she fusses about everything. You do things the way you planned."

He told me once that sometimes, people just needed to fuss before they were ready to see reason. Other people would always think they knew better, but as long as we had a plan, they were entitled to their opinion. Dad was funny, but he also said arguing was what he did for a living.

I thought he was a lawyer, but Mom would grin and say, "same thing." I bit back another laugh at the memory. Because usually, they started doing the icky stuff then with the kisses and the hugs. If I tried to escape it, they'd drag me in and kiss the sides of my head and blow raspberries until I was a giggling mess.

That was fine at five. At six? I couldn't be such a baby. Another reason for Mom to not drive me to school. I didn't mind giving her hugs and kisses, but I didn't want other kids to see me doing it. After breakfast, I carried my plate from the table to the sink and set my plastic cup up there too.

Dad mimed for me to go get my backpack because Mom and Nana were still arguing. I grinned at him and raced out. My backpack and lunch were already together by the door. I pulled on my coat and my hat then the backpack, and stuck my head around the corner to look in the kitchen.

With a wink, Dad motioned me to go, and I blew a kiss to Mom and Nana where he could see it, so he could tell them. Then I bolted as fast as my little legs would carry me. The bus picked up at the corner by the stop sign. We were five houses down. The rain was coming down steadily, but I resisted the urge to jump in the puddles, barely.

Didn't want to get yelled at before I even made it to the stop sign. I had my fingers crossed all the way. There were already a bunch of kids waiting, including the older ones who took over the back of the bus. I sat near the front 'cause they were super rowdy and picked on the little ones back there.

The bus pulled up, and I was one of the last ones on board and got a seat right near the front. I wiped the rain out of my eyes and looked out the fogged window. Mom and Dad were standing in the driveway with an umbrella over their heads, watching me.

I made a face, but Mom blew me a kiss with both hands and I mimed catching it. Hopefully, no one else saw it but me. The bus gave a hiss of air and a squeal as we started rolling forward, and I settled back in my seat. Another day won for me.

The best part of first grade was we had recess twice still, but we didn't have to nap after lunch. On rainy days, instead of going outside, we either went to the library or we watched a movie. Today it was a movie, 'cause we'd gone to the library the day before. The dark and gloomy weather outside made the room extra dark.

I liked *The Lion King* though, even the scary part where Mufasa died. Thunder outside joined the stampede on the screen, and there were a couple of girls crying. They were hugging Ms. Bell 'cause they were scared. A lot of what went wrong was Simba listened to the wrong people.

A knock at the door distracted me, and I glanced over my shoulder to see a pair of police officers standing there. That was weird. Was there a show and tell today? But when I looked at Ms. Bell, she wore a frown. With care, she stood and made her way over to the door. Then she went outside with the officers.

I went back to watching the movie, but a couple of minutes later, Ms. Bell tapped my shoulder and I stared up at her. She did a curling motion with her fingers to tell me to go with her, so I got up. I didn't want to miss the next song, it was funny, but at least I knew what happened next.

In the darkened hall outside the room, the officers stood waiting. I stared up at them. I'd never been this close to a police officer before. They were awesome.

"Kellan Traschel?" the lady officer asked, and I nodded my head.

"Am I in trouble?" I glanced at Ms. Bell and buried the urge to hide behind her. There was another woman in the hallway, but she hung back. Like the officers, she wore a long coat, and they were all damp from the rain.

The male officer squatted down and shook his head slowly. "No, son, you're not in any trouble. But we do need you to come with us." He motioned to himself and the other officer, then to the lady behind him.

"Why?"

Ms. Bell made a soft sound, and I jerked my gaze up to find her wiping her eyes. Fear ballooned inside of me.

"Oh, sweetheart," she said, then put her hands on my shoulders. "Can I tell him?" The question wasn't directed at me but to the officers. I leaned back into Ms. Bell. I didn't know what was going on.

The woman stepped forward and gave me a smile. "Of course," she said. "And I'm here for you, Kellan. I need you to know that."

I didn't know who she was, but before I could ask, Ms. Bell turned me around and, like the officer, she squatted until we were at eye level. "There was an accident, honey…"

She said a lot of words after that. A lot of words.

Mom and Dad had been in a car accident with Nana. They were all dead.

I couldn't quite work out what dead meant. I mean, we'd had a goldfish and it died, but we got another one just like it. Did that mean I'd get a new mom and dad just like them?

I didn't want a new mom and dad.

At some point, I started crying, and Ms. Bell hugged me for a long time. Then I had to say goodbye to her. To the classroom. To my friends. Ms. Stephanie, the lady, was there to take me with her. The cops walked us all out. I had my jacket, my hat, and my backpack.

Once I was buckled in the car, I stared out the window. I should have let Mom drive me to school.

CHAPTER 17

KESTREL

The last couple of days had been challenging. Jasper had checked out. He wasn't in his room. Not answering his calls. His car was gone. I had a suspicion about where he'd gone, but since he'd left the bat—and his new axe —behind, I told him I'd give him three days. After that, we'd find him.

He needed the cooldown. Finding Emersyn and Vaughn fucking wasn't something he was likely to forget any time soon. Hell, it wasn't anything I was going to forget. I rubbed a hand over my face and stared at the coffeemaker as it spilled the brew of life into the carafe.

It was like some kind of cosmic fucking joke. Drop her in the middle of all of us, the one person we'd do anything to protect, and half of us were ready to tear each other apart because the other half wanted her too. And I knew something had happened between them. I wasn't an idiot.

But I tried not to think about it. Tried not to think what it meant. Definitely didn't focus on how it made me feel. Instead, after Jasper had stormed out, I caught Emersyn before she chased after him, all naked, soft, and looking genuinely well-fucked.

Vaughn scooped her up and took her back in her room and closed the door. They argued, but it wasn't long before Vaughn proved he'd found a way to distract her. So I sat there, listening to them and ignoring the hardness in my cock while I kept watch.

The next day, Vaughn had to work, and rather than take her with him, he asked if she would keep an eye on Freddie. None of us wanted her leaving the clubhouse, but at least this time, we didn't have to make up excuses to try and not scare her.

The attempted kidnapping and the very real assault at the shop seemed to quell some of her rebellion. Though when Vaughn kissed her before he left, he did it in full view of me, Rome, and Freddie. When I pointed it out to him later, his only response had been, "Be clear, I'm not backing off and I'm not surrendering what we have. It might not seem like much, but it's a start."

"And the rest of us?" I countered.

He shrugged. "That's up to you. I've never been opposed to sharing with you guys. Can you say the same?"

Asshole.

Rome hadn't said a word, but Freddie had started cracking jokes. I left it alone when she smiled. I had to check in at the shop, and we still had a guest.

That was where I'd spent most of my second day. Rome stayed with Emersyn and Freddie, though it wasn't his favorite, and I interrogated the other investigator. Everyone had a breaking point, you just had to find the right place to apply pressure.

He'd cracked enough to tell me that they'd been after a

bounty. It was an open contract, and no, they hadn't told anyone about spotting her. But what he wouldn't tell me was *how* or *where* he'd spotted her.

That meant we needed to do some backtracking. I also needed to make sure no one followed me from the garage back here. All of us would have to be more careful. The rats had their orders, and I wanted them scouting. If there were more bounty hunters in the city, we needed to know about it.

The 19Ds had been making some moves too. Their flesh peddling had been stepped up a notch, and that brought with it the chance for a more unsavory clientele. The kind that could shit where they slept, and we didn't need that kind of trouble here.

Raptor was still in the hole. How long he would be stuck in fucking solitary was anyone's guess. It bugged me to not know why. His attorney didn't return our calls. I asked to be notified the minute Raptor was out. I'd make the drive up there and tell him in person.

The only thing giving me any kind of respite was the fact he couldn't know Emersyn was "missing" according to the news. Those stories, which had heated back up, had cooled again. The fact he'd been in solitary for months didn't help my mood any.

Doc agreed to help out. We couldn't leave Emersyn here alone. She'd gotten out. That much I'd already deduced. Gotten out and then come back of her own volition. That meant something. And as much as I didn't want our world to touch her, I was as selfish as the rest of them. I wanted her *here*.

"Kestrel?" The soft cadence of her voice roused me from my stupor, and I glanced over my shoulder.

"Good morning, Sparrow," I told her, summoning a smile far more easily now that I could drink in the sight of her. She'd showered, or Vaughn had woken her up with sex again.

I didn't think he'd left her bed for longer than to go to work since she'd come home the other night.

At least, the night before, he'd taken her to his room. It was one thing to accept they were screwing. It was another to have to listen, and I'd rather learn the details of her moans when I made her do it. My blood seemed to flow south at the very idea.

Yanking my mind away from that track, I said, "Would you like some coffee? Not sure what we have for breakfast. No one has done a supply run. I'll take care of that today. I can send one of the rats out for something though."

"Toast is fine," she said, padding into the room. The gear she wore suggested she was heading into the dance studio Jasper had insisted on building for her. At the time, I'd objected because I didn't want her staying here any longer than necessary. Now, I suspected we needed to make some other alterations. We'd already taken to locking the clubhouse, and there would be new cameras installed.

The rats weren't allowed in after a certain time, and definitely not when she was here. She didn't wait for me to respond before she pulled out the pitiful plastic bag with just the heels of the bread inside it. No complaint came from her though as she dropped them into the toaster.

I pulled out a second mug and set it next to my own. We worked in an almost companionable silence. Coffee poured, I moved it to the table, where I'd already set the newspaper. She joined me and smiled at the coffee, then offered me one of the pieces of toast.

"I can eat on my way out later," I told her. "If you're hitting your studio, you're going to need the calories."

"I'll be fine, it's better to dance without too much in my stomach." She lifted her mug carefully with two hands and took a sip. It was scalding hot, the way I liked it. I took a deeper drink, enjoying the burn.

"Why?"

"Hmm?"

"Why did you come back?"

That wasn't where I'd been going, but after what she said the other night? It was about time one of us did. If Vaughn discussed any of this with her, he'd been mute on the subject.

A slow, long sigh escaped her, and no eighteen-year-old should ever sound that burdened. Ever. More, the way her gaze turned inward and the darkness in her eyes? It was that right there that had captured me from the first night I introduced myself as her driver. I couldn't peg what went through her mind when that expression hit.

Was it loss? Sadness? I wasn't sure. I just needed to fix it. To fix it, I had to know what caused it.

"Because I was so focused on getting away, I didn't think about what I was running away to get to." She picked at the crust on the toast. I wasn't entirely sure if she was aware of what she was doing. "I...I didn't have my wallet or my phone or any money. I didn't have a plan. Get away. Then what? I suppose that seems stupid, huh?"

"Foolish, maybe," I said after a moment. "Not sure I'd call it stupid. When a person is desperate, they make the choices they can with what they know. Was it so bad here? With us?"

"You know it wasn't." She made a face. "But I still don't know why you guys kidnapped me or why you all seemed to know me or why... I don't know. I guess I don't know that why or what comes next. It comes down to trusting all of you. That's hard...with some more than others."

Fair. "Will you tell me what happened after you left?"

She gave me a long considering look, and I tried to keep my expression as open as possible.

"Sparrow, I'm not mad. I just need to understand." None of which was a lie. I did need to understand. If all of us were going to survive the changes she'd already wrought, much less what her presence could continue to cause, then yes, I needed to understand all of it. Her monsters. Ours.

What needed eliminating first.

"I walked. I just picked a direction and started walking. I really wasn't sure where we were, and to be honest, I didn't even remember the name of the city." Her grimace was almost adorable, and the element of embarrassment in it made me want to reach over and comfort her.

Instead, I kept my fucking hands to myself and took another sip of coffee. Emersyn rolled her lower lip between her teeth. She'd finished pulling the edges off the first piece of toast and went to work on the second. None of that was eating, but I let it go. Not like she could remove the whole crust on a heel of bread.

"It was cold and I was tired and I was trying to figure out what to do. Like I said, you had my wallet, my ID, my phone… Someone…offered me a ride, so I took it."

"Excuse me?" The words come out a snap. A quiet snap, but still a snap, and I studied her, looking for any clues in the nuance of her behavior as I lowered my coffee mug.

"Someone safe."

"A stranger is not safe." Then it hit me. It wasn't a stranger. "Doc."

Her startled blink confirmed my guess, and I tucked that information away to take out later and examine.

"Okay," I said on an exhale. "Doc picked you up. Which is better than a stranger. What next?" I rather doubted Doc brought her straight back here.

"I fumbled for somewhere to go, and finally, we headed to the hotel that I'd stayed at. Yes, I know you took my stuff, but they would've recognized me. If nothing else, I might've been able to trade on my name until I could access some ID that would let me get into one of my accounts."

At the third mention of her ID, I got it—that part still

irked. I still had all of that securely stashed away. If she wasn't a prisoner, she had the right to her own information.

"I had Doc drop me off," she continued, her gaze still a million miles from here and her voice going more distant. "He didn't like it, but…I thought it would be better to not have anyone with me if I turned up and suddenly cops were everywhere. Maybe it was stupid to go back, but my face has been on the news. The last thing I wanted was for anyone to get blamed for my kidnapping."

"You wanted to protect us." That shouldn't surprise me, but it did. We'd done her no favors. Not really. Yes, we'd tried to make her comfortable, but we'd also ripped her away from the only life she'd ever known. Fine, we took care of Eric, but a bullet to the head would have solved him without the torture.

That had just been a perk.

"I guess," she admitted, then let out another long sigh. When she lifted her chin and straightened her shoulders, I braced. Here was the admission I'd been waiting for. "I was across the street from the hotel, all set to cross and go inside, when I saw my uncle and some of his men come out." Nothing warm inhabited the frigid tone she used.

Her uncle was not an ally. I knew enough about the Sharpe family to know Bradley Sharpe was a key figure in their corporate maneuverings. Her father, Reginald Sharpe, was the CEO and aloof. His younger brother, Bradley, though? He was unpredictable. They had more money than god and seemed above approach.

And the heiress to all of that performed in shows that traveled across the country and had since she was a child. Something about that picture had always rubbed me the wrong way.

"Not a friend," I said when she'd gone quiet.

A quick shake of her head. "No. And not someone I would ever go to for help. I'd bleed out first."

Bradley Sharpe was going to die. By inches or with a bullet to the back of the head, all I needed were some details.

She finally took a bite of the toast, and I let her have the delaying tactic. If the Sharpes were in on the threats to her, that was a whole other rat's nest of problems.

"I shifted gears. I couldn't go back. So I headed away, and I didn't know where I was going. No plan. No ID. No money. What the hell was I going to do? I've always prided myself on being independent, and at the same time, I've been in a cage my whole life. A schedule told me where I would be, a car arrived to pick me up, handlers shuttled me from one location to another. For a while—"

The sudden sheen of tears in her eyes had me pushing aside my empty coffee cup and circling the table. When I held out my hand, she took it, and I pulled her into my arms and did the one damn thing I'd been wanting to do since the day I met her.

I gave her a fucking hug.

I swore she shuddered, and then her whole body seemed to relax into me. Tucking my chin against her hair, I said, "You're safe here, Sparrow. You're safe with us. I know it doesn't always feel like it and sometimes we can be real bastards, but there's not a man here who wouldn't take a bullet for you or tear apart anyone who tried to hurt you."

Gladly and with relish, but I kept that last part to myself.

"But why?" she asked, pulling back enough that I had to loosen my grip so I could meet her gaze. "Why do all of you care so much? Before the show, I'd never even met you."

"That's not entirely true," I said. "But we've followed your career for years. Kept an eye on you from a distance. You always seemed fine, but I'm starting to get that was the public face you put on and that the picture behind the scenes was a lot uglier. A lot more dangerous *for* you."

"Well, you know about Eric."

I nodded.

Closing her eyes, she sucked in a slow breath, but she didn't pull away. If anything, she leaned in and rested her forehead against my chest. "I just want to understand all of you. You kidnapped me to save me. You saved me from Eric…"

"There are other threats," I told her, and while Jasper hadn't or hadn't wanted to, she needed to know. "That swipe in the garage, I'm pretty sure that was an attempt to kill you."

She tensed, but I pressed on.

"More than once, someone tried to follow us from the theater back to your hotel. I lost the tail each time."

Her nails dug into my arms.

"The night you wanted me to watch you, someone messed with the silks. One of them tore, and you damn near fell for real."

Finally, she pulled back to look at me. I met her gaze, then raised a hand to caress her cheek. I couldn't help myself. I really did want to just wipe away all the pain and sorrow in her eyes.

"Your world was supposed to be safe," I told her slowly. "A world of wealth, privilege, and family." The last came out a little more bitter than I wanted. "But we're all discovering you weren't safe, and we didn't see it soon enough."

She swiped her tongue over her lower lip. It left a glistening trail that I had a hard time not thinking about.

"So, we took you. We brought you here to protect you."

"You didn't want me here." It wasn't an accusation, but at the same time, it kind of felt like one.

"No," I admitted. "I didn't. But not because I didn't want *you*."

Surprise flickered across her face, and I didn't let that scratch at me. She had no reason to think I'd be attracted, since I'd made a point of keeping her at arm's length.

"I wanted you safe. Our world isn't safe." The last time I'd been safe, I'd been six years old and I got on a bus in the rain. "But it turns out yours isn't either."

Her laugh lacked any real humor. "No, I guess not. My uncle, he's not a good man. He's—-" Real fear inhabited her eyes, and I added filleting the son of a bitch to my list. "He's just not. I'd rather live in anonymity than ever go back to him." She swiped her tongue over her lips again. The urge to kiss her bore down on me like a physical weight, but I shut it the fuck out.

What Emersyn needed was comforting, and I needed information. If I kissed her, I didn't think I'd be able to fucking stop until she moaned for me like she had for Vaughn. I swore my dick damn near throbbed at the prospect.

"If you really knew me," she said finally. "I don't think you'd want anything to do with me."

"I'll let you get away with that," I told her, but I cupped her face so I could keep her gaze on me. "Because you don't know us well yet. We're going to change that. All of us. We're going to make a new path forward, and you're going to find out that nothing you could tell us—literally nothing—would change how we feel or your place here."

Surprise parted her lips. She searched my face, and I hoped like fuck my expression confirmed every single word I'd just spoken. Because I damn well meant it.

"He's right," Jasper said, his voice rough. I glanced past her to see my brother standing in the doorway, eyes bloodshot, hair wet, and clean clothes on. "Keeping you safe is our priority." He took a couple of steps into the room, and Emersyn turned around in my arms. I loosened my hold, but when she stepped back against me, I kept them around her.

Jasper looked like hell.

"You can tell us or not, we're all entitled to our secrets," Jasper added. "No one will force you." Then he exhaled and flicked his gaze up to mine before looking back at her. "You're not a hostage. You're not a prisoner. We'll give you all your things back, and if you want to leave for real, if you want to be somewhere else, we'll get you there."

Fuck.

Was he for real right now? I frowned. I'd said all along she didn't belong here, but the truth was, she fucking fit us in a way no one else ever had. "Maybe we'll discuss what challenges she had at—"

Jasper raised his hand and then shook his head. "Sorry, Kel, I just…I need her to know that I'm not a total asshole, even when I'm an asshole." The level of hurt and pain in his voice killed me, but he kept shoving it down. "In fact, Emersyn, if you would, would you come and talk to me? I think you and I have a lot of things we need to say."

It was my turn to blow out a breath. Emersyn glanced back up at me for a moment, but I tried to shoot for neutral. She and Jasper absolutely needed to talk, but I wanted to get him a beer and pull out of him where he'd been.

"Please?"

It was the please that got her moving. She stepped away from me and said, "Yes. You're right—we need to talk. Maybe all of us do, but…" Then she glanced back at me and smiled. A real one. One that warmed her eyes and bled the shadows out of them. One she'd reserved for when I picked her up at the hotel room and I hadn't seen since she realized 'I was in on the kidnapping.'

It was a kick to the nuts in the right way.

"But Kellan's told me some things and it helped." She

glanced back to Jasper. "If we can find that same honest footing, I'd like that."

"Me too," he said in a hoarse voice. "Come with me?"

I had zero doubt she'd take his hand, and I folded my arms. I wanted to keep her *here* with *me* and talking to *me*. That wasn't what she or Jasper needed.

"Stay close," I advised. "Let me know if you decide to leave."

"We're going up to the roof," Jasper said. "Don't worry." He lifted his shirt to show the gun tucked into the belt there. "I'll protect her."

I only nodded. I didn't have the heart to ask who was going to protect him from her. Because as much as I was invested, Jasper was in love, and while I'd never seen him so deep into a girl before, Emersyn wasn't just any girl.

Fuck.

HELL'S WAITING ROOM

EMERSYN

The dress itched. The collar was too tight. The lace poked at me. The shoes were the wrong size. I said nothing as they dressed me up. The instructions had been specific. No sooner had I arrived than one of the maids swept me upstairs.

I'd at least expected to see my mother and father first, but the event that evening was very important and appearances had to be kept. As much as I tried not to fidget, the woman plaiting my hair kept yanking it. I glared at her in the mirror and opened my mouth to say something as the door opened behind her.

"There's my princess!" The deep timbre of his voice rolled over the room. The maids attending me scattered as he approached. "Jeanette, don't pull her hair back. It makes her look too severe, and she doesn't like it."

I lifted my gaze to meet his in the mirror. "Thank you, Uncle."

He smiled, smoothing a hand over my hair and untangling the plaits. My scalp still tingled from where she'd been yanking it.

"Yes, sir," Jeanette simpered and stared at my uncle with a kind of adoration. All the maids did. In his house, he was worshipped. He was the king, and I was his princess.

"Where is my hug, Princess?" His hand skated down to my shoulder, and I turned before he pulled me back. I wrapped my arms around him, careful of the dress, and let him press me to him. My head only reached his belly, and I held my breath to not breathe in his cologne. "That's my girl. You can all leave us."

"The party…" Jeanette began.

My uncle didn't say anything. He didn't have to. The maids scurried out of the room, and then we were alone. He stroked my hair, and I didn't move away from the hug until he leaned back and caught my hands.

"Come here, Princess. Tell me about school." He settled neatly into the armchair in the room he'd had decorated for me. It was a suite of rooms, or so the maids said. It came with the bedroom, the small sitting room outside, and the bathroom.

With a sigh, I climbed into his lap. When I would have perched on the arm of the chair, he tugged me down to sitting on his thigh. I was too old for this, but Uncle Bradley never wanted to hear that. When we were alone, he liked to cuddle me.

His favorite part of the day.

I tried not to shift around, but the dress itched. They hadn't made me pull on stockings or shoes yet, so I braced my toes against the arm of the chair. I could at least free some of the itchy stuff away from the backs of my thighs.

"It's fine," I said, answering his question about school. "Mrs. Holloman is really neat. She lets me read whenever I'm done with assignments. I don't have a roommate anymore."

VICIOUS REBEL

I'd liked Lainey. It had been the first year the school assigned me a roommate, but I'd made the mistake of mentioning her to my mother and she must have told Uncle Bradley.

"Good," he murmured, rubbing my back. "You should have a space of your own at the school. What about your riding lessons, how are they going?"

Equestrian lessons had been added to my daily routines, but it cut into my dance time and I made a face. I loved the horses, but I loved dance more. Madame B was brusque and strict, but I had learned so much from her. A compliment from her was a worth a thousand from anyone else, and she'd given me a great compliment the day before.

"They're fine," I said, fidgeting before I could stop myself and then pressing my toes into the arm of the chair and digging them in to try and keep myself still.

"Just fine, Princess?" He chuckled, still rubbing a slow circle against my back. "You don't like them?"

I made a face and then sighed. Glancing up, I found his steady stare on me. The corners of his mouth lifted at my attention.

"You can tell me," he prompted, looping his arm around me and tugging me closer.

"It's not that I don't like them," I hedged. "I love the horses. They're very sweet, even if they are huge. It's just—"

Again, I hesitated, because I didn't want to admit this to him. I couldn't even tell him why I didn't want to tell him. He never got angry at me for not liking his presents.

Sometimes, I didn't think he cared if I liked them or not.

I bit the inside of my lip.

"It's just?" he said, tapping my lower lip with his finger. "No biting these pretty little lips. We don't want them to chap."

I stopped immediately and squared my shoulders. "It's just I had to give up two days of dance."

"And that's important to you?" He tightened his hold until I settled more firmly against him, and I had to stop pressing against the other arm with my toes and let him have all my weight.

Grasping my courage in both hands, I met Uncle Bradley's stare head-on. "Madame B says I'm a natural and gifted." Two words that made me beam with pride. "She said she recommended me to the Poppy Teague troupe and sent them tapes of me dancing." I licked my lips, because despite rehearsing this, my heart fluttered so fast, it made me feel a little sick and there was sweat dampening my back. "I will need Mummy and Daddy's approval, but if I get in, I could travel and perform with them."

All over the country.

All over the world really.

Few breaks.

I might not even make it home for the holidays.

The minute Madame B warned me of how grueling the schedule could be, I'd gotten excited. I wanted to perform. I wanted to spend all day, every day on my dancing, and I wanted…

"The Teague company," Uncle Bradley mused, rubbing a finger against his lower lip. "I know Anya Teague, she's the original Poppy's granddaughter. Nice enough girl, family doesn't make the best choices."

I held my breath.

"Though I would say the dance company is distinguished."

I went to bite my lip again and stopped because my uncle watched me with these deep, black eyes. It was almost impossible to tell where the pupil ended and the iris began. I thought his eyes were neat.

Uneasiness fluttered through me.

"How important is this to you, Princess?"

"Very," I admitted. Because…

He nodded slowly. "Give us a kiss, and I'll let you know at the end of the weekend. I'll talk to your parents too."

"Really?" Genuine surprise fluttered through me. I'd expected that to be much harder. I'd *liked* having a roommate. I *loved* my first dance teacher. I *loved* my old school.

Uncle Bradley liked to fix things, even if they didn't need fixing. Sharpes didn't need roommates. Andrew, the dance instructor, was neither skilled nor focused enough to push me to my best. My old school was too far away, Uncle Bradley preferred I could come home on weekends without a flight.

"Really," he promised as he tapped his cheek. Excitement threaded through me, and I leaned forward to press a kiss to his cheek. He turned his head and pressed his lips right to mine. The band of his arm and surprise kept me in place. It didn't last longer than a few seconds, but it seemed forever.

When he leaned his head back, he laughed and brushed another kiss to my forehead.

"Let's get you out of this awful dress," he suggested, sweeping me up and walking with me into the closet. My heart began racing, and my stomach tightened as bile itched up the back of my throat, but I swallowed it back down.

"I can do it, Uncle Bradley," I assured him as he put me down on the round cushioned stool that occupied the center of the huge closet.

"Don't be silly, dressing up my princess is one of my favorite things to do." He moved to close the door and pressed a finger to his lips. "Shh, don't tell Jeanette or the others, but they have horrible taste and that itchy dress can't be comfortable."

It wasn't. "I can wear it. I know you wanted me to be presentable…"

But he was already undoing the dress and freeing the

buttons. I sighed and looked up at the shelf above, fixating on a box with some ribbons poking out of it. Uncle Bradley liked to make sure I was okay. No hurts or injuries anywhere. Sometimes he squeezed. To check. Sometimes he poked.

He used to wait for my baths.

Sometimes for when I got ready for bed.

"We have plenty of time," he promised. "We can find the perfect one."

I flicked my gaze to the door, and not for the first time, I wished someone would walk in. But no one would.

No one interrupted Uncle Bradley.

"My beautiful princess."

CHAPTER 18

EMERSYN

A part of me didn't want to leave Kestrel after that discussion. I wanted to trust him, badly. Of all of them, he'd been the one I trusted *before* they took me. He'd also been the most distant since they had. But if anything, his attention had been consistent, and I couldn't deny the want for that semblance of friendship back.

Even if it couldn't mean to him what it meant to me. I wouldn't lie, when he'd hugged me, I swore a huge weight lifted. The last few days had been a bit surreal. I was still a little horrified that Jasper had seen me and Vaughn together. Vaughn didn't seem to care.

His exact words had been, "Jasper's a big boy, Dove. He can handle it."

"And if he can't?" I'd challenged, because Vaughn hadn't seen the look in Jasper's eyes. The hurt.

"Then he'll get over it eventually." Vaughn had tried to soothe me and he'd been stroking his hands up and down my sides, but it didn't seem to help the restlessness invading my soul. I needed Vaughn. I didn't want to need him. I didn't want to need any of them. The idea that they'd all been carving out a place for themselves under my skin left me a little uneasy and at the same time...exhilarated? Was that even the right word?

The next morning, Jasper had been gone and no one would tell me where he was. Freddie speculated a lot of things, but he was too lost in his misery to really focus and I didn't want to make him feel worse. At least watching the cupcake shows turned out to be fun for him and a distraction.

When Jasper arrived this morning, profound relief had swarmed through me, followed quickly by concern. He looked just awful. Kestrel couldn't quite cover his concern fast enough, which confirmed for me I was right to be worried.

Not saying a word, Jasper led me out of the clubhouse into the main warehouse. There was no one around. In fact, there'd been almost no rats around anytime I'd stepped out since Rome ordered them out. Had they taken that to mean permanently? I both did and didn't want to ask.

In the corner of the warehouse was a ladder tucked neatly against the wall. It kind of blended into the shadows. Well, it was too obvious for my escape, but... I glanced over to where the hooks and chains secured my silks and where I'd climbed to before.

"I know you're not afraid of heights, so I'm going up first," Jasper said. "That way I can open the hatch."

I nodded. More than reasonable.

Five minutes later and after I'd climbed up behind him, we were standing on the roof. The sun was damn near blinding, and the air cold and fresh. It was definitely chilly, but when Jasper said where we were going, I'd snagged one of the hoodies off the sofas as we passed it.

Tucking my hands into my pockets, I gave it a faint sniff and smiled. Rome's. It was weird that they all possessed distinctive and different scents. Or maybe not weird. I didn't know.

Not saying anything, Jasper headed up the roof, and I followed him. He balanced against the slats, following where the support beams had to be beneath, and just over the lip of the top was a small table and a couple of lounge chairs. Well, more like seven, but only six were useable. One had been ripped and the fabric looked rough and worn.

Even more fascinating? The chairs *and* the table were bolted to the roof itself. The wind wouldn't move them or the bad weather.

"This is the best spot in winter," Jasper said as he motioned to the lounge chairs. "The morning sun warms up the roof and that warms up the chairs…"

A fact I confirmed as I slid into one of them. I turned sideways, mostly so I could just look at him, and also because wow, the chair was a lot warmer than I'd expected. It sent the heat right through my leggings.

Perched on the lounger next to mine, Jasper pulled a pack of cigarettes and a blunt out of his pockets. He held them both up, and I eyed the blunt. I'd planned to dance. If I got stoned, that wouldn't be happening.

If I got stoned, it would take the edge off a lot of things. I'd always avoided drugs before…when given the option. I'd kill for a cigarette, but I nodded to the blunt.

They kept saying I was safe here, and so far, none of that had proved a lie. The guys were all… They were tough and they were fierce, and fuck, in some ways, they scared the hell out of me. But the desire to trust them burned ever brighter.

Maybe I was just asking for trouble.

Or maybe I had long since learned there was always a bigger fish.

"Thank fuck," Jasper muttered before stuffing the cigarette pack back in his pocket and lighting up the blunt. He took a long draw on it before he passed it over. The smell of weed encircled us, the scent invading everything and permeating clothing. For the first time in my life, I didn't give two fucks if it did. No one here would say anything.

I took in a lungful and closed my eyes, holding the breath in for a long moment before letting it out. "Should I make sure I clean up before I see Freddie?" I didn't want to mess with his recovery. His mood swings were unpredictable enough.

"He won't care," Jasper commented as I handed him the blunt. "Or at least that's what he'll say, but yeah, probably better for a while. Weed won't hurt him and might take the edge off a bit. But it's when he goes looking for the harder stuff that we have a problem."

I nodded. That seemed fair. Still, we just sat there passing the blunt back and forth and saying nothing. The world softened a little. Some of the harsher edges weren't so jagged. Weirdly, the constant pressure in my chest had also evaporated. Maybe that was what he was waiting for...

With my next long drag, I closed my eyes again. The sounds of traffic in the distance muted. The sun against my skin seemed even warmer, and the fact Jasper sat there in silence nibbled at me.

"You wanted to talk," I said finally when I couldn't take the silence anymore. I'd been determined to wait him out, but the other night and the look on his face still haunted me. Dragging my eyes open, I focused on him.

A faint smile turned up Jasper's lips. "I did...but this is nice and I don't want to spoil it."

Laughter burst out of me because...well, he wasn't *wrong*.

"This is nice," I admitted as he stared at me for a moment before offering me the blunt again. Our fingers brushed, and for a moment, he didn't pull away as we both held the blunt, together. "I was worried."

His brows drew together. "Why?"

"Because you looked...mad or upset or both the other night, then you just disappeared. Everyone told me to leave you alone, that you would be back, but..."

His slate-gray eyes seemed to shutter, and the atmosphere seemed a bit darker despite the sun still shining down on us. "Because I walked in and found you fucking Vaughn."

No trace of emotion punctuated that sentence. If anything, the monotone voice ignited another round of warning bells. That and the icy expression on his face. He blew so hot, his temper a vicious and vibrant thing. But this?

This wasn't Jasper. Or maybe it was. Maybe I'd not seen the real Jasper until now, but I didn't think so.

No? asked a snide little voice. *You don't think so, or you don't want to think so?*

I shoved that voice to the back of my head with another drag on the blunt before I nodded.

The lift of his shoulders dragged a little, like he couldn't quite bring himself to shrug. "You fucking Vaughn wasn't the issue, Emersyn."

"Then what was?"

He locked his gaze on me. "Vaughn fucking you was the issue. That's something he and I need to deal with, but later."

I opened my mouth, but this time when my fingers touched his, Jasper took the blunt with his other hand before locking the fingers against mine.

"I am a possessive man," he said, and I clamped my jaw shut. "I'm also a raging asshole at people who fuck up. There's been a lot of fuckups around you. But *you* haven't been the one to fuck up and I…I don't know why you think I was mad at you."

Surprise filtered through me. "When did you hear I thought that?"

"I'm not blind, Swan. You held yourself aloof. You are more open with the others. You slept with Rome. You're hugging Kellan. Apparently, you're fucking Vaughn, and you're looking after Freddie. He can't shut the fuck up about you and your pretty pussy."

My lips pursed as I fought back a laugh. "That last is not my fault."

"No," Jasper admitted with a long sigh. "That's all Freddie, irreverent little fuck. But the point is…you even trust Doc to help you while you're naked."

He was a doctor, and he'd been really careful to only touch me when absolutely necessary…

"My point, Swan, is you seem to be building something with everyone around you, but you're keeping me at arm's length. You kissed me back, I know you did. I tasted it, and then you shut me out."

Wait. I shook my head. Okay, maybe I was more stoned than I thought already. Totally a possibility, so I used the grip he had on my hand to pull me forward so I could sit up. This was better done face-to-face, and apparently, kneecap to kneecap.

An utterly inappropriate giggle burst out of me. I clapped a hand over my mouth, and Jasper squinted at me.

"It's not funny."

Bullshit.

"No," I muttered behind my hand. "It's fucking hilarious."

Surprise raced over Jasper's expression, and he snorted. "Well, I'm glad I'm a joke to you." The sourness of his tone jolted me right out of my humor, and I squeezed his hand.

"You're not a joke," I argued. "And what was funny was

that you kissed me and then looked so damn angry for having done it and walked out. I didn't see you for *days* after that."

His brows drew together tighter. "We had to find Freddie."

"I'm aware of that *now*." I ran my tongue over my lips and suddenly regretted my choices in life. Because I needed some water, bad. When Jasper offered me the blunt this time, I shook my head. "I need to get my thoughts together."

"I feel that," he admitted, then let go of me long enough to clip off what little was left of the blunt and set it in the ashtray before looking back at me. "I wasn't mad at you."

"Then why did you glare at me?"

"I don't know... Probably because someone knocked on the door and interrupted us. Probably because I wanted to throw you down on that wood floor in there and strip you naked as we went to pound town. Probably because Raptor is gonna have my balls for garters when this is all done. But mostly, I think because I had to leave you."

"Pound town is a very attractive description for sex. Or at least I'm hoping it's for sex and not for technique." Right now, the blunt was the best idea ever, because apparently, it took the edges off both of us.

Jasper snorted. A genuine, loud snort, and then he shook his head. "Trust me, I can do more than pound. I don't need a dick piercing to get my partners off."

My jaw dropped a little. "That's rude."

"Depends," Jasper commented. "If the piercing is why you decided to fuck him, then yeah. If not...eh, Vaughn's a big boy, he can take it. Besides, piercing your dick is for masochists."

It was my turn to snort. "I can't believe we're having this conversation. This is not what I thought we were going to talk about."

"No?"

"No."

"Then what did you think we were going to talk about, Swan?" The sudden intensity in his eyes told me that the shutters he'd closed earlier were wide open now, and I swallowed, not that I could even manage to form spit at the moment.

"Sending me back," I said slowly. "Or why you brought me here. The threats. Kestrel said…he said he thought there were other threats besides…you know, besides Eric."

"Did he rape you?" The sudden question jolted me, and I frowned. "He said he did. He admitted it. He was abusing you."

"Then why are you asking me?"

"Because I need to know why you let him keep doing it, Swan. Why didn't you say something? Why didn't you stop him?"

"Because saying something doesn't always fix things, Jasper." Not that anyone around me would have done anything. Except my uncle. And I'd drag myself over broken glass before I'd ask him for help with anything. "Sometimes, what you have is better than the alternative. Even if someone else thinks it's awful."

He pinched the bridge of his nose, and I swore I could almost read the complicated parade of emotion. From fury to pain to confusion and back again. All I hoped was he wouldn't ask me to explain.

Some things? Some things I would never talk about.

"I need more than that, Swan," he finally said, and I shook my head.

"You killed him. Eric's gone, right?" I pulled my hand from his so I could fold my arms. "It doesn't matter anymore."

"Yes, it fucking matters." He clenched his fists, and a vein throbbed in his forehead. So many unspoken thoughts fluttered through his eyes as he glared at me. There it was. It was almost the same glare he wore that day in the studio.

Angry with me, but not angry with me.

"What do you want from me, Jasper?" I asked the question in as even a tone as possible. "What do you need from me?"

I had a feeling it was two entirely different answers, and if I couldn't figure it out, I needed him to tell me. Or we were going to keep cutting at each other for no reason.

Or maybe he was just working his way up to getting rid of me. Considering the way they'd started to fight the other night…

"You said you've been caged and shackled your whole life," he repeated my declaration slowly. "You know if we'd known…"

"Apparently," I said with a shrug. "While I think that's a nice thought…I have to wonder why you would have known?"

He opened his mouth and then snapped it shut with a look of aggravation. The silence between us elongated, growing stiffer and more uncomfortable with each passing second, despite the haze of being stoned. Maybe we should have stopped way sooner than we had.

"What do you want?" he asked quietly, and I glared at him.

"I asked you first."

"I know," he said. "What I want…it doesn't matter right now. I need to know what you want first. Do you want to go back? Like I said in the kitchen, we're going to give you your things. Including your phone. It's been powered off since we got it, and Kestrel pulled the sim card."

I nodded. "I suppose you guys were very good for not-kidnappers."

He snorted. "Do you want to go home?"

Ice flowed into my veins. Arms still folded, I shook my head. "I was leaving the company at the end of the tour. My contract was up. The tour ended a few weeks ago, so it wouldn't matter anyway."

"I meant go home to your family." He studied me for a long moment.

"I know what you meant." My answer didn't change. "My ID would be great, so would my bank cards." I wouldn't touch the credit cards, but I had one small bank account I'd squirreled funds away in, one not attached to the family accounts. Those I couldn't touch. Uncle Bradley would know where I was in minutes, if not seconds.

"Okay, if you stay, I want to take you out. You and me. On a date."

I raised my brows. "That's your way of asking?"

"You kissed me back." Apparently, that was his way of answering.

I pursed my lips. "I want to see Doc."

He snarled, his nostrils twitching.

"And I want you to stop fighting and attacking every single one of the guys for even looking in my direction. They've been looking after me too, and some of them have even become my friends." Admittedly, Vaughn was more.

"Friends." I swore Jasper spit the word.

"Yes, Jasper, friends. It can happen." I glared at him. "You can't keep going for people because they care, especially when these guys are your friends too."

"Doc is *not* my friend," he insisted, and I shrugged.

"Okay, but he is mine."

Jasper clenched his fists again, then forced them to relax before he dragged out the cigarettes. "Fine. He's your friend. He can see you here."

"At his clinic."

"No," Jasper snapped. "Not right now. Not while…"

"But it's safe enough to take me out on a date?"

"You'd be with me." Like that cleared everything right up.

"You said downstairs you didn't want me to think you were a total asshole, even when you were an asshole."

"I know what I said."

"Then stop being an asshole about Doc when he clearly cares about all of you." Did he not understand how amazing it was that they all had each other? That there were people willing to come out swinging for them? I sighed. "I want—I *need* to get out of this place. I know it's not necessarily *safe* to be out in public, but Doc has a clinic, right? I can hang out upstairs in the community room or in his office. No one else has to see me, and I can spend some time with him. I like him…"

Jasper's eyes narrowed on me thoughtfully.

"And I need you and Vaughn to get along. Like I said—stop hitting everyone. I still don't even know why you and Liam were fighting the other night."

"It's not important." He rubbed his lower lip. "So I stop knocking the shit out of the punks hitting on you and trying to get you naked, and you'll go out on a date with me?"

One would have thought he'd eaten a Sour Patch Kid or something.

"More or less."

He grimaced. "I'm perfectly capable of not being an asshole, but which is it? More or less?"

"I'm not asking for a miracle, but more with the guys here and Doc."

His upper lip curled. "You including the rats in that?"

I blinked. "Um…no?"

He nodded slowly. "Fine, okay." Rising, he held out his hand, and I stared up at him. "Let's go," he said. "I'll take you to Doc's."

I shook my head. "I didn't mean right now."

He sat down abruptly. "No?"

"No."

"So, you're free to hang out with me?"

"Unless you have work you need to do."

A grunt escaped him, and I wasn't sure if that was agreement, disagreement, or just something noncommittal. He retrieved what was left of the blunt and lit it up, then picked up his phone and dialed a number. Once it was lit, he passed it to me, and I watched him as he exhaled. I swore the stress began to melt off of him.

"Asshole, we're up on the roof. We need food and drinks and another blunt."

A pause.

"You can fucking join us since I have to be fucking nice to everyone."

I gaped at him, but Jasper just grinned.

"Yeah, fuck you too. Emersyn is thirsty and stoned, and she's adorable..." He held the phone away from his head and laughed.

"Do I want to know?"

"Kellan," he admitted. "I stole you away from him. Figure the least I can do is share you the rest of the afternoon or at least for another..." He checked his watch. "Fifty minutes until he has to work." The smirk on his face bordered on way too damn arrogant.

"You're proud of yourself, aren't you?" I took a drag off the blunt and passed it back. Honestly, it was all kinds of funny as fuck. Spending the afternoon up here with food, drinks, and weed sounded like a great plan. Not Emersyn Sharpe's scene at all.

Sign. Me. Up.

"Told you I was more than capable."

I chuckled. "You passed the first test. Let's see how you are when I go to Doc's."

His expression soured. "Don't remind me."

"Oh, I intend to remind you."

This time when he grunted, I was pretty sure it was a polite way of telling me to fuck off.

You know what? I'd take it.

LET ME FLY

EMERSYN

"Fifteen minutes." The call came from the area leading toward the arena. The troupe had been preparing for this tour for four months. Not only had my audition gone well, I'd made it all the way up to the owners. I'd been torn between excitement at the callbacks and fear that it was due to my uncle's influence.

However, he hadn't been as enthusiastic when it came up at the family dinner we all attended on Sundays. It was a formal meal. My parents dressed up, as did my uncle. He always picked out my dress. Since most weekends I was required to stay at his home while my parents traveled—they were always traveling—Sunday dinner always took place there.

When my mother looked surprised by my announcement, my uncle had jumped in to say he'd given me permission. Then my father asked me more probing questions about it. Eventually, they took my side against my uncle. It was an opportunity, and my mother thought I had a future as a dancer.

She'd always said she wanted to be a prima ballerina but lacked the true talent. It was one of the only times they took my side against Uncle Bradley. He'd been noncommittal but arrived at my boarding school on Thursday and fetched me himself, rather than sending a driver, and accompanied me to that audition.

It meant an extra night and day with him since he didn't bother to take me back to school, but I won my spot. Me. More, the troupe moved to Los Angeles to train, and that put hundreds of miles between me and my family.

A tutor was hired and a chaperone. I was to have my own driver at all times. I was also to have my own room or suite of rooms. Uncle Bradley made all the arrangements.

It was two heavenly months without seeing any of them. I trained every day. Did all my work. I was a little lonely, except when I was at the theater. There, even the oldest dancers were my allies and my friends. I learned more from them than I ever had from Madame B.

When Uncle Bradley flew in to spend a weekend with me, some of my joy diminished. But he left immediately the following Monday. After that, I was required to go home one weekend a month until the tour started.

It couldn't start soon enough for me.

Four months of preparation had led to the twenty-five-city tour we were currently on, and I'd loved every minute. I'd only seen Uncle Bradley a handful of times.

I'd seen my parents less. Though my mother called me most days or at least texted.

Daddy was often at the office late or in meetings or whatever it was he did. But he sent presents. The night of my very first performance, he sent me six dozen roses, a huge box of chocolates, and a bear that was nearly as big as me. It was stupid, but I loved it.

Tonight was different though. Halfway through the tour, the troupe director got an idea, and I'd worked with the other performers for three cities. Tonight was my huge debut, and I couldn't wait. Nervous excitement ticked away inside of me—a countdown clock that only I could hear.

"You ready, Emmie-Bug?" Marjorie asked as she flounced down in her sequined outfit and feathers. She looked ridiculous in the brash light of the dressing room. The colors were too bright and her plumage too full to look like anything else, until she was on the stage. I swore the woman floated as she danced.

She could fly, and I'd told her the first time I'd seen her dance I wanted to dance like her. I wanted to fly.

Tonight?

Tonight, I'd fly for my performance for the first time.

I glanced in the mirror. My costume was a full bodysuit, though it wouldn't look like it on stage. There were glitter and shimmery pieces located like I had on dance shorts and a strapless top, but the rest was sheer stocking. My hair was pulled completely back into a single ponytail.

They'd used so much hairspray when they did it, I thought I would die of suffocation. Then there were bits of sparkle and glitter in my hair. Marjorie had done my makeup herself. There was so much of it, but every time the light caught me, I seemed to shimmer more.

I wanted wings, but they would get in the way and I'd learned to fly without them.

"Ready!"

I clasped her hand and let her lead me toward the stage. Outside, the music was already booming, and the crowd was applauding as the first show began. There were eighteen separate routines in the first act. I used to be in four of them.

Now I would have a routine of my own mid-show, vanish, then again, every four routines after that until the finale, when I performed with them—only from above.

My heart raced as Marjorie and I followed the long narrow hall toward the ladders that went up. Christian was waiting for us, and he grinned at me. Christian and Jaime had been my trainers and they'd been super patient with me, but they were also very encouraging.

Since my chaperone preferred to watch movies during practice time, I'd managed all of this right under the radar. It was easier to ask for forgiveness than permission. My mother's favorite saying.

I started up the ladder with Christian right behind me.

Jaime was at the top, and her grin was wide. She held out a hand to me, and I let her pull me up the rest of the way. Normally, I practiced with a safety, but I couldn't for the performance.

Jaime and Christian would be on ropes and ready to catch me. But I wouldn't fall.

I'd worked too hard to get up here.

Too hard to learn to fly.

Below, the crowd went wild for the next series of dances that included Marjorie. The land-locked birds moved with so much grace and color, they were mesmerizing. I leaned against the railing as I watched them and the crowd.

Up here, the world was so far away. It was just me. The music. The dance.

Jaime and Christian murmured to each other, but they'd been on the verge of boyfriend and girlfriend so long, I'd actually asked *why* hadn't they kissed yet. They'd both sputtered and turned red.

I probably shouldn't have laughed, but it cracked me up. I bet they kissed before we left this city though. I hoped so. They were cute together.

"Two minutes, Emmie-bug," Christian said as he gripped my waist and lifted me up. Jaime had a hold of the hoop, and she kept it still while I settled into it. Man in the moon—or girl in the moon really. Feet braced against the sides, I leaned back and relaxed my arms out.

"You ready?" Christian asked.

"Of course she is," Jaime murmured, and then she added, "Emmie, look."

I glanced over as she let go of the hoop and wrapped her arms around Christian. He looked utterly stunned when she kissed him, and my smile was so big, it made my face hurt.

Then the music shifted and I settled back as the hoop lowered, then there were gasps and the lights came up.

The next four and a half minutes would be all me.

And I was going to fly.

CHAPTER 19

EMERSYN

We ended up hanging out on the roof for hours. Kestrel joined us with food and a thermos of hot chocolate that he gave me then flipped off Jasper when Jasper looked like he wanted it. Rome arrived a little while later, Freddie in tow. He eyed all of us a little on the apprehensive side, but I patted the chair next to me and Freddie grinned as he took it. Before I could say another word, Rome plucked me out of my chair, sat, and then settled me in his lap.

I stared at him a beat. "So that's how it is?"

"Yep," he said, shifting me around so I could lean back against him and see the others. Kestrel and Jasper stared at him with equal parts irritation and amusement. But I had to give Jasper a lot of credit—he never yelled.

We finished another blunt, and though Freddie looked at it longingly, he never asked and no one offered it to him. Despite his pallor, he did look better, and I wanted him to stay that way. I made him promise to watch movies with me later, and that earned me a grin.

I half floated from the second one. Kestrel offered to get us more, but I kind of half-smiled and waved him off. "I'm floaty, and this is kind of nice." Floaty and warm. Rome had me all tucked up against him, a blanket over me. Not sure when someone grabbed that. I did eat the tacos though.

They were amazing. The conversation seemed to flow around me. They talked about everything and nothing, but I couldn't quite zoom in on everything. Instead, I stared up at the sky and watched the clouds floating by. The bunny rabbit. The Volkswagen Bug. The wizard hat.

Eventually, rain rolled in and we'd abandoned our perch. But now that I knew this was up here? I totally planned to come back. There were rats at work in the warehouse moving boxes when I dropped down, and Kestrel caught me around the waist rather than let me land on my own. Then he set me on my feet.

I flashed him a grin and then, because there were so many people about, I motioned to Kestrel to come closer so I could whisper in his ear. "Thank you." I also pressed a kiss there, more to his neck than anything. It was hidden from the rats, and Jasper landed right after.

Kestrel gave me a studying look, flicked his gaze behind me to Jasper, then back to me again. "You're welcome." When he offered his arm, I looped mine through his.

"I think I'm pretty stoned," I told him, and Kestrel chuckled.

"That you are," he agreed. But there wasn't an ounce of recrimination in any of their faces as we made it inside. If anything, there was indulgence. A couple of the rats called out to Jasper, and he let out a grunt.

"It's okay," I murmured. "I'll save you a spot on the sofa next to me."

"I got dibs on the other one," Freddie said as he dashed forward to the door.

Rome snorted, but he and Kestrel shared a long look and Kestrel gave me a little nudge toward Rome. "Be with you soon, Sparrow, stay with Freddie and Rome."

"Okay." Then I stared after him and Jasper both as they headed over to the rats. But Rome tugged me to the door and then inside. He guided me to the little sitting area and the sofa. Freddie already had one side of it. Rome settled me in the center. He vanished on us long enough to fix more food. He came back with hot popcorn that made my stomach rumble and large sodas, then settled into the seat next to me and offered me a box of Whoppers with a near shy smile.

"Um, where's mine, asshole?" Freddie asked, leaning around me. "I know I'm not as pretty as Boo-Boo, but the least you could do was make me some too."

Rome just flipped him off, and Freddie threw his head back and laughed. Without a word, he pushed upward and pointed at the sofa. "My spot."

I twisted and stuck my feet in it for him, then Rome lifted me up and scooted over so I was in his lap and I giggled.

"You like picking me up," I informed him. Amusement softened his face.

"Hmm-hmm." He popped open the box of Whoppers for me. "What movie do you want to watch?"

I was hopeless at movies. I barely watched television in all the hotels I'd stayed at over the years. Particularly because the bill always included what paid for movies you got. I didn't feel like "apologizing" for not asking, so I just skipped them.

Popping a Whopper into my mouth, I sucked it into my cheek, then held up one for Rome. "You pick?"

I swore everything in me tingled when he wrapped his lips around my fingers to suck the Whopper from them. In fact, my ass clenched and my thighs went tight. Considering the fact I was pressed right up to him, there was no way Rome couldn't notice.

Okay, now I was happy that I was stoned, because I might start drooling. Especially when he sucked my fingers into his mouth.

"Get a room," Freddie grumbled as he came back with a bag of tacos. How many had they bought the night before? It might have been a lot, but I wasn't clear on that. I went to move my feet, but Freddie tugged them back after he sat so they were propped in his lap.

It was weird, but fun. Rome picked a movie about samurai. I shared my Whoppers with Rome and munched on the popcorn. The warm, humming sensation on my insides spread out. Jasper joined us, and when I offered to restart the movie, he shook his head. He'd seen it before.

Though he sat in the empty spot next to me and Rome, he gave Rome a dirty look, but he didn't say anything. I offered him a Whopper as a way of saying thank you. I also shared my popcorn and drink. Rome shook his head but didn't say anything. My eyes were getting heavier, and I ended up stretched out over all three of them.

Maybe that should be a problem, but some distant part of my brain had already labeled these guys as 'safe.' I'd been around bad people. I'd been around some pretty awful people.

Even with all his yelling and threats, Jasper didn't qualify. When he began stroking his fingers through my hair, I closed my eyes and just passed out. The next time I opened them, Vaughn muttered a curse.

"What the fuck are you doing in here?"

"Sleeping," Rome said. "Get in bed and shut up or get out."

I was wrapped up around Rome again, my head on his shoulder and my leg between his. Vaughn made another sound, but the next thing I knew, the bed depressed and the naked length of him pressed up against my back.

When I woke up the next time, I was alone.

Pity.

Still, I was cocooned warmly in the bed and the pillows smelled like Rome and Vaughn both. The day before was a kind of hazy memory, but it was also a comforting one. Jasper and I had talked. I'd hung out with all of them. Cuddling had been involved.

Oh, I fell asleep during the movie. I made a face as I got out of bed. I'd apologize to Rome later. After I showered and got dressed, I found a note with my old phone, my new phone, my purse, and my wallet. On the front, it only said, *As promised.*

Jasper and Kestrel both promised to give me my things back. Everything was there, but the phone was off and I left it off for now. I'd rather not have anyone tracking it. Even if it did have a lot of useful information in it. Surely I could transfer that and not the phone number?

I'd figure that out later.

The inside of the folded piece of paper was written in the most elegant script.

Dove,

I got you a phone for a reason. Hang on to it so you can get my messages and I can get yours.

Vaughn

Guilt assaulted me immediately. I'd forgotten all about the phone. The flowers were also sitting there in a vase, looking pretty and filling the air with sweetness. But it was less about the flowers than the reasoning behind the phone. I picked up the new one and turned on the screen.

There were a dozen messages from Vaughn, and my face heated. Well, clearly, I sucked at this.

After reading through them, I sent him a simple message.

Me: *Good morning. Sorry I forgot my phone yesterday. I won't today. Are you working?*

His response hit my screen so swiftly, I jumped.

Vaughn: *Sadly, yes. I'd much rather have woken you up, but there's a street fair down by the docks and the shop has me out here doing cheap tattoos for a few hours. I'd invite you, Dove, but until we know...*

He didn't finish the thought, but he didn't have to.

Me: *It's okay. I think I want to see Doc today if Freddie is all right.*

Vaughn: *Be careful. Doc's smart, but stay with him if you go to the clinic. No wandering around by yourself.*

I rolled my eyes but just sent him a kiss emoji back and shut off the screen. Kestrel's room was quiet, in fact, the whole building seemed to be as I made my way down. Freddie was on the sofa in the sitting room, passed out cold. The debris of our movie watching still littered the table.

Clearing some of it away, I carried it into the kitchen to put in the trash. There was a note on the coffeemaker that read,

To turn me on, flick the switch.

I snorted. But one button hit, and it began brewing. There was another covered dish on the counter with a note that read,

Food. A little too much sugar, but we need to shop. I got you donuts.

The note was signed with a J, and under the lid was two boxes of donuts. There were all kinds, including pink frosted ones with sprinkles. The coconut dusted ones too.

I didn't wait, I stuffed one of the pink ones into my mouth immediately before liberating a pair of the coconut dusted ones. You didn't bring donuts into a theater full of dancers and expect any to survive. You were either fast or you starved. And here were two enormous boxes just for me and filled with all kinds of sugary goodness.

Donuts on a plate, I poured a mug of coffee and then carried all of it to the table. My phone buzzed in my pocket, and I went utterly still...for about three seconds, then it hit me.

No one but Vaughn and the others had this number. It couldn't be my parents, Marta, or worst of all, my uncle, texting or calling. I wanted to pee, the relief hit so hard. After licking my fingers clean of the stickiness, I took out the phone.

Kestrel: *Awake?*

Me: *Just got up a bit ago. Found the coffee and my wallet. Thank you.*

Kestrel: *Welcome. At the shop until six. If you need something, text me.*

I smiled.

Me: *Will do.*

I'd no sooner sent that message than my phone buzzed again.

Jasper: *On a run. Didn't want you to think I disappeared on you again. Might not be back before tomorrow. Stay close to the clubhouse. If you go out, take one of the others, please. Text location at all times.*

I considered the message.

Me: *I slept very well. How about you?*

Jasper: *I'd have slept better if Rome hadn't stolen you away.*

I laughed.

Me: *Can I ask what kind of run?*

Jasper: *I'd prefer you didn't.*

Preferring I didn't wasn't an outright denial or a shutdown.

Me: *Okay. I won't. I wanted to see Doc today. Safe or no?*

If he was going to make concessions for me, then I could

for him. This weird world of theirs had become almost strangely normal very quickly.

His answer was not quick in coming, so I set the phone down and finished my donuts and coffee. I'd cleaned up and washed my hands before the phone buzzed again.

Jasper: *Doc is going to pick you up around lunchtime when he would normally close the clinic. If no one else is back, can you take Freddie with you?*

I smiled. His concern for Freddie softened him in a way. As much as I needed and wanted to talk to Doc by myself, I wouldn't abandon Freddie.

Me: *I can do that. Thank you.*

He'd taken so long because he'd been making arrangements.

Jasper: *I meant what I said.*
Me: *I appreciate that. A lot. Be safe.*
Jasper: *See you when I'm back.*

I checked the time, it wasn't quite ten, which meant lunch was at least ninety minutes away, maybe longer. I was dressed and ready to go, so I went to check on Freddie. He lay with an arm across his eyes. The rise and fall of his chest indicated breathing, but it was a little too deep and fast to be sleeping rhythm.

Perching on the table, I propped my chin in my hands and studied him. "Why are you hiding from me?"

Freddie pulled his arm back slowly and eyed me. "I'm not hiding." But the faint grimace said that was a lie. I just waited, and he sighed. "Maybe I'm hiding a little."

I nodded slowly. "Can you tell me why?" Because if I'd done something, I wanted to fix it.

Swinging his legs to the floor, Freddie sat up slowly. He scrubbed his hands over his face and looked anywhere but at me. "I fucked up." The admission seemed to cost him.

"Okay."

Shock rippled across his expression, and he finally met my gaze. "I fucked up," he repeated. "I was supposed to go get you food and I let you down, then I got high and fucked up and...yeah."

"Okay."

"How can you just say okay?" he demanded, and I shrugged.

"I got high yesterday. Wasn't my plan, but I did it."

"But that's weed. That doesn't count."

"My point was—I don't judge. I've seen a lot of people do drugs. Sometimes...running away is all you have."

A frown deepened his brow. "What makes you think I'm running away?"

"Nothing," I admitted. "I was thinking of going to the studio for an hour to dance before Doc gets here to pick me up." I'd have to shower again, but it would be worth it if it pulled Freddie out of this funk. There was absolutely nothing to be done about the past. Just the present and hopefully the future. "There's more coffee in the kitchen, and Jasper got me donuts..."

"If I touch your donuts, Jasper will cut my nuts off."

"If they're my donuts, you can touch them if I say so. Grab some donuts and some coffee, then come meet me." I winked at him as I stood. "If you want. You don't have to."

I was halfway to the stairs when Freddie said, "What changed?"

I paused and glanced over my shoulder. "What do you mean?"

"Between before I fucked up and after. You didn't want anything to do with us, Boo-Boo. Now you're..." He studied me.

"Now I'm...?" I turned to face him, arms folded, more curious than anything else.

"You're...present and you seem happier."

I didn't really have an answer for him. "You're not the only one still figuring things out," I said. "But I think you're lucky."

"How's that?" He raked his hand through his tumble of messy hair and seemed both far too young and too old in the same breath. Maybe it was his baby face or his bruised eyes.

"You have a lot of backup. The guys will do anything for you."

"Then you must be lucky too," he said with the first real smile of the day. "'Cause I'm telling you, Boo-Boo, they would do anything for you." The smile turned cocky and his playful expression turned almost leering as he wagged his eyebrows. "Hell, I'd do anything to you or for you too, and not just 'cause I want to tap that sexy ass."

I laughed and pirouetted before facing the other way. "My sexy ass is going to the studio, follow if you want."

I was almost to the door of the studio when he called, "So is there a prize if I follow? Like the secret to tapping that ass?"

A real snort of laughter escaped, and I shook my head. At least he was cracking horrible jokes. Inappropriate or not, that loss and sadness in his eyes seemed too achingly familiar, and I wanted to make it go away. Shoes off, I stripped down to just the tank and dance pants.

There was something to be said for basically only having workout gear. I was going to have to figure out the money situation because I was going to need new clothes. I went to drop a CD into the player and glanced at the closet with all the dance shoes.

They'd covered those for the time being, and I had a whole other list of questions about the guys and how they knew me. Why I was so important. Why they wanted to protect me so much. None of them had really answered me so far.

And I hadn't forgotten.

I set the phone down with my other stuff and backed up as the music began to play. I needed to stretch before I did anything, but the music chased away the whirlwind of thoughts and let me be present.

Stretch. Dance. Fly.

Freedom was the place between the notes, the moments in between the steps, and when I let go and just flew.

At least *this* hadn't changed.

CRASH

EMERSYN

Laughter eddied up from every table in the place. The whole of the show was here from performers to tech crew to the costumers and musicians. Even our much beloved director, infamous for his shrill meltdowns and scathing tirades was tucked away in a corner booth, cheerfully slaying a bottle of vodka.

The tour was over. Eighty-one cities. One hundred and ninety-four performances. Nine thousand four hundred and sixty-one miles traveled. I'd lost track of how many actual hours spent in studios, on stages, and practicing in hallways, busses, and planes.

It had been my largest tour to date and the troubled economy had kept my uncle very busy with corporate maneuverings. There'd been an SEC investigation and more. Not that I paid much attention other than to be utterly relieved that our visits began to stretch out further and further in between.

My only regret was that with the ending of this tour I

would have to go home. There would be a car waiting for me in the morning, probably before dawn, and a drive to the airport, where a private plane would whisk me home. A part of me wished that I were brave enough to just walk out of the bar and keep walking, to disappear into anonymity and never be found again.

I wasn't entirely sure what I could do for a living. At fourteen, I wasn't even old enough to get a job in most states, and my salary from the tour was handled through electronic deposit. In theory, I'd made a hell of a lot of money in the last six years since my first tour. In reality, I couldn't touch it without my uncle, since he controlled all of my finances.

The allowance from my parents was one oversight he'd made, and I'd gotten one of the dancers to help me open a different account and put as much money into that account as I could. But it wasn't enough. Not yet. I stared across the bar to where Eric was making out with one of the line dancers and let out a little sigh. He was gorgeous, and he could be as impulsive and hot-tempered as the director, but he was also sweet.

The last thing I needed was a crush.

"Psst, Emmie-bug," Christian said as he and Jaime swung by where I was seated. They had glasses in their hand, including a Coke for me. "Just for you tonight. And just the one." He winked and slid the drink over to me.

At my quizzical look, Jaime laughed and took a deep drink of her wine, then gave her glass a look before looking at my Coke. Jaime and Christian had let me have my first sip of vodka at New Year's. She was always willing to share her wine, though she used to tease it was probably too cheap for my refined palate.

I always laughed, but it wasn't like that at all. Still, I lifted the Coke and took a sip, and I swore my eyes watered and it took everything I had not to cough. Christian burst out laughing as he reached over and dropped a kiss on my head.

"Killer tour, Emmie-bug, and you're turning out to be the best aerialist we've ever seen."

"No lie," Jaime agreed. "We're going to miss you for the next few months. But you're doing the Mysterious Movement tour, yes?"

"Yes," I promised. "Already signed the contracts. Rehearsals start in ten weeks?"

Ten weeks was so long.

"I know," Jaime said with a groan. "I was hoping for a longer break."

Not me, but I couldn't tell them that. Instead, I summoned a smile and touched my glass to theirs and took another drink before I stood and gave them both hugs. They were already ducking out early. Probably going to celebrate privately.

The best thing I ever did was tell them to kiss. They said if they ever got married, I'd have to be the best man. Or at least that was what Christian joked. All too soon, they were gone, and I nursed my alcohol laden Coke slowly as the conversation in the bar washed over me. It was nice. There was music playing somewhere

Some of the dancers were leaping up and pulling their partners with them to show off or just play. Renae and Jules were out there dancing together, and I laughed when she skipped across the floor and tugged me out of the booth.

"Stop hiding, you sweet little thing, and come shake that moneymaker." The music kicked up a notch like someone turned it up, or maybe it was the alcohol and where the makeshift dancefloor had formed, but I was liquid and loose and I let the throbbing beat dictate my movements.

I danced with the girls. With the guys. I danced by myself. I was sweating by the time we'd moved through a dozen songs and headed to the bar to get some water. The bartender slid across the requested water, and as soon as I'd downed it, he winked and gave me another Coke.

A part of me said I should refuse, but it wasn't like I'd ordered it. "Thank you."

"Sure thing, hot stuff. If you're around in a couple of hours…I'll be free."

"Thank you," I said and my face was hot, but I hoped that was just from the dancing. He gave me a wink and a grin before he leaned against the bar.

"I'm…"

"Yo, asshole, drinks down here and hit on the pretty girls later."

My face truly flamed at that comment as the bartender glared down at whomever had called him. I laughed and saluted him with my drink. It was very sweet. Jaime was always telling me how attractive I was, but most of the company saw me as a kid and I was okay with that. The weird fluttery feeling at the bartender being so sweet was new.

Eric had gotten me to feel that once or twice, but he seemed to like the girls with real tits and I didn't think I was ever getting mine. I hadn't even started my period until the year before, and it was so inconsistent that I never knew when I'd be getting it, so I got birth control just to make sure I didn't have it on performance nights.

That was the best explanation for it and I stuck to it.

Drink in hand, I headed back to the table. More of the troupe had left. The director had snuck off with one of the choreographers. They were both married. To other people. But neither of their spouses had been on the tour, and everyone else knew they'd been having sex.

I'd walked in on them twice.

I never needed to know my director had a mole on his ass.

Ever.

I knocked back most of the soda before I let Renae drag me back out to dance. If I'd been warm before, I was on fire now. But we laughed. We danced. The bartender kept sending over drinks. The third one made me woozy, even after I ate some chips, so I just started passing the drinks to Renae or Jules.

Eventually, it was just too damn hot in there, even after the water, so I went to the bathroom, washed my hands, and then splashed some cold water on my cheeks. When I came back out, Renae and Jules were heading outside with Renae miming smoking.

That sounded good. It would be cooler out there, I hoped. The floor proved a bit more uneven than it had earlier, and I had to focus to avoid staggering and tripping.

Outside, the girls laughed at me, but passed me a cigarette and helped me light it. No chaperone. No tutor. No leash and eyes on me. Tonight was my last moment of freedom for ten weeks. The girls were chatting about some guys in the bar, but other than the dancers and tech people I knew, I hadn't paid attention. Well, except to the bartender. He was cute.

My phone buzzed in my pocket, and I pulled it out. My uncle's name flashed across the screen, and I clicked ignore, then turned my phone off and shoved it back in my pocket. Oops, dead battery.

A shudder raced up my spine, and my stomach twisted. Renae and Jules headed back inside but I leaned against the building, eyes closed and letting the cool air dry the sweat on me.

I didn't want to puke.

Dammit.

Just the thought, and I stumbled away from the building

and toward the side. I didn't want anyone to see me. Doubled over, I threw up until there was nothing left in my stomach to throw up anymore.

I swayed. The world flashed hot and cold.

It even took me a minute to realize someone was holding me up. Then there was a cool cloth being washed over my face and a bottle of water was held out.

"Rinse your mouth out," a voice suggested. My eyes were watering so bad from throwing up that I could barely make out the dark eyes and dark hair. I thought he might be one of the techs.

Good enough. I rinsed out my mouth twice, then spat. Then took a drink. It barely hit my stomach before it came back up.

A soft chuckle tickled my ears.

"Fuck you," I growled, though I was pretty sure it came out some kind of mewling whine. "Not nice to laugh at people being sick."

"I'm laughing because you danced your ass off while tossing back rum and Cokes like they were candy and then started smoking like you do it every day."

"How do you know I don't?" Who the hell was he?

"'Cause you're puking and you look like shit. Here, drink more, just slowly this time. Sips."

I groaned and sipped the water. "I hate you."

"Not the first time I've heard that. You want me to get one of your friends from inside?"

Seriously. None of the people left were my friends, and very shortly, I wouldn't see a lot of them again. The shows and the tours changed. The performers came and went. I could count on my hands how many people I knew now that I'd known since I was eight.

The world swayed, and the sidewalk shifted.

"Easy…" The voice came and went.

VICIOUS REBEL

"I need a taxi," I said and tried to turn toward the street.

"Yeah," my new companion said. "You do."

"The ground is moving."

"Is it?" He sounded almost amused.

"Yes."

I frowned. I had excellent balance, but I couldn't seem to stand straight or still for very long. It took me a minute to realize we'd started moving again. Only, my feet weren't moving. I frowned at them because they were visible directly and I wasn't looking at the ground.

Head tilting back, I stared up at the man holding me. "Where are we going?"

"To your hotel."

"I need a cab."

"One is on the way."

A car pulled up somewhere, and he turned us.

"You should put me down," I said.

"You're not heavy."

"Yeah, it's not that. I'm going to…" I threw up. He barely got me turned away from him before I yukked up mostly water. My throat burned and so did my eyes. "Sorry."

"It's all right, sweetheart," he said in a soft voice, but his tone shifted when he continued, "Get something she can use as a barf bag. We're going to get her to the hotel. You two deal with Romeo in there."

"Got it," came the lazy response. "She gonna be okay?"

"She better be," my savior muttered. Then we were in the back of the car and moving. I leaned my head back against the seat. I was hot, miserable, and tired.

"This is a very nice cab." Probably the nicest one I'd ever been in. "I have money." I patted my pockets for the spare cash I'd brought with me in case I needed it.

"I got it."

"But you don't know where you're going—Oh wait. Of course you do. You're with the show."

"Yeah," he said, his tone almost droll. I must have dozed off 'cause his voice hardened again. "Break his fucking kneecaps."

"Ow."

"You okay?" He was all soft and soothing questions again.

"Fine. Broken kneecaps would suck. Can't dance with broken kneecaps. Be stuck at home." I shuddered. The last place I wanted to be stuck.

"No one's touching your kneecaps."

"Yay."

"We're here," a new voice said, and I tried to peer forward at our driver, but all I could make out was dark hair. I was so tired. Out of the car and under the bright light from the hotel, I peered at the tech. He looked familiar, but I couldn't place him.

There were just so many different backstage responsibilities. I tried to be nice to everyone though, so I held out my hand. "Thanks for getting me back here...?"

I waited for a name, but he just wrapped an arm around me and guided me toward the hotel doors. They opened with a whoosh and let a wash of chilly air out, and it felt amazing against my fevered skin.

"Where are we going?"

"I'm making sure you get to your room, and you're going to deadbolt the door once you're inside. Clear?"

"Clear."

I would have argued, but my head had started thumping in time with my heartbeat and my eyes were so heavy. I leaned against him, and the guy was nice enough to keep me up.

"If I don't remember to thank you now, I won't remember

in the morning," I told him. "Sorry about that. Never…not even sure why it's this bad."

"Well, getting hammered on an empty stomach when you can't weigh even a hundred pounds wasn't the brightest idea."

He had a point.

"Sorry."

"It's not your fault."

Kind of was. "The bartender wanted to impress me."

A grunt was the only response. It seemed an eternity later, I opened the door and he stood there. I kicked off my shoes and walked over to the bed. I just wanted to fall on it.

"You have to lock the door."

Oh, he was in my room, and he was setting water next to the bed and there were a couple of small white aspirin packets.

"Right," I said as I turned around. "Thank you again…?"

"You can thank me by not getting drunk without having someone there to watch your back."

"Deal." Mostly 'cause I was never, ever doing this again.

At the door, he frowned at me. "You're going to be alone?"

"Yeah, it's just me." I tried to smile, but all I did was yawn. "I have an early pickup tomorrow, so I'm just gonna sleep."

"Put your trashcan by the bed in case you need it. Night, little dancer. Sweet dreams." I swore he said something else, but he muttered it, and then he was out the door and gone.

I managed to brush my teeth and wipe off the last traces of makeup that I hadn't sweated off and then just collapsed on the bed.

The hangover the next day sucked.

CHAPTER 20

EMERSYN

Jasper wasn't back the next day. In fact, he wasn't back the day after that, either. But he answered my texts, and I didn't want to press him about where he was or what he was doing.

As promised, Doc had picked Freddie and me up at lunch, and we'd swung through a sandwich place he liked. He and Freddie got these enormous subs, but I'd picked out a salad because seriously, the guys never bought vegetables. Not that I'd asked or even participated in the need to put food in the fridge.

Maybe I should start doing that too. At the clinic, I hung out with Doc in between his patients, and Freddie was in and out, though he got super restless at the clinic. I couldn't figure out why at first, and he wasn't forthcoming. In fact, by the time Kestrel showed up to pick us up, Freddie was ready to climb the walls.

Doc caught my arm as Freddie and Kestrel headed out the

door. "She'll be with you in a moment," was all Doc said to Kestrel when he paused to glance back.

"Sorry," I said as the door closed behind them. "I wanted to talk to you today, but Freddie…"

"Needs all the support he can get, Little Bit. You don't have to apologize for that. In fact, I really appreciate your patience with him." Now that we were alone, he let me go, and I tried not to think too closely about it. Doc always seemed to be pretty respectful.

Eyes intent on me, Doc studied me for a long moment. Long enough, I worried about the silence, then worried maybe he'd said something else and I'd missed it.

He'd been in scrubs all day and I had to admit, it was a great look on him, especially the blue against the tattoos decorating his arm, even if it hid everything except the ones that crept up his neck. As much as I wanted to study them, I did my best not to stare.

"What?" I finally asked, because my nerves jangled with awareness of his gaze.

"How are you doing?" A soft smile accompanied the question, but his eyes were lasered onto mine and I couldn't look anywhere else.

"I'm okay," I said slowly. "It's been… Weird isn't the right word, but it's been different."

He nodded once. "But you're all right?" When I glanced down, he tucked a finger under my chin.

I summoned up a smile for him. "I promise."

"And you and Vaughn?"

Heat flooded my face. Doc had been there the other night… "You saw Jasper." It wasn't really a question, and I wasn't altogether sure why I was embarrassed.

"Hey, Sparrow," Kestrel said as he pushed the door open. "We should go. Freddie's got a hair up his ass, and I'd rather we had him locked back down before he decides he'll be fine and wander off."

Crap.

I glanced back up at Doc, and he tapped my chin gently. "Go on, I'll see you soon."

"I'll text you." I'd confirmed his number in my phone and sent him a text so he'd have mine. I should have done it sooner. At the door, I hesitated and then paused with one hand on the handle, not looking at him. "You're not mad, are you?"

"No, Little Bit. Long as you're not being coerced or forced, I'm not mad."

Tears burned in my eyes, and I released a breath. "I'm definitely not being either of those." I almost tacked on the words "not there," but that would open the door to questions I didn't want to answer. I already had enough of those.

"Then I'm not mad," he confirmed, and at the sound of the smile in his words, I looked at him as I opened the door. He stood there, hands in his scrubs pockets, a wry smile on his face and a five o'clock shadow on his jaw and everything about him beckoned me to stay, but Freddie needed us around right now and... "Go on, Little Bit. I'm not going anywhere. I promise."

I blew him a kiss and then hurried out. Kestrel sat in the driver seat of his car, the engine idling like a purring beast. I slid around to the passenger side. Freddie slumped in the backseat and stared off into the distance, his whole expression shut down.

When Kestrel held out his hand to me, I slid my fingers into his after I buckled my seatbelt, and then we were pulling out of the lot with his gaze everywhere but me. The next day, I stuck close to the clubhouse because Freddie locked himself in his room and wouldn't come out. Vaughn told me to leave him because when he got like this, there was nothing to do about it. They were checking his room daily for drugs.

That might explain his sour expression in the car. When Vaughn left for work, I took one of the new books that had appeared on the dresser in my room and carried it down the hall to Freddie's door.

Sitting down, I opened to the first page of what said *HAVOC at Prescott High* on the cover. The spine wasn't cracked, so I didn't think Jasper had read it, and it didn't look like the other books he'd left for me. There was a couple on the cover, and I kind of liked the girl's hair.

"She's got this long blonde hair with pink tips, or maybe like pink streaks from halfway up to the tips. It's kind of neat looking." I'd knocked before I sat, then told Freddie I could hang out right there and I'd read to him if he liked. Hopefully, his door wasn't soundproofed or something. I'd look pretty stupid sitting out here. "I wonder if I should dye my hair." I tugged a lock of my endlessly dead straight brown hair around and stared at it. "Maybe bleach all the color out and then do like blue or purple or something. Food for thought."

Back to the book, I began on the first page and started reading aloud. I hadn't even made it a handful of pages in before I grimaced. What a bunch of *dicks*. I kind of liked Bernie, but the whole thing about her stepfather set off warning bells inside my head. Still, I kept reading along, even when my throat dried and my stomach twisted.

I kept reading even after my butt went numb, my throat scratchy from not crying in a couple of places, and my eyes burned. A shuffle of sound along the hallway pulled me out of that world, abruptly jolting me back to the present. But no one was there when I looked.

My bladder hurt, and I needed to stretch. I'd read about half of the book. "Sorry, Freddie, I need to pee and find lunch. I'll come back after and read more if you want." Or if you don't. 'Cause it wasn't like I was going anywhere else today.

There was food in the kitchen. I could make a peanut butter and jelly sandwich. I used to make those at rehearsals in the little kitchen they had at the old theater in Los Angeles. Peanut butter was good protein, and on a heavy dance schedule, I had to eat a lot.

I found water, made up a couple of extra sandwiches for Freddie, and after I ate and washed up, I carried the extra back with me. I covered them and sat them on the floor before letting him know I was there. I was still sitting on the floor reading when Kestrel arrived.

The door thudded down the hall, and I glanced up from the page in time to see Kestrel arrive at the top of the steps. He stared at me and then at the closed door as he approached.

"No sign of him?"

I shook my head. "I don't even know if he's in there." That thought had actually occurred to me a couple of hours earlier. "I might have been sitting out here reading aloud for just myself all day."

Leaning over, Kestrel hit the door with his fist in a rapid beat. "Freddie, open your fucking mouth and tell Sparrow thank you for spending her whole day sitting on this hard, fucking cold ass floor for you."

Mouth agape, I stared up at Kestrel as he extended that hand to me. I clasped it and let him pull me to my feet. I ignored the soreness radiating up my butt from where it had gone numb again down my legs, that also protested the absolute lack of movement all day.

A few seconds later, the door opened to the near pitch-dark room. I couldn't see Freddie, but I could smell him, and the scent of sweat and body odor was a little strong.

"Thanks, Boo-Boo," he said in a raw voice. "I really liked you reading."

"There's a sandwich here for you. A couple of them."

When I would have picked them up, Kestrel tugged me back from the door. "He's a big boy, he can get them. You've looked after him all day, let's look after you, shall we?"

I wanted to argue, but Freddie's lack of objection coupled with the expression on Kestrel's face had me biting my tongue. He led me to his room and, by default, to where mine was.

Though he wasn't wearing the overalls from the shop, I could smell the hints of dirt, exhaust, and motor oil on him. There was also the familiar scent of the soap from the garage. It had a kind of lemon tang to it, but it cut through the grease smell.

Inside his room, Kestrel closed the door.

"Did I do something wrong?"

At my question, he blinked, then shook his head as he stretched. It was only when he turned the lights on in his bathroom that I got a good look at the weariness on his face. There were shadows beneath his eyes. His jaw was a lot scruffier than I'd ever seen it. I couldn't remember if he'd been clean-shaven that morning or not.

He aborted his stretch with a faint grimace before he rubbed his shoulder. "You didn't do anything wrong. Freddie's...Freddie's fallen off the wagon before. We can pick him up, clean him off, and throw him back in the wagon, but the choice to stay on it has to be his."

There was a hitch to his step as Kestrel reached into the shower and turned it on before turning to face me.

"You did a good thing, sitting out there while he was in his room feeling sorry for himself. But now you have to wait for him to come back out and reach out for help."

Oh.

The feeling was returning to my butt and the backs of my thighs. The pins and needles weren't the worst I'd ever felt, but it made me want to stretch out.

"I'm going to shower. Then look into finding food for dinner. You got any preferences?"

Not looking at me, he tugged his shirt off and threw it toward the basket in the corner before he freed his work boots. Every motion he made had him gritting his teeth, and the muscles didn't quite finish their stretch before they contracted.

"You hurt yourself."

"I'll be fine, Sparrow." He sent me a smile as he straightened. "Nothing to worry about."

I mouthed, 'Liar,' as he undid his belt with one hand and closed the door with the other. I let myself into my room and went into the bathroom, where I ran some hot water into the sink. Kestrel took fast showers, and I was already back in his room when he came out wearing nothing but a towel around his hips. Droplets of water decorated his chest and slid over the pair of guns he had tattooed to his pecs.

"On the bed," I ordered and ignored the surprise on his face. He moved over to sit on the end and watched me as I walked back into my room. I wrung out one of the hot towels, then came back in. With care, I wrapped it around his neck and did my best to not catalog the other tattoos he had. It wasn't any of my business, and I wasn't doing this to ogle him.

"What's up, Sparrow?" He tracked me with those cool eyes as I reached for the liniment that had been in my bag. At least when they returned some of my stuff, I had some of my basic supplies.

"You're hurt." I rubbed it on my hands to warm it, because it would turn my hands to ice at first application, and then moved to his left shoulder. At his swift gasp of air through his teeth despite his stoic expression, I nodded. "I'm not wrong. You can't stretch the arm all the way up. You did something to your shoulder. Either to a tendon or to the muscles. Hyperextended maybe?"

Not waiting for his answer, I just dug my fingers in as I spread the liniment around. The minty scent soothed me with its familiarity. The heat from the shower had already warmed the muscles, and the hot towel on his neck kept those muscles loose, because too deep a pull could start dragging on the rest.

"Had to shift an engine today, that's all," he said almost noncommittally, like it was no big deal. I moved onto the bed behind him and went to work along the scapula, tracing the tautness in the rhomboid as I slid another hand down the back of his biceps. "I've had worse."

I found a scar on the back of his arm. Mottled skin where it had fused. Probably a burn. There was a puckered spot of flesh just below it. At my nudge, he raised his arm, and the rhomboid went taut before he even made it to ninety degrees.

"Tell me about your day if you're going to poke and prod at me." Despite the evenness of his voice, he couldn't hide the fact he gritted his teeth.

"Mostly spent my day reading to Freddie," I admitted. "No idea where the new book came from."

"Do you like it?"

There it was, a knot where the muscles interconnected, probably ligaments or tendons. Didn't matter, I had it now, and I began applying pressure with my knuckles as I braced his biceps to keep his arm where I wanted it. "Don't let me shove you forward." At my order, his legs stiffened and so did his back as I leaned all my weight into that knuckle on the knot.

"Right," he said, then forced a laugh. "A tiny thing like you isn't moving me anywhere."

"Uh huh," I said, as the knot rebounded again and again. Digging one of these out could be excruciating, but oh so worth it when it let go. "The book was fine. A little... disturbing in places. Lots of violence."

Easier to focus on that.

"Also, they were real dickbags to her and I'm not sure why she likes them."

Kestrel let out a laugh that turned into a pained grunt. "Motherfucker..." The knot gave and he half sagged, but his arm raised as the rhomboid relaxed and he could stretch his arm over his head.

I chuckled as I ran my fingers over the line of muscles again. Less pressure, but still firm. It wouldn't be the first time more than one knot caused the problem.

He caught my hand as he twisted to look at me. "Magic hands."

"Hardly." I snorted as I wiggled off the bed and bounced to my feet. "Just years of dance practice and having to help other dancers while they helped me."

His eyes narrowed.

"Does it hurt anywhere else?"

"No," he said slowly. "Does it have to hurt to get you to finish the massage?"

Trapped in his gaze, I shook my head slowly. "If you need more, I'm okay at it. My feet are stronger than my hands but...I've got a good grip."

He dragged the wet towel off his neck and then moved to stretch out on his bed. The towel stayed around his hips, narrowly. Though as he sprawled, it had definitely loosened.

"I wouldn't normally ask," Kestrel admitted, finally looking away from me and folding his head down to lay against his forearms. "But that felt fucking amazing when you weren't torturing me and it's been a long damn week. You give me a massage, Sparrow, and I'll get you anything you want."

"Hang on," I told him, biting back a smile. I swapped the liniment for a little body oil. It would be better if I could warm it, but I kind of liked lazy, all sprawled out Kestrel and it was the first time he'd actually asked *me* for something for him.

Back in his room, I climbed back on the bed and knelt next to him. "Just let me know if I'm too rough."

He chuckled against the comforter. "No worries, Sparrow. I trust you."

The words startled me and so did the first flush of pleasure that spread out at the declaration. I went to work on his back, slowly spreading the oil out and moving from his neck down. Every muscle interconnected, so tension in one could pull on the next, which in turn strained another. A pulled neck could wreck your back, and a strain in your lower back could leave your neck aching.

Bit by bit, he seemed to melt into the bed. He didn't say anything about just stopping at his back, so I worked on the back of his thighs, then down his calves and to his feet. I was careful to keep the towel from slipping. Though he'd let out a grunt when I massaged his glutes.

To be fair, he had a nice ass, but it was tight in a way that said it would probably pull on his back if he wasn't careful, so I worked to loosen it too. At some point, his half halting comments had faded away and his breathing deepened. I worked my way up to his occipitals and then used my knuckles to gently massage the back of his head. I didn't want to get oil in his hair, but I swore he just seemed to sink deeper into the bed.

His breathing came in slow, regular fashion. He was out like a light, and the tiredness in his expression also seemed to have eased. I slid off the bed carefully and then eased the towel off him because it was still damp. On quiet feet, I went to the bathroom and hung it up before I slipped into my room and snagged the comforter off the bed.

Back in Kestrel's room, he hadn't moved. I spread the blanket over him, and yes, I looked at his naked ass. I'd seen plenty of nude bodies, but he really did have a nice ass. After I tucked him in, I indulged myself and brushed a kiss to the top of his head before I shut off the light and slipped out to go downstairs.

The next day, I got Vaughn to drop me at the clinic on his way to work. He wasn't thrilled with the idea, but he had pulled an afternoon shift and I'd spent the whole morning in bed with him. I ached in all the right ways, and if he hadn't had to go to work, I don't know that we would have gotten up.

Fortunately, we grabbed food on our way to the clinic. It was really busy when I got there, and Vaughn ushered me into Doc's office and out of sight. With the sound of crying babies and more than one upset mother out there filtering through the walls, I used my new phone to surf the internet. The connection at the clubhouse was garbage on the phone.

I could barely get a webpage to load, and it lacked some of the fancier features of my other phone. The one I still didn't dare to turn on. But while I was in Doc's office with no audience and no one to ask questions, I could do some research.

It took time to scour the news sites. My disappearance had been downplayed at first. Then came the first false claims for ransom. A whole spread in one of the lifestyle magazines discussed my mother's mini-breakdown and her commitment to a facility for exhaustion.

Not quite rolling my eyes at that, I skipped over the family drama to find the actual news pieces. Apparently, some industrious types had decided to "ransom" me after I'd been declared missing for ten weeks. The ransom was paid, but a cooperative effort between the FBI and agents working for Sharpe Financial tracked the money and the would-be kidnappers.

All but two had been killed in the raid. Those two admitted under questioning that they had never had me and just tried to bank on the effort. The article then continued to detail my uncle's profound efforts to find me.

My upper lip curled at his statement that the family would never give up until I was safe and home again.

That site had links to other articles. In some, there were rumors that I had run off with Eric, but Eric's disappearance at the same time as me made him a person of interest in my missing person status.

The mentions grew further and further apart. The reward for information leading to my discovery had continued to rise. One video showed up, and it was my father making a plea for my return. My uncle stood just a foot to his left and right behind him, but he said nothing.

He rarely did, in public. My father was the figurehead, the face of the company. He and my mother handled all of the public appearances. Yet even as my father's quiet, well-worded if somewhat impersonal plea sounded up from the tinny speakers, I couldn't look away from my uncle.

It was like he knew I'd be watching.

I snapped it off when it got to the end, then began to erase my search history, clearing it all before curling back up in the seat.

Months, I'd been gone. Months. And from all appearances, they hadn't given up on finding me.

PAYING IT FORWARD

EMERSYN

It was my dumb luck that the show's two-week break fell during the charity ball season for the Manhattan elite. I'd already attended four with Uncle Bradley acting as escort. He loved the pageantry of the events. He'd also made a point of purchasing me a new dress for each one. After all, I couldn't be seen in the same one each evening.

Tonight's dress was a deep forest green. Strapless, the bodice was ruched and shaped what breasts I had nicely. The rest of the dress fell in a straight line from the empire waist. Slits along both sides allowed for reveals of my legs. The shoes were expensive and dyed to match. The emerald choker on my neck seemed to dig into my skin just a bit. There was a tail of diamond encrusted platinum gold that fell from the back like a leash.

Since it was the third such choker my uncle had put on me this week, I had a feeling he was making a point. The hickeys Eric had left on me hadn't quite healed before I returned.

Uncle Bradley's reaction had been…incensed.

Fortunately, the galas meant he couldn't leave visible damage. That was something. The diamond and emerald shackles on my wrists glittered as we ascended the red carpeted stairs toward the Met. While this gala was only a precursor to the main event, it was still important that we mingle.

I'd expected my parents to show up, but they'd been called away at the last minute to represent the company at another event. Better to divide and conquer, as Uncle Bradley always said.

"Smile, Princess," Uncle Bradley murmured against my ear as we reached the top step. My arm was firmly tucked into his with my hand on his forearm. It showed off the bracelet to great effect against the Saville Row jacket. A breeze stirred my skirt and bared my left leg just in time for one photographer to snap a picture of us.

The scrape of his teeth against my earlobe before he pulled away was a warning. My smile was firmly in place when the second shot was taken, though a part of me wondered at the first picture. We slowed as men greeted my uncle, and I kept my smile in place as he glad-handed his way through a dozen well-wishers.

I only half listened to the exchanges. Most regarded business that I couldn't care less about. We were near the main doors when I caught sight of a familiar face.

Lainey.

She seemed to have spotted me at the same time. Her smile grew, and mine became so much easier. We were almost to them. His hand stayed firmly on my lower back for nearly all of his interactions. When he released me, I let out a relieved breath. It was a flaw in my performance, a chink in my armor. No way he hadn't noticed it.

Rather than dread what was to come later in retaliation

for that rather public faux pas, I took Lainey's extended hand and let her pull me away. "You look amazing," she told me. "It's been ages."

"I know," I said, only wishing I wasn't admitting this within my uncle's earshot. Lainey wasn't good enough to be a Sharpe roommate. Whatever. Lainey had kept in touch on and off. "Was it last June?" I'd lost track somewhere. Where had we even been?

"It was last April," Lainey said with a laugh. "At the show in Paris. You were fantastic, and I was so surprised to see your name."

Right. I shook my head. "I barely got out of the rehearsal rooms. I never did get any sightseeing in."

"You went to Paris and didn't actually *see* Paris?" Utterly scandalized, Lainey shook her head, but her eyes sparkled. "Unacceptable. I insist, girls' trip at some point."

"That sounds wonderful." It really did.

Her smile dimmed a fraction as she gazed past me, then her mouth set in a thin line as she shook her head. With the kind of effort I recognized and was all too familiar with, Lainey refocused her attention on me. "Good. Let's make it happen…"

"Elaine." The greeting came from behind me. Pivoting, I glanced up at the good-looking guy in the tuxedo. He wasn't much older than us, tall, lean built, with dark hair and dark eyes. Everything about him seemed to hold a chill except when he focused on Elaine. "Aren't you going to introduce me to your friend?"

"I didn't plan on it," Lainey said. "Go away."

He laughed, but it held less mirth than his smile suggested. Transferring his cool attention to me, he held out a hand. "Adam Reed, and you are…"

"She is utterly unimpressed," Lainey informed him as she hooked her arm through mine. "And we're going inside."

Okay. She didn't want me to talk to him. Got it. Lainey was my friend, not whoever Adam Reed was.

"Adam," my uncle said in a booming voice. "Good to see you." It was hard to miss how easily Adam shifted gears to steely politeness as he and my uncle shook hands. They clearly didn't like each other.

Oh, that put points in Adam's corner. Sorry, Lainey.

"How is your father?"

"He's well, sir. I'm sure he'll be terribly upset to have missed you."

I almost snorted but managed to restrain it because the temperature around us plummeted. My uncle did not like to be dismissed. "Not to worry," he responded. "The shares I just secured will see me seated on the board. I'll catch up with him at the board meeting next week. Enjoy your evening. Princess."

The snap of command on the last two syllables had me casting an apologetic look at Lainey before taking my uncle's arm again.

"You didn't introduce me," Adam mused, a damn near sadistic grin on his face. If I weren't right in the middle of this nightmare, I'd want to egg him on.

"You're right," my uncle told him smoothly. "I didn't." Then Uncle Bradley slid an arm around my waist. His fingers bit into my side. There would be bruises in the morning. While we were hardly running, he directed us into the Met itself. We nodded and exchanged cordial smiles, but he kept us moving.

It didn't take long for him to direct us behind a velvet rope to a darkened hall and an executive, and very private, bathroom. My heart sank as he unlocked the door. As soon as we were inside, I found myself pinned to the wall.

"You will stay away from the Benedicts and the Reeds, Princess." Each word slapped me. "Do you understand?" But it was his hand under my dress where he gripped my cunt, his fingers pinching brutally. The bruise on it wouldn't be visible, but I could barely breathe around the pain.

"Yes," I said as calmly as I could. I refused to cry. I hadn't shed a fucking tear for him since my tenth birthday when he rewarded me with a long weekend away.

A weekend I wish I could tear out of time.

Forever.

He studied me intently, then removed his hand and feathered the fingers of his free hand against my cheek. "That's a good girl, my sweet princess. That young man will do nothing but bad things. He'd use you to get to me, and we can't have that. I won't have anyone else touching you."

There was the warning.

I nodded when he paused and stared at me. Then he brushed a kiss to my cheek, all smiles as he moved to the sink to wash his hands. "Freshen up, Princess. It's going to be a long night."

It already had been.

"We're going to have so much fun together," he promised, the softness in his voice a velvet gloved lie. "I promise."

CHAPTER 21

EMERSYN

"Come on in," Doc said as he held the door open for me. He'd closed the clinic early. But he said he did that at least once a week because he did most of the work at the clinic himself.

"Do you not have any help there?" I asked as I walked inside his place. His apartment was in a building not that far from the clinic. We'd barely driven a couple of blocks before he pulled into a parking lot next to a ten-story building. His apartment was on the fourth floor. Thankfully, they had an elevator, rickety as it was.

It made me laugh when I realized it used the old-fashioned and manual accordion doors. Not so much when it gave a distinct shudder on our way up. I'd gripped Doc's hand abruptly and squeezed it. He chuckled and pulled me into his side.

"It's safe enough, Little Bit. Don't worry."

Yeah, easy for him to say. The shudder it gave when we

stopped at his floor made my teeth ache. The place had to have stairs. Fire code would demand it. I could easily take the stairs.

Good exercise, anyway.

Better than the possessed elevator from hell.

Doc chuckled at me all the way to his apartment door. The scent of Indian food, rich curry, and spices perfumed the hall. My stomach rumbled in appreciation. It was pretty institutional in the hallway. Bland colors, clean floors, and otherwise empty.

His apartment was different.

It had spots and splashes of color *everywhere.*

"I do have help at the clinic," Doc told me as he set his backpack down on the floor below a row of hooks. He hung up his keys and his jacket next. There were four deadbolts on the door, and he threw all of them once he'd closed it. "Just only a couple of days a week. A nurse comes in to help out if I have female patients."

He'd mentioned that.

"But you do everything else? Administration? Cleaning? Seeing the patients? Opening? Closing?" It seemed like a lot. I traced my gaze over the prints on the wall. Most of them were photographs. Some were of Doc, in the military. There was desert behind him in one shot. Ocean in another. Still, a tree-lined pathway in another. I didn't know any of the people with him.

"It's my clinic," he answered. The sound of the fridge opening and closing echoed through the quiet room. He walked back out with a couple of beers. He held one out to me. "Have a drink and a seat. I need to grab a quick shower and change."

"Thank you," I murmured when he handed me the beer. "I'm going to kind of miss the scrubs." No lie. He really did look good in them.

His chuckle was genuine and aching with a hint of disbelief. "If you say so. Remote is there," he said, pointing to the coffee table. "There's chips in the pantry if you can't hold out until I fix us some grub. The sofa is moderately comfortable, the chair is better. I'll be back in a sec."

"Mickey," I said before he took two steps, and he paused. "Thank you for having me over."

The corner of his mouth hitched a little higher into a near lopsided smile. "Little Bit, you're welcome anytime."

"Great, as long as I can skip death's elevator."

He threw his head back and laughed. "I'll hold you on the way down, I promise it will be better."

Snorting, I raised the beer to my lips and turned away so he could go grab his shower. No door closed after him, so either he had the softest doors on the planet or he hadn't closed them.

I took another swallow of the beer rather than consider what that meant. Instead of sitting, I explored the living room. Instead of art, he had pictures of places—a house, a community center, and the clinic were all featured prominently. There was a shot of a woman with dark hair and kind eyes. She was older, and that photo sat on a bookshelf with a lot of well-worn copies of everything from Tom Clancy to Gandhi. Fiction. Non-fiction. I studied the titles before I continued my circuit.

More pictures. I picked out a younger Doc—Mickey in one of them. Here at his place, I should probably call him by his name. He had a kind of carefree smile on his face, and he had his arm around another guy, a kid really, in a kind of headlock and was rubbing his head. They were both laughing.

Everything about the picture just made me smile. When I spotted Jasper and Rome in a shot near it, I studied it closer. Mickey was seated on what looked like a picnic table, and he was in deep discussion with Liam and another guy. They were all younger in the photo.

A lot younger. Liam still looked a bit like a cocky asshole. I tracked my gaze to where Rome stood. He held himself back, hands in the pockets of a hoodie that seemed familiar. It probably should, since I was wearing it. I couldn't tell if he was irritated by the conversation or just focused. But Jasper was right behind him, and he mugged straight at the camera.

He flipped it off, mouth open and tongue out like he was saying something.

It probably shouldn't make me laugh, because everything else in the image was so intent and focused, but Jasper radiated fuck off energy as clearly as if he were standing here. There was history on these walls.

A lot of history.

My heart squeezed at a picture of Doc in a graduation cap and gown. He looked determined but pleased. He would have been my age there. But his eyes seemed older. A shot in the frame next to it had that same dark-haired woman, and she beamed proudly at him.

Had to be his mom.

Envy slid through me, side by side with pleasure. I was glad he had someone who cared.

I found more pictures of kids and Doc. The other kid from the picture with Jasper, Liam, and Rome was present in more than a few. More than any of the others. I didn't find Kestrel in any shots, but I did find Freddie.

He was all the way in the background of a shot, and I leaned in close, squinting. In the picture, he looked too thin, too pale, too shaky…

"That was taken three days before his first OD," Mickey said quietly. If I hadn't been expecting him to come back, the fact he was right behind me might have sent me leaping. He was so silent on his feet.

"First one? How many times has he?"

Mickey shrugged. "Three unintentional ones that I know of."

Unintentional. Lifting my chin, I studied him. "How many intentional?"

"Only one," he answered. Then raised his beer and took a long swallow. "He's not suicidal, Little Bit. Not that I've seen. Not anymore. Depressed? Yes. Dealing with his addiction? Yes. Maybe a bit in denial? Oh, for sure. But he's not suicidal. Especially not with a certain new face hanging out."

I rolled my eyes at his teasing smile and followed him into the kitchen. "Sorry I was being nosy."

"I don't mind you looking." His hair was damp and slicked back from his face. He'd changed out of the scrubs like he said he would. Dressed in an open collar Henley with three-quarter sleeves and a pair of faded, relaxed jeans, he looked comfortable. More at ease. The bare feet added to the overall picture. "Tell me, is there anything you don't like before I fix you something to eat?"

I gave a little shrug. "Most of the time when I'm on tour, I eat a high protein and dense vegetable diet. Carbs are only for fueling after a performance. But I have to watch my weight. Probably need to watch it more now, since it's not like the diet lately has been particularly healthy."

At the sheer amount of takeout I'd consumed, Marta would have had an aneurism at this point. Madame B too. Dancers could not afford to be too thick. *Lean muscle. Lean muscle.* The words were like a whip cracking in the back of my brain.

"Little Bit, if you weigh more than a buck, buck and a nickel, soaking wet, I'll eat my shoes." The lack of amusement in the dry look he gave me had me laughing.

"It's different when you're a performer."

"Yes, starving yourself for your art, so I've heard. You

probably burn what? Four or five thousand calories a performance?"

I shrugged. "Maybe. Doesn't change the fact that I still have to watch what I eat. Or did. It was all monitored. For the most part."

His eyes narrowed, and I needed to change the subject. I pointed my beer at him. "Just make whatever you would if you were by yourself. I kind of invited myself over."

The studying look he gave me had me shifting a little, and then I lifted my chin. Fidgeting was a tell. I needed to not do it. The retaliation…

"Fine," he grumbled. "Come here." Surprised, I obeyed, and he set his beer on the counter. "Gonna pick you up, Little Bit."

"Okay."

Then he settled his hands on my hips and lifted me to perch on the counter. "Stay here." The last he delivered with a light tap to my nose before he went to the fridge.

From my angle, I could see the fridge clearly, everything neatly placed. A drawer of vegetables. Milk. Yogurt. Cheese. He also pulled out a package of defrosted chicken breasts.

"Tell me how it's been since you decided to go back." It was the first time since the day I asked him to take me back to the clubhouse that he broached that topic. "Better? Worse?"

"It wasn't…it wasn't terrible before. I mean, Jasper was bossy and controlling, the guys kept a lot of secrets, they all wanted to look after me, and they were a mixture of frustrating and adorable. Most of that is still the same."

He chuckled and shook his head.

"I wanted… It's hard to remember a time I wasn't here. I mean, not here, here." I wasn't making much sense. I tipped the bottle up and took a long swallow. "I wanted to escape because I didn't understand why they took me and why they were keeping me. I saw they had Eric all chained up and beaten bloody…and I liked that. Not sure what that says about me."

He turned on the heat under a pan and started warming it. There were fragrant onions and garlic being added with a little oil, and the sizzle made my stomach clench. I was hungrier than I thought.

"It says you're human and he was a piece of garbage that needed taking out."

"I hate that you know that about him."

"That he hurt you?" Doc—Mickey frowned at me. "You getting hurt by someone who was easily more than twice your size isn't something to be ashamed of."

"Jasper doesn't understand why I didn't stop it." I needed to shut up.

"That's because he's been in a fight to survive for as long as he can remember. Fighting back is how he survives."

That made me sad. "But that's his story."

Mickey nodded slowly.

"And why he's so angry with you."

"That too, Little Bit. Give him time. I know he doesn't blame you for not fighting back, he just hates the idea you were being hurt. Frankly, so do I. That's why you shouldn't lose any sleep over his removal."

"I haven't," I promised. "It's kind of funny…being back, I'm dancing. Maybe not every day, but even before I got out, I was dancing. That studio…it means more than I think they understand. For so long, dance has been my escape, my ticket to get away. What I loved about it became less important than what it meant for me."

He'd added the vegetables to the pan and started searing the chicken in another one. I'd finished my beer and so had he. He pulled out two more bottles silently and opened them before offering me one. I'd never really cared for beer, but I sure as hell drank it more now. I had no idea what this one was other than it had an earthy kind of taste, but it was darker than the ones Jasper and the guys drank.

"But here, here I get to love dance again and just dance for the sheer joy of it."

"I'm glad. I'd love to see you sometime."

I bit back a smile. "If all of you came to watch me, you'd have to make the studio bigger."

"Private performance then." He winked. Heat flushed to my cheeks, and I took another sip of the beer.

"I guess, better is the short answer. There's...there's still so much I don't understand and decisions I need to make."

"I get that too," he said as he covered the chicken and turned down the heat. The whole kitchen smelled amazing, and Mickey was as dexterous and controlled at cooking as he was at everything else. When he pulled a fat loaf of bread down and split it, he asked, "What do you want to do? For real. If you could go anywhere, be anything, what do you want, Little Bit? First answer that rolls off your tongue, don't think about it..."

"Someone else."

I didn't even have to think hard on that. Blowing out a long breath, I shuddered.

"Someone else?" he prompted.

"Not Emersyn Sharpe." It would mean giving up a career I'd built over the last decade. But it would also mean walking away from a life that had held me prisoner for so much longer. "What about you, Mickey? Who would you be?"

There was no mistaking the hint of pleasure in his face when I used his name. It still felt a little weird on my tongue, but I was determined. Names were important. The names we had. The ones others gave us.

The ones we never wanted to hear again.

"I'd be me," he said as he slid the bread into the oven. He'd buttered it and added some seasoning to it. Oven closed, he drained half his beer and then looked at me. "But you're wondering if I'd give up my scars."

It wasn't a question, but... "That wasn't what I was thinking about. The scars say you survived." He told me that. The memory was a little foggy. A lot of my damage was hidden away, safe from prying eyes. But he wore his on his flesh. "I think your tattoos are beautiful and the skin beneath it is too."

Real surprise flickered across his face. "Who are you, Emersyn Sharpe?"

I laughed, because it made me want to both scream and cry. "That's the million-dollar question."

Maybe my discomfort translated because he changed the subject after that. Soon, dinner was ready. Grilled chicken, seared with lemon and pepper, along with grilled vegetables that were crunchy and savory and hot, plus crunchy bread seasoned with garlic.

I was so hungry, I devoured everything, even the whole half a loaf of bread he'd sliced for me, though he kept teasing me he'd take care of my carbs. We talked about the clinic. About his going into the army. Why and how he went to med school. He'd trained as a paramedic and worked as emergency medic in the field.

Something had happened, but he didn't offer and I didn't pry. By the time we circled back around to the fact that he valued the clinic and his work there, I was yawning. "Sorry."

"Nope," Mickey told me as he rose from where we'd been sitting on the sofa. "Let's get you back. It's after ten, and I'm surprised they haven't come to kick my door down."

I wrinkled my nose. "Jasper is working on that."

It wasn't long before he had his shoes on and we were in the rickety elevator of death. I wanted to use the stairs, but Doc promised me it would be better. "Just look in my eyes."

The fact he was cupping my face and tracing his thumbs against my cheek had nothing to do with the wild fluttering. "We empower what we fear when we focus on it."

"Is that so?"

"Hmm-hmm." The soft hum of sound zinged through me. Everything was a lot easier with Mickey. "Because we're giving what we fear the power when we focus on it. Nothing robs something of its fear faster than ignoring it and basically flipping it off."

My mind slipped to thoughts of my uncle, and I shoved his face and memory away. I didn't want him in this moment. He tainted too much already. I focused on the sense of Mickey's heartbeat where my hands rested on his chest and the way he stared at me, the faint part to his lips.

"See?" Mickey said as the elevator stopped, and he lowered his hands. The fact he didn't kiss me disappointed me more than I cared to admit. We walked to his truck, and he stayed at the passenger side door as I buckled my seat belt. "Little Bit, the kiss you gave me..."

My heart sank, I could almost hear the rejection in his voice.

"It might be best if we just let that go."

I frowned. "Why?"

"Because I'm a hell of a lot older than you for one, and for another, your boys aren't going to welcome the idea of me and you together."

"They aren't mine," I said. "And...age is just a number. You see me. You see me in a way a lot of people never have." They all did. It was scary how many of them saw the disparate broken pieces of me that floated under the surface of my skin. "I meant that kiss."

Eyes closed, Mickey leaned his head against the truck frame. "I know you did," he murmured softly. "But it would be better if we let that go."

"Do you want to let it go?"

His eyes flicked open, and heat seared me. But instead of answering, he closed the door and walked around to the driver's seat. I guessed that was an answer all its own, right?

The silence in the car added to the chill, but I didn't push. He'd already gone out of his way for me. Better to ease back. It took almost no time to get back to the clubhouse. He pulled right up to the little door on the side. It was quiet out here, but that didn't mean anything. It could be a hub of activity inside.

"Thank you, again," I said as I unbuckled the seat belt. "I really did have a good time tonight."

I reached for the door handle, but he caught my hand and tugged. I slid over the seat, and he closed his mouth over mine in a swift, searing kiss that burned all the way through me. The stroke of his tongue was demanding, and finding access had me sliding my hands up into his hair. While his grip was firm, there was no bite to his fingers, no force, nothing keeping me still if I wanted to rip away.

Then he released my mouth, dragging out my lower lip slowly with his teeth. My heart thundered, and his eyes were blazing in their intensity in the dark.

"No, I don't want to let it go," he told me. "But it would be better for everyone if we did. Now get your ass inside, Little Bit. Go now."

The order shivered over me, and I had already slid out of the truck before it occurred to me to say no and argue.

"Go, Little Bit," he commanded again when I hesitated. I glared at him.

"I'm not letting it go."

And maybe it wasn't the most mature of me, but I slammed the truck door before I marched over to the door to the warehouse. I didn't look back before I was inside. The sound of it closing behind me was a little ominous, and I shook off that chill. Arms folded, I headed across the warehouse floor. Like I'd thought, it was definitely busy in here. Two huge trucks were parked side by side, and the rats were moving one set of boxes from one truck to the other.

The feeling of being watched crept over me, and I glanced around. I half expected to see Jasper or Kestrel keeping watch for me to come back. Instead, I found the rat Rome had punched staring at me.

He gave me a tight smile when our gazes met, and I moved a little bit faster. The weight of his stare followed me all the way and I half wanted to run to get away from it, but I forced myself to go at a normal pace.

Once inside the clubhouse, I let out a shuddery breath and fell back against the closed door.

Sweat prickled along my skin, despite the cold. There was something wrong with that guy.

Really wrong.

BLOOD IN

JASPER

I blew the smoke straight upward and stared through the empty branches of the tree at the blue sky beyond.

"You're supposed to be in school," Milo said as he dropped onto the bench of my picnic table. Mine 'cause I'd fucking claimed it this morning when I sprawled flat on my back smoking. The hangover was real, and my head thundered. Liam had brought a bottle of whiskey with him and the best fucking cookies we'd ever had. They were called something French or some shit, but goddamn, they were fucking awesome.

"So are you," I countered, taking another drag. The sunglasses were dark enough the light didn't bother me too much. But I couldn't quite bring myself to give a fuck about social studies, Shakespeare, or science. Unlike Milo, I didn't do any sports, so I'd just headed for the park rather than the school.

"Some asshole went missing, so I came to make sure you were okay."

I squinted at him. He wasn't looking at me. In fact, his posture seemed relaxed, with the way he leaned back against the table, arms stretched along the edges. A muscle twitched in his jaw despite his expressionless face. Like me, he wore sunglasses, but I swore I could hear his teeth grinding.

"You pissed at me or something?" 'Cause last I checked, I hadn't pulled anything recently. Not that I remembered anyway, and all the shit we got up to the week before had been his idea.

"Not at you," he answered. "You see Freddie this morning?"

Three years younger than us, Freddie had showed up at the group home the summer before last. We were all damaged, but he was a special kind of broken. The kid had a death wish or something. Scrawny as fuck, he kept writing checks with his mouth that his body couldn't pay. The shit that came out of him seemed designed to get his ass kicked. Milo and I had started watching out for his punk-ass, mostly 'cause he didn't seem malicious or stupid, just nuts.

We could live with nuts. Admittedly, watching him piss others off was fun.

"Nope," I said, then exhaled another long stream of smoke. "They go to school before us." He wasn't at the high school. Hell, he seemed small for sixth grade. I didn't remember being that short then, but what did I know? "He shit in your backpack or something?"

Milo snorted. Freddie had legit done that to one of the kids at the community center when the jerk slammed into Rome on purpose and knocked over the painting he'd been working on.

So you know that might be another reason Milo and I kept an eye on him. I loved a good fight.

"Why are we here?" Kellan asked as he dropped onto the

bench, on the other side of the table, with a thud. "I have a test today."

"'Cause Milo told us to meet him," Vaughn said as he joined us. What the fuck...?

I sat up and peered at Milo. "What happened?" 'Cause he was a goddamn straight arrow who didn't skip unless forced. He'd gone to school with a hundred and two temp before and then fought the nurse when she tried to send him back to the group home.

Of all of us? He was the one going places. His plans had plans. The only other one with a straight A average was Rome. They often jockeyed for first and second in the class. I'd bet Liam would be up there with them if he was at our school, but his "parents" had enrolled him in some fancy fucking prep school.

"You guys see Freddie?" Milo asked Vaughn and Kellan rather than answer me.

They both shook their heads. "Do we need to cut over to his school?" It wouldn't be the first time some losers thought that ambushing him between the group home and the elementary building was the way to go. We were at school longer than he was, but that didn't mean we couldn't act, and the paybacks we delivered were a hell of lot more fierce and twice as bad.

We wanted people to get the point the first time. The second time was a lot worse. So far, no one had tested us with a third time.

"He wasn't in at bed check," Rome announced as he arrived. We'd all been drinking at bed check, so technically, we hadn't been there either. The blond shrugged at my raised brows. "I asked." Like that should have been obvious.

"I'm guessing no one knew where he was?" I put out the cigarette before sliding off the table. My head thudded thanks to the hangover, but I ignored it for now.

"No." Succinct. One word. Then again, if Rome knew more, he'd have said more. He didn't hold information hostage.

"Fuck me," Kellan groaned. "Did he run away?"

"You mean again?" Vaughn asked. Freddie had run away over the summer with no word to any of us. He'd eventually turned up, almost mute in his rebellion. The thing was, I'd told him the next time he wanted to go, to get one of us. He was too damn scrawny for the streets.

Vaughn was the biggest of us all, and he'd still had the occasional asshole try to pay him to suck his dick. The fact everything was for sale wasn't lost on me. Still...

"I know where he went last time." At least part of it. He'd been rather closed-mouth on his plans, but he'd admitted that he'd holed up at a warehouse down near the docks. No one used it anymore, and they had old shipping containers inside.

Milo cut me a look. "Where?"

"Docks. Near Waterston and 105th."

"Let's go." Milo followed me along with the others. We didn't even make it to the edge of the park before Liam showed up. Rome's twin wore a suit with a fancy patch on it for the school he'd been enrolled in. Sweat dampened his hair, and his tie was askew.

"Sorry," he grumbled. "Took me a minute to slip out and get down here." Since the school was on the far side of town, I was impressed. "Where we going?"

"Docks," Rome answered him. "Freddie's missing."

Unlike me, Liam didn't look like he was sporting a hangover. Dick. I was glad for the backup though. As we walked, he shucked off the tie he'd been wearing and stuffed it in his pocket.

"Nice outfit, man," Kellan commented with a grin. He

probably meant it, but Vaughn's soft chuckle and Rome's snort made me smile wider. Liam raised his middle finger at Kellan. But he wasn't done as he added, "You're gonna totally screw up that perfect attendance record."

"Fuck you," Liam said with a laugh. "And I left after attendance was taken, so unless one of the teachers gets his panties in a bunch, I'm in the clear."

Fucker. They only took attendance once a day at his school. Must be nice. The thud in my head matched the pound of my heart as we moved together. Sure, we looked like a pack of troublemakers, but most of our neighborhood knew us, even Liam.

They left us alone. Even the cops tended to look past us. The beat cops at least. But we avoided them anyway. We'd had a run-in with a real bastard of one a couple of years earlier, and he'd gotten nightstick happy with me and Milo. The only reason we hadn't fought back was he was a damn cop. If it hadn't been for Mickey J, our asses would probably have ended up in juvey.

It was a hike, but we made it down there in an hour. A lot of this side of town had gone to shit over the years. It was like as the businesses shuttered, nothing new was added to replace them and the derelict buildings were left to rot.

"Which one?" Milo asked after we slid under the broken chain link fence. I pulled out a cigarette and tapped it as I studied the buildings.

"The one he used before is on the south side. You can see the water from it."

"Split up?" Liam asked as he scanned the area. "We'll hit more buildings."

"Agreed," Milo said. "Kellan and Vaughn, you guys head toward these first buildings, just do a sweep and keep an ear out for him. Rome and Liam, go to the north side, but on the far gate and work your way south. Jasper and I will find the building he knows and start there."

"Everyone have their phones?" Kellan asked. Another gift from Liam—he'd bought us all cheap cell phones with limited minutes. It was a way to reach out in emergencies.

Okay Freddie, where the fuck are you?

CHAPTER 22

JASPER

Kellan had given me a look that said I was a sad sack when I planted myself on the sofa and kept watch for when she got back. We watched the game in silence. Freddie was still holed up in his room, having a pity party for one.

I'd checked on him earlier, but his embarrassment outweighed his need for approval at the moment, so in his room he wanted to stay. Something about being at the clinic had set him off. I asked what, but he didn't want to tell me. I needed to talk to Emersyn about what they did. Maybe if I could figure it out, we could kick his ass back to NA.

If absolutely necessary, I'd go with him. It had done him good before. The fact I'd gone through three cigarettes in rapid succession had me shoving them away before I lit another.

"She texted that they were going to have dinner and Doc would drive her back," Kellan said without looking up from the accounts book he'd been reconciling. "Rome's probably working on something over near Doc's building just in case."

A door slammed and I sat up, but it was Vaughn—not Emersyn. He slowed when he saw me, and we stared at each other. The silence stretched, and I clamped my jaw shut. He pulled the knit cap off his head slowly, and the only sound came from the announcer on the television.

"Yeah, I'm going to do this shit in my room." Kellan stood and shut the television off before leaving the remote on the table and grabbing his beer. "Just don't fucking break the furniture or spread blood around. Pretty sure Sparrow likes your ugly ass faces the way they are. No rearranging."

Vaughn and I both jerked a look at Kellan as he tipped the beer up for a drink.

"Fuck you, Kes," Vaughn growled out.

"Not my type." He smirked. "Play nice, boys." Then he left the room and headed for the stairs.

Vaughn focused on me once more. "Do you care if I get a beer before you start your bitchin', or do you want to go straight to fists? I don't plan on wasting the beer."

"You're a real dick," I grumbled. "Go get your fucking beer."

He chuckled. The asshole.

I downed the rest of my own beer, then lit a cigarette. Maybe if I had it in my hand, it would keep me from punching him in his smug face. I'd told Emersyn I would try to be less of an asshole and not start fights.

Didn't say I wouldn't let him start it and then dive in. Course, Vaughn didn't usually start the damn fights. Fucker.

Not saying a word, he dropped to sit in the chair and spread out his legs like he had all the time in the world. His expression was damn near serene. Well, if I'd been merrily fucking Emersyn to my heart's content, I'd probably be fucking serene too.

"You want to just spit it out?" Vaughn asked.

"Not particularly," I groused. I hated the knotted tangle of emotion gnawing away in my gut. "You fucked her."

"I did," he said.

"When you knew how I felt," I said slowly, glaring at him. "You did it anyway."

"Hawk, I love you like a brother, but you're not fucking stupid. We all want her. We have for a long time. You are *not* the only one who cares." He raised his bottle and pointed it at me. "And I want her to trust us. We fucked ourselves when we took her how we did, and before you tell me we had to, I don't disagree. That asshole needed to die, slowly and painfully. But she didn't deserve the terror and the worry."

No, she hadn't.

"She didn't deserve you being a dick to everybody because you want to piss on her leg and mark your territory."

I glared at him before stabbing the cigarette out. "I don't just want to fuck her."

"Me neither," Vaughn said. "I want to take care of her."

Goddammit. "I want to date her. I want…" A lot of things.

"You realize it doesn't matter what either of us want, right?" He tipped his beer up and knocked the whole thing back before adding, "It only matters what she wants, and eventually, Raptor. 'Cause I'm not sure any of us are gonna survive when he finds out."

The weight dropped onto my shoulders, and I pinched the bridge of my nose. My pulse throbbed in my head. "We'll deal with it." We'd figure it out. "But I'm not backing off of her." Not now. Not when she'd shown serious interest. Even if I'd seen her coming apart in Vaughn's arms. Even if he'd tasted her pleasure.

"Are you telling me to back off?" The weariness in that question made me look up. Fighting with my brothers wasn't my favorite thing to do. But this wasn't over just anything.

"No," I said slowly "I would love it if all of you did, but Kel's got his eye on her. Rome's nuts for her. That dick Liam keeps sniffing around." Like he thought I hadn't noticed how often he'd started popping up now that she was here. Then having Rome take her to his place?

Asshole.

At least him I got to pummel before Emersyn asked me to not do it anymore. I ground my teeth. "Doc wants her too."

Vaughn chuckled. "I don't know a red-blooded man alive that wouldn't want her."

"You're okay with it?"

"With you guys?" Vaughn shrugged. "It's always been us against the world. Now it can be us *with* her, against the world."

That...didn't sound so bad.

"Just try not to scare her off by being an asshole," he continued as he stood. "Is she here, by the way?"

"Nope, she's still with Doc."

His jaw tightened just a fraction and that shouldn't have pleased me, but it did. At least he wasn't *totally* immune to jealousy. "Okay. I'm gonna grab a shower."

"And I'm waiting up for her, so don't make any plans like crawling into her bed naked."

Vaughn chuckled. "Ask me no questions and I'll tell you no lies." He left the empty bottle on the table as he headed for the stairs. "And if she's not back here in an hour, we go get her."

Fuck yes. Then I could tell her it was all Vaughn's idea. "Done." He threw me a peace sign and then disappeared up the stairs. I still wanted to kick him in the nuts for touching her, but I didn't want to kill him anymore. The desire to pound him bloody or shoot him had ridden me the night I found them until I had to leave. I'd had to get the hell out of here before I did something we'd all regret.

The door opened again thirty minutes later, and she walked through the door. At her expression, wide-eyed and a little pale, I stood. I'd kill him. "Are you all right?"

"Fine," she said, pulling off the hoodie. "Just a lot of rats working out there, and it was kind of creepy with it being dark."

Dammit, I was an asshole. I should have thought of that. "Sorry," I said, circling the table. "Maybe next time, you text us, then one of us will meet you at the door." If any of the rats looked at her sideways, we'd deal with it.

"You don't mind if there's a next time?" The unguarded question floored me. I loved her whisky brown eyes with the hint of gold around the edges. It had to be an optical illusion, but I didn't give a fuck.

"Do I mind if you go out with Doc?" I clarified, and she raised her brows. "Yeah, I mind." It was the truth. "But I won't stop you." No matter how much I wanted. "So, if or when there's a next time and you're out and coming back without one of us, text."

Doc should have fucking walked her all the way *to* the door. Her sudden smile cracked my bad mood into a dozen pieces. "Thank you," she said. "I really appreciate that."

"I'm trying."

"I know you are," she said softly. "And that means more than you realize."

"You wanna…sit for a bit with me? I can get you a drink. Then we can talk?" And I just got awkward as fuck. What the hell was wrong with me? I had moves.

"I'd like that, and I'd kill for a cigarette too." I didn't hesitate. I got the pack and pulled out one for her and lit it before passing it over. When her lips wrapped around the same tip I'd just touched with mine, all my blood fled south.

"Beer. Coming right up." I had to adjust myself to a little more comfortable position. She'd taken up residence on the sofa, right on the center cushion, so I dropped back onto the seat I'd had before. "Here you go."

"Thank you."

"Should I ask how it was?" That was a question you asked, right? "How your night went?"

She eyed me over the bottle as she raised it and then frowned a little before taking a drink. It wasn't until she lowered it that she said, "It was good. I like talking to Mickey."

Oh, do not fucking call him that. I bit that thought back before it could escape and tried to swallow it. The lump of it got stuck in my throat but I pressed on. "Good."

Her smile ticked a little higher. "Thank you for trying, Jasper, but you don't have to hurt yourself at the same time."

I frowned. "I'm not…"

"Biting your tongue so hard there's got to be blood in your mouth?" Her raised brows dared me to say otherwise.

"Fine, I don't like it. In fact, I fucking hate that you enjoy talking to *Mickey*." I half spat his name. "But I made you a promise and I'm going to stick to it."

When she settled her hand against my cheek, I went totally still. Her palm was chilly from holding the bottle. "Thank you. That means a great deal to me. I enjoy talking to Mickey because he never seems to judge a single word I say. Even when I talk about leaving."

My gut bottomed out. Rather than snap, I ground my teeth together and pulled back a bit to grab my phone. Even if I'd rather touch her and be touched by her, I needed to get my shit together. Leaving was a *bad* idea. We hadn't tracked the actual source of the threats yet.

We had some feelers out, and there were people who owed us, big time, who were looking.

"I saw pictures of you there, at his place. Pictures of you and the guys. When you were younger."

That didn't surprise me. Mickey—Oh fuck no, I was not giving him that consideration. *Doc* had always been something of a damn sap. "We knew him when we were younger. He grew up here in the neighborhood. Used to look out for some of the younger kids when they got into trouble."

"Did you get into trouble?" The innocence in that question ribboned around the amusement. She knew the answer, but at the same time, how could she possibly fathom the depth of it?

"More than once," I admitted. Turning on the sofa, I faced her. With my knee touching hers, I leaned on the back of the sofa and studied her. "Tell me about this conversation regarding leaving."

"He asked me if I still wanted to go," she said softly. "At one point, I asked him to help me escape."

The tension snapped through me, but her featherlight fingers on my thigh yanked me back toward her.

"And I'm telling you this, not to piss you off, but to clarify a couple of things. I'd asked him to help me. He kept telling me none of you would hurt me, but I still wanted to escape."

I waited.

"Now? Maybe not as much." That wasn't a full admission, but she frowned as if she were mulling her choice of words. "I don't know where I'd go, and being here has been safe enough. But…"

"But this wasn't your plan," I said softly. Kellan had been saying that all along. She didn't belong in our world. He was right—she didn't. But I wanted to make a place for her. Especially if she wanted to stay.

"No." She shook her head. "I have different options now, especially since I'm not a prisoner. But I might need to get a job…"

"You don't need to."

"I do. You guys have been taking care of me, but I have to plan for what's next, if I figure that out. Until then, I'll just…"

"You'll stay here. You'll have a place here, and we can help you figure it out." That hopefully didn't come out desperate, even if it felt a tad on the desperate side. "I don't want you to leave."

Emersyn lifted her gaze and locked on mine. I forgot what it was like to take a deep breath as she stared at me. It felt like she was reaching into my soul and examining it. Fuck, I hoped I was worthy.

"Why?" The quiet question ricocheted through me.

"Because I care," I confessed. It was about all I could tell her of the truth until we talked to Raptor. Granted, I'd broken nearly every other tenet where that was concerned, what would be one more? *The same difference between a friend who messed up for the right reasons and a raging asshole.* The little voice in the back of my head supplied the answer readily. "Because your safety and your happiness are important to me." To all of us, but I wasn't going to speak for them right now.

"I want to own you," I added quietly, and she blinked. For a split second, something akin to fear flashed in her eyes and her pupils swelled to the size of saucers. "Not like a possession," I quickly added and took her nerveless, limp hand in mine as she continued to stare at me. "And I'd kill anyone who tried to chain you up. But I do want you to just be mine. I don't…I don't want to share you with my brothers."

"Oh." She exhaled the single syllable on a shaky breath.

"Are you all right?" Concern swelled within me. Her hand was like ice. The words she'd snarled at us the other day when we'd gotten back from Liam's echoed quietly in the back of my mind. She'd been shackled and caged her whole life. "You can tell me," I promised her. "Whatever it is, I'll take care of it."

Another smile curled her lips. "Thank you for that. For wanting to make it better."

"Always." I frowned. Then with care, I reached up to push the hair back from her face. "Can I do anything now?"

"Give me a hug?" The request startled me, and I plucked the bottle out of her hands and then tugged her to me, right into my lap. Her arms threaded around me, and I wrapped mine around her. She was so damn tiny. There was almost nothing to her and I didn't want to hurt her by squeezing too tight, but at the same time, I never wanted to let go.

When she buried her face against my neck, the soft hush of her breathing tickled. I raised a hand to stroke her hair. I'd fucked up when I said I wanted to own her. Something about that messed with her. I filed that away for later. Right now, I needed to fix what I'd fucked up.

"I know I said I want you for myself," I murmured softly. "You confuse the hell out of me, Swan. You're beauty and elegance, but you're also fire and rage. In my mind, you're fragile…"

A soft laugh escaped her, but the sound could equally be a sob. "And the reality?"

"So much better, still fragile, but a strength that cannot be defined." I needed Vaughn's poetry or Rome's simple, cut to the heart of it observations. "You're nothing like I imagined, and at the same time, you're everything I imagined."

Emersyn pulled back slowly, and I forced my arms to loosen instead of keeping her softness pressed against me. "You know I can't be both, right?"

It was my turn to laugh. "Who says?"

"Well, logic."

"Fuck logic." I shrugged. "You're both to me, Swan. Beauty and power. Grace and strength. Flower and fire."

"Fowl and funny?" The tart response cracked me up. A

real laugh escaped me, and her eyes brightened. Whatever darkness I'd tempted out of hiding retreated.

"Fine, I'll leave the poetry to the experts."

I leaned away, but she swatted me lightly. "Don't do that. I thought it was lovely, but you said flower and you don't call me something floral like tulip or pansy or marigold."

"Because to me you are a swan. Elegant. Exceptional."

Another smile graced her lips. "I think you're pretty cool too."

I snorted.

"You know," she continued. "Despite your temper and anger issues, you take care of everyone. Even me. Even if I didn't see it until you built that studio for me. You're an amazing guy, Jasper. That's the guy I want to get to know."

I didn't really have a response to that. My anger had helped me survive for far too long. The rage…we needed it to keep us all going. But she didn't want my rage. I wasn't sure what I was without it.

At my silence, she sighed and then she leaned in and pressed the softest kiss to my cheek. Like the caress of her hand earlier, it burned through me, branding me.

"Thank you for trying," she murmured. "I think I'm going up now."

Two steps.

She made it two steps before my baser instincts overrode the brain stutter locking me up. I was on my feet and after her. When I touched her arm, I barely closed my fingers around it, and then she was tumbling into me. Capturing her face in my hands, I locked gazes with her before I sealed my mouth to hers. One brush of my tongue, and she opened to me, the sweetness of her a tease on my lips as I breathed her in.

Maybe I didn't have the poetry to communicate what I felt, but I could damn well show her.

FIRST BLOOD

JASPER

The walk from the fence to the warehouse Freddie had shown me took us almost ten minutes, even when we quickened the pace. Urgency thrummed in the air and beat against my skin in a staccato rhythm like razor bladed raindrops. Milo said nothing as he kept up with me while I weaved through the closed and derelict warehouses. Once upon a time, all of these warehouses had been used to keep cargo, sort it, and move it—some inland, some back out to sea, and still more into the city.

Now?

It was a lot like the rest of Braxton Harbor—crumbling and forgotten. Shoving the litany of thoughts cascading through me, I focused on where we were. The deeper we ventured, the eerier the warehouses looked. Some even took on an air of menace, doors open like gaping holes into a broken past.

Even for an abandoned area, the quiet was too much. I forced myself to blow out a breath before taking another.

"There," I said in a much softer voice than I'd intended. Then again, this whole place pressed in on us. There were other warehouses deeper into the city yet still along its perimeter. Places where the foundation had surrendered completely. "That's the one."

But here? Here, the battle had long since been lost. I didn't want to think why a place like this called to a kid like Freddie. Milo caught my arm before I could walk right through the door of the building, cracked open like someone had tried to close it and the latch simply hadn't caught.

I looked at Milo, and he nodded silently toward some debris on the ground. Abandoned tools. Crowbar. Metal rods.

Got it.

After tossing my cigarette into a puddle, I scooped up the crow bar. It was heavy as fuck. I flexed my grip as I rebalanced it, so I could swing it. Milo tested a couple of metal rods before he picked up one that was about the same length as the crowbar and had a huge screw bolted to the end.

One could never be too careful. We'd learned that lesson the hard way. Without a word, I cut through the small space ahead of Milo. His glare burned against my back. We always jockeyed for who took point. I wanted him to hang back because if there was trouble, let me get into it. He wanted me to shut up because I was too hotheaded—his words, not mine —and let him take the first crack.

On this, I doubted we'd ever agree.

I'd just have to keep being faster. The interior of the warehouse was dark. Oppressive. Almost hateful and haunted. I shook my head to clear the thoughts. The air was rank, populated by mold and mildew.

One hand on my shoulder, Milo stood like a silent sentinel as our eyes adjusted to the dark. Bit by bit, shapes began to distinguish themselves. Shipping containers. My brain supplied the source of that funky smell as metal rust.

I started forward, but Milo tightened his grip and I stopped as he tugged me back. He tapped my ear, and I cut a look to him. In the shadows, I could barely make him out, but he had a finger to his lips, then he moved the same finger to his ear.

Listen.

I was trying too hard to see, so I closed my eyes and focused on what I could hear.

Scuffling and scratching. Rats probably.

Slow drip. The distance between the plops was probably a roof leak, because it had rained overnight.

Creaking of boards. The wind hitting the building?

Crying. Almost inaudible.

Freddie.

Now that I'd heard it, the sound scraped against my senses. It was coming from the right. Eyes open again, I found the dark less ominous and just harder to see in, but I could make out enough to navigate.

This time when I moved, Milo tapped my shoulder and stuck with me. I didn't worry about what was behind us because he'd warn me while I made sure we got where we were going. Back-to-back, we weaved a haphazard path through the dilapidated building and its abandoned shipping containers.

The jagged sound of crying grew louder. The hammer of my heart thrumming in my ears threatened to drown out the sound, but we needed to find the person sobbing so brokenly.

After what seemed like an eternity, the sobbing was right next to us. We moved along the side of the shipping container when the first end we'd reached was closed and smooth, no doors. On the opposite end, we found it was cracked open like the door had been.

More, there was some kind of light in there. It burned my eyes so adjusted to the dark. Behind me, Milo had begun typing something on his phone. I dug my hand into the pocket and looked for the button on the side to turn it off. I didn't want mine to ding.

Done, Milo shoved his away, and when I glanced back at him, he nodded. The crying shredded me. It was too close to how my mother would sob after one of Dad's beatings. How she would try to stifle the sound, smothering it, even if I was right there trying to hug it better.

My stomach rolled, and the sound of my father's fists raining down blows as she tried to cover her face with her hands and arms flooded through me. Not worried about the quiet anymore, I raced forward.

We had to get in there and save...

The metal of the door screamed as I yanked it open. The light inside came from a couple of portable lanterns. Their dim light was still too bright against my dilated eyes, and tears gathered as I squinted to find Freddie curled in the corner with some filthy bedding.

He was naked, and he had his arms around his knees, rocking himself. The sobs grew louder and his whole body flinched as I rushed toward him. I skidded to a halt and stared around the empty space.

Only it wasn't empty.

Freddie wasn't alone.

A man lounged, half dressed on another pile of blankets.

Hate swelled within me as the man opened his eyes. "Shut your fucking crying," he muttered. "You know you wanted it, and I told you I'd bring you back home."

Then it registered I was standing there as the guy's unfocused eyes locked on me.

Freddie let out another sob that he choked off. The man growled and lunged toward me, and I swung the crow bar. It connected with a meaty *thunk*, and a spray of warm blood hit my face. The man howled, more in pain than fury, and I rammed into him and swung the crow bar again. Bone crunched and more blood sprayed.

I wasn't alone. Milo was there, cutting off the guy's escape, and he crashed his pipe to the guy's kneecap. The sound was vicious, visceral, and so fucking satisfying.

He needed to hurt. Like he'd hurt her. Hurt Freddie. My father's eyes blazed fury up at me as the guy roared, and he took a swipe at Milo with a fist. The blow missed when Milo danced back out of reach, and I swung the crow bar again. This time, I got his wrist and shoulder.

The man went down. My next blow missed because he managed to drive his shoulder into my chest. I couldn't breathe as all the air whooshed out of me. The move slammed me into the side of the shipping container. Something cut through the shirt and bit into my skin.

One minute, he had me against the wall, and the next, he was howling on the ground. Vaughn let out a damn near preternatural growl of sound that made my skin shiver. He'd broken the guy's arm, and it was twisted at an unnatural angle.

I felt my brothers more than saw them.

Liam. Rome. Kellan. Vaughn. Milo. We were all here, and the predator had become the prey.

No one said a word as Kellan slammed his foot into the guy's face. Liam went next, driving his foot into the guy's groin. Rome landed on him like a savage, kicking his back and shoulders repeatedly.

Milo and I went next. We skipped the weapons. Fists and feet took longer to inflict the damage we wanted.

I didn't know who he was or why he'd done it, but he'd hurt one of us.

We'd extract that cost in blood. Freddie's sobs quieted as the man's sounds died away. Soon, the only thing left were our blows, and even those stopped.

Bathed in blood, we'd extracted vengeance without remorse.

CHAPTER 23

EMERSYN

I literally couldn't get enough of the way his mouth felt against mine. Jasper didn't just kiss, he breathed me in as his lips took control. Anticipation gave way to curiosity, and that still left me wanting. I thrust my fingers into his hair as his arms banded around me. I'd left the floor, but I let him have my weight.

The slam of my heart against my ribs was almost painful in its intensity. The tickle of his beard on my face as he pushed past my tongue with his own, only to suck my tongue back into his mouth, made for competing sensations.

More.

I needed more.

"You can have it, Swan," he promised in between drugging presses of his lips. I could barely open my eyes as I swayed, then he dragged my head to the side as he nipped my lips, then my jaw. "You can have everything."

A door opened and then we were in the dark, but he hit a

switch on the wall, and suddenly, stars seemed to illuminate everywhere. It was enough to chase through the haze of passion as he sucked and bit a path along my throat. I tilted my head back to stare up at the lights.

Faerie lights.

They were all over the walls in crisscrossing patterns, like a network of stars surrounding us, and I gasped as he pulled at the collar of my shirt and laved his tongue over my collarbone.

"You taste so good, Swan," he whispered, his voice rough and hoarse. With calloused fingers, he traced my jaw and then pressed his thumb to my lips. I opened my mouth and sucked it against my tongue. His head snapped up to lock onto me. The slate gray of his eyes was lost to the dance of low light over his face, but their intensity burned into my soul and I swore my pussy clenched.

When he sat down abruptly, I folded my knees to straddle his lap and then, with a hand in my hair, he pulled my face to his. It forced me to release his thumb, but the taste of him lingered.

Long, soul searing kisses alternated with biting sucks and hungry swipes of tongue. "I want you," he whispered in between the kisses, and I rolled my hips against him, grinding against the feel of his erection. Reality tried to tiptoe back in, but his hands were under my shirt and cupping my breasts through the bra. The rough thumbs teased the hard points of my nipples.

We were rapidly tumbling out of control. My heart thundered in my ears, and my breath came in panting gasps. An ache unfolded within me that I didn't have words for. Vaughn had awakened it, and Jasper seemed to do the same. That need was like a black hole inside of me, devouring every touch, kiss, and soft word.

"Be mine," Jasper demanded in a harsh voice as he shoved

my shirt upward. Momentarily blinded, my arms trapped as he jerked the shirt back, it forced my chest forward and blind panic erupted, even as he sucked one desperate nipple against his teeth. Even through the bra, the heat of his mouth seared me. A rush of warmth soaked my panties, and I clamped my knees tighter to him as he bent me half backwards.

A scream clawed its way up my throat, and I bucked under his touch, wanting him desperately and needing to be free in the same breath. Shudders rolled through me as he bit down on the nipple, just a hint of teeth, and pleasure blacked my vision.

My shirt was gone and I was cuddled against his chest, sobbing for air, as Jasper rubbed my back. "Hey," he said as I pulled back and looked at him. "You back with me?"

The worry and fear in his expression sobered me. Concern rolled off him in waves, the energy snapping at the air. I swore he was furious. Yet none of that fury was present as he kept rubbing my bare back. My pulse still raced, and I blinked at the wetness in my eyes. I wiped the dampness away with trembling fingers.

"What happened?"

"You freaked out a little," he offered with the barest hint of a smile. "I know it's been a while for me, Swan, but it felt like you were enjoying it." The sheepish note covered for something much deeper. The words crackled with everything he wasn't saying, and while I might not have a Jasper decoder, it wasn't hard to decipher.

"The shirt," I said after a moment, piecing it together. The hot and cold flush racing through me prickled my skin. "You were trying to kiss my breasts and you trapped my arms and I couldn't see..." Dark memories I refused to examine surfaced to bite at me like swarm of angry mosquitos, each one sucking just a little more of the blood out of me.

"Won't happen again, Swan," he swore. "I just got eager to play with these beautiful tits of yours."

A laugh slipped out of me as I wiped at the tears on my cheeks. I still couldn't quite catch my breath.

"Who scared you?" The hairs on my arms stood at the very real menace in his tone. "That fucker Eric?"

"He's gone," I reminded him and pressed a hand to his chest. The wall of muscle beneath his shirt tensed at the contact.

"Was it him or someone else?" Undeterred by my answer, he tilted his head to study me. "Just give me a name, sweet girl."

Uneven laughter escaped me at his attempted coax that came out as a growl. He curved his hand against my ribs, leaving tingles to ripple over my flesh, creating goosebumps in their wake, even as my nipples tightened again. When I shuddered this time, it had nothing to do with fear or the past. I was very much present.

Despite my reaction and the way he stroked his fingers against my ribs, almost lazily petting me, he said nothing. The contact both soothed and stimulated in equal measure. I studied his lips, the firm shape of them, how they were compressed as if he held back the words by sheer force of will.

We were still in the darkened room, surrounded by the faerie lights. The taste of his lips was still on my tongue as I put myself back together. We'd been on a promising path…

"When are you going to trust me?" The question raked through me, slicing through the warmth ribboning around me and leaving us in the shredded remains. Though I sat on his lap and his erection was very much still in evidence, anger threaded through the sensuality.

"It's not about trust," I said, uncertain of how to even put this in words beyond adding, "I don't want to talk about it."

He frowned, the lines deepening across his forehead. "Swan, I can't fix it if I don't know what it is."

"Maybe it doesn't need to be fixed." Maybe I had learned a long time ago to leave it alone.

With care, he cupped my face, and the tilt forced me to meet his gaze. I licked my lips and blinked slowly. "Swan, what am I going to do with you?"

"Well, I was going for fuck me, but I have a feeling you're pulling away." The words didn't shock him into action. If anything, he just swiped at the tear tracks with his thumbs. Taking a chance, I pushed forward and brushed my lips to his.

The barest hint of salt flavored the kiss as he opened his mouth, but he wasn't kissing me back. I went for nibbling bites as he had, then traced the outline of his lips with my tongue. His groan vibrated through me.

"Do you need to get off, Swan?" The mood burst with the roughness in his voice. "Is that what it will take to get you to trust me?"

Real hurt echoed in that last question. The sting of it was like alcohol on open scrapes. Suddenly, he dropped his hands to my thighs as he stood and lifted me with him. I landed on the bed abruptly, bouncing as he let out a growl of sound that bounced right to my pussy.

With deliberate motion, he yanked the shoes off my feet, then peeled down the socks. His temper licked along my skin as he hooked his fingers into my dance pants, snagging the panties at the same time, and then he dragged them off me with such painful slowness, I wanted to scream.

Until it registered. "Jasper…"

He stilled.

"Swan?"

"What would you do if I said 'no' right now?" I had to know.

Chin down, he let out a long breath, and his fingers twitched against me where he gripped them against my thighs. I'd stopped him halfway. "I'd stop."

I closed my eyes. No hesitation. Just control. Even with the quiet fury punctuating the words. That anger wasn't at me. It might be there, filling the room with us, lashing out like static tendrils shocking when contact was made, but he wasn't angry with me.

"Do you need me to stop?"

For so long, I'd had no choices. Only the illusions of them. For so long. "Please don't."

"Thank fuck." He breathed the words with such vehemence, I laughed, and he tossed my pants behind him as he straightened. The miniature lights in the room blessed him with a corona, and I swore an almost crooked halo resting atop horns formed by his hair where I'd been pulling on it. "You're beautiful."

I pulled my knees up, then spread them, not hiding from his view as I unsnapped my bra and then tugged it off. When I tossed it to him, he caught it and lifted it to his nose. He sniffed it slowly, and a shiver trembled inside of me like he was running his nose against my breasts.

When he started forward, I slowed him with a foot pressed to his chest. Not that it had much affect as he ran his hand over my calf and then cupped my ankle in his warm palm. With absolute care, he pushed my foot up onto his shoulder and then began nuzzling kisses along my leg as he climbed the bed.

A moan escaped me as my toes curled. "I wanted to see you." Pushing those words out took some effort, but Jasper didn't halt, even as he made it to the inside of my thigh. The tickling softness teased my senses, while all the air backed up in my lungs when his breath teased over my cunt.

"So fucking sexy," he murmured, then he buried his whole

face against my pussy and I arched right off the bed. The overwhelming stimulation of his beard against my inner thighs and along my slit coupled with his mouth kissing me with so much tongue, he damn near seemed to be fucking me, had my ass clenching.

All of the earlier need roared to life, and I was going up in flames. He didn't hold me down, just rode upward with me, locking my legs around him and keeping his face buried against me. The pressure of his nose against my clit wasn't quite enough, and with far too gentle fingers, he cupped my ass and then vibrated his tongue against my channel.

The fucking sound he released pushed me right up to the edge, and I dug my fingers into the sheets as he began to lick, suck, bite, and stroke in earnest. Too much, the pressure was too much. The tongue was too much. The heated brushes of his beard as he delved deeper threatened to rip away my sanity.

"Come," he ordered, and fuck, I wanted to, but it was too much. A scream built in my throat as I flexed my thighs, and Jasper growled. The deep, chest thrumming sound slammed into my pussy, and I lost it. I came, screaming. Not once did he stop licking and sucking like I was his favorite fucking treat, and he could curl his tongue in such a way that I damn near came again from the pressure of it

Sweat decorated my skin as he eased his mouth up, and I fought the shaking in my thighs to get them to let him go. The intensity of his gaze seared up my body.

"Swan..." Sex drenched his voice. "Tell me who hurt you."

I groaned at the intrusion of that reality. I didn't want to talk about that.

"You need more," he soothed as he spread my legs wide and pushed me up higher on the bed. "Brace yourself, sweet girl, and when you've had enough, you let me know..."

Enough of...?

He went back to eating me out like I was the only thing he wanted on his tongue, and the tremors in my system built again. This time, he added his fingers to the teasing thrusts, curling them just so with each deep push, and he sucked my clit until I swore I came so hard, I squirted a little. It was something I'd only ever heard of happening, not experienced. He laughed.

His soaked beard glistened in the half-light. Fuck me. I was floating. First Vaughn, and now Jasper… I'd had no clue it could be so fucking good. I was a boneless mass on his bed, and Jasper still had on all his clothes.

Where was the justice in that? No sooner would I complain then he'd dive back into my pussy like he planned to live there, and my brain would white out all the noise until we were all that existed in his room of stars. It wasn't until I ached almost as badly as I wanted his touch that he let up. He pressed a damp kiss to my lips, searing in its intensity, then eased back with another sweet peck before he pushed off the bed and went to the bathroom.

The light came on in there, and the brightness against my closed eyelids teased me. I swore I was both hot and chilly. Sweat dotted my skin, my heart raced, and I had to be flushed from head to toe.

Jasper's tongue was a dangerous weapon, and the anger fueling him had been like a drug, highly addictive and devastating to my system. Not once, no matter how many times he asked and I refused to answer, did he direct that rage at me.

The sound of the water running pierced the haze of pleasure. I told my limbs I wanted to roll over, and they didn't even have the energy to flip me off. Lying there, I suffered not knowing if he was changing his clothes or, even better, getting naked.

Eventually, he returned to the bed with a tease of his fingers along my thigh. "You still with me Swan?"

I managed to open my eyes, just barely, and I smiled up at him. He really was a good-looking man, and his eyes... "I love your eyes," I admitted, maybe a little too drunk on the orgasms he'd pulled from me one right after the other.

"Really?" I swore there was a smile in his voice. "Good to know."

He kissed me again, then helped me sit up enough to drink some water. While I sipped that, he ran a chilly cloth against my swollen cunt, and I closed my eyes and blotted out any discomfort. I'd had far too much pleasure to let that bother me.

Instead, I focused on the simple way he'd taken care of me. It wasn't until he rose and vanished back into the bathroom that I forced my eyes open. I'd forgotten to look. The lights went out in the bathroom, plunging the room back to semidarkness, and he crossed the room to the bed.

Shirtless.

Pantsless.

Sliding in on the other side, he gathered me to him, and I sighed at the contact of his skin on mine, but instead of kissing me, he rolled me onto my side and spooned against my back. The brush of fabric against my ass betrayed that he hadn't gotten completely naked.

Pressing a kiss to my shoulder, he said, "Go to sleep, Swan."

"But I didn't get to see you." The distinct warbling note of whining in my voice made me cringe.

"When you trust me," he said, smiling. "Now sleep." How the hell was I supposed to do that? Even boneless and spent, I wanted...I wanted to do something for him, but he had me tucked tight against him and I wasn't even sure I could move anyway.

The flash of his phone came on, and I squinted up as he typed something, then chuckled as it made the whoosh sound when it sent. After, he turned off the screen and set the phone down.

"What was that?"

He nuzzled a kiss along my nape and gave my waist a gentle squeeze. "I told Vaughn to enjoy your bed, you were sleeping in here tonight."

The genuine pleasure in his voice had me shaking my head. I should get up and go to my own bed. Sleeping in Jasper's, just like when I'd slept in Vaughn's, it set a bad precedent. But the truth was, I didn't want to leave his bed. I didn't...

The next time my eyes fluttered open, I shuddered through the first blush of confusion in not knowing where I was. The shift of movement in the bed had me half ready to bolt lest *he* wake up, and then my bed partner rumbled a sound and pressed a kiss to my shoulder. The tickle of his beard would have betrayed him if the half growl in his voice hadn't already given him away.

"Go back to sleep," he ordered. Even mostly asleep, he was a bossy ass. A smile pulled at my lips as he rubbed his face against my shoulder. The brush of his beard and the combination of soft and bristly reminded me of the way cats like to rub against people.

Marking them.

My nose wrinkled.

With Jasper, he might be doing it as much for that reason as for just being cute in his sleep. I tried to listen to him and go back to sleep, but the rush of adrenalin when I woke up somewhere unknown made that impossible. I listened to him breathing. The brush of his breath against my shoulder soothed, as did the weight of his arms around me.

He'd cuddled right up to me. I didn't think he'd moved away when he was asleep, that had probably been me. I looked up at the lights, letting my eyes lose focus as I tried to make my mind relax.

But random images kept dancing behind my eyelids each time I closed them. Time seemed to slow, or maybe I was just imagining it. Jasper slept so still and warm. I rolled over carefully, and he eased onto his back. The arm he'd had around me went up over his head, and I raised up on one arm so I could study him in the dark.

Asleep, his face seemed...not peaceful. No, but it did seem less tense, but no less guarded. Did his demons not leave him alone, even when he slept? The light was too dim to make out the tattoos on his chest, but one looked like a vine wrapped around a letter, or maybe it was a ladder? I leaned in a little closer to peer at it. Not that it helped.

And ogling him in the dark while he slept wasn't exactly the best behavior. The ache in my pussy from him making me orgasm so many times reminded me that I'd gotten off multiple times to his talented tongue, his gorgeous lips, and that tongue... Fuck me, his tongue.

It had seriously fucked me. I closed my eyes and pressed a kiss to where the vine was. His breathing didn't change and he barely moved, so I nuzzled a path toward his belly, enjoying the way his muscles moved beneath my lips.

He wasn't huge or jacked, but he was definitely cut. Strength marked the lines of his body, and the scent of him was all warm and clean. Had he showered before he slept? The minutes between that last orgasm and when he'd cuddled up to me were hazy at best.

Kissing along his abdomen, I paused at the top of what looked like a pair of black boxer briefs. I pulled the blanket back some as I sat up. I wanted to... Even as I reached out a hand to explore, I pulled it back.

"Something wrong?" His voice startled me, and I jerked my gaze up to find him watching me.

"You didn't want me to see you."

"Didn't say that," he admonished and yawned. "Said you should sleep 'cause you were tired, and I wasn't going to push for more when you need time to learn to trust me."

"So I have to trust you to see your cock?" I tilted my head.

"Well, I have to keep my temper under control so you'll date me." The tone said deny it if I dared.

I pursed my lips. "Those things don't seem equal, and you—"

He sat up abruptly and touched a single finger to my lips. "Don't you dare."

Surprise filtered through me. "Don't I dare what?"

"Don't you dare say it's not fair that you got off and I didn't. This isn't about tit for tat or quid pro quo." The remonstration in his voice silenced any argument I might have made. "I wanted to chase away whatever scared you. You wouldn't tell me who…" He brushed the hair away from my face. "So I did the only thing I could think of, Swan—I made sure the only thing crowding into that beautiful mind was me and the only thing you could feel was me…"

Tears pricked my eyes.

"Now," he said, holding out a hand, "come back and sleep with me? I like feeling you against me. Even if you move that ass so temptingly."

That made me laugh. "How does one move temptingly while asleep?"

"You breathe in and out, that's all the temptation I need." Okay, I was really glad for the darkness when my face heated, because the absolute sincerity in his growling tone floored me. It took him very little coaxing to pull me up against him again.

While it took me longer to go to sleep than I cared to admit, his breathing never evened. He was as awake as I was, but he let me choose quiet or words. He waited for me to sleep, and the idea that he kept watch finally let me relax enough to drift off.

The next morning, I showered in his bathroom, and he grabbed me clean clothes from my room. His smirk when he carried them into the bathroom and watched me shower while he sat on the vanity spoke volumes.

"What did you do?"

"Nothing," he said. "Didn't have to. Vaughn was already up and heading downstairs."

I groaned and ducked my face under the water. At some point, I needed to work through the tangled knots of all these relationships, but right now, I just wanted coffee.

Maybe pancakes.

A whole stack of pancakes.

Jasper seemed to take great pleasure in watching me get ready. Thankfully, I wasn't body shy, or the way his gaze seemed to devour me might have put me on edge. As it was, there was something proprietorial in his eyes that niggled at me, but the rest was just…open admiration.

Downstairs, we found *everyone* present in the kitchen. Well, everyone except Doc. They all turned to look at us as I came in with Jasper right behind me. Kellan was already at the stove, and he nodded to the coffeemaker. Vaughn leaned against the counter next to the coffee.

Wordlessly, he pulled down a mug for me. I met his gaze, and when I offered a small smile, he answered with one of his own swiftly enough. Rising on my tiptoes, I kissed the corner of his mouth and murmured, "Sorry you waited for me." I tried to keep it low, because frankly, not a discussion for everyone.

Vaughn just grinned and caught my chin in his fingers and gave me a real kiss. It was sweet, searing, and with enough heat to make me feel like I'd just stepped out of the steamy shower all over again. "It's fine," he murmured against my lips before letting me go.

Aware of all the speculative looks, I poured myself a mug and made my way over to the table. Freddie sat on one side of it alone, so I sat next to him.

Rome and Liam were opposite me, and Rome bumped my foot with his before hooking his ankle around mine. I grinned before a cough-snort from Liam made me glance over to where Vaughn and Jasper glared at each other. If one could have a silent war, it raged right there.

Kellan walked right between them with a platter of pancakes. He set the whole mess down in the center, and I swore my eyes had to grow. My stomach growled, and Freddie grunted when Kellan told him to eat.

It was the first time I'd seen Freddie out of his room since we'd gone to the clinic. He really did look like hell. "Look," Kellan said. "I know you don't like it, but everyone has work today. So it's go with Liam or I'll take you to the clinic with Sparrow."

I blinked. "I'm going to the clinic?" Everyone hushed and glanced at me.

"You don't have to," Rome supplied. "But I won't be back for a few hours and everyone has work."

"No one wants you here alone with the fuckup," Freddie said with a grunt.

I frowned, then speared two of the pancakes with a fork and set them on my plate. With care, I cut them up and added a bit of butter and a little syrup, then traded my plate for Freddie's empty one. "Eat," I told him. "We can hang out here today. Maybe finish the book we started, or you can pick out some horror movies to watch."

More silence rippled through the room, and Kestrel grimaced. "Sparrow, that might not be the best idea. Freddie's still…"

"He'll be fine," I told him and then glanced around the room. "We'll be fine together. It's hardly the first time I've been around someone coming down. He's clean, he's just in the fight to stay clean. That means he needs distractions and not stress."

As much as I liked the clinic, Freddie had not. Ignoring them, I grabbed a few more pancakes. Freddie stared at me in disbelief, and then I pointed at his plate. "Eat, wasting pancakes is a crime."

The desire to carb up was intense. The silence weighed in as I bathed my own stack in syrup. Not willing to engage on this topic, I just glanced at Liam. "When did you want to start those boxing lessons?"

The temperature in the whole room shifted, as did the tension.

"What boxing lessons?" Jasper asked as he and Vaughn ceased glaring at each other and focused on Liam. Kestrel frowned, and Rome slanted a look at his brother. All at once, the four of them hit Liam with a dozen questions. The man at the center of it just shot me an amused look.

And if I read that right, one that promised to get even.

I could live with it. Freddie was off the hook and eating his pancakes, which meant I got to eat mine.

THROUGH PAIN

EMERSYN

The show had four days between performances. Technically, ten days, but I'd lied to everyone when I booked my flight. The show was traveling to the next city, but there would be a lot of technical setup required at the new venue that would keep the show shuttered until it was complete. A lot of the performers were taking advantage of the extra time to take breaks, visit family, or whatever. I'd told them, and Eric specifically, I was going home for the week. Home thought I was still performing.

I had ten days to travel, take care of things, and come back. Hopefully with no one the wiser. The whole flight, I gnawed on a hangnail. My manicure was a mess, but it was the least of my problems. I looked like every other teenager on the flight, and I'd pretty much kept to myself.

Since I left most of my gear with the show to transport, I'd only brought a backpack. Lainey was waiting for me beyond arrivals, and I almost tripped, the relief hit me so hard. Without a word, she opened her arms, and I hugged her tightly.

"Thank you for coming," I managed around the tears in my throat.

"Of course I came," she countered, pulling back to stare at me. "You look like shit."

I laughed and shoved my sunglasses on before she could see the tears in the corners of my eyes. "I love you too."

"I know," Lainey murmured and brushed hair away from my face. The almost faint tut-tut underscoring her words made her seem like someone older than me and not the same age. "I booked us a great place. It's private, and I paid well to make sure no one bothers us."

Relief scoured through me at the news. More at the fact Lainey didn't ask me any questions, she just led the way out of the airport to the short-term lot, where she'd parked in a no parking zone. I eyed the convertible, then her, and she gave me a careless shrug.

"You wanted to get out of here fast."

Another watery laugh escaped me as I dropped my bag into the backseat and climbed in. With the hat on, it would help protect my hair. "You know where the clinic is?"

"Yep. What time is your appointment?" She barely waited for me to buckle in before she accelerated out of the spot and we were zipping through the lot to the access road.

I checked my watch. "Two hours?" I was cutting it close.

"No problem," Lainey told me, all confidence. "We'll make it."

"Have I said thank you yet?" As much as I was chewing on that hangnail again, I couldn't emphasize enough what a lifesaver she was. I didn't know what impulse drove me to call her three days ago, but when the tests turned pink one right after another, I'd thrown up—again—then her name popped into my head and I had my phone in my hand, calling her before I'd even registered choosing her contact.

"About ten times too many," Lainey told me. The wind racing at us as she accelerated chased away the heat and the humidity.

She had no reason to even answer my call, much less make such hasty arrangements when I'd burst out with the *"I need help."*

"Where does your grandfather think you are?"

"Visiting Andrea, she'll cover for me," she said with an easy smile. "Andrea's stuck at the apartment this month in New York. She's supposed to be going to her dad's, but that douche canoe canceled at the last minute and Mom already had an appointment in Paris. So Andrea basically told them she'd be fine here and that I'd come and keep her company. Which I will, after we're done."

"Oh shit," I swore. "Who is going to look after her if you're…"

"She'll be fine. The current governess is actually pretty biddable, and both the housekeeper and the cook accept bribes. So I paid them well, Andrea will be spoiled and actually get to do whatever she wants for a week, but if she rats me out, I'll make sure they send her to boarding school in Switzerland."

I didn't pretend to understand her family politics, but one thing about Lainey I knew for damn certain… "You would never."

"I know," she said with a grin. "But Andrea needs both stick and carrot when it comes to cooperation at this age, and it's more so she doesn't call Adam if she gets bored. 'Cause then that prick will want to know why I'm not there and he'll try to track me down. I don't need that grief."

Fair. "Thank you for going to so much trouble for me."

"Girl, you'd do the same for me."

In a heartbeat, but I wasn't sure I had access to the resources to do it as easily as she did. Either way, I was fucking grateful.

When she said we'd make it, I didn't think she'd meant she'd break every speed law leaving the city as she got on I-95 North. Her car zipped in and out of traffic smoothly, like we were in a race rather than just trying to get to an appointment.

Despite not having eaten or drunk anything for about twelve hours, I wasn't hungry or thirsty. I couldn't have anything anyway. When we pulled into the lot at the clinic and parked, she grinned at me. "See, thirty minutes to spare."

"You're crazy."

"You fall, willingly, from great heights with just a bit of silk between you and going splat, and you call me crazy?" She raised her sunglasses and gave me a look.

Fair. I looked past her to the clinic, and everything in me clenched. She pressed a button, and the top rose on the car, sealing us inside with an element of privacy.

"Here," she murmured, handing me a wallet. "My credit cards, and the ID you needed."

"You had two days?"

"I know people," she said. "And you need to make sure there's no paper trail."

I couldn't swallow around the dryness in my throat. Unbuckling the seat belt, I reached over and hugged her. She returned it fiercely. If my uncle found out... No, I couldn't risk it. He might actually kill me. Thanks to Lainey, I didn't have to.

"I'm not asking, but if you ever feel like you can tell me, I'll happily tell Adam and his dick friends it happened to me."

I laughed as I pulled back. "You'd talk to Adam for me."

With much drama, Lainey rolled her eyes. "Damn straight. We've managed this friendship thing without any parental support or approval. You're my badass entertainer friend who doesn't give two shits about bloodlines or protocol."

If she only knew... "And you're just my best friend." Maybe my only real one, and even she didn't know me. "I don't...I don't know how long this will take."

"Doesn't matter, I'll be here. I'll take you back to our exclusive spa after, and we'll have all the chocolate, wine, and bad reality shows you want. Or we can have complete quiet. Whatever you need."

I sucked in a noisy breath and then let it out. The tension riddled my muscles and my stomach rebelled, but I had nothing to vomit and I ignored it. I'd danced through pain and agony before.

Pain didn't scare me.

I could do this.

I needed to do this.

"Ready?"

At her quiet question, I nodded and we let ourselves out of the car. My backpack, ID, and other items stayed in the vehicle. We walked into the clinic together, and I signed in. They took the ID and payment information without batting an eyelash. It was one of the few states that didn't require any parental consent or notification. Lainey sat next to me as I filled out the paperwork, and I added her name as the person taking me home after.

The whole appointment and process took about ninety minutes from start to finish. After a birth control shot, I left with a sheet of instructions and a lot of cramps. Bless Lainey, the only thing she asked me after we got into the car was, "What do you need?"

I couldn't tell her the truth, so I went with the next best thing. "I need carbs. A lot of them."

CHAPTER 24

EMERSYN

The wind blowing today was practically frigid, and I rather hoped Freddie didn't freeze to death up here. A part of me was uneasy about leaving the door unlocked, but the guys did it all the time. There were only a couple of rats out in the warehouse when we left the clubhouse. The rats were also nowhere near that door.

Freddie grumbled as I headed for the ladder. He hadn't wanted to come out. If anything, he'd seemed content to just stare sullenly at the television no matter what was on. The reality show marathon hadn't even given him an inkling of his smile back. Maybe a change of scenery would help, but I wanted it to be something with no other people in case it was the people at the clinic that got to him.

The only reason he came with was because I said I wanted a smoke and I didn't want to go up on the roof alone. First, that involved finding cigarettes, but I let myself into

Jasper's room and stole a pack from his dresser. Then I texted him to let him know I'd stolen them.

His response had been swift and teasing.

Jasper: *It's hardly stealing if you're telling me. Let me know if you want a different brand.*

Me: *Your brand is fine.*

Jasper: *So you like me. Good to know.*

I rolled my eyes, I couldn't help it, and at the same time...

Me: *Pretty sure we cleared that up last night.*

Jasper: *Pretty sure we asked a whole new set of questions. Shall we try to answer those tonight?*

A shiver went straight through me at the flirting. It was weird and refreshing. I wasn't entirely sure how to handle it, but at the same time, I wanted more.

Me: *We'll have to see what happens tonight.*

There were no other messages, so I'd stored the phone in my pocket and *borrowed* one of his jackets as well to wear over Kestrel's hoodie. We really needed to get me more clothes of my own. I had hesitated in the hall. I really needed to reach out to some people too.

Caution held me back.

For now.

Freddie climbed up behind me as I went up the ladder. I had to fight the urge to glance back at him. I flipped open the roof door easily enough and scooted right through it. Grunting, Freddie pulled himself after. We were both squinting in the sunlight, and fuck me, it was *cold*.

He shot me a look. "We could go back down into the warehouse for a smoke. Hell, you can smoke in the clubhouse, no one will care."

"I don't want to smoke with the rats." Not remotely a lie. "And I need some air." Also, not a lie. As much as I hated to give him the out, I said, "But you don't have to look after me. I know where the chairs are."

His snort spoke volumes. We made our way across the roof to the bolted down chairs—a feature I truly appreciated now—and I curled up into one. It offered some shelter from the wind, but the cold was like a burn against my face.

It took three tries to get the cigarette lit. Freddie took the one I offered him and lit it up, then flipped open the top of the table and grinned at my surprise. There was a stove in there. It didn't take much for him to fire it up.

"Thank fuck," he said, talking around the cigarette while he adjusted some knobs. "If no one refilled the propane, we'd be shit out of luck."

In almost no time though, heat wafted up, and while the breeze cut through it, there was also warmth on my face. I stared at Freddie, mouth agape. "Why the hell didn't we light it the other night?"

"'Cause they wanted an excuse to snuggle you," he said. "Besides, it wasn't this cold. We only put it up here last year I think, when Jasper took to sulking on the roof."

I frowned at that description. The question of why he was sulking died unspoken on my lips. Probing Freddie for information on the others seemed…wrong. "Well, I'm glad they did."

The hand he used to hold his cigarette shook. Not from the cold, or at least I didn't think so.

"What do you need?" I'd wrestled with the question all morning. I wanted to help. While I might not be able to do much, Freddie needed to know someone was in his corner.

"Why do you care?" The question probably hurt more than it should. "You know what, Boo-Boo, just ignore me. I'm a fucking dick like this. I could almost be Jasper." A ghost of a smile touched his lips.

"Almost," I said. "But you look more like you hate yourself than the rest of the world."

He wrinkled his nose. "Maybe. I hate a lot of things right

now. As for what I need? I could do an eight-ball, that'd be sweet. But I figure you aren't going to go for that, and the guys would kill me."

"No, they wouldn't."

He shrugged. "Fine, but they'd want to. Anyway, what about a blowjob? Yeah, I think I need a blowjob." There was just the barest glimmer of meanness in the humor flashing in his eyes. He didn't even give me a chance to respond before he said, "Fuck a goddamn motherfucking duck in the rubber hole with a rubber dick, dammit."

Okay, my mouth fell open that time, then Freddie slapped himself in the head and the crack of sound made me wince.

"Boo-Boo, don't ask me questions right now. I'm begging you. I think you're the best fucking thing I've ever seen, and I already look like a pathetic jackass loser who can't do shit right except maybe make you laugh. I'd like to hold on to that illusion. At least for a little while."

Instead of responding right away, I took another drag and considered how to address it. "Okay, but I'm running out of things to talk about. If I can't ask questions, you're going to get bored and leave me."

It was a gamble.

"Fuck," Freddie said, his cigarette already finished, and when he reached for the pack on my lap, I passed it over to him. "Fine. You're right and you are not boring, Boo-Boo. Not even a little bit. Did I mention that I'm proud you figured out where Jasper hides his cigarettes?"

"They were hidden? Not a very good hiding spot if they're in the top of the drawer."

Freddie paused, just before he lit the lighter, and stared at me. "Huh."

"What? Sorry, that was another question."

"Oh, what hell," Freddie grumbled and flung himself back in the chair. Cigarette lit, he exhaled a long stream of smoke.

"Just, he used to hide them somewhere else. So if they're in the drawer, means he's probably hoarding something else."

"Do I want to know why he hoarded cigarettes?"

"Yeah, Raptor fucking hates them. Gives Jasper shit about it all the time. Or he used to, you know, before…"

"Before?"

Freddie gave me a wan but real grin, and I rolled my eyes. "Fine, no questions. Tell me about the hoarding."

"Oh, that I can do." He warmed a bit. "I know where they all stash their stuff. It's kind of fun to be the runt sometimes."

"You're not the runt."

"Ha," he said with a bark of laughter that at least verged on being real. "I am. I don't have trade skills like Kel, I'm not a strategist or a moneymaker like Jas and Liam, definitely not an artist like Rome or Vaughn. Mostly, I'm the loser everyone takes pity on. Or sometimes, I'm the funny guy."

"Well, does this pity party have room for one more at the table, because if we want to compare being runts, I'm way smaller than you."

He stared at me a beat, then snickered. "You have a point."

"Thank you. Besides, pity parties by yourself are boring. Who brings the booze?"

His lips twitched. "So, do you want to know what they hoard or not?"

"Is it giving away big secrets?" Because to be fair, I had a fair set of my own and I didn't want to pry into their business without them knowing. Hell, we still hadn't cleared up why they took me in the first place and maybe they never would. Maybe they'd just seen me that day at the theater and it had been some kind of kismet.

Course, that didn't explain how Kestrel became my driver, because I knew my uncle. He would have used a private company. He always hired private. He wanted to be able to control them. Just like he controlled…

"Hey," Freddie said, shattering the dark thoughts. "Where'd you go?"

I fought to swallow the lump in my throat before it threatened to choke me. My cigarette had gone out, so I coughed to cover for a moment and then reached for the pack.

"Maybe that was enough," he commented, and I bared my teeth at him.

"Yeah yeah," he said, this time with a real laugh. "I'm hysterical. But where did you go?"

"If I can't ask questions, neither should you."

"Yet, you keep asking them."

"I'll stop," I promised, crossing my heart before I lit the second cigarette. The drag on it helped some, but the images of my uncle were too sharp. Too…fresh, like I'd just seen him, rather than the months it had been. Then that hit me, and it helped *some*. It had been months.

Maybe he was still determined to find me, but right now? Right now, I was free of him.

"Kel hoards the best weed," Freddie said. "He knows all the right people, and sometimes they pay him in the good stuff. Vaughn's got stimulants, but I'd bet money those have been moved, and before you worry, he's not a junkie. He needs them to stay focused if he pulls a double at the tattoo parlor. You do not want your tattoo artist falling asleep while they're drawing on you."

That made sense.

"Rome's a little weirder, but weird cool not weird bad or anything. He hoards candy. Butterscotch candies were the big ones he always kept. You could find them anywhere in his room. Pockets of his jackets. His pants. It was kind of hilarious. He used to wash them in his clothes."

"Oh man."

"Also, peanut butter candies. Those are another big one.

Not just peanuts, peanut butter. Then there are these weird truffle things he got into last year. Like, so expensive, you have to go to one of those fancy shops uptown to find them."

"Kalouda's?"

"That's it," Freddie said, almost warming to his topic. "Crazy ass expensive, but he always gets a whole box. Who pays three hundred bucks for some candy?"

I frowned, but I didn't answer him. There had been an article about me the previous year. The reporter had wanted to talk to me as one of the youngest members of the company, and they'd ended up reorienting the article on me rather than the whole company. Eric had been pissed. He'd been mentioned as barely a footnote with the appellation of 'current partner' like they expected him to be replaced.

A box of those chocolates had been on my dresser. Lainey sent them so I'd have something sinful and fun. I loved them and they were ridiculously overpriced, but more, they were from *her*. I'd loved every damn morsel of them, extra calories be damned.

The same article had also listed my favorite kind of ballet shoe.

That...explained a lot.

"People who love exquisite chocolate," I offered up with a wry smile, and Freddie cackled, some of the doom and gloom around him dispelling.

"I should have known it was something you loved." But he didn't dive further into that. Instead, he said, "Liam used to always have the best booze when he lived with us. You wanted a nice whiskey, he'd have it in stock. His tastes are almost as snooty as yours in chocolate."

I wrinkled my nose. "What do you horde?"

Freddie looked me dead in the eye and said, "Porn. Wanna see my collection?"

"See, and here I thought you'd say something like hookers and blow."

Freddie laughed. A real one this time, as he put out his smoke. That real glimpse of him eased some of the worry I'd had since they'd disappeared with Freddie to the clinic.

"Would you fall over from shock if I asked if any of the porn was any good?"

"Nope," Freddie said, this time with an honest grin. "But I would need you to tell me how you define good. For example, have you ever seen two dicks in one hole?"

I laughed. "Pretty sure it's all subjective."

"Woo! Next binge-watch session—porn." He gave me a sly look. "Wondering how Vaughn and Jasper will respond to that with you in the room?"

My face heated. I wasn't before. "I am now."

He was still laughing when I swatted his arm.

"Just for that, you're going to come down and dance with me."

"Woah...Freddie doesn't dance. Unless it's the horizontal mambo, and I got your pelvic tilt right here, a little bump and grind action." It was like he'd been rebuilding his walls while we sat there, and I'd helped him glue them back together. I couldn't fault him though. We all needed our walls. His play leer accompanied his body contortions.

I snorted as I rose and pointed to the stove. "Turn that off and follow me."

"Awww, do I have to?" He did the whole pout thing well, and I grinned.

"Yes, you have to. I want company, and if you hate it, you can just watch me dance."

"Strip show?" He waggled his eyebrows. "'Cause that perfect pussy of yours has been in hiding for a while. I might need a memory refresher."

"You do know that you don't have to get my attention with the crass come-ons, right? You had it before?"

He paused, the wind ruffling his hair, and stared at me with the saddest eyes. "You know, life isn't all pretty. You're clean and soft and bright. The crass…it just helps to laugh and keep the ugliness from touching you."

Leaning up, I brushed a kiss to his cheek. "Freddie, some of the warmest smiles can hide the darkest pathways of all. Don't believe everything you see in magazines or imagine from the stage." I squeezed his arm. "Never feel like you have to be anyone other than who you are with me."

Then, before I confessed more, I cut across the roof to the door, leaving him to deal with the heater. I needed a minute to get my own walls back up. Freddie didn't show up in the studio right away. But he did come. While he didn't dance, he sat on the floor and watched me.

No, I didn't strip, but the sad eyes he watched me with seemed a little less alone, and that was worth cutting myself open. Closing my eyes, I let go and let the music carry me, as I moved from one routine into the next. It was just instinct to leap for the silk and to dance with it instead. Higher I flew, twisting, twining, and wrapping it around myself, a bandage for the soul, and at the same time, wings to set me free.

More than once, I wished the wings were real, and even as I did, I worried the freedom I'd found was an illusion.

Like all illusions, it would come crashing down.

FAMILY VACATION

EMERSYN

By the time I'd turned twelve, I understood more about sex and reproduction than I'd ever wanted to know. For some reason, the tutor decided this was the year for the safe sex conversation. Sex was never safe. I finished the lecture, the video, and took the test on my laptop. There were some other "health" material we needed to cover to qualify for the end of year material. Honestly, I didn't care. I knew how to treat my injuries for the most part and how to avoid them. The rest of it just didn't seem all that interesting.

The last thing I expected was my mother to appear at the hotel in Los Angeles where we'd taken up residence as the show retooled. For the next six to eight weeks, the choreographers would pull the show apart and put it back together again. Some performers would go, and others would join us. Once the new show was readied, we'd spend two weeks in grueling rehearsal and then hit the road again.

The last two years, my uncle had plucked me out for a month each time. An ice-cold shudder raced through me.

Time just for us. This year, he'd let me know that we'd have to postpone our "vacation." Apparently, some business had pulled him away, so instead of bringing me "home," I would spend my break at the hotel. He'd even sent me flowers and gifts in apology and the promise to join me on the road as soon as he could.

Maybe he'd get in a wreck along the way.

When Mother walked through the door in a cloud of Chanel and dressed from head to toe in a perfect white pantsuit and wearing stilettos that let her tower over me, I could have cried.

"There's my beautiful girl," she greeted me with a smile and leaned into brush an air kiss against my cheek. "Don't hug, we don't want to wrinkle." Then she paused to remove her sunglasses as she eyed me. "What are you wearing? You look like some crude ad for an amusement park catalog."

Nothing worse than being an ad in a catalog.

But I glanced down at my pajama bottoms—dark blue with 'Sully' wrapped around one leg and the tank top that matched it with the *Monsters Inc.* logo. My feet were bare, but my toenails were electric blue, courtesy of Lauren down the hall, who'd given me a free pedicure while we ate pizza and cinnamon breadsticks and watched romantic comedies on Netflix. I'd stayed up *way* past my curfew, and she totally covered for me with my jailer—my chaperone.

"I'm in my pajamas, Mother," I said slowly. "I just finished the last of my classes before the break, and I didn't have anything to do today." I had an entire suite to myself. Unlike some of the dancers who had to share and then only had hotel rooms, mine had a sitting room and a mini bar—locked—my own bedroom with a king-sized bed in it, and a whirlpool bath.

Most nights, I just slept on the sofa in front of the television. It was more comfortable.

"Well, clearly I can see that, Emersyn. Why aren't you ready to go?" She did a slow circuit. "Where are your bags?"

"Go where?" I asked slowly. I hadn't even showered today. After the test was done, I'd fully intended to pull up Netflix and binge-watch some of the shows I never got to watch on the road.

Irritation marred her perfectly smooth forehead as she whirled to face me. "To Singapore."

I had no idea what she was talking about, and apparently, she grasped that. With a huff of exasperation, she settled her sunglasses atop her perfectly coifed hair and set down her Birkin bag and pulled out her phone. While she was distracted, I did a quick scan of the room. There wasn't anything visible that would get me into any trouble.

Not that she focused on the room at all. Her fingers flew over the keyboard on her phone, and I waited. Her absolute huff of disgust, however, as she raised her head and stared at the ceiling almost made me laugh.

Almost.

Because there were only two people I knew that irritated Mother like that.

"Your uncle," she said in clipped tones, "does not get to decide if you're going with me. Do you have your passport?"

Actually… "I do." I wanted to smile, but I didn't want to disturb the moment. Mother *never* argued with Uncle Bradley. With Daddy? All the time, but never my uncle. "We did two shows…"

She waved a hand. "I don't care why you have it, as long as you do." One perfectly manicured hand on her hip, she began to smile. "This is what we're going to do. Go shower and change. I don't care what you wear, just look vaguely presentable. I'll rearrange our car and have Jacques update our flight."

Update… "I'm going to Singapore?"

"Yes, my darling. *We* are going to Singapore. We're going to the fashion festival. We'll shop, we'll drink wine, and we'll act like civilized people, and your father and your uncle can rot." Lips pursed, she shook her head. "Don't worry about it. It's time you and I ran away."

Those were the words I'd always wanted to hear. I took a step closer to her, and she made a shooing motion.

"Go, go. You smell like bad vending machine food. How you are that skinny with the junk you eat…"

I went and took the fastest shower ever, though I made sure to use all my hair products. Mother hated frizzy hair. And despite what she thought, I did have presentable clothes, I just hated wearing them. I kept my mental fingers crossed the whole time as I threw everything clean I owned into one of my suitcases and dug my passport out from under the bed where I'd hidden it, and then hurried back out to the sitting room.

Mother emptied a glass of champagne and gave me a brilliant smile. "Now *there* is my beautiful girl. Shall we go and be rotten together?"

It took two hours to get to LAX in the traffic, and Mother spent as much time on her phone as she did talking to me about everything we were going to do. I didn't care, there was a warm fizzy feeling in my stomach that I hadn't experienced in so long. I saw my uncle more than I ever saw my parents. They sent presents. They sent cards. They sent flowers.

They rarely appeared.

At the airport, we checked our bags in one of the commercial terminals rather than the private.

"It's an adventure," my mother said, pouting almost playfully before she pressed a finger to her lips.

We had dinner in the first-class lounge at a quiet table for the two of us, and Mother ignored her phone and focused on me. She wanted to hear about my shows, my travels, and what my plans were. It was more words than she'd spoken to me in years.

By the time we boarded our flight, it was late and Mother's phone had blown up with messages, vibrating with calls she ignored, and more. She took a sort of savage satisfaction when she turned it off.

I never found out why she'd been so angry with my father or my uncle, but the next three weeks were the best we ever spent together.

CHAPTER 25

EMERSYN

A routine formed over the next couple of weeks. Breakfasts were with everyone present, even Liam, who showed up more often than not. Enough that his absence was conspicuous on those days he wasn't. Or maybe that was just to me.

Everyone took a turn at cooking. That meant some days, there were pancakes. Other days, eggs and bacon. Donuts appeared twice, and since one box was labeled 'Swan Only' and filled only with the donuts I always ate from the other boxes, I had to admit, it tickled me. Jasper never said a word, but they were absolutely from him.

On the day it was supposed to be my turn to fix breakfast, the boys made a rude discovery. Well, one of the boys did. I had zero idea how to cook. Always up early, Kestrel took pity on me and showed me how to make more than just peanut butter and jelly sandwiches. He could flip eggs with this little wrist maneuver. I tried it, and we lost one egg to the ceiling.

The second egg died ignominiously on the floor. Kestrel scooted right up behind me, put his hand over mine, and helped me flip the next ones. "See, not so hard," he murmured. Right, that was all him. Though I had to admit, the lessons were fun. Jasper's snarl at our position when he came in cut off abruptly. When I twisted to look, it was to find Liam with the egg dripping off his head. Apparently, the one on the ceiling lost its battle against gravity. Jasper suddenly burst out laughing. It was probably one of the most joyous sounds I'd heard in a long time. Even Liam's aggrieved face seemed to relax into a smile.

It was the most ridiculous scene. Beyond the pair of them, I caught Rome's slow wink and approving look. Vaughn snorted as he pushed past all of them, waiting only long enough for me to finish the next round of eggs before he tugged me away from Kestrel for a very thorough good morning kiss.

Still breathless, nothing readied me for Jasper swooping in for a toe-curling, tongue twisting kiss that seemed to shut off my brain cells as he walked me back toward the coffeemaker. The heat Vaughn ignited burned through me as I melted into Jasper. The smugness in his smile was almost adorable. My lips were still tingling as I turned to go back to Kestrel, only to bounce off Rome's chest. He picked me up, carried me to a counter and pressed me right up against the wall as he kissed me. The sweep of his tongue and the firmness of his lips erased the rest of the room.

"If I'd known Boo-Boo's lips were for breakfast, I'd have gotten up earlier," Freddie announced into the sudden silence, but I couldn't see him beyond Rome taking up my whole view. He rubbed his thumb gently against my lower lip before he gave me a gentler, sweeter kiss that felt more like a promise than a demand. The tingles racing over my skin turned electric, and if Vaughn and Jasper soaked my panties, Rome burnt them up.

With a nod, Rome left me to grab his own coffee. I locked gazes with Liam and shivered under the intensity of that stare.

"Not done with breakfast yet, Sparrow," Kestrel said as he rescued me by stepping between us and cutting off my view. I hopped down and retreated to the stove. It didn't matter if he stayed between us, Liam's stare seemed to drill right through me.

I stayed with Freddie most days and found myself in Vaughn's bed most nights. Jasper's schedule had him away more than at the clubhouse. He seemed exhausted too, but he didn't tell me what was going on. I tried to respect his wishes and not ask. Kestrel, Vaughn, and Rome took turns hanging out with Freddie and me, but there were days they were all gone. Once, Liam had come by, but all he'd done was kick back in a chair and watch cooking shows with us. Actually, he watched me like he was trying to figure me out.

Instead of confronting him about it, because I had a feeling it had to do with all the kissing, I retreated to my dance studio. Freddie still wouldn't dance with me, but he came in most days and watched me practice. The color was coming back into his cheeks, he showered more often, and we finished the Havoc series together.

Well, most of it, there were some sex scenes I just wasn't ready to read aloud, so I skated past them until Freddie figured it out. Then he took over reading those parts with such gusto, he would have me in tears laughing.

"It's just good, old fashion dirty fun, Boo-Boo," Freddie told me. "Haven't you ever had a threesome? Or a foursome? A daisy chain? How about letting a girl go down on you? Or watch you while a guy did? I bet you like to be tied up. All those silks…strung up and spread wide…"

The rapid-fire questions went from teasing and playful to kind of horrific. I shook my head. "No," was all I managed to squeak out before I escaped. I barely saw Kestrel as I headed for the stairs, but the look on his face said there was no way he hadn't heard what Freddie had been asking.

I didn't want to talk about it.

At the top of the stairs, the sound of a thump carried and Freddie's aggrieved, "Ow, I was just playing. Jesus, Kestrel."

The rest of it faded away as I gave up decorum and ran all the way to my room. Inside, I shut the door and closed my eyes like I could shut out the past. Months since I'd seen him as more than a blip on a newsfeed, and I could conjure his face without trying.

My uncle seemed to have carved out a space for himself in my head as deftly as he had my body.

Nothing made it go away.

I hid in my room for the rest of the day. I was supposed to be watching Freddie, or at least hanging out with him. But I couldn't face him. I couldn't face any of them. Kestrel was home, so at least I knew that Freddie wasn't alone. I ignored the messages on my phone, curled up under the covers with the bear that had been in the room since I arrived. The old, somewhat worn but still soft bear absorbed invisible tears as well as real ones.

Twice, the door opened, and I pretended to be asleep both times. For a little while, I'd forgotten the kidnapping, the life before, my uncle, all of it. It was like I belonged here. Then just like that, it was all gone again. I was the missing heiress with an uncle swearing repeatedly he wouldn't stop looking for me. My captors had become my friends? Lovers? How did I even describe them?

Did they count as kidnappers if I came back of my own volition?

I wish I could just forget again. Just go back to the little bubble we'd made. But that bubble was just another illusion, and I knew better.

I did.

As elusive as peace and sleep seemed, I didn't even notice I'd drifted off until I woke to Jasper setting me into the back of a car. I frowned at him, but he just shook his head and shut the door. Kestrel slid into the driver's seat as Jasper circled around to climb into the passenger seat.

"Is something wrong?" I moved to the middle as Rome opened the door to my right and climbed in, but before I could scoot over further, Vaughn climbed in on the other side.

"We gotta go," Jasper said, not looking back at me.

Kestrel sighed and shook his head. But if he had any objections, he didn't offer them up. It was pitch black outside, the headlights barely cut through the gloom, and no matter how hard I squinted, I couldn't see past the haze of light as it seemed to disperse against heavy fog.

"Where are we going?" My question barely seemed to register with any of them. Rome was in the seat next to me, but he wouldn't look at me. Kestrel tightened his grip on the steering wheel.

"Rome?" A muscle ticked in his jaw at my plea, but he still didn't turn his head. I twisted in the seat. Vaughn was my last hope, right?

The shadows hid his expression from me until another set of headlights hit us. The sadness in his face wrenched my heart.

"What happened?"

But no matter what I asked, they just kept driving and no one answered. I finally gave up, and after what seemed like an eternity in this purgatory, I wasn't ready for the car to stop or Kestrel to say, "We're here," in a tone that rang with such finality.

"Stay in the car," Jasper ordered, and then he was out. I tried to lean forward, but I still couldn't see where we were. He wasn't gone long before the door opened on Vaughn's side. He let out a little sigh before he climbed out, and then Jasper reached in for me. "Let's go."

"Where are we?"

"Just…trust me."

I swallowed hard at the request, but that was what he'd been asking me for all along, right? Wasn't that what they'd all been asking me for?

Vaughn wanted truth.

Rome wanted secrets.

Jasper wanted trust.

Kestrel? I glanced at the front of the car, his gaze fixed on mine in the rearview mirror. He'd betrayed me once before. Did I stay in the car? Or no? I hope that question conveyed in a glance. For the longest moment, he didn't do anything. Then as Jasper's fingers closed over mine, Kestrel shook his head.

I opened my mouth, but with one solid pull, Jasper hauled me out of the car. The misty air dampened my face, but it wasn't the fog or even Jasper that had all the sound dying in my throat.

Uncle Bradley stood next to another car, his hands in his pockets and his expression dark.

"Jasper?" His name came out a strangled whisper, but it didn't slow his steps as he dragged me forward. "Please don't…"

"I told you to trust me," he commented finally. "Maybe you should have." Then he snapped his gaze up to my uncle. "Here she is, as promised." Then he shoved me away, and when I would have stumbled, my uncle caught me and I swore, the moment his hands touched me, I screamed.

My struggle did nothing. It didn't stop Jasper from

turning his back and walking away. It didn't pull Rome out of the car to avenge me in silent fury. It didn't keep Vaughn from getting back in the car like I was already a memory.

Kestrel stared at me from the driver's seat and I reached for him, but it was too late—I was trapped in the car with my uncle, and the Vandals were gone.

"Sparrow!"

"Come on, beautiful girl, open those eyes."

A sob ripped out of me.

"C'mon, Sparrow, open those eyes."

The softness of that voice was a lie. They'd left me. I beat against the arms holding me, but they didn't relax. If anything, they squeezed me closer. Not tighter. Not harder. Just closer.

The rasp of stubble rubbing against my hair and the warmth of flesh beneath my chilled fingers made me shudder.

"Please, Sparrow, c'mon, open those eyes for me." My captor released me long enough to cup my face, and gentle thumbs swiped at the hot tears leaking from my eyes.

"Kestrel?" He came back? He…

"I'm right here, sweetheart," he promised. "Open your eyes."

Terror fisted my heart. What if… Violent trembling rocked me, and I forced my eyes to open. The world wavered. Instead of fog, there was diffuse light stinging my watering eyes. Backlit, Kestrel's rumpled hair stood up like he'd rolled right out of bed.

"Kestrel," I repeated slowly, blinking to get the tears out of the way. I'd forgotten how to cry, how much it hurt, how it choked the air out of my lungs and left my throat raw. The broken sounds in the room were alien. More so when I realized they were coming from me.

"I'm right here, Sparrow," he whispered. "Right here.

Pinch me if you have to, I'm real." Then as if to prove the point, he pinched me. The sharpness of the contact burst through the iciness, and what little of the dam I'd managed to erect against my tears collapsed.

I flung my arms around his neck and half climbed out of the tangle of blankets and onto his lap. Kestrel didn't say a word, just bundled me right up to him.

"I'm here," he repeated as the sobs just poured out of me. I wanted to stop. I desperately wanted to stifle those tears and shove them all back into the dark corner that had been blown open. "I'm here."

At some point, he started to stand, and I scrabbled hard to hold on, but he just carried me with him.

"Shh, I have you," he whispered, not even seeming to mind that my nails were leaving half-moon shapes in his skin or that I'd locked my arms and legs. Then he settled again and freed one of his arms to drag the blankets up and around my shoulders.

I'd gone to sleep in a T-shirt and panties. Shivers kept skating over me. Eventually, I seemed to reach the bottom of the well and the tears slowed. My eyes and my nose hurt so bad. It felt like I'd swallowed glass, and Kestrel's chest beneath my face had been soaked with tears and snot.

Oh, that was so gross. I tried to pull away, sniffling badly, and Kestrel loosened his arms.

"I'm sorry, I just—Oh, I snotted all over you."

"Oh, who cares," he muttered and dragged me back. "I won't melt, and that's hardly the worst thing that's ever gotten on me." It was so decidedly practical that I settled against him and used my shirt to wipe my nose. He gave me a moment, and then with a gentle hand that I could easily resist, he turned my face up so he could see me.

There was still a light on, and it had to be coming from

his room. The door between our rooms stood wide open. It was still dark in here, but not so cold or lonely.

"You want to talk about it?" No pressure lived in that question.

I swallowed, dipping my gaze to the pair of birds tattooed on his pecs. They were arcing away from each other. Wings spread. Kestrels, I'd bet. I licked my lips.

"You don't have to," he told me. "I can stay right here until you go back to sleep if you want though."

"I don't want you to go." Admitting that took everything I had.

"Then I'll stay."

My lower lip trembled until I compressed my mouth closed. I couldn't breathe through my stuffed up nose though, so I swiped at my face with a hand before I dared to look at him again. The chill in his eyes was all but gone. The man gazing at me was the one I'd begun to nurse a crush on back when he was just my driver.

The one I'd let myself fantasize about.

The one…

"Please don't tell the others?"

"That you had a bad dream?" He raised his brows. "They won't care except to make sure you're all right. Hell, if they'd heard your screams, they'd have ripped down the damn doors themselves."

"But I don't want them to know." I opened my mouth, then closed it. "I need to trust you again. I need to know you won't tell them my secret."

Sadness crept across his expression so briefly, I must have imagined it. "I'll keep your secrets, Sparrow. I won't betray your trust again. I promise." When I would have opened my mouth, he pressed a finger to my lips. "But believe me—we all want to protect you, and we're all very familiar with nightmares."

That was probably true. Might even explain the faerie lights in Jasper's room, though I hadn't asked him. Nor had I slept in there again. Every night I was in Vaughn's bed, there was a light on somewhere in the room. There were lamps in here. Lights around the ceiling in Kestrel's room.

So yeah, maybe they did know.

"If you don't want me to tell them, I won't," he promised again. With careful hands, he reached up to smooth the hair back from my face, then carefully swiped away the dampness on my cheeks. "Or you can just curl up here and let me hold you while you sleep. Whatever you need."

I wanted to believe.

I needed so desperately to believe him.

"I dreamt that you guys took me back." There was only so much I could tell him. "You didn't tell me where we were going or why. You put me in the car, and Jasper dragged me out of it when we got there." Then pushed me toward my uncle, done with me. "Got rid of me because I wouldn't trust you."

His smooth expression turned fierce as he frowned. "You know we would never do that." Then, without waiting for my response, he sighed. "Of course you don't, or you wouldn't have had that *dream*." Something about the way he said 'dream' told me he understood there was so much I wasn't saying, but he didn't press.

Head back, he shifted me on his lap, and it hit me that he was mostly naked and I had a hand spread over one of the tattoos on his pecs. There was another at his abdomen, a cross all intertwined with vines. Focusing on the tattoos helped me to get my breathing under control, because I didn't want to move, even if the gradually stiffening erection in his shorts pressed against my leg.

Still, he'd been… "Are you okay with me sitting here?"

"I'm fine, ignore my dick. Dicks do that." He was so

matter-of-fact about it. "Right now, I want you to know and to try and believe me when I say nothing—and I mean *nothing*—you could do or say would make us force you to go anywhere you don't want to go. In fact, I'll kill the first person who tries, whether they're my brother or not."

He held my gaze as he issued that quiet threat in a deadly calm voice.

"Why did you take me?"

"Because leaving you there seemed like a far worse idea. I can't say we thought it all the way through," he admitted. He touched his tongue to his lower lip, then said, "You know what, fuck it. Jasper has had plenty of time to clear this up with you. When we found out you were going to be in town, we just wanted to be close. To see you. Make sure you were all right. But you weren't all right." He flicked his gaze over me. "You were far from all right, although you are very talented at hiding it. Maybe better than I realized, and that's a discussion for another day, hopefully when you believe me about being able to trust me."

I swallowed again.

"But that asshole hurt you…and you needed medical help. We could have just taken you to Doc, gotten you patched up, and taken you back. But we didn't trust anyone there. Not after seeing those bruises and injuries. Not after realizing those assholes at the show just let that abuse continue. You were safer with us, and then you needed to heal."

"And then and then…"

He gave me a small smile. "Precisely. Once you were here, none of us wanted to let you go back."

"Except you."

"I didn't want to let you go, Sparrow." He covered my hand on his chest. "I thought…I thought it was the best thing for you. Do I want you? Absolutely. Did I want you to have to be in our world? No. I thought yours was better."

I glanced down to where he rubbed his thumb against the back of my hand. He'd said that before. "Not everything they write about us is true."

"I'm figuring that out. More, you came back. You got out, and you came back all on your own."

I bit my lip, then let it go. "Don't ask me why."

"I'm not going to," he said. "You'll tell me when you're ready. Until then, you're safe here. I promise."

This time when I looked into his eyes, I saw nothing but him blazing back out at me. Sniffling once, I leaned close and just pressed my lips to his, not asking for anything but needing the contact. He returned the kiss, the pressure of it, but he didn't try to deepen it, even when he lifted a hand to cradle the back of my head.

We stayed there, suspended in that moment, and some of the fear slithered away. I closed my eyes, and when I opened them, I pulled back. "I believe you," I whispered.

I did. He meant it.

"You ready to try and sleep again?"

"I need to wash my face."

"Okay." It wasn't until I was halfway to the bathroom that it occurred to me he might leave, and I turned to find him just sitting at the edge of the bed. The black sleep shorts he wore just seemed to emphasize the line of muscles along his thighs.

"You'll still stay?"

He glanced up and smiled at me. "If you want me to stay, or you can come sleep with me in my bed. You won't be alone."

It took me a couple of minutes to wash my face. My eyes hurt so bad. I couldn't remember the last time I'd just cried. It took several attempts to blow my nose, and then I just brushed my teeth, 'cause I couldn't remember if I had before.

When I came back out, Kestrel waited for me. "Where are we sleeping?"

"Sometimes Vaughn comes in here early to wake me up," I admitted.

"I'm aware," Kestrel said. "Trust me, I have no problem shoving his naked ass back out."

A laugh escaped at the utter dryness in his tone, and his smile gentled. When he held out a hand, I shut off the light in the bathroom and went straight to him. The door between our rooms was still open. The main light was off in his room, but the soft lights around the ceiling were on. The blue chased away the shadows.

Kestrel ushered me into my bed ahead of him, then followed behind. He wrapped me up and tucked me to his chest and chuckled when I pulled the bear over to cuddle it too. "Rome will like that you love his bear so much."

The soft words made me smile. "It's his?"

"Hmm-hmm. He left it in here so you wouldn't be alone when we brought you here that first night."

The absolute and utter sweetness in that gesture floored me. I didn't even have words for that. I hugged it tighter. "Thank you for telling me."

He pressed a kiss to the back of my head. "Go to sleep, Sparrow. No more bad dreams."

"Good night, Kestrel."

"Think you can start calling me Kellan, by the way."

Kellan.

"It's my name."

"I know it's your name, smart ass," I retorted, and he huffed a laugh. "I just...I've always called you Kestrel."

"I don't mind that either, but my friends call me Kellan or Kel. But you can call me whatever you want."

Kel.

"Good night, Kel."

"Good night, Em."

I grinned. "I like Sparrow."

"Good to know." He gave me a squeeze. "Now go to sleep."

Honestly, I didn't think I would. I really didn't. When I was still awake a few minutes later, Kestrel—Kellan shifted us again so I was facing him this time and he tucked my head to his chest, right over his heart, and then began to stroke my hair.

I was asleep before I hit the count of ten beats.

NO BROKEN PROMISES

KELLAN

"Are you serious right now?" Milo demanded from the doorway.

"Yes," I told him. "I've been thinking about it. I didn't say I was committed."

He let out a breath and then pushed into the room and closed the door behind him. I turned eighteen the following day, which meant it was time for me to go. Just like Vaughn before me. Though Vaughn had gotten a place not far away, crashing in the spare room of the guy teaching him how to ink. He'd said I could stay there for a while. I might, but the group home didn't let us stay beyond our eighteenth birthdays.

There was still a couple of months of high school left. I could finish up and then graduate.

"But the army?" Milo raked a hand through his hair.

I shrugged. "Training. Paycheck. Free place to sleep. Money later for school, if I decide I want to go to college. It's something."

"Yeah, but is it what you want?" Milo pinned me in place with those dark eyes of his. "You've never said a word about it before."

No, because I rarely talked about my future plans. We talked about Vaughn focusing on getting an apprenticeship, because ink was something he loved. He'd already started practicing on himself. We talked about Jasper taking business classes at the local junior college and how we could afford it. We talked about Rome and the art school in Easton. We'd done his application and managed to sneak more than a few of his pieces from the clubhouse to submit him for consideration.

Then there was Liam and the Ivy League plans his parents had for him. They'd already tried to send him up there for that private prep school the first school year after they'd adopted him. He'd been gone for three weeks. While he never admitted what he'd done to get kicked out, his parents acquiesced to the private school here instead.

It was still not with us or with Rome, but he was close enough the twins could see each other. It still baffled me why they hadn't adopted Rome too. But the one time I brought it up, Rome said they could go fuck themselves. He wasn't leaving us. At the same time, he never once blamed Liam for the way they'd gone after him.

Liam would never have cooperated without Rome's blessing anyway. All they had to do was say the word, and we'd all have taken off. "Who's getting Freddie today?"

"Jasper," Milo said. "Don't change the subject." Ever since the day down by the docks, we kept an eye on Freddie to and from school. We made it clear to everyone that he wasn't to be touched or messed with. Pick a fight with him, and it was all of us you would get. We bled for each other, no one was allowed to bleed us.

Turning, I dropped to sit on the edge of the bed and

studied Milo. We'd known each other too long for bullshit. "I'm tired," I told him. "I know what you're trying to build, and I support that. I can send home money to keep helping…"

"Talk to me, Kel." Like me, Milo dropped to sit on the other bed in the room. We'd gone from six in a room to three, now to two as we'd gotten older. Freddie rotated between our rooms because he was still bunking with the younger kids. His hell raising and recklessness nearly landed him in juvey, but if we let him crash with us, he slept and stayed relatively sober.

Vaughn had broken the arm of the last dope dealer who sold to Freddie. Then again, who could fault the kid for wanting an escape? We all needed one. Wasn't that what I was doing?

"Jasper's getting out of control," I said. "He leads with his temper, and he's *always* on edge these days. He almost beat that asshole to death. If we hadn't been there…"

"But we were there," Milo replied. "That's what we do, and the rage…it's part of who he is. We know that. We know what he saw, and he's only ever mentioned it once."

Yeah, once when we'd all gotten puking drunk and confessed our pasts. That had come right in the aftermath of saving Freddie. Killing a man finished bonding us in a way that years of knowing each other had begun.

I sighed. "You've got plans."

"I do, and those plans need you." Milo raked a hand through his hair and shook his head. "If this is what you want, then I'll support you. But no lie, brother, it doesn't feel like something you want. It feels like you're running. Nothing wrong with that, but I'd rather you ran toward something than away. If you need this, then fuck it all, we'll make sure you get it."

"I saw him the other day."

"Your father?"

"Sperm donor." I would never refer to that man as anything else. "He looked right through me, even though the woman with him did a hard double take." I had the face of a monster. A man who had used his money and influence to buy and sell whatever he wanted, including my mother. Some facts I'd never needed to know. Didn't change who *my* parents had been. But that asshole? Learning about him had definitely cracked something inside of me.

"Want me to kill him?" Milo asked. "Or do you need to be the one to do it?"

This right here was why we were brothers and always would be. A wordless promise we'd made a long time ago. No questions asked, if I said let's do it, we'd leave and get it done. If I said no, he'd leave it alone until I was ready.

CHAPTER 26

KELLAN

The next couple of nights, I just slept with Sparrow. Vaughn wasn't amused when he found me there, but I enjoyed the hell out of answering his sinful little come-on. The best part of it all was when she burst out laughing. I could have left them in peace and he could've cheerfully fucked her into a better mood, but I didn't.

One, because I was an asshole and if my dick had to behave, so did his.

Two, because even though Vaughn had his hard dick out in all its glory, she'd remained cuddled up to me.

So Vaughn was shit out of luck.

After breakfast, Rome pulled Sparrow out before she'd even finished her coffee or gotten anything to eat. And I wasn't the only one irritated.

"Hey," Vaughn said. "What the hell?"

"We'll be fine," Rome said over his shoulder. "She needs a

break." From what, he didn't have to say. I had a feeling it wasn't just a break from Freddie, but from all of us.

"I'm more worried about her being spotted." I kept my tone even as I sipped my coffee. Rome had been there. He knew. We still hadn't had much luck tracking down the source of the bounty. I assumed it had to be her family or someone close to them.

That didn't endear any of them to me, because the kind of people a bounty brought to the table were downright dangerous. Rome poked his head around the corner and flipped me off.

That translated well. Fuck off, he had it covered. Blowing out a breath, I shook my head and checked the time. Jasper was overdue for a check-in.

"You have something you want to tell me?" Vaughn asked, and I spared him a look. Sounded like someone's balls were aching.

Well, I'd feel worse if I hadn't had to listen to them on and off for days.

Who was I kidding? No, I wouldn't. Vaughn was a good guy, but every once in a while, it was good to remind him that he couldn't talk himself into or out of anything he liked.

"Nope," I said, draining my mug of coffee. "I'm running by the diner before I head to the shop."

"I thought you were off today."

Well, before Rome pulled his disappearing act with her, I had been. It was fine. I had a couple of old beaters I was rehabbing, and I needed some time to think.

"I'll see you later." At the entrance to the kitchen, I paused and glanced back at him. "Stick close for Freddie and keep an eye on the rats. They're being extremely obedient lately."

"Maybe because Rome knocked one of JD's teeth out?" Vaughn said dryly. "And not all that long ago, Jasper took an axe to a guy's hand?"

I shrugged. "Not the first time...well, maybe the axe." The sword was put away neatly in my room. "Still, keep an eye on them. I got that itch at the back of my head."

Vaughn frowned. "I put a GPS chip in her phone."

That was good to know. Burners didn't always come with them. Vaughn was pretty good with delicate work, including adding devices. "Thanks, keep track of her. I don't think it's her but..." I couldn't shake the feeling. It had been there before her nightmare and that blood-curdling scream of despair ripped me out of a dead sleep.

I'd come through that door with a gun ready to shoot whatever was attacking her. The moment I'd touched her, she'd fought. I took the blows 'cause I needed to get through to her, but it was the sobs that killed me.

Absolutely fucking gutted me. Something had happened. Something she didn't want anyone to know. We knew about the now very dead and gone partner. So if it wasn't him, then what?

Fuck. "I'll be back." She'd begged me not to tell anyone, and I'd kept this promise. The quiet gratitude in her eyes when I said nothing that next morning and pointed out her room was dusty when Freddie noticed her reddened eyes made me feel like a jackass.

I was halfway to my car when my phone rang. Half expecting Jasper's name to pop up, I paused at Doc's. He'd taken a huge interest in Sparrow. I hadn't said much because she also seemed to take a lot of comfort in him, still...

"Hey," I said as I unlocked the car and slid inside. The Jeep was gone. Vaughn's car was there, but Jasper's was missing and the refurbished Jeep I'd fixed up a couple of years earlier was gone.

Probably better Rome took her out in a car than on foot. It irked though.

"You seen Jasper?" Well, so much for pleasantries. Maybe

Jasper had been spending too much time with Doc. "He's ignoring my calls."

"He's working," I told him as I started the engine and scanned the warehouse. There were a pair of rats on guard duty. There should be three, and there he was walking out of the bathroom and zipping up his fly. All three of them were decent enough. "What's up?"

"Raptor knows."

All the blood in my body chilled at once, and I let out a long breath. A stream of curses danced through my brain, but I gave voice to none of them. "He was in solitary."

"I'm aware, he's not anymore. He's also getting cut loose today."

"What?" I barely managed a nod to the guys at the doors as they rolled up to let me out. The phone had transferred to the hands-free. "I thought he had…"

"It doesn't matter," Doc continued in a very guarded tone. Almost too guarded.

"What do you know?"

"I know you dumbasses should have found a way to get him a message."

"He was in fucking solitary, how were we supposed to do that? Not every guard is on the take, and we're supposed to be keeping it clean out here as much as possible." Fuck. Fuck. Fuck.

"Yeah well, he called me. He found out she was missing. It was literally the first thing he checked as soon as he was able to get news."

"You told him." It wasn't a question.

"I thought he had a right to know, and he was going to lose his fucking mind."

I slammed my hand against the steering wheel once, then sucked it up. "How is he getting out?"

"I don't know. He just called me for a ride. He didn't want to take the bus back in…"

No, that wouldn't be safe. "Where are you?"

"My place," he said. "I closed the clinic for the day."

"Stay there, I'll pick you up." Then I hung up before he could tell me no. I called Jasper next, but the call went straight to voicemail. He either had his phone off or he was out of range of a cell tower.

Fuck. At the beep, I said, "Hawk, call me back when you get this. I don't care what time." A part of me wanted to leave him the warning and a part of me knew better. We never left messages that might compromise anything.

It was just safer.

To my surprise, Doc waited at the curb when I pulled up. The look he gave me said he could have skinned me alive. He pulled open the passenger door at my arrival and eyed me. "Don't ever hang up on me."

"I wanted you to stay put." I shrugged. "And I want to know what you told him. Exactly."

"You can ask him," Doc said as he slid into the car and settled in. "Where's Little Bit?"

"She's with Rome. And no, she doesn't know. You called me after they left."

"Wouldn't matter if I called you before, you punks have had time to put all the pieces in a row and you haven't." He sounded so damn aggrieved.

"Why does this piss you off so much?" I swung back out onto the road and headed for the highway. We could grab food when we got to Camden. We had at least ninety minutes to get there, and I had plenty of gas.

He just shook his head. "You wouldn't understand."

"A lot of that going around, apparently." I barely resisted rolling my eyes as I tightened my grip on the steering wheel. We needed a plan, not an argument. At the same time,

Mickey J wasn't just the kid who bailed us out when we got in over our heads anymore and we weren't kids.

We hadn't been in a long time.

"What's going on?" Doc asked. "Freddie holding out?"

"He's having good days and bad." I had to bite back the retort of he wouldn't understand, especially after the crap he'd given me. "As for the rest, it's just shit...more shit than we need to deal with."

Doc made some noncommittal sound, but he didn't say anything. The silence filled the car, and even though I was tempted to turn on the music, I waited him out.

"What's eating you?" I asked after we'd gone thirty minutes without saying a single word. "For real?"

"Raptor," Doc answered. "You kids...Jasper. The choices you guys all made."

"They were our choices. We made them." I wasn't going to justify any of them, not to him. "Just like you made yours. You saw a way out and you took it. No different for us."

"Are you shitting me with that?" Doc asked. "I'll grant you guys are better than some, but you're still a bunch of bangers who are playing at bigger business, cutting off the hold of bigger gangs and interrupting their trade. Not to mention, you're slowly but surely extending your grip over this city. Don't think I'm fooled by some of the moves you've been making."

I didn't confirm or deny anything. "We did what we had to do."

"The mind that came up with this plan could have done a hell of a lot more," he said with another long sigh. "All of you could."

I chuckled. "Doc, you worried about us? Still?"

"You guys were family."

"We still are." I left the rest of that sentence untouched. As angry as Jasper was and as determined as he was to keep Doc at arm's length, Raptor's return was going to change a lot of things. "That's why we stuck together."

Why I stayed.

I could have taken the same out Doc had. I thought about it, every once in a while, what life would have been. But then I wouldn't have been here when… Yeah, I just wouldn't have been here.

"You guys should have told me," Doc said finally. "I get it, Raptor was in solitary, but you should have told me that night you brought her in."

"You didn't need to know," I said with a shrug. "I didn't think we were keeping her." Maybe I shouldn't admit that, but it was something he needed to know. "But she's better off here. She's better off with us. Jasper was dead right about that, and if I hadn't believed it before, I do now."

"Why now?"

"It's complicated."

"That little fucker you guys were tearing apart? He's dead, right? She said he was dead."

I nodded. "He won't touch her again."

Doc nodded. There was a coldness in that nod, and more, there was a sense of satisfaction. "Did she get to see it? "

"No," I snapped. "What the fuck, Doc? She doesn't need to see that shit." Hell, she'd already seen a couple of dead bodies, and that was two too many.

"Maybe she needs to see it when she was the one who suffered. Killing him probably felt good. He got what he deserved. But what about her?"

I opened my mouth to argue that, but I couldn't. I snapped it shut. She didn't need to see that side of our lives. That was literally the first thought that crossed my mind, but she had seen it. She'd seen it when those 19Ds had tried to go after her for no other reason than she was there. She'd seen it when those investigators tried to steal her out of the shop.

She hadn't broken.

Then the image of her sobbing against me flooded my mind, and I squeezed the steering wheel. Was that what made her cry? She hadn't seen that fucker die for real? She didn't have the guarantee that he wouldn't come back?

Fuck. Me.

There was no way to fix that.

A dull headache formed behind my eyes. "What would you have done?" Because really, if he thought he knew better, I'd like to hear it.

"I don't know," Doc said slowly. "I might still be skinning the little fuck."

"He wasn't so little." Laughter escaped me. "And aren't you supposed to be all about healing?"

"It would be therapeutic," Doc said.

"And here I thought you didn't agree with what we did."

"I didn't say that, I just said she should have had the opportunity to see it. And you should have cut his dick off."

"We did."

He cut a look in my direction. "Good."

Well, at least on that we agreed. It was the last we said on the subject. We still had another thirty minutes to go and then... Well fuck it all, I really didn't know what happened next.

Raptor was coming home. It was about damn time and it worried the fuck out of me all in the same breath.

US

ROME

"You could come, you know," Liam said for the fourteenth time since he'd met with the O'Connells. "They know I'm a twin, and I told them I wouldn't go without you."

I shrugged. "They don't want me."

"They don't *know* you." Liam folded his arms and leaned against the wall of our room. I didn't look up from my sketchbook. I almost had the look of her face right. "You could try," he said softly. "Just this once. For me?"

The last two words halted my pencil. "Liam, I'm not like you. I like it here. I like our friends. I like—"

"Being left alone," he said, finishing the thought for me. "Where no one has any expectations and you can do what you want. But we could have a family again…"

"I have a family." Resuming my focus on the sketching, I refused to look at him. I didn't want him to see the fact I'd already made peace with him going. He needed the challenges. He would thrive. They could give him a lot more than they could give me. "You're my family. The guys are our family. Whether you stay or go, nothing changes between us."

"Goddammit, Rome," Liam snarled as he stomped over to the bed, then froze. He'd seen what I was sketching. "Dammit." This time, the curse came out a lot softer, far more resigned.

It was Liam with the O'Connells. They looked happy.

So did he. But he wouldn't let himself be happy if he thought he was abandoning me.

"I don't want to do this without you," he admitted as he sank down to sit on the floor next to the bed. I rolled on my side and touched the back of my head to his. His sigh weighed on me. "You think I should."

I didn't say anything.

"Why the hell do you think I'd choose them over you guys?" The wounded note hit me, and I sighed. "I wouldn't. Ever." His sigh echoed my own. "That's not what you're saying, is it?"

We sat there like that in silence.

"No, you want this for me. Why?"

"Because," I told him softly. "You were built for that life. You could do amazing things. Just because you go home with them, it doesn't change who you are, just what you can do."

I'd thought about this a lot. The foster parents, they didn't like me much. Too different. I didn't react like the other kids. I was too quiet. Kept too much to myself. There were always criticisms, quietly offered and never mean, but I heard them.

I heard them all.

They weren't wrong.

"Rome…"

"I know."

And I did.

"You're my brother."

"Always," he swore aloud, not that he needed to. "You're

my better half," he said without an ounce of irony. "I won't go if they take me too far from you."

There it was. He did want to go. Even if he hadn't been able to admit it to himself. He wanted the opportunities the O'Connells offered him. He liked the couple. Genuinely.

"Will you think about going with me?"

I couldn't lie to him. "No," I murmured, then rolled back to where I'd been sketching and went to work. "I don't belong there."

"You belong anywhere I am."

"Then I'll already be there, won't I?"

I glanced at him, and our gazes locked. This was absolutely the last thing he wanted, the desire for more conflicting with his need to stick with me, but that was why I could do this.

He would leave for us.

I would stay for us.

Because, as always, we were us.

CHAPTER 27

EMERSYN

When we left the clubhouse, all Rome said was he wanted to show me something. The quiet intensity he delivered the request had made me say yes without hesitation or a second thought. Vaughn's disappointment weighed on me as much as his lingering stare when I gave him a quick kiss farewell to follow Rome.

Whatever Rome wanted to show me was not in town, or at least not close, because we took a car. I had on a hat and sunglasses with a heavy hoodie to hide my face. As it turned out, the spot he wanted to go was down the coast from Braxton Harbor. I was glad for the breakfast and coffee he picked up for us, because we made a picnic of it, sitting on a large rock below an overpass that overlooked a stony shoal. The water washed pebbles were all different shades, and the sun glinting off the water made them glitter.

We'd had to climb down from where he parked, following a shallow set of sheer steps with only a rope for railing.

Rome had on a heavy backpack and he went first, but I had no trouble navigating it. At the base, I discovered exactly why this was one of Rome's favorite spots.

On the underpass, still half shrouded in shadows, were massive paintings. There were ropes attached to the underpass, and I had a feeling the climbing harnesses he'd pulled out of the pack were for those. I studied one as we ate, trying to make out the different features, though half of it was still too dark to truly make out.

They were people.

I had to think they were the Vandals, maybe. Hey... "Are you the reason that you guys are called the Vandals?"

He quirked an eyebrow at me, and a smile flashed across his lips before he hid his mouth by taking a drink of coffee. "Do you think the paintings are vandalizing anything?"

Laughing, I shook my head. "Only in the absolute best ways."

The softness of his chuckle stroked over me. Between the warmth of the sun on the rocks and the sound of the waves gently lapping against the rocky shoal, a kind of peace invaded me. Maybe I was still too raw from the all too realistic nightmare. At the same time, the thought of any of them handing me over to my uncle made me sick to my stomach.

Not wanting to think about him here, I continued to study the painting, but more, I watched Rome from the corner of my eye. His head tilted upward, like he, too, was enjoying the sunshine. The relaxed posture of his shoulders and the hints of a smile still on his lips warmed me even more than where we were.

"Thank you for bringing me here."

"We just got here," he said. "Did you want to leave?" The matter-of-fact way he asked didn't carry even an ounce of disappointment.

"No," I assured him. "I'm good right here. I want to see

you paint." But it was safe. Maybe not when the tide came in, but right now? We were out of sight, nowhere near the place we'd run into trouble before, and we were alone. "You wouldn't have brought me here if it wasn't okay for me to sit and watch while you're up there."

Then it hit me. I glanced at the *pair* of harnesses.

"You want me to go up with you." There was no way to play that off in a teasing or joking manner, not when I grinned. I loved heights. It would be hard to explain, but I just loved being up in the air where no one and nothing could reach me.

"Yes." One word, nothing more, and yet I heard the invitation and the hope all rolled up into it. He could say so much with so little. "And no."

"What?"

"No, we aren't Vandals because of me."

I'd almost forgotten I even asked that question. Laughter swelled up in me again, and I drained my coffee. With both of us done, he collected the trash and stored it in a small plastic bag that he tucked into his backpack. Then he handed me one of the harnesses. I stepped into it and then tightened it up to fit me. Clearly, whoever had worn it before me was a lot bigger.

When he had his on, I followed him to the wall, and this close, I could see the rigs and divots he used to climb. Excitement thrummed in my veins as I began my climb. The ropes were higher, and we'd need to hook carabiners once we got to the top. There was a climbing rope attached about a third of the way up, and I scrambled over it to where it had been looped near the abutment.

I slid a carabiner on it and then followed it upward to the first beam. Once up there, I checked the slack on the rope. It would catch if I fell, but I'd have to be careful of the swing so I didn't haul Rome off too.

There was only about five feet of space above the beam to where the overpass began. I didn't even try to stand up straight, I just scrambled across it to where the ropes were attached closer to the wall itself.

"Which one do you want me to use?"

I didn't have to look, Rome was right behind me. The comfort of his presence was like a warm blanket wrapped around me.

"The blue one."

That was helpful, I leaned over to look below the beam. The blue one was right there. I caught the rope and pulled it up, then began to thread it through my harness before detaching the carabiner and situating myself.

Rome watched me for a beat, then smiled before he moved over to grab the red rope and did the same for himself. We dropped down at almost the same time, and I closed my eyes for the fall. The light bounce as the ropes caught made me grin even wider. I glanced over, and Rome wore another smile.

That was like three this morning.

From this angle, I could twist and see the rest of the painting I couldn't make out. It was Liam on his motorcycle. There was no mistaking the smirk on his face. Granted, he was wearing a helmet, but his face shield was up. He sat astride the bike, cocky as hell. It was in his posture and his expression.

But there was something else there.

Joy.

Real, open, honest joy.

Envy flooded me, and I shook my head. It was absolutely stupid to be jealous of a painting. It wasn't like I'd ever seen that expression on his face for real. Still, I loved it. This was *Rome's brother* and not just Liam. Turning, I found Rome watching me. He flicked a look to the painting then back to me, and I grinned.

"I'd pay to see that expression in real life," I admitted. "It's beautiful."

It was a little too shadowy out of the sun and I was glad for the extra layers to keep off the chill, but I could have sworn Rome's cheeks flushed a little deeper pink. Yet at the same time, he nodded.

"What are we painting here today?" I glanced to his blank canvas, and his expression shifted, minutely, but to something more enigmatic.

"You'll see."

In some ways, it turned into the perfect morning. We spent the next few hours hanging there, and I only had to climb up and then back down once to find a spot to empty my bladder. Rome nodded to deeper beneath the underpass, and he'd handed me toilet paper. I loved how prepared he was.

He'd also followed me down and planted himself with his back to me. I was hardly shy, but it was a bit awkward to squat and pee with the chilly wind tickling me and Rome standing not five feet away. But at the same time, I utterly appreciated the gesture.

I wasn't alone.

When I finished, he motioned that he was going to do the same, so I took up watch for him, and I didn't miss his low chuckle or his wink. The fact he had hand sanitizer, however, just made me laugh all over again, and I leaned up to kiss him after we'd washed our hands.

The brush lasted all of about three seconds before he wrapped me up and gave me a real kiss. The slow, devastating pressure of his mouth massaging mine as he half lifted me up onto my toes sent tingles racing through my blood. When I parted my lips, he darted his tongue against mine, then away. Once. Twice. On the third stroke, I sucked against his tongue, and his laughter sent a pulse straight to my cunt.

With one hand, he tugged my hood back and cupped my nape as I tilted my head. The slow swaying motion as he kissed me and turned us in a circle was like dancing in a way. I opened my eyes and gazed up at him as he teased my tongue with swipes of his own. It was both erotic and playful. The serene expression he wore made me smile, and that clacked our teeth together and then I laughed aloud.

Rome chuckled as he lifted his head. The laughter shining in his eyes just made me grin wider. It was ridiculous and carefree and…

"So this is where you two have been hiding." Liam's voice sliced right between us and I shivered, but Rome didn't turn around.

"Fuck off," was all Rome said, then he winked at me. That open joy on Liam's face in the painting above, it glowed in Rome's eyes right now, and not for the whole world—or a stubborn Liam—would I move and ruin this moment.

"Love you too, bro," Liam retorted as he crossed into my line of sight. He wore his motorcycle jacket and boots. The intensity that had been in his gaze for the last couple of weeks burned right through me as we locked gazes.

Shifting, Rome turned us in a circle until my back was to Liam and he could meet his brother's gaze over my head. The gentle way Rome cupped my nape asked me to keep looking at him and not to turn, but he wouldn't stop me.

The brothers said nothing. The hairs all across my body seemed to stand up as if charged by an electrical current. The air around us positively crackled with all the words they weren't saying to each other. The silent argument seemed to explode all around us, but I kept watch on Rome. His eyes narrowed. His nostrils flared. For a moment, a smirk tilted his lips before it vanished and they compressed again.

It was like being outside in the midst of a gathering thunderstorm—all that static and kinetic energy preparing to unleash flooded the air. Maybe I imagined it, but the longer this went on, the angrier Rome seemed to grow. While I couldn't understand the content of their argument, it involved me.

Closing my eyes, I curled into Rome and pressed my forehead to his collarbone. He settled his chin against my hair as he shifted his weight. Some of the tension drained out of him.

"Fine," Liam said. "But Hellspawn and I have a date."

"Excuse me?" That actually brought me back into the conversation, and when I lifted my head, Rome loosened his hold so I could turn.

Liam smirked at me. "Yeah, Southpaw, we're going to work on that swing." There was a devilish gleam in his eyes. "I'll pick you up on Tuesday, you're spending the day with me. Be ready to get that little ass of yours in shape. Some of us have jobs."

Rome's hand came up in a perfectly formed middle finger, and Liam just grinned.

"Tuesday," he reminded me, then pivoted on his heel. For a split second, he paused to look at the painting of himself, then to the one Rome had just started on the far wall. Without another word, he stalked off.

I leaned back against Rome. "He was serious," I murmured. I'd brought up the boxing lessons mostly to get everyone off Freddie.

"Yeah," Rome said, lifting my hand and kissing my knuckles. I tilted my head back, but he wasn't looking at me. Instead, his gaze tracked where his brother had gone. "He likes you."

I didn't know. "You sure about that?"

"Yes," he said. "Just not sure if it's a good idea."

I licked my lips and pivoted to face him. "Because of you and me?"

Rome spared me a real smile and stroked my cheek. "No." Without another word of explanation, he kissed me lightly, and then we went back up for more painting. Oddly, the lack of words didn't bother me. Then again, I wasn't bringing it up either. It took a while, and he was nowhere near done when he called for us to leave, but I recognized the shape of my face and the flow of my hair.

He was painting me here. In his favorite place.

The warmth that blossomed grew brighter when he pulled my hand over to rest on his knee. We'd barely pulled back into the warehouse when Jasper appeared at my car door. A grin pulled my mouth wide. I'd missed him the last few days. The texts had been fun and funny, but it wasn't the same as seeing him.

"Hello, beautiful girl, did you have fun?" The question held none of his surly grumpiness.

"We did," I said. "Welcome back."

"Miss me?"

It was midafternoon, and there were dozens of rats here offloading a truck and sorting them onto different pallets. But I ignored all of them at the singular note of hope edged by teasing in Jasper's voice. I threaded my arms under his and then around his torso.

"Yes."

He gave a little jerk of surprise. That made me ache a little. Things between us had been complicated. But I thought he understood some of my feelings. Then again, I wasn't terrifically skilled at discussing them. When his arms closed around me, I smiled against his shirt.

The scent of him was crisp, clean, and freshly showered. I recognized the hint of spice from his soap. "Did you miss me?"

"Hell yes, I did, my beautiful girl." Then he leaned back. "Go out on a date with me?"

I blinked slowly.

"No big plans, we'll just go. Right now. You and me."

I glanced down at my outfit. Not that I had anything really nice.

"Trust me," he said, and an echo of what he'd said in my nightmare rushed back. *Maybe you should have.*

Licking my lips, I glanced over at Rome. "Do you mind?" I had been spending time with him.

He just winked, then gave Jasper a long look.

"I know how to look after her," Jasper said, sounding aggrieved for the first time since I'd arrived, before he looked back at me. "What do you say?"

"Yes."

His eyes lit up. Without glancing back, he palmed some keys from his pocket and threw them to Rome. "Make sure they all head out on time? And find out what Kel needs. He left me a message, then didn't answer his phone."

Rome nodded, a bemused expression on his face as Jasper clasped my hand and led me to his car.

"Oh," Jasper said as he held open the passenger door. "Don't call me. I'm taking a few hours off."

I laughed as he made a show of turning off his phone.

Rolling his eyes, Rome just flipped him off before he began to stroll toward the trucks, spinning the keys in his hand.

Jasper slid into the driver's seat and started the car up.

"Are you sure you can just turn everything off?" He'd been so busy lately and...

"Yes, I'm sure. I've been gone more than I've been here, and I want some time with you without the world burning down. One night won't kill anyone."

I chuckled. "I'd offer to turn my phone off, but I think it's still in Rome's car." I'd set it in the cupholder.

"That's perfect. It's just you and me. Trust me?"

Maybe you should have...

"Yes," I said slowly. "I do."

"Then let's go have some fun." He turned up the music, and we peeled out in a screech of tires that made me wince and laugh at the same time. I wiggled my shoes off and put my feet up on the dash as Jasper headed away from the clubhouse.

I could have asked where we were going, but I decided to trust him.

Just like coming back had been my choice, this was going to be my choice too, and the warmth from earlier burst into a thousand butterflies in my stomach.

"Jasper?"

"Hmm."

"Would now be a good time to tell you I've never been on a date?"

CHAPTER 28

EMERSYN

We drove north for almost two hours, following the coastline. I had to admit, it was a stunning drive. The ocean views alone were worth it. Even with the sunny skies, the water looked gray and stormy. It foamed where it crashed against the rocks. We alternated between listening to music and Jasper telling me stories.

"There," he said, pointing ahead of us to the far side of the bridge we were crossing. I sat forward and squinted. Even with the sunglasses on, the angle of the sun gleaming off the cars made for a glaring effect. "That's the cliff."

"You all jumped off that cliff." It wasn't a question.

"Yep, the night I turned eighteen. We came out here, cracked open a case of beer, got drunk enough to not give a fuck, and jumped." The absolute glee in his voice made me stare at him sideways.

"That's insane."

"It was fun as fuck, Swan." He shot me a look, and the

reckless grin he wore seemed such a stark contrast to his normal grumpiness. The expression filled me with such an inexplicable joy. "Trust me. Having seen you perform? The way you just float on those silks and fall with such rapture? You'd fucking love it too."

Okay, while I wasn't arguing with that... "When's your birthday?"

His expression turned sly. "Do I get a present if I tell you?"

"Is it today?" Well, two could play that game. "Because if it is and you jumped in that water, I'd be worried about your balls surviving the cold."

Deep throated laughter escaped him, and he reached over to squeeze my knee. "I would love to tell you my birthday is today, Swan. Maybe it is 'cause you said yes to a date, but trust me when I say my balls are just fine."

"That still doesn't answer the question." I raised my brows and lowered my sunglasses so I could make a face at him over them.

He chuckled. "Fine, it's in the late spring. So while the water was chilly, it wasn't frigid. My balls are perfectly intact."

"Hmm." I shoved my sunglasses back up. It had been just around two when Rome and I left the beach. My stomach grumbled, but I'd gone hungry plenty of times. Though honestly, I'd eaten more in the last few months than I was used to. I was gaining weight, so I needed to work out more and make sure I wasn't losing muscle.

"Don't believe me?"

I bit back a smile and gave a little shrug. "I mean, you could be lying about your birthday."

His snort followed by a smirk had me biting down on the inside of my cheek. "You worried about my present or my balls?"

"Both?" I suggested. "Neither." I gave it a beat and made a point of glancing out the passenger window because this was far too much fun. "I mean, I suppose I could answer both concerns at the same time."

The brief, albeit distinct, waver in the car's course coupled with the way his hand flexed on my knee made me smile. "Swan, don't tease me."

Facing him again, I leaned my head against the seat. "I'm not teasing. I may not know how to date, but I do know sex." I'd learned a lot more from Vaughn and from him. "I know about attraction."

He cut a look at me. "I want to take you out somewhere nice. I was going to buy you a pretty dress and we could go dancing…or play pool or…at least have a fancy dinner. I know I don't have everything you're used to but…"

No, we needed to stop this right here.

"Jasper," I exhaled his name slowly. "I don't need pretty dresses or fancy dinners. Believe me when I say I've had more dresses bought for me than I ever wanted to wear or will wear again. In fact, I'd cheerfully burn every single one of them." All of them. "Fancy dinners are boring and filled with staid rules and requirements. The food is expensive, the portions are small, and sometimes they're just awful, but we're all supposed to pretend that because it's served on some pretty platter it's not rubber chicken."

Sadness curved through me at his frown. Yeah, I was revealing a piece of myself here. I was telling him something I'd told no one else…except Lainey. But then, she felt the same way I did about society.

"Money is useful for making things expedient and for getting away with whatever you want whenever you want." I sat up more in the seat and put my feet down. "What I want is to spend time with you. To get to know you more to… build on my choice to trust you."

"And you want to have sex?" Far from disinterested, I swore he seemed to be fact-checking that one part of my statement.

My lips twitched. I couldn't help it because it was fucking funny. A giggle escaped. Then another.

"What?" He shot me another look, clearly divided between watching the road and watching me.

"Just, I confess all of that to you, and the part you focused on was the having sex part." It was hilarious.

"First, that's not all I focused on, I heard the bit about money and dresses you hate that were bought for you and the hints of misery and unhappiness beneath all of that."

Well if that didn't sober me, nothing would.

"Second, I got the message that you don't like the fancy, anonymous dinners in places where you're on display. I should have fucking figured that part out on my own. You perform on stage, you don't want to live there."

Even when it was the only life I had, living my life one song at a time.

"Third, I'm a guy, and you had a real issue when we were fooling around. Do I want to fuck you? Yes. Can I fucking wait? Also yes. So if you want to have sex with me, I'm in, Swan. All in."

The blunt directness of every statement paired with how straightforward he was in his delivery without an ounce of anger to taint the atmosphere had tears clogging my throat again.

"Fourth, let me be explicit—I asked you out for a date because I want to do this right. I want more with you than just a casual fuck."

I swallowed the lump forming.

"You're way more to me than that. And while I'm not one hundred percent sure about this whole sharing thing, 'cause I know you and Vaughn are having sex still—not that you could miss it."

I bit my lip so I didn't laugh.

"And there are times when I want to dislocate his jaw for putting his mouth on you, much less that metal filled dick of his." The last was a damn near growl, and he adjusted his grip on the steering wheel—both hands. He was trying so hard. I reached over to slide my fingers through his hair, and he let out this long breath. "He's my brother and I want you to be happy. So I'm working on all of that. But that means when I think you're telling me you want to have sex with me, I want to make absolutely sure that you want to have sex with me."

I want you to be happy.

I turned the words over and over in my head.

"Emersyn?" Jasper's voice seemed to come from a long way away, and I snapped my gaze up and back to the present. The frown he wore was dark, and his eyes were intense. He'd even yanked off his sunglasses. I still had my fingers in his hair, and I sighed. "Talk to me."

"Sorry, I think that's like the second time in my life someone's said that to me."

"I need a little help here, Swan. Which part? 'Cause I promise, I must threaten one of my brothers at least weekly, and I know you've heard me do it."

A watery laugh escaped. He wasn't wrong about that. "The part about wanting me to be happy."

Fuck, I sounded so small, and Jasper's knuckles went white on the steering wheel. I licked my lips.

"Sorry. I really don't know how to date, apparently. Maybe deep existential stuff falls under the no column."

"There was nothing existential about that statement."

The tears clawing at the back of my throat refused to be dislodged, but I couldn't let them out again. Not after the nightmare. Not after breaking like I had with Kellan. I couldn't do that. Not again.

"Fuck it," he growled abruptly. "Did you mean it when you said you trusted me?"

That question held so much meaning in it. Every movement in a silks routine had a moment to release and a moment to catch. You had to know when to do both. You had to trust the silks to catch you. You had to trust your body to let go. You had to fall to fly.

"Yes," I promised him, sliding my hand down his arm and catching his hand as he released the steering wheel to grip mine. "I mean it. I trust you."

All in. Catch. Release. Fall. Fly.

"You'll catch me." I didn't know if he would understand what that meant, but in the last few weeks, he'd done everything I could have asked for and more. He'd pushed himself because I asked him to, and all he'd asked from me in return was to trust him.

The raw tension holding me hostage let go at that admission. It was scary as fuck the first time you fell. But that was how you knew you were still alive. We didn't exchange another word as he finally left the highway and turned down toward a hotel that sat on another bluff overlooking the water.

It was a gorgeous, colonial revival style set of buildings with a huge main structure and what looked like bungalows beyond two wings that curved off to the sides of the central building. White columns marked the entrances, and there was a red, almost sandstone roof crowning it. The road winding from the highway to it had some beautiful landscaping, even if it was mostly brown and faded under the wintry sun.

Speaking of which, that sun was rapidly sinking in the sky, and I reached for my hat and tugged it back on. The guys didn't want anyone to recognize me. This place was pretty upscale, if somewhat deserted. "I don't know if they're open," I said as we drew closer.

"They are," Jasper said, grinning. "Trust me."

"Don't abuse it," I murmured, but his grin didn't diminish one iota.

"I promise, I won't." He followed the road around to where a parking area held a few vehicles. After choosing a slot for us away from the others and backing into it, he slid open the glove compartment.

The gun present inside surprised me. It shouldn't. But it did.

"I don't suppose you know how to use this?"

"What gave me away?" I wasn't sure if it was my reply or my tone that made him grin.

"Okay, we'll fix that soon enough."

A thrill barreled through me. He was going to teach me how to fire a gun? To use one?

Before I could totally grapple with that, he pulled something else out of his pocket and depressed a button. A knife flicked out the end. "Easy enough, yeah?" He snapped it closed, then pressed the button and the blade flicked out again.

"Um, how long am I going to be in the car?"

"Not long, Swan, I promise. But I'm not leaving you exposed without protection. So, car is on, heat is on. Gun is in there. It's very simple—point and shoot. Just press this button here on the side before you squeeze the trigger. The knife, far more basic, but slashes work. Cut them across the palm or the eyes, that will slow them down. If you have to stab them to get away, you fucking stab them."

"Groin work?" I should probably feel worse about this whole plan, but all I had to think about were those guys at the park or the man in the kitchen at the shop.

Or Eric.

Or Uncle Bradley.

"Bloodthirsty," he murmured, then kissed me hard and swift. "I like it. I'll be right back. If you need me, you slam your hand down on this horn and blare it for all its worth."

I licked my lips.

He pushed open his door after giving me another hard kiss that sent feeling sizzling through me. "Lock the door." Command filled those three words, and I was tempted to flip him off, even playfully. But I didn't.

Instead, I just reached over and hit the door locks as he waited and watched. His pleased smile sent another pulse of heat to bounce through my system, and I clenched my thighs.

Between waking up between Vaughn and Kellan that morning, playing with Rome all day, and then the drive, I ached with wanting so bad, and more...I just wanted to spend more time with him.

With all of them.

But I really had missed Jasper.

I twisted in the seat and tracked him across the parking lot. It wasn't until I sat back and let out a little girly giggle, hand fixed around the handle of the knife, that it hit me.

In front of me, the sun had begun its descent toward the water, and I let out a slow smile. If I were to compile the list of amazing days I'd had in my life, this one already counted in the top ten. Maybe the top five.

Probably the top two, who was I kidding?

Six months.

Six months without a show. Without a rehearsal. Without my uncle. Without Eric. Without *pain*.

Tonight, I was going out on a date...for real.

As promised, Jasper was back at the car in less than ten minutes. He slid inside as soon as I unlocked the doors and leaned over to cup my face. The swift seal of his mouth to mine sent my pulse racing, and I leaned into the touch, clasping his wrist, as eager to hold on to him as he seemed to be to taste me.

"Fuck, that was too long to be gone," he whispered.

"It was ten minutes."

"Trust me, felt a fuck load longer." Another hard kiss that made me want to climb over into his lap, and he let me go. "Hang on, we're almost there."

We were almost…

But he pulled out smoothly and instead of heading out the way we came, he took another route through the lot to a hidden drive. Curiosity burned in me, but I held fast to his hand as he navigated the curves in the rapidly dropping darkness. The sun was a red ball sinking into the water, and a part of me was torn between watching it and watching Jasper.

Jasper won.

Every time.

Just around a bend, out of sight of the main buildings, was a little bungalow in the same colonial revival style with what I supposed was a red slate roof. Jasper backed into the slot clearly marked for it and grinned. "Told you we were almost here."

I handed him the knife back, and when he took that and then the gun out of the glove compartment, I didn't say a word.

"Stay put," he ordered again, this time though, he turned off the car. He tucked the gun into his belt at the back and pulled his shirt over it to cover before circling the car and opening my door. "My beautiful swan?"

I laughed and clasped his hand. The effect was kind of ridiculous when you considered what I was wearing, but I'd never felt more like a lady than when he winked and pushed the door closed before locking the car. The air outside was even colder than it had been back in the harbor. The breeze coming off the ocean was almost a gale. I shuddered almost immediately, and Jasper pulled me into his side, one arm around me. He guided me up onto a darkened porch that lit up at our approach. Motion sensor lights. Nice.

It also let me get a good look at the windows. The place had them on all sides, and the interior looked like a huge room.

"What is this?"

"This," Jasper said as he unlocked the door with a key card and held it open for me, "is one of five staff bungalows on the property. They look really nice 'cause they are, but they aren't fancy. They are warm, comfortable, and have great views." He locked the door behind us and moved over to the fireplace. He flicked on a switch, and it flamed to life.

Gas fireplace.

He adjusted a dial. "There's another one upstairs," he told me. "I'll get it turned on. Between them, they can warm this place pretty well."

I followed after him, more curious than anything else. The big wide room we were in had a couple of sofas, a pair of armchairs, a six-seater dining table, and what had to be a little kitchen off to the side. There was a deck on the back and a pair of doors that opened out onto it. The view was spectacular with the setting sun filling all the windows.

Upstairs, Jasper had gone into a huge room to the right. There were three doors up here, and I toed off my shoes as I followed him into the bedroom. He was turning on another fireplace.

"And they let you just check into a staff bungalow?" I unzipped my hoodie as he turned around. The lights were still off, and only the fire illuminated the room. Unlike downstairs, the windows were all shuttered up here. So maybe they were closed for the winter months.

"The summer most of us were sixteen, we got jobs up here," he told me, gaze fixed on me as I set the hoodie down, then reached for my shirt and tugged it over my head. "The group home wasn't always fun in the summer."

I swore I could feel his caress as his gaze skated over me, even as I dropped my hands to my borrowed sweatpants and peeled them off. The dance pants under them came next.

Jasper chuckled, then cleared his throat. "Anyway, the summer job came with lodging. So all of us got to stay here for the summer while we worked."

I nodded slowly. "Sounds like fun. What did you do?" I left the pants and sweatpants atop my borrowed hoodie. My nipples were on point, but the heat from the gas fireplace couldn't quite compete with the fire in his expression. The bra unsnapped with one hand, and I slid it down my arms and tossed it behind me before I slid my thumbs into the sides of my panties. "Jasper?"

He snapped his gaze up to my eyes.

"What did you do?" I repeated the question and just barely managed to stifle my laughter at the stunned expression on his face. Considering he'd turned me inside and out pulling orgasm after orgasm out of me and he'd definitely seen *me* naked, the fact he was so riveted filled me with a quiet kind of pleasure.

"Pretty much whatever they needed. Sometimes bellman, that kind of sucked, but the tips were good. Lifeguard backup, too young to be an actual lifeguard, but we could help keep watch. Waiter. Sometimes at the cabanas or the restaurant. Little bit of everything really."

He licked his lips, and I peeled the panties down and stepped out of them. The hungry way he tracked me with his gaze encouraged me to pose, just a little. He was right about one thing—I did love to perform, even if I didn't want to be on display.

Halfway to him, I stopped and put my hands on my hips. "Sounds like fun."

"It was," he admitted, a strangled note in his voice. "I think—Why are we talking about that?"

"Because you're still wearing clothes and I didn't get to see you last time, so I let you watch me... Now I want to see you."

The firelight flickered over his face as he rubbed his beard. "Yes, ma'am," he said slowly as I retreated toward the bed. I swore my mouth had gone dry with anticipation as he moved to follow me. "I promise, you can see anything you want."

At his nearness, I slid up onto the bed on my knees, still retreating a little as he closed the distance.

"What was your favorite part about that summer?"

He set the knife and the gun down on the nightstand. I ignored both, keeping my attention fixed on him. I swore my cunt pulsed every time his gaze flicked to mine, and my breasts were damn near aching. He hadn't even touched me yet. The taste of him lingered on my lips.

"The freedom," he admitted, unbuttoning his shirt with far more swiftness than I had used in stripping. He tossed it to join my clothes and already had his belt undone and out before I processed he'd lost his shoes.

"I get that," I said softly. "There's nothing quite like freedom."

"No, Swan," he agreed as his jeans hit the floor and took whatever briefs or boxers he'd been wearing with them. "There isn't."

Holy hell. He wasn't built all in beautiful lines and colorful muscle like Vaughn, but there was a raw kind of beauty to Jasper. To my delight, he held still under my perusal. His cock was as thick as I'd imagined it, long and curved toward the tip. There was a fine dusting of hair everywhere from his chest to his legs to the deep brown curls at the base of his dick.

Compact muscles flexed and rippled in his legs and his arms. Toned. Fit. But there were scars too—scars that made me ease forward, one step at a time on my knees. A circular one below his breast bone. Another longer, more ragged one on his side. The tangled vines I'd seen on his chest before formed over his left pec, almost like a circle with little strands escaping.

When I reached out with one hand to smooth over the tattoo, I swore his chest muscle flexed. He was tight, compact, built more like I would expect a crewman. He could pull his weight.

I trailed my fingers down his arm. The tattoo was just the one sleeve that went up to his elbow. But there was more, on his side, words that I hadn't seen before.

"Swan," he said in a near strangled tone, and I pulled my gaze up to his. Want burned back at me. "Emersyn." He said my name like a caress. "Is there anything else you want to know?"

"I want to know everything."

Bless him, he swallowed hard but nodded. "Ask away." Not once did he move a muscle, even though I was touching him. If there had been even a minuscule amount of doubt left in me about trusting him, it vanished.

"But it can wait. I want you more."

"Oh, thank fuck," he whispered before his mouth crashed down on mine and we went down on the bed in a tangle of naked limbs. His hands were fucking everywhere, stroking, teasing, pushing, pinching, and his mouth only left mine to trace kisses along my jaw or to suck on one of my nipples.

The moment he brushed two blunt fingers against my clit, he swore again. I was soaked and aching for him. The minute he went south with his kisses though, I gripped his hair and tugged, pulling up those sultry gray eyes that stared right into my soul. The firelight turned them almost molten silver.

"I want you," I repeated. "I need you to fuck me, Jasper. I need to feel all of you this time." Heat swept over my face, and I wrapped my legs around his hips, arching my back. I'd barely gotten to brush his dick with the fingers of my free hand when he caught my wrist and pinned it to the bed.

When he caught my other hand and eased it from his hair to pin it next to my head, I met his stare openly. "Fuck me, Swan, I don't know if I can be gentle."

"I didn't ask you for gentle." To be honest, they all needed to stop acting like I would break. "I want you. I want your anger. I want your rage. I want your heat. I want—" His mouth slammed down and cut off the rest of my words as he pinned me in place. When his cock slid against the dampness of my cunt, I swore we both groaned, then we reached for his dick together.

As soon as he was at the right angle, he slammed into me in one relentless push that had me seeing stars.

"More," I begged as he threw his head back and groaned. The rock of his hips pulled him out and then slammed into me again, and on the third thrust, I arched up to meet his lips, nipping at his teeth as I kissed him.

The little bite did what nothing else had. Jasper pinned both of my arms this time and took over the kiss, matching the thrust of his tongue to the rhythm of his cock, and both drove into me at such a frenetic pace that I couldn't catch my breath. My heart thundered in my ears, and the glide of his skin on mine, the rasp of his beard where it rubbed my face while his lips kept me prisoner, matched only to the pounding of his cock hitting deep inside me.

The first orgasm startled me, and I screamed against his mouth. He slowed only to power me through it as I spasmed around him, and then he picked up the pace, not once letting up on the kiss.

My lips were going to be bruised. My face would be burned. My cunt was already raring up for round two when round one hadn't even ceased.

"More?" he asked in between brutal kisses, and I pulled at my wrists. He released me in a second, and I dug my nails into his back.

"More."

"Oh fuck yes, Swan, more." I swore he made me come twice more before he let himself go. The shattering sensation as he stiffened against me and the hot flood of his release were perfect. We clung to each other, and I cradled him as he collapsed. His muscles shook and trembled in tandem with mine.

With a kiss to my shoulder, he eased himself upward and then kissed me again. I shivered as he pulled out, and I swore my cunt was already crying for more.

I clenched around the emptiness, wanting him back.

"One second," he whispered as he walked through a door to a bathroom. A minute and one toilet flush later, he came out and held up a hand. "One more minute."

I chuckled, because the firelight did wonderful things for his ass shifting and clenching as he moved. He wasn't downstairs long before he returned, this time with two beers in hand.

At my raised brows, he said, "I asked for a favor, and they delivered them. There's food down there too, but I'll get that for us in a bit."

"You ordered dinner?"

I sat up slowly—holy crap, I was shaking—and held out my hand to take the open beer bottle he handed me.

"It's a date, Swan. I even got you a big fat piece of chocolate espresso cake."

I stared at him.

"My dessert is right there," he murmured, pointing to me. "I suppose I can eat you out again now, yes?"

He took way too much delight in grinning at me as I forgot English for a second.

"I'm going to take that expression as a compliment to my prowess and not your lust for chocolate espresso cake."

Laughing, I dragged myself into sitting in a cross-legged position. He leaked out of me, and I swore for a moment, he just stared at my cunt, licking his lips.

Fuck me. "Definitely your prowess."

"Finish that beer, sweetheart. I'm really fucking hungry all of a sudden."

When I shot-gunned the damn thing, his grin turned positively sinful. Two seconds after he took the empty bottle from my fingers, he had me flat on my back with my legs over his shoulder and his face buried in my cunt.

The next orgasm took him time to get there, but he fucking knew how to apply himself and that tongue of his could curl on the inward thrust to stroke me in ways I didn't know were possible.

At some point, we took a break for food and another beer. I might even have napped, but it wasn't for long, and then he filled me with his cock again and I came crying and screaming.

While he hadn't let me suck him off yet, he promised that he would, on our next date. In between bouts of sex and sleep, he told me a little about his childhood and the group home and the friends who became his brothers—the Vandals.

It twisted my heart into all kinds of knots. I told him a little about growing up, not a lot. I'd been working since I was eight, and when he complained about that, I told him that life on the road was so much better than life at home. I swore for a moment, he looked like he would press me for more, and then he said, "Yeah, homes don't always mean happy."

And I think that made me want to cry. Eventually, we slept. Or I did. I wasn't sure Jasper did at all. He woke me so early, it wasn't even light outside. At my grumbling, he teased me out of the bed and carried me into the bathroom, where we took a shower and he fucked me right against the tile until I was wide awake and aching.

I hated having to leave the place so early, but Jasper couldn't take more than the night away. As it was, he said the guys were probably gonna be pissed at him for disappearing with me all night.

"Should we call them?"

"Nope," he said once we were back on the road. "We still have a couple of hours of it just being us, and I'm going to be selfish and take it."

The drive back, we talked about the different jobs he'd had. He also, apparently, knew how to drive a big rig and he had a degree in accounting and business.

I must have looked surprised, and that made me feel like an ass when he said, "What, didn't expect more from this pretty face?"

"No," I said, then winced and he laughed. "That's not what I meant."

"I know, most people don't look at me and see a businessman. But we have to make money, and making money in business is a lot about who you know to begin with, but it's also about mining opportunities."

That was far too close to something Uncle Bradley had told me once, but I shut out that little voice and stuck a gag in it. Jasper was *not* Uncle Bradley. Also, Jasper's stories about punk-ass bitches—his words not mine—that he went to the local community college with and then later in the online courses he took at the state university to finish his bachelor's degree entertained me.

"How can you know they were 'punk-ass bitches,'" I asked, using air quotes, "if you were in an online class with them?"

"They posted snotty."

I snorted, but he gave me an unrepentant smirk.

We grabbed fresh coffees, and I talked Jasper into getting donuts for the guys as a peace offering before we pulled up to the warehouse. It was still early. We'd made way better time on the way back than we had on the way out. A part of me debated calling Lainey. Of all the people who didn't know where I was, she was the one I wouldn't mind knowing. If only to tell her that I was all right.

I'd talk to the guys about it later. They were the ones worried about someone else coming after me, and I was more worried about Uncle Bradley finding me. Inside, it was quiet. There weren't even any rats around.

Jasper frowned as he scanned the empty area. The trucks were both gone, but he didn't look bothered by that.

"Maybe they aren't here because the guys are?" I suggested, and he flicked a look at me, then smiled.

"Probably. They have work to do too, and we don't need guards all the time..." Still, despite the easy expression he wore, his eyes remained cooler, more assessing. "Do you mind carrying the donuts?"

He had them, but I had a feeling he wanted his hands free. Sucking in a deep breath, I said, "Want me to wait here?"

One shake of his head. "It's not that bad." At my raised brows, he sighed. "I promise. I just prefer three being on duty all the time. The others think I'm paranoid. So probably just a way to fuck with me, but carry the donuts and let me go in first?"

I nodded. His swift smile and gentle kiss went a long way as a thank you. Then he took point.

The door was unlocked, but it always was. He didn't make any discouraging sounds, so I followed right behind him. Jasper didn't even make it to the living room area before a blur with dark hair slammed into him. His coffee went flying, and he went down in a wild fury of pounding fists.

I froze. Jasper was already coming up swinging and I started forward, but an arm looped around me. "Don't, Dove," Vaughn said, his voice strained. That was when it hit me—everyone was here. Kellan gave me a pained look, and he sported fresh bruises on the side of his face. Freddie stood a couple of feet behind him, fidgeting miserably. Rome and Liam were like silent sentinels near the kitchen.

Rome flicked his gaze from me to the fighters, but Liam never took his eyes off them.

Who the fuck...

"Let go," I said as Jasper and his assailant broke apart. Blood poured from Jasper's nose and from a cut on his face. "Stop it!"

The man beating on him froze and cut a look at me. His chest rose and fell as he panted. His hair was cropped close, and there was a shadow of stubble on his cheeks. He had tats running up both his arms, and his knuckles were bloody and broken.

Everything about this guy screamed threat. Jasper raised a hand. "I—" He didn't get more than that out before the guy lunged forward and slammed his fist into Jasper's face.

I dropped the donuts and slid out of Vaughn's arms. I didn't know why no one was stopping this, but I got right in front of Jasper. If the guy wanted to hit him again, he'd have to hit me.

"Sparrow—"

"Starling—"

"Little Bit, don't…"

"Boo-Boo!"

"I don't know who you are," I said, glaring up at the guy towering over me. "And I don't care. Leave him the fuck alone." I didn't know when Jasper stuck that knife in my pocket, maybe he'd done it outside, but the weight of it was there and I pulled it out, flicking the blade open.

No one moved, not the bruiser, not the guys, no one.

"It's okay, Emersyn," Jasper said from behind me. "He has a right."

"The fuck he does."

But I didn't dare look at Jasper. The guy staring at me blinked slowly. "Ivy," he whispered, in a tone so raw and broken, it didn't quite sound human.

"What?"

"Little Bit," Doc said slowly as he moved toward us. "This is Raptor." They'd mentioned him. Great, so Raptor was an asshole. Good to know. "Your brother."

What?

Emersyn and the Vandals will return in *Ruthless Traitor*.

To keep up with Heather and all her series join her reader's group:
Https://www.facebook.com/groups/HeathersPack/

RUTHLESS TRAITOR

At the heart of it all was a secret and a lie.

A secret we didn't tell her.

A lie we told ourselves.

Emersyn Sharpe is more than just the girl we watched over. She's very much the woman who fits us.

The last thing we should have done was take her and the worst thing we did was keep her, but she needs us. I think, more than one of us—myself included—needs her.

The secret wasn't ours to share and the lie?

I bought into the lie that keeping her was saving her. The lie that persuading her to trust us was needed. The lie that falling in love with her was as natural as breathing.

It didn't matter if I wasn't alone in falling into this trap. It mattered that when the trap closed, it put her on one side and us on the other.

Damn and we were so close too…

My name is Vaughn Westbrook and I'll be damned if I give up now.

RUTHLESS TRAITOR is a full length mature college/new

adult romance with enemies-to-lovers/love-hate themes. This is a reverse harem novel, meaning the main character has more than one love interest. This is book three in the series.

AFTERWORD

This is one of those rare books that poured out of me. I think I was on chapter five when the entire book just flooded my mind in one go. I sat down and wrote out an entire book's worth of chapter breakdowns.

From that point forward, I was full throttle writing this book. It wanted out of me and while I was stuck on bedrest with a herniated disc in my spine waiting to find out whether I'd get to have surgery or not, this was my distraction and my joy. It was also sometimes my agony because I couldn't always keep up with the words I wanted to pour out.

Scarily enough, the next book in the series is doing the exact same thing, so I cannot wait to see where we go from here.

Thank you for being on this journey with me. I'm so excited to see where we go from here.

xoxo

Heather

ABOUT HEATHER LONG

USA Today bestselling author, Heather Long, likes long walks in the park, science fiction, superheroes, Marines, and men who aren't douche bags. Her books are filled with heroes and heroines tangled in romance as hot as Texas summertime. From paranormal historical westerns to contemporary military romance, Heather might switch genres, but one thing is true in all of her stories—her characters drive the books. When she's not wrangling her menagerie of animals, she devotes her time to family and friends she considers family. She believes if you like your heroes so real you could lick the grit off their chest, and your heroines so likable, you're sure you've been friends with women just like them, you'll enjoy her worlds as much as she does.

Follow Heather & Sign up for her newsletter:
www.heatherlong.net

ALSO BY HEATHER LONG

Always a Marine Series

Once Her Man, Always Her Man

Retreat Hell! She Just Got Here

Tell It to the Marine

Proud to Serve Her

Her Marine

No Regrets, No Surrender

The Marine Cowboy

The Two and the Proud

A Marine and a Gentleman

Combat Barbie

Whiskey Tango Foxtrot

What Part of Marine Don't You Understand?

A Marine Affair

Marine Ever After

Marine in the Wind

Marine with Benefits

A Marine of Plenty

A Candle for a Marine

Marine under the Mistletoe

Have Yourself a Marine Christmas

Lest Old Marines Be Forgot

Her Marine Bodyguard

Smoke & Marines

Bravo Team Wolf

When Danger Bites

Bitten Under Fire

Boomers

The Judas Contact

Deadly Genesis

Unstoppable

Chance Monroe

Earth Witches Aren't Easy

Plan Witch from Out of Town

Bad Witch Rising

Her Elite Assets

Featuring:

Pure Copper

Target: Tungsten

Asset: Arsenic

Fevered Hearts

Marshal of Hel Dorado

Brave are the Lonely

Micah & Mrs. Miller

A Fistful of Dreams

Raising Kane

Wanted: Fevered or Alive

Wild and Fevered

The Quick & The Fevered
A Man Called Wyatt

Going Royal

Some Like It Royal
Some Like It Scandalous
Some Like It Deadly
Some Like it Secret
Some Like it Easy
Her Marine Prince
Blocked

Heart of the Nebula
Queenmaker
Deal Breaker
Throne Taker

Lone Star Leathernecks
Semper Fi Cowboy
As You Were, Cowboy

Madison, The Witch Hunter
Every Witch Way But Floosey's

Magic & Mayhem
The Witch Singer
Bridget's Witch's Diary
The Witched Away Bride

Mongrels

Mongrels, Mischief & Mayhem

Shackled Souls

Succubus Chained

Succubus Unchained

Succubus Blessed

Space Cowboy

Space Cowboy Survival Guide

Untouchable

Rules and Roses

Changes and Chocolates

Keys and Kisses

Whispers and Wishes

Hangovers and Holidays

Brazen and Breathless

Wolves of Willow Bend

Wolf at Law

Wolf Bite

Caged Wolf

Wolf Claim

Wolf Next Door

Rogue Wolf

Bayou Wolf

Untamed Wolf

Wolf with Benefits

River Wolf

Single Wicked Wolf

Desert Wolf

Snow Wolf

Wolf on Board

Holly Jolly Wolf

Shadow Wolf

His Moonstruck Wolf

Thunder Wolf

Ghost Wolf

Outlaw Wolves

Wolf Unleashed

Spirit Wolf